Along the Way Home

by
Christi Corbett

Along the Way Home
by Christi Corbett
Published by Astraea Press
www.astraeapress.com

Paul,

thank you so much for all your help in making every part of Along the Way Home have good word choice, and Realistic "guy" talk.

Christi Corbett

In *Along the Way Home,* author Christi Corbett unfurls an unforgettable epic romance inside of an epic Western adventure. Beautifully crafted, this debut novel is a tender journey of the heart as well as a treacherous journey of many miles. *Along the Way Home* is a squeaky-clean historical romance with authentic period details and deep emotion. Much danger, risk, courage and compassion will make you long for more books from this talented author. As heartwarming as *Christy*."

Eve Paludan, author of *Taking Back Tara* (Ranch Lovers Romance series)

A breath-taking account of courage and adventure along the Oregon Trail. Travel this dangerous journey with characters you will treasure as they cope with heart-wrenching difficulties they never thought to encounter in a search to fulfill their hopes and dreams. Christi Corbett's debut novel, *Along the Way Home,* will both surprise and delight.

Jillian Kent, author of *The Ravensmoore Chronicles.*

A dash of action! A touch of intrigue! Loads of sweet, clean romantic promise — a chick flick 1840's historical western that will tickle young adults and ladies!

Reid Lance Rosenthal, Winner of 15 National Awards, #1 Best Selling Author of the *Threads West, An American Saga* series.

To Dalen—For your unwavering support of my dream.

To the M's—Never give up on your dreams

Chapter One

Kate's Decision

Charlottesville, Virginia
Wednesday, April 5, 1843

Every Wednesday Kate stood on the same front porch, her hand poised inches from the door, willing herself to do the unthinkable — walk away without knocking. However, during the hesitation, her courage inevitably fled.

Wednesdays were a long-standing tradition, and one she couldn't disrupt.

She rapped her knuckles on the wood. Familiar footsteps clicked toward the other side of the entry, and she forced a smile as the door opened to reveal an overdressed, overfed, overbearing woman.

"Katherine Davis, how dare you appear at my doorstep bareheaded like some commoner? Get your bonnet on this instant!"

Kate's smile faded. "Yes, Aunt Victoria."

She slid the velvet cage over her head, knowing she'd only remove it after stepping across the threshold. Under the guise of propriety, her aunt had tortured her for years. Recently she'd expanded her teachings to include the fine art of manipulating men and viewed snaring a husband as the ultimate goal.

Kate followed the bitter spinster's perfume cloud into the parlor. Cream and gold wallpaper, the best her father's money could buy, adorned each wall. Marble-topped tables stood between overstuffed chairs and a matching sofa. After taking a seat on the sole wooden chair in the room, she smoothed a wrinkle from her skirt in preparation for the weekly inspection.

"A lady's appearance is of the utmost importance." Aunt Victoria paused to wriggle her fingertips into her taut sleeve, tug out a handkerchief, and dab a line of sweat from her upper lip. "Might this be the week you finally manage to pull yourself together?"

Secure in her dressing room choices, Kate held steady under the probing gaze. Her auburn curls were captured in a perfumed knot at the nape of her neck. She wore a dress of the finest green velvet, custom dyed to match her eyes and brushed by servants to a soft sheen. A silk ribbon accentuated her trim waist, not that she needed any help. Her petite frame misled many. She was a grown woman with the responsibilities to show for it.

"Though the color is garish, the style of your dress is appropriate." Aunt Victoria clucked her tongue. "Too bad the same can't be said for your hair."

With an indifferent shrug, Kate poured herself a cup of tea. She'd long since given up on winning the woman's approval. After a glance at the wall clock, she added a pastry and a melon wedge to her plate. It was early morning, but she'd been up for hours without breakfast.

"Don't take too many sweets. They'll ruin your figure." Aunt Victoria hefted a wedge of Brie and three pastries on her own plate and then leaned back against the upholstered sofa. "I assume your servants have improved their work ethic since my lecture last week?"

After discovering muddy footprints on the front porch during an unannounced visit, her aunt had lined up the household staff and disparaged each and every one. Three had left the room in tears. One had quit on the spot.

Kate merely nodded.

"Good. They have to learn to serve their betters with more respect. Now, did you enjoy the Ladies' Society meeting yesterday?"

Kate grimaced at the thought of wasting an afternoon listening to a herd of fussy, jewel-laden women congratulate themselves on bettering the community.

"I didn't attend."

At this, her aunt's tone hardened. "Securing you an invitation required delicate negotiations among the most influential women of this town. Your position in society is not guaranteed, so I trust you have a good reason for embarrassing me. Again."

Undaunted, Kate met the narrowed eyes with ease. "I needed to review a contract and finalize the monthly profits and losses."

A wrinkled hand flew into the air and the familiar rant began, as always, with an exaggerated sigh.

"Your father should hire a bookkeeper instead of forcing the task upon his only daughter."

"Father doesn't force me," Kate said, dropping her plate on the table hard enough to garner a wince from her aunt. "I rather enjoy it."

Actually, tracking accounts was the highlight of her day. Numbers were logical and consistent — little else in her life was as uncomplicated.

"The intricacies of business are useless knowledge to a woman," her aunt declared with a disdainful sniff. "At twenty-two years old, your focus is better spent on more ladylike pursuits, like improving yourself to attract a husband." Pinched lips gave way to a taunting sneer. "Unless Crandall finally proposed?"

Kate met her aunt's hard stare with her own. "No, ma'am."

"Maybe if you paid attention to my advice, you wouldn't have to pass your evenings with only your father and dim-witted brother for company."

Kate sprang from her chair even as the cruel words still hung in the air between them. She would bear the brunt of her aunt's insults and had for many years, but drew the line at attacks upon her nine-year-old brother, Ben.

"Father trusts me with our livelihood, and I won't flit about town sipping afternoon tea, obsessing over the latest fashions, or hosting parties when there's real work to be done. As for my evenings, you needn't worry. They are far more fulfilled than your own."

With a dismissive nod, Kate started toward the doorway.

"Wait."

The single word confirmed again Aunt Victoria's one weakness — money. Kate's father paid handsomely for the weekly lessons, and her aunt wouldn't allow a few harsh words to stop the lucrative practice. Kate returned to her seat not because of her aunt's command, but because she couldn't bear the thought of disappointing her father.

An hour later she donned her shawl and bonnet, stepped into the bright sunshine, and exchanged a last round of false niceties. When the door closed behind her Kate raced down the stone path to freedom. Six glorious days lay ahead before her expected return.

When the visits had begun nine years ago, she'd been a child teetering on the verge of womanhood, unable to protest the absurdity of piano lessons twice a week, French instruction with a private tutor, and Aunt Victoria's vicious style of imparting etiquette. Now she was long past caring what anyone thought. Anyone besides her father. The lessons made him happy, and since little else did, she continued the weekly farce.

Kate walked along the dusty boardwalk toward her father's store. When she stepped down onto the street, intent on crossing, the sight of five boys caught her attention. They were crouched shoulder to shoulder, peering under the boardwalk. She frowned to see her brother's sandy-brown head in the middle of the group.

As she approached, a boy spun around, scanning the street in a search for potential interferers. Sighting her, the lookout nudged Ben.

"Your nosy sister's coming. She's gonna ruin everything."

Kate closed the distance with three steps. "What do we have here?"

Ten hands scrambled for cover behind backs and into pockets. Trouble obviously brewed.

"Hands out. All of you."

Grubby hands reluctantly came forward.

"Open them."

Fingers uncurled, revealing chunks of bread in each palm.

"What are you boys doing?"

When no one answered she looked to her brother. "Ben?"

"N-n-n-n-nothing."

Ignoring the other boys' snickers, Kate focused on her brother. "Certainly seems like something."

"It was Ben's idea," the lookout said.

"Yeah," added another with a defiant sneer. "It was all his idea."

Kate knew better. Ben tried too hard to fit in with boys his age and was often a scapegoat when they were caught during mischief.

Rustling under the boardwalk quieted the remaining boys. Kate wondered at their silence until a small black nose emerged and began sniffing crumbs scattered in the dirt. Moments later a black-and-white head appeared, followed by the well-fed body of a skunk.

All kept still as the creature plodded across the street, and only when it disappeared under Smith's Hardware did the boys take flight. To his credit, Ben stayed behind.

"What were you thinking?" Kate asked in exasperation.

Soft blue eyes pleaded understanding and her heart melted. To a point.

"You have to stop getting in trouble, Ben." She crossed her arms and attempted a firm stare. "Or have you forgotten how last week Mr. Sherman brought you into the store, sopping wet?"

"You never let m-me have any f-f-fun," he cried.

With a sigh of defeat, she reached to comfort him. Too late. He recoiled and she dropped her hand. Ben desperately needed what she and her father could never provide — his mother's love.

Kate watched her brother's lanky frame as he galloped down the street. Knowing he would hide and lick his imagined wounds for the remainder of the day, she continued on toward the store. When she entered she greeted their stock boy and then sat at her desk in the back room. With January through March's ledgers opened before her, she began tallying all supplies purchased for the first quarter.

Hours later, the stock boy whispered news of a visitor. She walked out front, smiling to see Marie Ann, her dearest and closest friend, lumbering past the displays.

"What are you doing here?" Kate scolded her *enceinte*, yet stubbornly mobile, friend. "You should be resting. Robert will be furious when he discovers you've escaped from your bed."

Marie Ann leaned against the counter, her burgundy curls bouncing with each panting breath. "I heard the news about you and Crandall."

Safe and predictable, Crandall Hewitt was the one constant in Kate's life. During her youth, he'd pulled the ribbons from her hair; later he'd led her through her first dance with a man besides her father. They'd courted exclusively for the past year, but recently he'd begun pressuring for more than attending social functions together. Maybe one day she would grow to love him.

Kate frowned in confusion. "What news?"

A torrent of giggles accompanied Marie Ann's gleeful hug. "I'm so happy for you! Crandall confirmed to Robert he's engaged."

In a daze, Kate grasped Marie Ann's shoulders and pulled away. "Not to me."

Honey-brown eyes widened in dismay. "If not you, then who?"

"I'm going to find out." Kate rushed behind the counter, snatched her door key off the wall hook, and pressed it into Marie Ann's hand. "Lock up for me."

Ignoring her friend's look of disbelief, Kate grabbed her shawl and marched out of the store. Within minutes she stood in the doorway of Crandall's apothecary. Her eyes swept the room and located the back of his blond head behind the counter. For the moment, she held her fury in check — Marie Ann could be mistaken.

"Is this talk of your engagement true?"

Slowly, Crandall turned to face her, his eyes filled with wary hesitation.

"Is it true?" she demanded.

Instead of answering, two slender fingers pinched the edge of his wire-rimmed glasses and settled them higher on his nose. It was a move she recognized from their school days together. A move he used to stall for time.

"Well?" she asked, not bothering to suppress the brittle edge in her tone.

"I've asked Mary Wells to be my wife."

"Mary!"

Crandall pursed his lips, pointing to where a huge bear of a man stood studying a display. Ignoring the stranger, she continued.

"Why would you ask for her hand when you're courting me?"

"You're not the marrying type, Kate. You're too busy doing the work of a man, instead of behaving like you want to marry one."

A rush of feelings boiled over, leaving behind the stench of her failed dreams. She'd thought Crandall respected the life she chose to lead. That she'd been so blind to his true character hurt more than his betrayal.

Anger rapidly overtook anguish.

"How dare you judge my behavior, you lying cad!" The stranger jumped at her shout and she lowered her voice. "You believe my willingness to manage the financials after my mother's death as a hindrance?"

"Yes, and a time-consuming one." Crandall gave an unapologetic shrug. "I've found a woman who does what you wouldn't — focus on my needs and make me feel like a man."

Kate heard a snicker from across the store. Mortified, she whirled on her heel and stalked toward the stranger. He stood well over six feet tall and had to be two hundred pounds of solid muscle, neither of which dissuaded her from standing toe to toe with him.

"Shame on you for eavesdropping."

Instead of slinking away, the man swept off his hat, took a step back, and bent into an exaggerated bow. His hair was jet black, and, as evidenced in the curls at the nape of his neck, in need of a haircut.

"My apologies," he replied, insincerity in his tone.

"I hope you at least have the decency to leave," she snapped. "Now."

The interloper straightened, startling her with the brilliant blue of his eyes. "Last time I checked this is a free country, and I have purchases to make. What I can't understand is why you're so irritated with me—" his lips twitched in amusement as he nodded toward Crandall "— when he's right over there?"

As he replaced his hat and gave her a slow, lazy smile, Crandall's soft cough brought their conversation to a halt.

"Kate, if you'd let me help this gentleman we can finish our conversation in a few minutes."

Crandall gestured to a chair against the wall, and because she wanted the stranger gone she sat. But beneath her skirt, one foot tapped an angry rhythm against the wooden floor. After a glance at her shaking hands she forced herself to think of something, anything, besides Crandall's betrayal. Her eyes fell on the towering man now wasting her time with too many questions. Brooding, rugged, bold — a definite man's man, and every giggling debutante's secret desire. A stark contrast to Crandall, who her father often referred to as "delicate".

"This liniment is guaranteed to soothe, almost on contact." Crandall's voice brought Kate back to the present as he answered yet another question from the lingering stranger.

"If it'll ease a leg that aches in the rain I'm willing to give it a try." The man fished a coin from his coat pocket and tossed it on the counter.

When he glanced her way she stiffened, waiting for the inevitable compliment on her appearance. But as his eyes took in her polished shoes, freshly pressed gown, and upswept hair, she had the uncomfortable feeling he didn't like what he saw. Though what did it matter? She was there to speak to Crandall, not banter words with a drifter.

"Ma'am," he said, touching the brim of his hat. He walked away without a backward glance.

As the door closed behind the man Kate fired the first shot. "So, you believe the town trollop is the 'marrying type'?"

Crandall's face went pale, but to her growing frustration he kept silent.

"You owe me an explanation," she said.

"I do, but I won't tolerate you making a scene." He fiddled with a button on his jacket before settling his gaze on her. "Mary is expecting my child."

Furious, she lunged to slap him, but he caught her hand in midair.

"Your temper will be your downfall one day," he warned as she jerked her hand from his grasp.

"Crandall Hewitt, you are a despicable, dishonorable rat!" Kate spat out the words, wondering how she could have wasted a year of her life on such a worthless man. "You and Mary deserve each other."

Leaving him where he stood, she hurried for home and the one man she could always count on — her father.

When the line of oak trees signaling the start of their property came into view, she began her search. Oftentimes he took in an afternoon cigar on the upstairs balcony, but a glance revealed it empty. Same for the wraparound porch. Several trees stood guard across the front lawn, and the urge to hide up one and cry until the sting of disappointment faded was strong, but gardeners — hired by and loyal to her aunt — milled about the property.

The oak front door swung open and Kate nodded to their butler, Mr. Cribs, while stepping past him into the foyer. The click of her heels followed her across the marble tiles, then faded as she wandered down the carpeted hallway, peeking into doorways for her father. When she reached his study she opened the door and slipped inside, smiling as the warm, rich smells of leather and cigars surrounded her. Across one wall, floor-to-ceiling mahogany shelves held hundreds of books. She'd spent many lonely evenings curled on an overstuffed chair by the fireplace, losing herself in the endless pages.

Kate checked the kitchen, the parlor, and even the stables, all with no success. Upon her return to the house she sought out a maid.

"Have you seen Father?"

The woman's eyes showed a mixture of surprise and sadness. "Today is April 5th."

Kate's hand flew to her chest. How could she have forgotten? Untouched except for weekly cleaning by the staff, her mother's dressing room had, for nine years, remained exactly the same. Once a year her father entered — on the anniversary of her death.

****

Hours later, long after Ben had fallen asleep, Kate tiptoed through her father's bedroom to a second door and knocked softly.

"Come in," said her father.

Kate turned the cool glass knob and stepped into the dressing room. Her father sat on a chair, flipping through the pages of a small, brown book. The lamplight revealed a distinguished man with a thick, well-kept mustache and eyes the color of the sea.

"Father, you didn't come down to dinner. Shall I have a plate brought up?"

Shaking his head, he continued fanning the pages of the book she now recognized as one of the guides they stocked for customers heading to Oregon Territory. Intent on leaving him to his thoughts, she headed toward the door, but when her hand touched the knob his voice broke the silence.

"Sweetheart, are you content with your life?"

She was startled to see his normally smooth forehead now marred by wrinkles.

"Of course," she assured him. "Ben is happy. You love us, and provide all we need and more. What else could I want?"

He tossed the book on the floor, ambled to the dresser, and traced his fingertip around the lid of her mother's silver jewelry box. "Would you ever consider leaving?"

"Leaving?" At her cry of surprise he crossed the room and took her hands. "What do you want to do? Buy a house in another town?" There wasn't a home within a hundred miles that could compare to theirs. The manicured grounds alone were the envy of all who visited.

"Yes." His grip tightened as his expression changed to one of joy. "In Oregon."

"Oregon!" Kate was stunned. "I know it's become the latest craze, but I never thought you would want to go." While working in the store, she'd overheard eager discussions of opportunities available out west. Lately, their patrons talked of little else.

"This isn't a whim," he insisted. "It's been on my mind since the Parkers went last year. And while I appreciate the role you've taken in the business, the house, and with Ben, I want to see you enjoy life. I'm not sure it will happen living here."

She sank to the sofa, shaking her head in astonishment at her father's words.

"Sweetheart," he said, kneeling before her. "I'm a rich man. I never expected such success, but there was a need in this town — a need I had the opportunity, and the good fortune, to fill. On the other hand, all the money in the world cannot buy what doesn't exist."

"What?"

"Land," he said with a triumphant smile. "When your mother and I first married we spoke often of starting a horse ranch, but life got in our way. I have the time and the money, but too many people have bought up property for their orchards. However, there are acres of untouched land out west, waiting for the care of a skilled hand."

"With so many heading west each day, how long can the surplus last?" In addition to watching travelers prepare for their journey, she'd seen the ones who'd returned — beaten by the trail and their own unfulfilled dreams.

"We'll start with a general store," he continued, oblivious to her distress. "We already have the knowledge and the contacts, and with the way people are talking, the next ten years will see more people going west than ever before. After a year or two of certain profits we'll pick out a spread large enough to support a full-scale ranch. Then, we'll round up mustang stallions and start a new line with the mares we brought with us."

"It seems you've thought of everything," she murmured.

He rose, thrust his hands in his pockets, and paced the room. "New settlers will need supplies. Horses too. Horses from a ranch I can build with my own hands."

Kate leaned against the sofa, still reeling. Her father's idea, though unexpected, intrigued her. All things considered, she did lead a lonely life. Her days were spent hunched over endless piles of paperwork. Evenings passed entertaining her brother and discussing business and politics with her father. Irritating her aunt was one of her few sources of enjoyment, and one she couldn't push too far.

Then there was family, or lack thereof, to consider. All her mother's family had remained in England and her father's only sibling, Aunt Victoria, was ten years older than Father with no hope for children of her own. Kate pushed at the rug with the tip of her shoe. All the reasons to go were clear, but when it came down to it, could she leave?

"Does your hesitation have anything to do with Crandall?" he demanded. "I've held my tongue thus far, but no longer. I'm sure you've heard the rumors regarding him and Mary. Tell him to decide once and for all, or you'll decide for him."

Her father's fierce tone surprised her; he rarely lost control of his emotions. She eyed the floor, dreading her next words. What if Crandall was right and she wasn't marriage material? What if every man felt the same way?

"We spoke today on the subject."

"I didn't realize." He paused, his voice softened in uncertainty. "How did it go?"

"He's engaged to Mary."

As shame colored her cheeks, her father's strong arms surrounded her. "Sweetheart, don't worry over a man who won't give you everything you deserve, including his undivided love."

Stifling a sob, she nodded.

"Kate, I know I'm asking a lot, but I can't stay here anymore. This house, this town, anywhere, is a constant reminder of your mother and the life we once shared. I need a fresh start."

Her heart was torn. She loved her father and had watched his anguish throughout her mother's long illness. She'd witnessed his frustration and then desperation at not being able to comfort her, to save her. His panic when she'd died, leaving him with an infant son and a thirteen-year-old daughter.

"You understand, don't you?" Anxious eyes begged her to tell him she approved of his proposition.

"I'm trying." Though she was beginning to comprehend the magnitude of what he asked of her, one thing was clear — with a single, fateful decision she would either give up all she'd ever known or shatter her father's dreams.

Kate thought of the days to come. By next Wednesday, Aunt Victoria would have heard the news of Crandall's engagement, and their morning visit would be dominated by cruel assumptions of why she'd lost his interest. Nothing was ever going to change. Everything would stay the same day after day, year after year, until one day she settled down with a man who fulfilled none of her desires.

Oregon was the only way out of her predetermined life.

Before she lost the burst of courage racing through her body, she spoke the words that would change her life forever.

"Father, I'll go to Oregon."

With an exuberant shout he picked her up, swirled her around, and kissed her on the forehead.

"Kate, you won't regret this. I promise."

Chapter Two

Jake

Friday, April 28, 1843

Jake Fitzpatrick rode his horse along the dusty road into Charlottesville. His last time in town had earned him a useless bottle of ointment from the apothecary and a bitter conversation with yet another pampered woman. This time, he hoped for a more productive visit.

He dismounted and tied his horse to the hitching post in front of Grey's Place, a restaurant known for obliging women and hearty portions. Though the smell of fresh bread drifted from the doorway, he swallowed hard and kept his boot heels to a steady rhythm against the boardwalk. The breakfast he wanted — steak, eggs, fried potatoes, a slice of apple pie, and a cold glass of milk to wash it all down — was a far cry from the cup of three-day-old coffee he'd poured for himself that morning.

When he reached the mercantile he stepped inside. As he waited for the storekeeper to finish with a customer, he noted the wares were orderly and clean, much like the impeccably-dressed storekeeper. His own coat, threadbare and held together by patches, was a testament to how far he could stretch a dollar, and his pride.

A stove in the corner fought, and lost, against the damp morning air. Resisting the urge to build up another man's fire, Jake stayed put and rubbed at the stiffness above his left knee. The liniment from his visit to the apothecary three weeks ago hadn't worked. Nothing ever did. The ache was a reminder of a cross-country journey years ago — his fourth.

When the customer walked out the door, the storekeeper shifted his attention to Jake. "What can I help you with?"

"You the one who needs a trail guide?"

The man's eyes widened, and a stack of books he'd begun straightening slid unheeded to the floor. "Yes."

Jake came forward and leaned against the counter. "I'm here for the job."

While many considered him a veteran of the fledgling Oregon Trail, Jake tended to dismiss such talk. He was simply a man willing to share his knowledge — for a price. A few months of watching over a wealthy businessman seeking excitement would earn him enough for a wide stretch of land in Oregon Territory. His dream was a simple one — to raise cattle and crops. But dreams required money, and due to his foolish pursuit of a worthless woman he was broke.

"You're hired," the storekeeper replied without hesitation.

"You don't waste any time, do you?"

"No one else wants the job," he replied with a tense smile. "My name's Elijah Davis. And you are?"

"Jake Fitzpatrick. Well, Mr. Davis—"

"Please, call me Elijah."

"Well, Elijah, everyone going west left weeks, if not months, ago. There's little chance of catching up to a wagon train." Needing money was one thing; taking advantage of a man was something else. Elijah needed to know the stakes.

"I realize that, but I've already sold my home and this store." Elijah waved an arm over the room. "The buyers are here, and I can't ask them to wait any longer. We have nowhere to go but Oregon."

"Who is 'we'?"

"My son and daughter."

Jake's hopes sank. Children made every aspect of the journey difficult compared to men with only saddlebags and a horse. This unexpected development was a deal breaker. Now, in order to arrive in Oregon with enough money to purchase seed and animals, he'd need to tighten his belt. Good thing he wasn't a stranger to tough, hungry living. Oftentimes when food and bullets were low, he pan-fried dandelion greens and survived off the bitter leaves and stems. While he wasn't eager to do it again, each dollar saved meant more opportunities out west.

"You could spend the winter with family and go out with next year's wagon trains," Jake suggested, feeling a twinge of guilt at the desperation in Elijah's eyes. "Leaving this late would be a foolish undertaking with children."

"My daughter's an adult and my son is almost ten."

Jake frowned. "I'm only willing to take on a riding partner. Best of luck." He spun on his heel, already calculating the cost of a ration of coffee and beans to get him started.

"I'll pay twice the going rate, plus compensate you for all your supplies," Elijah called as Jake neared the doorway.

He stopped walking. Provisions for one man could run hundreds of dollars. Slowly he turned and eyed Elijah, taking another measure of the man.

"It could get dangerous at the end if the weather turns bad."

"A risk I must take." Elijah extended his hand across the counter. "Do we have a deal?"

One word.

One word stood between Jake and an amount of money that would put him months, if not years, ahead. For a moment he could only stare at Elijah's palm, his mind rampant with possibilities. Then, before reason overcame reality, he changed his future.

"Yes," Jake said, sealing their deal with a firm handshake. "As for supplies, I'm figuring since you're the storekeeper you know what's needed and how to load the wagon?"

"Consider it done."

"Then we'll meet at your house a week from today. At dawn."

Chapter Three

Preparations

Tuesday, May 2, 1843

Kate sat at the dining room table, draped a linen napkin over her lap, and prepared to enjoy dinner with her father.

"A toast," he said, holding his water glass in the air. "To our new lives in Oregon."

As their crystal clinked, Kate tried to push aside thoughts of the countless tasks awaiting completion. Between getting the store's books in order and supervising the packing of the house, she was exhausted. She hadn't gone to bed before midnight all week, and she still needed to be at the store each morning. Her father had worked just as hard purchasing supplies and wagons and overseeing their delivery.

"Where's your brother?" Her father motioned toward Ben's empty chair. "I hoped he would join us for dinner since tonight is one of our last evenings in our home."

"He's off with James and the Bloom brothers, stirring up all types of mischief, no doubt. He begged for one last night with them, and I didn't have the heart to say no."

A servant set a gold-rimmed china plate on the table before her. Flank steak, roasted red potatoes with a sheen of herbed butter, and steamed asparagus — just as she'd ordered that morning. After expressing her satisfaction, she dismissed the servant.

"I've purchased a building in Oregon City," her father said as he cut into his steak. "And a home two miles outside of town. Also, I've done some checking and it seems our trail guide is one of the best."

Kate had more pressing concerns than the abilities of a hired hand. To her dismay, Edith, her personal maid, had refused to accompany them to Oregon. Since childhood she'd had someone to care for her hair and manage her elaborate wardrobe. Each dress included a complicated system of corsets, buttons, and ribbons, making it impossible to don one without assistance.

"Were you able to convince the cook or any servants to come along?" she asked.

"It seems none share our daring spirit," he replied while buttering a roll with crisp precision. "We'll hire more the moment we arrive."

She frowned. Their diligent household staff was trained to anticipate their every need. Now who would cook their meals while they traveled? Wash and care for their clothes? Prepare her bath?

As fast as they'd risen, Kate dismissed her concerns. Her father wasn't worried, so he'd obviously made other arrangements. Either way, such trivial details were irrelevant.

When they were done eating, Kate rang the bell directing the servants to clear the table and then waited until they disappeared into the kitchen to continue speaking.

"Did you purchase oxen?"

"Eight. They were delivered today and are in the east paddock." He removed a cigar from his vest pocket. "How is packing going?"

"We'll be done in a few days."

"See it doesn't take longer. Thursday I finalize the sales of the home and store, and we'll leave the next morning."

"Consider it done," she replied.

During the past three years, her father had rarely made a business decision without sounding it out on her first. Kate was thankful he valued a woman's opinion, especially his daughter's. Many men wouldn't bother consulting their family before deciding to embark on any trip, much less one to a foreign land not yet belonging to the United States of America.

After dinner, Kate and two maids finished packing the eleven flat-bottomed trunks her father had purchased for their journey. No expense had been spared, including hiring a seamstress to line the interior compartments with velvet.

Her wardrobe took six trunks. Books, silver, linens, and other heirlooms filled another four. After spending over an hour spreading scented tissue between treasured quilts and placing them into the final trunk, Kate sighed in frustration at a maid's repeated attempts to close the lid.

"Pull out the top quilt," she commanded. "As for my mother's lace coverlet, try squeezing it in with the china. If it won't fit, put it in the case with my shoes."

"Excuse me, Miss Kate," a timid maid whispered from the doorway. "There's another group waiting to see you."

Rising to her feet with a groan, Kate headed downstairs for another round of goodbyes. It seemed the entire town planned on stopping by. Everyone except Crandall.

****

Late that night, Kate returned to her room for her bath. It was, as always, scented with rose petals from their hothouse garden. Lavender-scented towels sat in a basket nearby.

Her nightly routine included a rosewater cloth placed upon her face for five minutes to blanch her skin, then the application of a honey and witch-hazel solution to keep it soft. A chamomile rinse left a shine in her hair, while lotions and oils applied after her bath kept her skin smooth.

Edith helped her undress. Once she left the room, Kate unpinned her hair, allowing it to tumble down her back. This began the favorite part of her day — sinking down into the steaming water, resting her head against the rim of the tub, and feeling her tense muscles relax.

While her fingertips swirled grooves into the surface of the water, she began her latest evening ritual — reflecting on her failed relationship with Crandall. During the day, activity kept her mind off the cheating louse. Not so at night when she was alone with her thoughts. Then, her emotions ranged from anger to despair as she replayed their last conversation in her mind.

As for the stranger who'd witnessed her humiliation, she hadn't seen him since.

Chapter Four

Reasons

Friday, May 5, 1843

Jake stood before his campfire, rubbing his left leg against the chill in the morning air as he watched the sun rise over the Blue Ridge Mountain range for the last time. His horses, Plug and Nickel, stood nearby, saddled and waiting.

Departure day had arrived.

Not wanting to be late, he finished his coffee in one gulp and reached inside his vest pocket for a handkerchief to wipe the cup clean. Instead of cloth, his hand brushed against crumpled paper. He swallowed hard, then slid out the note that ten days ago had shattered his carefully-laid plans for Oregon.

Jake,

Traveling across a barren land to spend a lifetime in a shoddy cabin is barbaric, and I want no part of such nonsense. It is obvious I want more for my life than you can give me. You needn't bother calling again.

Valerie

Even now, his pride hurt more than anything else. Out of sheer loneliness, he'd allowed himself to pursue a relationship he knew, deep down, had been destined to fail. As to why? Well, he had nearly three thousand miles to figure it out. When a man spent hours straddling horseflesh with nothing but the horizon ahead, the mind couldn't help but wander.

Done reminiscing, Jake crumpled the scented paper and threw it into the fire. Greedy flames browned the edges of the taunting reminder of his stupidity, and then consumed it entirely.

His time as a settled man was over.

Chapter Five

Burdens Collide

Kate awoke to the cry of their rooster and immediately summoned Edith. Departure day had arrived, which meant dressing in the outfit she'd planned down to the last detail. Her finest gown, green velvet with black ribbons adorning the bust, had been scented with rosewater. Satin shoes completed the look of perfection.

When Crandall watched her leave town, she would appear her absolute best — beyond impractical considering the journey ahead, but her best nonetheless.

Once her primping was complete, Kate went outside. Ben sat on the porch steps, watching their staff load trunks and furniture into both wagons. At her footsteps, he jumped up and ran to her side.

"I figured I'd find you in the middle of all the action." She reached to tousle his hair and he ducked away with a laugh. "Have you been out here long?"

"I saw the sunrise," he said, hopping foot to foot. "Father s-said he'd teach me to s-shoot when we get to Oregon."

"How exciting."

"I'll be a c-c-cowboy!" He vaulted over the railing and ran toward the stables.

Kate surveyed the organized chaos on the front lawn. Two men stretched canvas over one wagon while several more hoisted bags of flour into the other. A stable boy struggled to contain the oxen wandering about, and a carriage filled with well-wishers traveled up the lane.

It was happening.

****

Jake rode onto Elijah's property with a bedroll, four saddlebags, and two horses. As he approached the massive house he squinted, thinking once again his eyes betrayed him.

Supplies and crates were scattered across the lawn. A woman, her face obscured by a grandiose hat, called orders at an old man struggling to heft a trunk into a wagon so overloaded two of the sideboards were already split. He looked to the porch and noticed more luggage. Glancing back to the grass, he saw another wagon. Unbelievable.

Jake dismounted to gauge the full extent of their over-packing. A peek into a wagon revealed trunks stacked so ineptly the first hard jolt would bring everything tumbling down.

A boy with a coil of rope slung over his shoulder approached, climbed a wheel, and began to push up the doubled canvas. *This must be Elijah's son.*

"Helping your father pack?" Jake took the rope from him and tossed it into the wagon.

The boy nodded while flashing a wide grin.

Jake chuckled and stepped around him, intent on finding Elijah, but instead he ran right into the woman he'd seen earlier. Only this time a hat didn't obscure her face.

"You!" he said in disbelief.

Standing before him was the beautiful woman with the sharp tongue he'd met at the apothecary weeks ago. The same one who had been on his mind every day, no matter how hard he tried to forget her fiery green eyes and the temper to match. What was she doing here?

"Did you come for a reason?" Her fists slammed against her hips. "Or merely to ogle me?"

If she was surprised to see him she covered it well.

"So, do you remember me?" he asked, amused at her instant anger. "Or are you always this rude to people you've just met?"

"Do you always appear out of nowhere and scare women and children?" she responded in mimicking sarcasm. "I thought you were a friend of my father's until I noticed you poking around our wagons."

Jake recalled Elijah mentioning his daughter was grown. Could this wildcat be coming along?

"Would your father be Elijah Davis?"

"Yes." Her eyes narrowed with wary curiosity. "Why do you ask?"

"Name's Jake," he said with a tip of his hat. "I'm here to guide him and his family to Oregon."

He watched with odd satisfaction as she realized the man who'd overheard her conversation with her beau was the same man hired to bring her across the country. To her credit she recovered quickly.

"My name is Katherine, and this is my brother, Ben." She tucked an arm around the boy's shoulders and managed a hurried squeeze before he pulled away. Undaunted by the snub, she returned her attention to Jake.

"My father mentioned he hired someone to assist us. However—" she brushed imaginary lint from her sleeve "—you'll find I don't pay much attention to servants."

"I'm not a servant, ma'am," he corrected. "I'm your leader."

Her eyes locked with his and told the lie of her next words.

"Well then, you simply must forgive my harshness." After a long pause, her innocent expression turned smug. "You see, I took you for yet another of the dishonorable men milling around town lately. A woman can never be too careful."

Jake bit his tongue so hard it stung. This woman was the sum of Valerie and all her kind: big skirts and little substance. Even worse, she was completely unsuitable for trail life. They were to leave in minutes, and she wore a dress fit for an evening of parlor games.

Willing his face to remain expressionless, he tipped his hat once again then walked to his horses, intent on calming his rising irritation. *A servant! Dishonorable!* After adjusting Plug's harness and giving Nickel a handful of acorns, he saw Elijah emerging from the stables. Sighting Jake, the storekeeper walked over.

"You're right on time," Elijah noted before his expression changed to one of chagrin. "Unfortunately, we're not. My farriers are still checking over our fifteen horses to ensure their shoes are ready for the trip, and replacing any worn ones. They should finish within the hour. At least the eight oxen are ready." He smiled. "Have you met my children?"

This man needed his expectations reined in. Quick and hard.

"Yes," Jake replied, still smarting over Kate's words. "I suggest you go alone and send for them once you're established."

Elijah's eyes widened. "I couldn't leave them for so long."

Jake tried again. "It's dangerous out west for a woman. Especially one Katherine's age."

Elijah's lips twitched from hidden mirth. "She can take care of herself."

"Suit yourself. Let's move on to my other concern." While Jake would honor his agreement to lead this family, including the spiteful daughter, he wouldn't budge on the next matter. "We can only take one wagon. And you'll need to lighten your load or the axles will snap less than a mile out of town."

Jake had expected Elijah to either recoil in shock or plead frantic reasons for disagreement, but he appeared unaffected at the grim news.

"I'll bring what's necessary to make my children feel at home once we arrive. Though, you needn't concern yourself," Elijah said with a tense smile. "The second wagon is full of supplies."

"I disagree. Supplies are bags of flour, dried fruit, and spare wagon parts. Not bolts of cloth, heavy furniture, and trunks."

"I need those things to stock our store and furnish our home. Two wagons shouldn't be a problem."

Elijah's nonchalant replies and inability to understand the situation didn't bode well for their journey.

"Two's impossible," Jake corrected. "We don't have the manpower. And while we're on the topic, since leaving late means less grass and water, you can only bring two horses — any more jeopardizes the other animals."

Elijah cocked his head with a frown. "I'll remind you I'm paying a substantial amount more than the going rate for a trail guide, and I plan on giving you a bonus once we arrive."

Apparently Elijah was accustomed to getting his way by using wealth to smooth over conflicts. Well, today would be different.

"Money isn't the issue, and I'll remind you I was the only one willing to take the job."

Tenderfoots like Elijah always expected to transport themselves and their belongings across half a continent without problems. There were always problems.

"I'm a patient man," Jake continued. "Normally, I'd let you learn firsthand how your excess will tire the oxen until you're forced to abandon your load trailside. But in the interest of time, and for everyone's safety, I insist on one wagon and two horses." He paused, weighing his next words before continuing. "Don't take chances, Elijah. I've buried plenty who have."

Elijah started at the grim words and Jake softened his tone. "You can send for your things once you arrive. They're not worth the risk."

A stare-down with his employer wasn't how Jake wanted the day to start, but he held his gaze firm as Elijah's eyes ran through a gamut of emotions — resentment, anger, and frustration. Thankfully, they settled on resignation.

"I have to admit, I didn't expect an objection." Elijah ran his hand along the back of his neck. "While I appreciate your point, realize this will be difficult for my daughter."

"I understand. Once the wagon is loaded proper, I'll try and find room for a few of her treasures."

"Fair enough," Elijah said.

"And while we're getting things out in the open, know your family coming along means extra work. I won't have time to watch over them."

Elijah's eyes narrowed. "They're great children."

"I don't care how great they are. My concern is if they comply when I give an order." Jake knew he was pushing, but wanted this point understood. "I plan on supervising the repacking, but I'll need your help."

"You'll get it right after I find a buyer for the second wagon. It shouldn't take long."

"Sell two of those oxen while you're at it." Seeing Elijah's surprise, Jake added, "It'll mean more water and grass for the others."

Pulling papers from his pocket, Elijah headed toward the house. Jake spun on his heel and nearly knocked over Ben. The boy wore a hat two sizes too big, a smear of dirt across one cheek, and a toothy grin.

"Are y-y-y-you a real c-c-cowboy?"

Jake smiled for the first time in a week. "Not exactly."

Ben's face showed disappointment then changed to hope. "W-w-will I see one in Oregon?"

"I guarantee it."

"If you're not a c-cowboy, then what'll you do out there?"

"Well, first I need to get us to Oregon." He put his hand on the boy's shoulder and pretended deep thought. "Your father will be busy driving the wagon, which means I'll need a helper. Someone who can check gear, care for stock, and update me on how everything is holding together. You the man for the job?"

Ben stared up at him with utter adoration. "You bet! I'll get started." He ran toward the stables.

At least one member of the Davis family wasn't upset with him. Too bad the next one wouldn't be as easily swayed. Jake returned to where the older man continued in his struggle to lift trunks into the wagon.

"Sir, those appear heavy."

The man straightened and put a hand to his back. "Yes, sir. Most of Miss Kate's luggage has been rather burdensome."

"Go inside and relax. I'll take over."

Spotting the little spitfire fanning herself on the front porch, Jake decided it was high time for a lesson in loading a wagon. Her tantrum, at the least, would be entertaining.

"Could you come here, please?" he called, and then watched in amusement as she sauntered over.

"Can I help you?" Her tone left no doubt a different reply simmered beneath powdered skin and a lifetime of practiced decorum.

"I'm culling useless items from these wagons." He pointed to a nearby stack of trunks. "I assume these are yours?"

"You assume correctly."

"Well, Katie, since we're taking—"

She interrupted him with a quiet, yet somehow haughty, cough. "My family and friends call me Kate."

"Very well. Kate, since we're taking—"

"*You* can call me Katherine."

The hint of a smile behind her brusque words intrigued him, but he continued on as if she hadn't spoken.

"—one wagon, there isn't room for useless things." He motioned to the smallest trunk. "You can bring this one."

"Absolutely not," she declared with a look that betrayed her indignation. "We'll take both wagons, all my trunks, and anything else I desire."

"No, we won't."

"Where's my father?" she demanded.

"Selling the other wagon."

Her eyes widened and he saw fear lurking in their green depths. "You're lying."

"I'm not a liar and take offense when called one." A flash of regret crossed her face and he knew the point had been made. "You need to begin deciding what stays behind. We don't have all day."

"What are you going to do?" she stammered.

Jake took an apple from his pocket, enjoying her astonishment. "Eat my breakfast while you repack."

"I will do no such thing."

Ignoring her, he pointed to a mirror. "We'll begin with this. You can't take it."

Her jaw dropped. "My mother brought it over from England. I wouldn't expect you to know a valuable piece, but it's worth more than you could ever dream."

"Yep." He bit off a chunk and began chewing noisily. "It stays."

"No."

"Yes," he said firmly. "It will break the first week."

"Fine." Her pert chin raised a notch. "Are we done?"

He shook his head. "We're just getting started. I haven't even taken the canvas off the other wagon yet." He grasped the handle of a nearby trunk, lifted it a few inches, and then let it drop. "What's in here?"

Her lips flattened into a tight line of frustration. "Books."

"They're too heavy and serve no purpose. Pick a few and leave the rest."

"You aren't being paid to decide what we bring."

Everyone had their limits, and this woman was testing his. "I have the final say on what stays and goes. And I say this trunk of books—" he tapped it with his toe "—stays."

"Don't touch my things with your filthy boots." He might as well have kicked a newborn foal for the look of revulsion she wore.

He nodded to another trunk. "What's in here?"

"Dresses."

"There's no fancy balls where you're going. Choose three and call it good."

She gasped. "I couldn't possibly bring only three."

Taking another bite of apple, he focused on another trunk. "That one?"

Her eyes narrowed with contempt. "China."

"Nope. We'll use metal on the trail. How about this one?"

"I don't know," she muttered through clenched teeth.

"Check."

Swishing her skirt out of the way, she knelt down, fiddled with the lock, and opened the lid. Her eyes met his in unspoken challenge. "My trousseau."

"You can make more once you arrive," he said indifferently. "Though I doubt you'll ever have the need."

"How dare you!" Crimson anger stained her cheeks and warned him to tread lightly. After all, her father had agreed to pay him a life-altering amount of money and it wouldn't do to lose the job on the first day. He took a breath and let it out slow.

"I've made this trip four times, carrying only saddle bags. Suited me fine."

"Yes, but you obviously have no appreciation for the finer things in life."

Untrue, but Jake had no interest in debating his background. "And you're about to get a hard lesson in what's important for survival. Let me assure you it isn't books and dresses, princess."

"Don't call me a 'princess'. You don't know me."

Jake knew her type, and hated the charmed lifestyle and privileges that went with it. Kate was cut from the same cloth as Valerie: a typical female who wanted little more than to spend money, be indulged, and hear assurances of her flawless beauty.

He wasn't about to coddle yet another pampered woman's every whim.

"I knew everything there was to know about you five minutes after we first met," he said, matching her glare. "You're spoiled–"

"I'm not spoiled."

"I suppose everyone grows up in a house like this?" He waved his hand across the two stories of white grandeur. "You probably spend your days sipping tea and blushing at simple words from spineless men."

"Certainly not. I'll have you know I've worked in my father's store since I was thirteen, not that a shifty drifter like you comprehends real work."

If the hours weren't ticking by like minutes, he'd have been amused by the attempted slight. But arguing with her meant more of a delay, and time was one thing they couldn't spare.

"Quit stalling and go through your trinkets."

"I'm done with you," she said in a brisk, airy tone. "Wait here while I speak to my father. Upon my return, I'm certain you'll find my choices of what I'm bringing upheld."

She flounced off toward the house, swept up the porch steps, and vanished through the door. Jake sighed, knowing he'd gone too far. Once she told Elijah how he'd spoken to her, Jake wouldn't blame Elijah for sending him on his way.

****

Blinking back angry tears, Kate stomped through the house. *Why did the trail guide have to be him?* Not only was Jake a bitter reminder of her last conversation with Crandall, he treated her as if her opinion and feelings were of no consequence. She'd escaped the clutches of Aunt Victoria and now he clamored to take up her role.

She found her father in the study, sitting at his desk, staring at his deerskin billfold. Surely once her father learned of Jake's actions he'd straighten him out.

"Father, please tell the guide I can bring what I need," she said, dropping into the chair across from his desk.

The remorse in his eyes sent her confidence spiraling.

"I've already sold the second wagon."

She bolted from her chair and began pacing the room, trying to suppress her rising panic.

"He demands I abandon all of Mother's belongings." She cast him a speculative look. "What will we remember her by?"

"Those are just things, sweetheart. You can take your memories wherever you go. Besides, the sale of the wagon to the Andersons included the agreement they bring three of our trunks when they come out next year."

"When I agreed to this, you never mentioned a limit on what I brought," she countered, "or the accompaniment of a rude, uncivilized hired hand." Desperation roiled through her body. "I know the house is sold, but can't we stay in a hotel suite and go out with next year's wagon trains?"

He walked to the leather couch and patted the spot beside him, coaxing her to sit.

"Sweetheart, we're in a serious situation. I've spent a lot of money preparing for this trip, and we need to save everything we've got left for our new life in Oregon. This is our last chance for departure this year, and we need an experienced guide to take us. From now on we'll follow his orders — starting with repacking."

Chapter Six

Departure

Jake leaned against the porch railing and watched his three burdens roam the yard. Negotiations with Elijah, terse words with Kate, and reloading the wagon had squandered the morning. Nevertheless, he'd learned plenty.

Judging from the number of prominent townsfolk saying their goodbyes, this family was well connected and well respected. And though Elijah had been naïve regarding what they could bring, he'd selected the wagon and supplies with an admirable attention for quality. Even better, neither Elijah nor his son balked at tough work. They'd been at his side most of the morning, helping when they could.

Yet now, while oxen and horses waited with growing impatience, Jake's confidence waned. Didn't they realize every inch the sun crept up the sky meant less miles at day's end?

Half an hour later, the jovial atmosphere of the yard faded into one of somber hugs and handshakes. As the overdressed intruders returned to their carriages, Jake stepped off the porch. Time to take control of this group. If he didn't, they'd never leave the yard.

He crossed to where Elijah and his children stood, waving off the line of carriages winding down the lane.

"Ready?"

"Shouldn't take more than another hour," replied Elijah. "Two at the most."

Jake clenched his jaw. At this rate, his teeth would be stubs by midnight.

"The trail doesn't tolerate idle hands or wasted time. As of this moment, neither will I. We leave in fifteen minutes."

Kate whirled to face him. "Departure is on our terms, not yours."

While her challenge didn't surprise him, the uncertainty in her eyes did. And if he wasn't mistaken, fear lingered in them too. Was it possible she didn't want to go? Jake filed this consideration away for future pondering.

"Fifteen minutes," he repeated.

While two members of the family were less than enthused at his words, Ben let out a whoop of excitement.

"Hear that, Father? We're gonna get s-started."

Elijah held Jake's gaze as if testing the merit of siding with his daughter. After a long moment, he squeezed Ben's shoulder. "Yes, son, I believe we are."

Kate's smirk faded at the defeat. Jake took the opportunity her silence provided to lay out ground rules.

"This is my fifth time across and I assure you, trail life isn't easy. Your responsibilities won't be either. But I want one thing clear before we leave." He paused to focus solely on Kate. "I won't tolerate my orders, or my judgment, questioned. If I sound harsh then so be it. I was hired to do a job, not for my friendship."

She had no response — hopefully setting a precedent for the coming months.

"As for riding positions, Elijah, you'll drive the wagon. Katherine, you'll finish arranging supplies in the back. Ben, if your father agrees—" he nodded in deference to Elijah "—you and I will ride scout."

Ben's chest swelled under his father's thoughtful stare. With a chuckle, Elijah gave his consent.

"Sounds good."

Ben's eyes grew wide. "I've never s-scouted before."

"You've got to learn sometime." Jake resisted the urge to smile as Ben bounced from foot to foot. "You can start by checking over the horses and reporting back on how they're doing."

"You bet!" Ben scampered across the yard.

"I appreciate you taking him on," Elijah said. "Let me know if he's too much to handle."

"Not a problem," Jake replied. So far, the nine-year-old had shown himself as the most reasonable in his family. The boy deserved to learn. "Go ahead and round up the oxen. I'll help lift the yokes in a few minutes."

Elijah headed toward the paddock, leaving Jake alone with Kate and her inevitable complaints. She didn't disappoint.

"I won't leave town stuck in the back of a wagon." Her smooth tone portrayed a woman in complete control, but indignation ruled her eyes. "I'm capable of riding and have been doing so for years."

"Then you know a horse's back will suffer if it carries a rider day after day. If you prefer, you can walk." He glanced at the glossy cloth covering her toes. "Never mind. Until you wear suitable shoes—" he pointed to his well-worn boots "—you'll ride in the wagon."

She frowned and lifted her skirt a fraction. A diminutive foot, clad in no more than a slipper, twisted in the air for his inspection.

"These are custom made, imported from England, and the best money can buy."

"I see money can't buy common sense," he muttered as he dug into his coat pocket for a handkerchief.

The skirt dropped into position with a rustle. "What's that mean?"

He stopped searching. "It means those shoes, much like you, aren't strong enough for this trip. Both will fall apart in less than a week." After a quick check to make sure Elijah and Ben were out of earshot, he glared down on her. "I don't want to see or hear from you until nightfall. You can arrange your treasures or sleep away the day, but you'll stay in the back of the wagon."

She drew in a sharp breath and exploded. "No matter what my father says you're still our hired hand, which means I'm your superior. Therefore, I will ride today!"

Elijah turned from where he'd been coaxing the last team of oxen into their yoke to focus on his screeching daughter. With a frown, he strode to her side.

"Everything all right here?" he asked.

Jake clamped down on a cruel retaliation. After all, he needed this man's money and he'd given his word. Cursing himself for not backing out of this trip with these people when he'd had the chance, Jake walked to the rear of the wagon and untied Plug.

****

In the wagon indeed! How would Crandall see her leave if she sat hidden in the back? Kate had waited weeks to watch the gutless fool realize the final cost of his unfaithfulness as she rode out of town. Why couldn't Jake compromise just this once? She'd lost every fight, sacrificed nearly every belonging, now he intended to deprive her yet again.

To her relief, Jake unfastened a black-and-white paint and led it over.

As he held out the reins, she dared a dainty sniff. "This saddle is not for women and this is not my horse. I'll wait while you remedy your errors."

She regretted the words the instant they left her mouth, both for their spitefulness and for the certain retaliation they would bring. With a hint of trepidation, Jake's eyes shifted to her father. Seconds later, they returned triumphant.

Apparently, she'd lost another battle.

Her suspicion was confirmed when Jake's deep voice rumbled in her ear. "You'll ride this horse or none at all."

Cheeks burning, she shot him a surly glare but didn't challenge him again. Silently, she took the reins from his gloved hand and raised her left foot to the stirrup. Despite the layers of petticoats swirling around her legs, she mounted and settled astride the saddle with practiced ease.

Jake's smirk faded. "Let's move out."

While the others took up their assigned positions, Kate closed her eyes and prayed for safety throughout the journey ahead. Then, as her emotions flitted between excitement and panic, she rode away from the only home she'd ever known.

As she headed down the front lane the finality sunk in. Never again would she wander the garden paths, slide down the banister when her father wasn't home, or gaze upon their roses from the balcony. Worst of all, she wouldn't see Marie Ann's baby grow up.

Only by the strongest of wills did she win the battle against tears.

Sweat from Kate's hands darkened the reins as she followed the wagon into the heart of Charlottesville. Heart pounding, she summoned all her courage to see Crandall one last time. They would ride down Main Street and right by his store.

She'd envisioned the scene in her mind countless times. The ending varied between him standing on the boardwalk with his jaw dropped in surprise that she was leaving to him running after her, blathering apologies and begging her to stay. Either way she wouldn't say a word. She'd ride away, secure in the knowledge he was watching the best thing in his life disappear forever.

Moments later, they made their way past the apothecary. The steps stood empty, but not the window. As she rode past, two fingers moved aside the curtain and she caught a glimpse of Crandall. The companion of her childhood, the man she'd considered sharing her life with, didn't have the decency to stand outside and see her off.

Good riddance.

Head high and heart intact, she followed her new life down the street. But as Jake began the final corner out of town a faint voice made her turn.

Marie Ann plodded up the street, arms encircling her swollen belly. Kate dismounted, tossed the reins over the nearest hitching post, and ran to her friend's side.

"The baby's due in two weeks," she scolded as Marie Ann caught her breath. "You should be in bed, not out here chasing me."

"I couldn't let you leave without one last goodbye," Marie Ann replied, flushed and vibrant as ever. "So I snuck away from the nurse."

When their burst of laughter subsided into sobs, Marie Ann pulled a handkerchief from her sleeve, wiped her cheeks, and passed the cloth to Kate.

"Robert said you could stay with us for a while in case Crandall changes his mind."

Kate shook her head against fresh tears and false hope.

"I understand." Marie Ann's lip trembled as she pulled a box from her apron and slipped it into Kate's skirt pocket. "We're all rooting for you back here and—"

At her friend's dismay, Kate spun and saw the glossy black tail of Jake's horse disappear between the bakery and Smith's Hardware. Grimly, she followed the grooves in the dust left by the trailing reins, but only managed a few steps before the sound of approaching hooves halted her progress. Jake stopped his horse at her side.

"The first time I look back I find you on the ground and my horse missing."

She pointed to the alleyway. "I'm going after him."

"Don't bother," he muttered. He removed a glove and brought two fingers to his lips. Three sharp whistles pierced the air. After several tense moments the wayward horse returned. Kate didn't make a sound as Jake dismounted, checked over his saddlebags, and then led the horse away.

Marie Ann slid her hand around Kate's and nodded to where Jake stood, retying his horse to the back of the wagon. "Who's he?"

"Our trail guide," Kate whispered as Jake reappeared.

"I hate to make a scene in front of your friend," Jake said, tipping his hat in Marie Ann's direction, "but you're wasting time by not following orders. Now, get in the wagon!"

He mounted his horse and set off without a backward glance. Horrified, Marie Ann dropped Kate's hand and pulled her into a crushing hug.

"Kate, don't go."

The plea tested Kate's weakening resolve, but in the end, family won. With a shaking hand she smoothed away her friend's look of concern.

"I'll send a letter when we're settled."

****

Kate saw the last of Charlottesville through the gap in the gathered canvas at the back of the wagon. When the town blended with the horizon, she opened Marie Ann's gift. Nested inside the box was the pearl ring she loved, the one she'd always chosen when they'd played dress-up together as children. All her reservations about leaving returned as she slid the circle onto her finger.

"Sweetheart," called her father as tears threatened. "How about sitting with me a while?"

Getting through the wagon was a chore. She stumbled over a bag of flour, banged her ankle on a chair leg, and tore a hole in her sleeve climbing through the front canvas. Breathless, she settled beside him.

Oxen's hindquarters aside, the view from the seat offered plenty to wandering eyes. Tree covered hills nestled together under a cloudless sky. A lone oak stood watch over the road, its thick, gnarled branches offering refuge for travelers and wildlife alike.

"I see your first day is going well," her father said.

The simple words, meant to tease, unleashed another wave of doubt.

"Oh, Father," she cried. "I worked so hard, but nothing about our departure went as intended." She studied her extravagant dress with a sigh. "Crandall didn't even say goodbye, and I've fought with that horrible man all day."

"Give Jake time, Kate. He is rough, but success out west doesn't come easy, and certainly not to soft men."

Rough indeed. Jake knew nothing of her life, but hadn't bothered with one question as to her abilities. She wasn't soft. Her father had made sure she was skilled in practical matters — she knew how to ride, how to shoot, and could tie seven different knots fast and well.

"This morning didn't go as I'd planned either," he added. "However, anything worth having comes at a price."

The advice came from experience. Years ago, he'd left behind a successful business in the shipping industry to be with her mother. In return, she'd given up her homeland — England. The journey to America, her mother had always insisted, had been worth every minute of danger. Kate had grown up hearing stories of her parents' love and knew of their material sacrifices. Yet only now, as the wagon carried her away from all she'd ever known, did she fully understand all they'd surrendered to make a new life together.

And now it was her turn.

"No need to worry about me." She patted his arm, suddenly filled with newfound confidence. "I'll be fine after a nap."

Between farewells the previous night — which included a stilted, tearless goodbye to her aunt — and repacking, she was exhausted. She kissed him on the cheek and slipped through the canvas.

The featherbed came from her room, but the similarity ended there. Normally topped with down pillows and a satin duvet, her bed now lay beneath a grey wool blanket, a box of tools, a sack of beans, and rope. The base, three flat-topped trunks, was less than half the size of the bed frame she'd left behind. She shoved everything aside and closed her eyes, grateful for the chance to rest.

But her body had other plans.

The wagon jolting over the rutted road and no breakfast proved a terrible combination — she needed to be sick. Except how? Every kettle, pan, and dish sat in the kitchen box outside the wagon, and hanging her head out the back would stain the canvas. Asking her father to stop would bring Jake's certain ridicule — both for her weakness and for wasting time.

With Jake and Ben far ahead and her father busy driving, no one would see her slip from the wagon. Their pace was easy; she could be back long before anyone missed her. She eased under the canvas and balanced on the back ledge, her skirts fluttering in the wind.

The wagon hit a bump. Her stomach lurched, and before hesitation got the best of her, she leapt.

****

Trampled grass. A worn path leading over the rise ahead. Hot sun overhead. Freedom and endless possibility.

The trail, the one constant in Jake's life, welcomed him back like no other.

With his charges in close pursuit, he rode Nickel at a brisk pace. Ben held his horse named Old Dan, a dapple gray with a white mane and black tail, a few paces behind Jake. Twenty-five yards farther, Elijah kept the wagon at a steady clip. Half an hour later, both still tackled the rolling hills without difficulty. In fact, Ben appeared to be having the time of his life. Even the oversized hat couldn't hide the boy's enthusiasm.

"You ready to ride scout?" Jake called.

Ben nodded, nearly sending his hat tumbling to the ground. With a chuckle, Jake motioned him forward.

"Got a handkerchief?" he asked once the boy rode beside him.

Ben dug into his shirt pocket and produced a square of red cloth with a proud flourish.

"A scout's first duty," Jake said, plucking the hat from Ben's head and the handkerchief from his hand, "is to watch for danger. To do so, you need to see your surroundings." He re-folded the cloth into a long strip, eased it into the brim, and passed the hat back.

"Thanks!" Ben replaced his hat and studied the rocky hill ahead for all of ten seconds before turning to Jake. "We're doing g-good, huh?"

Jake grinned.

Between intermittent nods at the chattering boy and glances back to check Elijah's progress, his irritation soon faded. Clear sky, warm sun, and a crisp breeze — he couldn't ask for better.

They passed by open fields before the trail narrowed and veered to the left. At the top of the curve, Jake looked back. To his surprise, fabric fluttered in the wind at the back of the wagon.

Jake squinted against the bright sun. Was it the wagon canvas? He wiped a sleeve across his eyes and focused again. No, the canvas wasn't balanced precariously on the wagon's back edge, it was Kate!

Before he could shout a warning, she fell to the ground. Hard.

"Of all the foolish..." he muttered and added a few curses while reining in Nickel. Leave it to this woman to injure herself in the first hour of the journey.

Ben drew up alongside. "What's wrong?"

"Your sister jumped from the wagon."

"Is s-she hurt?"

"I'm heading to check. Stay here."

Jake pivoted his horse and thundered toward the wagon. When he passed Elijah he gave the signal to stop, but rode on without explanation.

Twenty yards further down the road Kate was trying to stand.

Upon seeing the darkened dirt spread out before her, he slowed his horse and his anger. Dismounting, he pulled a fresh handkerchief from his vest pocket. He wet it with his canteen and then crouched beside her.

"Riding in the wagon can be tough on the stomach," he said, offering her the cloth.

She dry-heaved into the dirt. While he waited, he noted the smear of filth across her bone-white cheek and the tear in the sleeve of her dress.

"Did you eat this morning?" he asked softly when she quieted again.

She shook her head. Warily, she accepted the handkerchief and held it to her mouth.

"Quite a leap you took back there." He bit back the lecture about respecting orders and trail protocol. Instead, he stood and focused on the wagon. "Your father's headed over."

She groaned at the sight of Elijah hurrying toward them. When she struggled to rise he took her by the hand and pulled her up.

"Since you have a delicate stomach, I'm willing to compromise," he said quietly. "If your feet can handle it, walk next to the wagon when you feel ill. But in the future," he cautioned, "never jump from a moving wagon. From the side the wheels could crush you, from the back you could get tangled in the canvas." He paused and studied her. "Though, if you're willing to brave a fall like that one I doubt much could hurt you."

Too bad she'd let Plug wander off in town. They would have been a perfect match; both had a strong temperament and a fine form.

Chapter Seven

Day's End

Kate admitted defeat after one mile. Jake was right; her shoes were no match for the rugged terrain. She returned to the dim wagon and rummaged for her riding boots while eyeing the bed.

The bed won.

She slept for an hour, dozed for another, and when Jake called for a break she sprang from the wagon. While the others cared for the animals, she spread a blanket on the grass, fetched four tin plates and cups, and then brought out the basket their cook, Sue, had placed in the wagon moments before they'd left.

Kate kneeled on the blanket, flipped open the lid, and smiled in delight. Their last meal from home would feature all her favorites: slabs of cold ham, buttermilk biscuits with strawberry jelly, pickles, and three types of cheeses. For dessert, an apple pie.

After arranging the food, Kate reached into the basket in search of silverware and gasped at what she found instead. Nestled beneath a stack of cloth napkins lay her mother's china teapot and a matching pair of cups and saucers. The ones Jake had demanded she abandon on the porch that morning.

Never had she been so grateful for a servant's defiance.

Her father's shadow fell across the blanket and she quickly closed the lid. The secret would keep until the first night in their new home.

"Everything all set?" he asked.

Not trusting her voice to conceal her excitement, she nodded.

"Jake should be along in a minute or two. As for your brother," he said, pointing to a mighty oak standing watch over open grass, "he begged and I couldn't resist."

Kate spotted Ben shimmying up the trunk and shared a chuckle with her father. Though a flock of crows wasn't so amused by his antics. Chattering their displeasure, they scattered and reunited in the air above as he pulled himself along a branch.

Moments later Jake joined them. He stood at the edge of the blanket, his eyes darting from one item to the next. However, when her father motioned toward an empty plate, he shook his head.

"No need. I got a saddlebag full of hardtack and jerky."

Kate frowned. Why wouldn't he share their provisions? She glanced at her father in confusion but stayed silent.

"In case I wasn't clear earlier," her father replied, "your payment includes meals."

Jake remained as he was — eyes locked to the food spread out before him, yet wrestling against some mysterious inner turmoil.

"I insist," her father added firmly.

Jake ran a hand across his jaw then knelt onto the blanket and pulled his hat from his head. "Thank you."

Kate loaded her plate and chatted with her father while surreptitiously watching Jake.

With quick movements that betrayed his eagerness he rolled up his sleeves, revealing thick, tanned forearms. Since their encounter in the apothecary he'd gotten a haircut. The change suited him, bringing focus instead to his square jaw and piercing blue eyes.

Had he expected to survive on what he carried in his saddlebag? No wonder he now sat on their blanket, his plate filled. Though for a starving man he ate with restraint, even waving off her offer of seconds.

Her father nudged her and pointed to Ben, now close to twenty feet high.

"My boy is fearless," he said with a proud smile. "I hope the new property is filled with trees."

Jake shaded his eyes and focused on the lone oak. "You may want to call him back. He won't get another chance to eat until dinner."

Her father's sharp whistle pierced the air.

As Ben hustled down the trunk, Jake tossed his napkin on his plate, brushed his hands together, and rose.

"Thank you for the meal." Jake looked to Ben, now standing flushed and grimy at his side. "We're moving on in ten minutes."

Ben fell to his knees at the edge of the blanket, shoved two biscuits in his pocket, then stuffed a slice of ham in his mouth. Chewing mightily, he dropped a wedge of pie into one hand and then poured a cup of water with the other. He drank greedily, wiped his lips with the back of his hand, and then got to his feet.

"Ready to scout?" Jake asked, smiling as Ben dug his fingers in the jar and fished out three pickles.

Meanwhile, Kate grimaced at his question. While Nina was their best mare and Old Dan was their most reliable gelding, all horses need time without a rider. Which meant either she or Ben would be walking at all times. Before her brother got his hopes too high, she spoke up.

"Ben, I'd like to ride now."

The crestfallen look on her brother's face almost made her reconsider. Almost. Leaving their other horses had been Jake's decision, not hers. Ben could take the issue up with him.

"You could ride in the wagon," she added.

Kate hated to see Ben look to Jake for confirmation before nodding.

Minutes later the group set out again. Jake took the lead, now on the black-and-white paint horse that had abandoned her in town that morning. His other horse, Nickel — brown, with a straw-colored mane and tail — was tied to the back of the wagon beside Old Dan. Her father drove the wagon with Ben on the seat beside him. She rode Nina and stayed far away from Jake.

The clear sky above, light breeze against her face, and favorite horse beneath her bolstered her spirits. So much so that hours later when Ben's subtle hints at wanting to scout moved to outright begging, she cheerfully agreed. After all, it was high time she changed into riding clothes.

After climbing back into the wagon, she began searching for her sole trunk. Moving aside several bags of flour and a spare wheel brought a sheen of sweat to her forehead, but she persevered until she saw gold locks against green metal. After opening the lid, gentle searching soon turned frantic as she recalled putting aside her riding boots and all practical clothes to make room for two dresses and a mink wrap. Though she'd intended to repack them in another trunk, in all the confusion they'd been left behind.

Dread swept over her as further rummaging produced only her long-retired stable shoes. She'd brought them for their memories — not for use. They were crushed flat and the folds were black from age.

Kate stuck a foot inside one and tied the laces. Much to her dismay, she found no amount of kneading would relax the crease below her anklebone. Stiff leather pressed against soft flesh and promised a blister. To make matters worse, they pinched her toes and the soles were already worn thin.

They would have to do.

Kate walked, and managed to keep up for over an hour before her throbbing feet demanded rest. Back in the wagon, each spin of the wheels brought more misery to her now roiling stomach. When dusk took the sky she lay on the bed, her head resting through the hole in the back canvas.

"Whoa," Jake called. "Better quit for the day. Don't want it dark the first time we make camp." Her father stopped the wagon, hopped to the ground, and began unhitching the oxen.

"Kate!" Ben's face peered at her over the wagon seat. "Jake said I g-get to help Father find a creek and later he will t-t-teach me how to whittle. Gotta go!" He disappeared with a shriek of glee.

Smiling at his joy, Kate climbed from the wagon. Three steps later the searing pain of raw skin brought her to her knees. She gingerly removed her shoes, revealing blisters on each heel and swollen toes that burned like they were on fire.

Jake walked over to her. "Your brother and father are searching for water. While they're gone, you need to..." He trailed off as he saw her feet. "Try walking barefoot. Calluses will form and you'll barely feel anything."

"My feet are accustomed to daily soaks and softening creams. I refuse to allow this trip to change my routine." She ran her fingertips over her heel and winced. "This is your fault."

"My fault?"

"If you hadn't been so stingy about what I could bring I'd have better shoes."

"I told you to wear sturdier ones. You didn't listen."

Her cheeks grew warm, but she wouldn't give him the satisfaction of knowing what she'd done. Her feet were already bearing the brunt of her mistake; she didn't need his sharp words adding to her pain.

Thankfully their conversation was cut short when Ben ran into camp, followed closely by her father. Both were bursting with the news of a nearby creek until Jake quieted them by assigning duties.

"Ben, while I water the animals you can get the horses' feed ready. Elijah, I'd like you to check over all the harnesses, saddles, and yokes. Katherine, you'll collect wood for the fire."

While her family rushed off to their tasks, she stared at him in disbelief. "You've seen my feet and surely realize I'm in no condition to walk."

"No one else can do your job."

With a sigh of defeat, she reached for her shoes. Gritting her teeth against the pain, she eased her foot inside. She ignored his outstretched hand and rose on her own.

"So it's true," she muttered. "A leopard can't change its spots."

"What?"

"Never mind."

"Fine," he said. "Your thoughts don't concern me."

Jake said the words lightly, but his eyes betrayed his interest and she was unable to resist a final slight. "When I took sick earlier you were helpful and kind. I see now you were merely acting out of character."

Movement across camp caught her eye and she noticed Ben watching them. Their constant arguing wasn't setting a good example for her brother, something she'd tried to do since her mother's death. Swallowing her pride, her temper, and another insult, she took a breath and tried again.

"I'm willing to help, but I can't walk far."

"You won't have to. There's plenty of wood available today. We're months away from using chips."

"Chips?"

"Buffalo droppings."

She drew back in horror. "Surely you're joking."

"I'm not, so treasure each piece of wood you find."

Kate grabbed the bucket from his outstretched hand and limped off. Before long, she'd filled the bucket and even found a chip. Pulling Jake's handkerchief from her pocket, she captured the chip with the cloth and tossed both in the bucket.

After returning to camp, she flopped down beside the wagon. She'd long since given up on keeping her dress clean. Soon enough, Jake peered into the bucket.

"You found enough. Can you start a fire?"

"Of course," she snapped in annoyance. "I'm not helpless."

He snorted and went to help her father and Ben picket the horses.

Starting the fire proved impossible. After making many useless attempts and plenty of smoke, she gave up. Jake returned and raised his eyebrows at the charred remains.

"No fire?" he asked with mock astonishment. "I figured you'd have it roaring by now."

She clenched her hands. "The wood is wet and won't light."

He squatted, brushed aside her efforts, and thoroughly explained the process. Once he had the beginnings of a fire, he shifted to face her. "There aren't servants to do everything out here. You've got to fend for yourself."

"I would have gotten it eventually."

"Right about the time we were starving to death," he muttered while placing another branch on the flames. "I hope you don't cook like you pack."

"You assume I'm cooking? With the amount of money we're paying you, *you'll* be the cook."

"Not unless you want only jerky and hard tack. Besides, I've got too many responsibilities out here to make meals as well." Rising, he gave her a skeptical look. "Can you cook?"

In reality, her only part in meal preparation was to order the weekly menu, but she spoke with all the arrogance she could muster. "I watched our cook when I was young. How hard can it be?"

His eyebrows raised in amusement. "Very well. The fire is strong and everything you'll need is in the wagon, so you shouldn't have any more problems."

"Fine," she said through tight lips.

But it wasn't fine. Over the next hour she spilled the coffee, burned the beans, overturned the pan of salt pork onto the coals, and the cornbread didn't rise. And, after all the trouble preparing the meal, the last thing she wanted to do was eat it.

When she summoned everyone to dinner, they sat around the makeshift table, joking about hunger pains and rumbling stomachs. Their mirth faded, however, once they saw their plates.

"I guess I've got some learning to do," Kate said, wincing as her father scraped ashes from his salt pork.

"Sweetheart, I'm proud of your willingness to make the effort, and I'm sure you'll get better over time."

With a smile of relief, she took her place at the table beside her father, folded her hands, and bowed her head. When her father didn't speak, she opened her eyes to see Jake gingerly setting his fork on his plate with an uneasy expression.

"Jake, we usually pray before our evening meal," her father said. "You're welcome to join us if you like."

Kate bowed her head again, this time watching surreptitiously as Jake lowered his head. With a giggle, Ben poked Jake's hand and pointed to his hat. Jake pulled his hat into his lap and gave Ben a wink before bowing his head again.

"Thank you, Lord, for this day you've given us," her father said, "and thank you for keeping us safe on our journey. We also give thanks for bringing Jake into our lives and ask you to help him guide us in the following months during our travels together. In your precious name, Amen."

Chapter Eight

The Warning

Saturday, May 6, 1843

Beneath the star-filled sky, Jake thrashed about in his bedroll, plagued again by the nightmare of his youth.

"Father, it's good to have you home," Jake said as he bent to pick up the ax. The woodshed was empty and they planned to spend the morning replenishing the supply.

"I'm glad to be back, son. I know it's been hard on you these last two weeks while I've been gone tracking the Gilroy brothers and then bringing them in to face their sentencing."

Jake felt his father's strong hand settle on his shoulder.

"You're only ten, but you've become a fine young man. I don't have to worry while I'm out on a job since I know you're back here taking care of everything." He eased the wedge in place. "We better get chopping. Your mother wants to make a pie to celebrate my return."

"Hey, Marshal!" The unfamiliar shout came from the direction of the house. His father walked to the doorway and peered outside.

"The Gilroys are here," his father said. Quick as a flash, Jake found himself pushed into the corner, an old horse blanket thrown over his head.

"Stay put," his father whispered. "Whatever happens, don't move."

Footsteps thudded across the floor and then softened as his father headed outside. Jake pulled his head from the blanket and scurried to a knothole in the wall. Pressing his cheek against the rough board, he saw two men holding his mother and younger brothers at gunpoint.

Although his mother's dress was torn at the chest and blood dripped from the corner of her mouth she stood quietly, her eyes narrowed in defiance. Jake saw the glint of a knife secreted within the folds of her skirt.

At six years old, Michael could do no more than stand protectively in front of their mother, his chest heaving with panic. Little Teddy, only three, sat howling in confusion with his favorite blanket clutched between his chubby fingers.

"Put your guns down," his father commanded before taking a step forward, hands in the air. "You don't want to do—"

Four shots rang out in rapid succession, and Jake watched in wide-eyed horror as one by one, his family slumped to the ground.

Jake woke, his blankets constricted around him in a sweaty tangle. His breath came hard and fast as he drew trembling hands across his eyes, a futile attempt at erasing the image of his bloodied family lying before him in the dirt.

Twenty-one years ago his life changed forever with one heartless act.

After the terrible day, he'd been sent to live with relatives in New York. Education, forced upon him until he spoke like one of them, had done nothing to tamper his plans for his life. Five long years had passed before he'd been able to break free and live as his own man. By then, the U.S. Marshals had long since seen to the fate of John and Jessie Gilroy.

Jake kicked aside the shambles of his bedroll, knowing sleep would elude him the rest of the night. Darkness surrounded him and hid his weakness, while the light from the stars and red-hot coals cast an eerie glow across the silent camp.

He rose, intent on checking yet again that all his charges were safe. Once he'd made certain all animals were tethered and calm, Ben and Elijah slept beside each other in their bedrolls, and the wagon canvas was securely fastened, he crouched and built up the fire.

All was well in the camp, if not his mind.

****

"We're burnin' daylight. Let's go!"

Jake's voice boomed through the canvas, jolting Kate awake. She'd drifted off two hours prior; doubt and the lumpy featherbed proved themselves as barriers to sleep.

Struggling upright, she caught a glimpse outside through the gap in the canvas. To her astonishment, the sky held bright stars. The man was a fool — even birds still slept.

She pulled a blanket over her nightgown, clutched it beneath her chin, and stuck her head out the back of the wagon. Jake stood beside the fire, filling a tin cup with steaming coffee. The flames reflected his frown as he set the coffeepot back into the glowing coals.

"It can't be past four in the morning," she called. "What are you thinking, waking this early?"

Jake strolled to the back of the wagon, cup in hand. As he grew closer, the smell of burned coffee filled her nostrils. How could he drink something so vile?

"We're weeks behind schedule. The time won't be made up by sleeping past dawn. If we'd have left when I wanted we'd have two miles in by now."

Leave earlier? Kate considered this while Ben's and her father's tousled heads began poking out from their bedrolls.

"I want everyone ready to move out in fifteen minutes," Jake said.

At this, Ben tossed his blanket aside and jumped up, fully dressed down to his boots. Dirt scattered as he scooped up his bedroll, wadded it, and then staggered toward the front of the wagon. Meanwhile, her father propped himself up on an elbow.

"I'm not as quick as my son anymore," he said, pausing to yawn and give his head a thorough scratching. "But I'll be ready."

Jake faced her. "That leaves you."

"Better watch yourself, Jake," her father said while kicking blankets from his legs. "Kate's never appreciated sunrises."

"How unfortunate." Jake's gaze didn't waver, yet his lips curved into a grin which incensed her even more than his taunting words. "Especially since she'll be seeing so many of them on this trip."

Kate did her best to slam the canvas shut, but had to settle for a rustle in the fabric. As she reached for her dress, every muscle in her body protested. Blistered heels rubbed against the rough wool blanket and she couldn't help but whimper. Stiff fingers fumbled, and then succeeded, against buttons and laces.

Taming her hair was another matter entirely. On her first attempt, the brush stopped halfway down her scalp. Minutes ticked by while she struggled to work through the knot. She tossed the brush aside, tried a braid, and eventually settled for shoving the tangled mass underneath her bonnet.

"Come on, Katherine. Time's a wastin'," Jake called.

"What about breakfast?" she yelled, eyeing her bed and wanting nothing more than to snuggle back into the warm feather lumps.

"We'll eat at daybreak," Jake shouted back.

By the light of the dwindling fire, Jake and her father yoked the oxen, hitched the wagon, and saddled the horses. Kate fought back yawns and listened as Ben chattered on about scouting.

"Let's move out," Jake said once he and Ben were mounted up, her father was in the seat, and she sat in the back of the wagon. After making her bed and straightening the wagon, Kate decided to sit with her father.

She climbed through the canvas and discovered the wagon seat, empty yesterday, now held a bag of cornmeal. Sacks of flour lay on the floorboard below.

"What's all this?" she asked, settling beside him.

"Jake mentioned redistributing the weight in the wagon. I guess this is his answer."

Within minutes, her right leg grew numb from hip to toe. Her father was a large man and even though she was petite, the seat was crowded. She shifted again, trying to find a comfortable position.

"I'll walk if you feel up to driving," he offered.

She reached for the reins, and then hesitated. The weight of the wagon and the temperaments of the oxen intimidated her. "No, I better not."

Nervous about walking in the dark, she returned to the back of the wagon. With nothing better to do and an endless amount of time on her hands, she lit the lamp, set it on the dresser, and dug out the trunk full of books she'd hidden underneath a stack of blankets.

While reaching for her favorite, *Mansfield Park*, the wagon lurched and she sprang to catch the lamp. Sighing, she blew out the flame.

Two hours passed before they stopped for ten minutes, long enough to eat the remainder of the ham slices and leftover cornbread. Hours later, as she lay on the bed contemplating how long it took for a person to go mad from hunger, she heard Jake's command to stop. She poked her head through the front of the wagon to see lush grass and a pond. Several trees offered plenty of shade.

Lunch consisted of baked potatoes — charred on the outside, raw on the inside — and fried pork. Other than singeing her palm removing the thing Jake called a spider-pan from the fire, meal preparation went well.

"Thank you for the meal, sweetheart," her father said after they'd eaten. "While you clean up, your brother and I will get started repairing the snapped bridle."

Ben followed her father across camp, and they knelt before the toolbox.

"Sounds like they've got a handle on the situation," Jake said. As her father's patient explanations on using a leather punch drifted through the air, he gathered the dishes and placed the stack before her. "Soaking these in heated water first makes it easier to scrub them clean. Wash bucket and soap are hanging on the side of the wagon."

To her disbelief, he strolled to the pond and sat against a tree trunk. When his head tipped back and his eyes closed, it was too much to take. She stomped over.

"What are you doing?"

"Trying to rest," he said. "But your yammering is ruining it."

She gasped. "We got up before dawn and now you want to spend the afternoon lounging?"

"Start early, rest during the heat of the day, travel late. That's how it's done. I suggest you try a nap. It might improve your outlook."

"I think not," she muttered, exasperated both with his words and his sudden drawl.

"Suit yourself," he said, lowering his hat over his eyes.

Fuming, she marched back to the wagon, snatched up a cloth, and doused it with water from Jake's canteen. Each plate and utensil received a quick swipe before she tossed it into the kitchen box. Satisfied, she climbed into the wagon and emerged with two books, her writing supplies, and the cloth bag containing her mother's sewing kit.

Intent on getting away from Jake, if only briefly, she disappeared over a small hill. Settling herself on the grass, she examined a rip in her skirt.

After ten minutes of attempting a repair, she gave up in frustration. Thread lay hopelessly tangled atop the material — material now dotted with blood from a pinprick to her thumb. During her childhood she hadn't time to pursue idle tasks like sewing. She'd been too busy caring for her ill mother. Basics like cooking and sewing were completely foreign to her, and now she would suffer for the lack of those skills.

Setting the kit aside, she thumbed through the books many considered vital education for travelers. They were filled with tales of adventure, survival, and Indians on bloody warpaths. Not wanting to think of such atrocities, Kate set them aside and unpacked her writing supplies. Two words into her letter to Marie Ann, she heard Jake shout it was time to leave.

****

Jake stood at the top of the hill, staring down at the cause of his problems. Kate sat small and alone, her dress and flowing hair the one spot of color amidst a field of grass bending in waves with the wind. Though she'd changed from yesterday, her attire was still more suited to an afternoon in a parlor than traveling across an unsettled land.

His footsteps broke the quiet as he headed down the hill. With a panicked glance over her shoulder, she began shoving items into a hemp bag.

"I'm sorry if I startled you," Jake said as he approached. "I wasn't sure if you heard me say we were leaving soon." He caught a glimpse of the two books as she slid them into her bag. "Have you studied much about Indians?"

"No," she replied with a hesitant shrug. "I found these among my mother's things when she died and figured I'd take them along."

"Don't let their exaggerations worry you too much. After all, there's plenty of actual danger out here."

"What are you talking about?"

"Dysentery, cholera, broken bones, frostbite, dehydration, hunger, getting lost, and death are the real threats. What this book says—" he plucked a title from her bag "—is the least of your concerns."

Her face went pale.

"I've seen weather so cold a man's legs froze from his hip to toe. I've watched a man drown trying to cross a swollen river. I've led searches for lost children and found them days later shrieking from hunger and fear. There are many things worse than Indians, few of which you can prepare for or prevent."

Hating himself for the terror he saw in her eyes, he went on.

"This trail isn't the place for a society woman. Never has been, and won't be for some time. But if by some miracle you do make it west, rest assured you won't be the only female. Oregon City is populated with soiled doves." Noting her confusion, he grimaced through his next words. "Do you know what that means?"

Eyes wide, she shook her head.

"I'll phrase it nicely for your ears." With a purposely leering look, he slowly rubbed his chin. "Ladies of 'easy virtue'."

Watching this innocent woman cower from his words made Jake's stomach roil, but she needed a sharp dose of the truth. Disgusted with his cruelty, but at the same time knowing time was running out for her to return to Charlottesville, he crouched before her.

"Women of your type won't be around until these parts need settling. Head back now. Your father can send for you once he's established and I am far gone."

Jake spun on his boot heel and walked away, not giving her a chance to respond.

****

Kate watched Jake retreat over the hill. She'd known of the dangers they could face; they'd been the focus of idle chatter for the past month. But hearing them away from her warm, secure home, from someone who had actually made the journey, made them real. She would be lying if she didn't admit she was afraid. But as she recalled his vulgarity, her fright grew to anger. She was a lady, and for him to talk of such vile things was highly improper — a fact any man knew, no matter how uncivilized.

When she returned to camp the oxen stood hitched, her father held the reins, and Jake sat in his saddle. Ben stood at Old Dan's side, an unspoken question in his eyes. Not trusting her voice, she nodded her response. Yes, he could ride.

Jake led the group off.

Kate walked all afternoon, her cheeks flushed with exertion and rage. As the sun sat on the horizon, she returned to the wagon, proud of her dual accomplishments. Not only had the hours outside stretched her shoes and muscles, they'd focused her mind on one thing. Jake couldn't keep her from going west, and his speech made her more determined than ever to succeed.

"We've gone nonstop for hours," Jake called. "Let's break for the night."

She climbed from the wagon and looked around in dismay. There were no trees to speak of, and they were at least fifty yards from a lake in the hollow below. "What are we supposed to do — haul water up a hill?"

Jake dismounted and walked to her. "Wildlife won't come close if humans are around. Stopping here ensures animals needing a drink will come to the shore." His expression grew fierce. "Instead of questioning my judgment, why don't you help Ben pull out a circle of grass for the fire?"

Knowing arguing was futile, she knelt beside her brother.

"I hate that man," she whispered.

"You d-don't hate him. Besides, Father says we can't hate anybody."

"I know." She yanked the stubborn, prickly grass, wincing as the sharp edges cut into her palms. "But if I was going to hate anyone, it would be him. He's disrespectful and impatient. I'm going to speak with Father about dismissing him."

Ben shook his head, wise beyond his years. "You d-don't know where you're going and neither does Father."

"We don't need him," she insisted.

"We need him like you need gloves." Ben laughed at his own joke, his own leather-clad hands continuing their newfound swoop-and-pull rhythm. "B-be quiet," he warned. "He's coming back."

Head down, she snatched up a handful of grass so hard a clump of dirt came up with it. She threw it aside, barely missing the tip of Jake's boot.

"Ben, your father wants to check on the squeaky wheel. Why don't you come along? Your sister can finish up here."

After Ben scrambled to his feet and ran off, a pair of gloves dropped to the ground before her.

"By the way, your brother was right."

Chapter Nine

Water Trouble

Sunday, May 7, 1843

Kate held scissors in one hand and a fistful of hair in the other. She'd fought against a snarl the size of an orange since dawn.

The snarl won.

Tossing the clump of hair aside, she picked up her mother's silver hand mirror and inspected the bald patch above her left ear. At least the rest of her hair shielded her latest failure at trail life.

Hiring a personal maid would be her first priority once they arrived. She'd succeeded in dressing herself, but her hair was another matter. Tight, smooth coifs were a past luxury; out in this forsaken wilderness she was fortunate to brush through a finger-wide section before Jake started in with his morning demands.

"Kate, you awake?"

Dropping the scissors onto the table, she fell prone across the bed and stuck her head through the hole in the back canvas. Her brother stood in the grass below, spinning the brim of his hat on one finger. His plaid shirtsleeve bore a new rip and a fresh circle of dirt covered one knee.

As always, he made her smile like no one else in the world.

"G-guess what?"

"What?" she replied, grateful for the small comfort of his cheerful presence. Back home he'd tagged at her heels, but now he only seemed concerned with Jake.

"Jake told Father I could s-saddle Old Dan and Nina every day and maybe water them too!"

Why did Jake hate her so? She'd done everything he'd asked and more when it came to getting wood, cooking, and making camp, yet still he undermined her efforts at caring for their horses.

"I better get started," Ben said, blissfully ignorant of his position as Jake's pawn in controlling her every action.

His retreating footsteps mingled with Jake calling her name. Part of her considered ducking back through the canvas, but she stayed still. She'd never acted a coward, and Jake wouldn't make her start. Besides, there'd be no avoiding his latest tirade — he'd already spotted her and was walking over with a confidence that bordered on swagger. When he stopped at the back of the wagon, their eyes met straight on.

"Katherine, you told me yesterday you wanted to be responsible for watering your horses. Ben's ready to saddle them, but they still seem thirsty to me."

She clenched the canvas until her knuckles grew white but held his gaze. "I'm still getting ready. I'll be out in a few minutes."

"Caring for your horses takes priority over whatever you're doing. Make it one minute."

And thus began another day.

They spent the afternoon break in the open sun with the wagon providing the only shade. After letting the horses and oxen drink sparingly from water poured into the men's hats, they moved on again. Evening found everyone hot, tired, and thirsty, but only a few swallows of water per person and animal were allowed. Dinner was forgettable and sleep couldn't come soon enough.

****

Monday, May 8, 1843

Kate stepped out into the crisp dawn air and built up the fire for coffee. Minutes later, she filled three metal cups with the strong brew — their one luxury during the water shortage. At Ben's hopeful look, she poured a mixture of water and coffee into a fourth cup. Anything to please her little brother.

Hours later, it was long past hot. Tired of the relentless sun beating through her bonnet as she walked, she returned to the oppressive heat trapped within the wagon's canvas. A canteen hung from the dresser knob, taunting her with each sloshing swing. When Jake called for the afternoon rest, the wheels were barely stopped before she bolted from the wagon. Stopping meant lunch and a full cup of water all her own.

"We'll make this a quick break," Jake said as she stretched the miles from her muscles. "If we push we might get to a creek tonight. Until then, drink sparingly."

After a lunch of beans and cornbread, she wiped the dishes with a damp rag and returned everything to the kitchen box. She then waved off Ben and her father's invitation of exploring the area, preferring instead to sit in the shade of the wagon and tame her matted hair.

The next fifteen minutes brought tears of frustration and pain, and a nest of brown snarls in the dirt before her. Sweat trickled down her neck and seeped through her collar. Her back grew slick underneath her dress.

Her efforts were rewarded in the form of two thick braids.

Setting her mother's silver brush aside, Kate leaned her head against the wagon wheel. If only she could have some water! The few tepid swallows with their meal had done nothing to cool her. Worse yet, it had been four days since she'd had a proper bath or a change of clothes.

Fanning herself with her sunbonnet gave no relief. Rolling the material idly in her hands she groaned, first at how filthy it had become and then again at the thought of putting it on. Rising, she went to the water barrel, intent on wetting her handkerchief and scrubbing the worst of the grime from herself and her bonnet. When they stopped for the evening she could finish both jobs properly.

Just as her arm plunged deep into the glorious wetness, Jake came around the corner of the wagon, beating dust from his clothes with his hat. Seeing her, he stopped mid-stride.

"What are you doing?"

How, with a simple sentence, he managed to be both irritated and demanding she would never understand.

"What does it look like?" She didn't bother keeping the edge from her voice. "I'm cleaning my bonnet."

Shaking her head in exasperation, she pulled her handkerchief from the barrel. After squeezing out the excess water, she rubbed the cloth over the darkest stain.

"That's all the water we have." His tone was as chilling as his words.

"You said we'd come to a creek tonight."

"No, I said we *might.*" He spoke slowly, as if she were a child. "What part of 'every available drop of water is for our canteens, the animals, or for cooking' was confusing to you?"

Her cheeks grew warm. He'd spoken those words just that morning, but she'd forgotten his warning once he'd given news of the upcoming creek.

"You're right. I should have waited and I'm sorry."

"Tell that to your brother tonight when he's thirsty."

The words cut like a knife. How dare he insinuate a tiny bit of water would bring harm upon her family, especially her brother?

Grabbing up her skirts, she hopped onto the log near his side. This man would tower over her no longer.

"That's it!" she shouted. "I've had enough!"

Chapter Ten

A Family United

Jake regretted his cruel words the second they left his mouth. He wanted nothing to jeopardize this job, and with it Elijah's money he needed to lay the foundation for a new life. First and foremost, he needed to calm her down. Elijah and Ben were within earshot over the next hill, and he didn't want an angry woman, and her father, on his hands.

Even if he deserved every bit of her wrath.

"You're out of line." Her eyes glittered with fury as she pointed a dirt-stained finger at his chest. "I've done everything you've asked for, yet still you thrive on making me feel useless."

"I'm only trying to teach you—"

"You don't teach! You order me about and then condemn my efforts. You show my brother and father every detail to manage their tasks, yet refuse me the same courtesy."

The log wobbled and he steadied her by the arm while she regained her balance. Why was she standing on it anyway?

He tried again. "Living out here means you've got to understand a few—"

"Oh, I understand all right. I've heard it all before." She began mimicking him. "You didn't get enough wood, Katherine; go get more. You got too much wood, Katherine; a waste of time since we can't carry extra. The horses need water, Katherine; why haven't you watered them? The horses don't need so much water, Katherine; you're wasting it." Her ranting faded with a weary shrug. "Jake, your endless criticism must stop."

Crossing his arms, he considered his next words. Time had nearly run out to send her back. And the woman before him, teetering on the brink of rage and tears, needed a final nudge in that direction. Really, it was for her own good.

"It will stop. If you go back to Charlottesville."

Her hands clenched into tiny balls of rage. "I wouldn't give you the satisfaction! I'm on this trip whether you like it or not, so get used to me and all my faults."

"I don't have that kind of time."

"Which still doesn't excuse you from being a decent, civil human being!"

Jake opened his mouth to reply, but movement over Kate's shoulder changed his mind. Elijah leaned against the corner of the wagon, watching them. Leaving Kate standing on the log, Jake headed straight for her father.

"I need to speak with you," he said, hoping this time the man would listen to reason. "Tonight."

****

Jake set a fast pace the rest of the afternoon and into the evening until he found what he'd been searching for. Actually, to his chagrin, Ben had seen the reflection first.

Jake urged Nickel back to the wagon.

"It's over there," he said, pointing to where trees nestled within an outcropping of rock.

"What is?" Elijah asked.

"The creek," he replied, then smiled as relief settled over Elijah's face. Hot weather had lowered the water level, but there was plenty for man and beast to drink their fill.

They made camp twenty yards away from water's edge, and soon a hum of activity filled the air. Ben unsaddled their horses and Kate brought them to the creek. When she returned, she cajoled Ben into helping her gather branches for the fire. Meanwhile, Elijah unloaded supplies from the wagon and then brought the oxen to the creek.

Jake followed with his horses.

The confrontation with Elijah was now or never. He'd resorted to finding fault with every task Kate had performed for the past two days, but to his surprise she hadn't asked to go home. Time to reason with her father.

"I don't know what you heard this afternoon—"

"I heard plenty," Elijah replied as he inspected an ox's leg.

"You need to reconsider your daughter coming along. She isn't suited for such an extensive journey and has already proven she can't handle the hardships. What you overheard earlier was a result of her blatant disregard of my order to save water."

Elijah said nothing, just continued massaging the ox's leg muscles.

"In addition, she's burned a staggering amount of food, she's argumentative, and still questions my orders."

Elijah rose, sent the ox off with a slap to the rump, and then faced him.

"First, I'm going to ignore the fact you're attempting to go back on your word — for now. Second, while I appreciate the guidance and patience you've shown Ben, I know you haven't done the same for Kate."

Elijah's face remained stoic, yet his eyes betrayed a sea of conflict and guilt.

"She's only twenty-two, but I suspect I've destined her to a lonely life. I raised her to be an intelligent, informed partner in my business. As a result, she is headstrong and speaks her mind without hesitation. She's also brighter than most men, which tends to intimidate."

Jake fought the urge to look away.

"So," Elijah continued, "although you've seen her consult me for advice, don't assume she can't handle herself. And coming to me about Kate does no good — she makes her own decisions."

Elijah's stare turned challenging.

"While I don't appreciate the tone I've heard you take with my daughter, it's always been my rule to let her fight her own battles. Furthermore, because I have confidence in her and believe she can handle the hardships, she will continue on this trip. Let me know now if you're backing out of our agreement."

Though Jake hadn't expected an immediate capitulation, Elijah's staunch support of his daughter was daunting. Could he have misjudged her?

"I'd like a few questions answered first."

"Ask away," Elijah said.

"She's argued her way into caring for your horses. Can I trust her to do it right?"

"She loves those horses and is more than capable of the task."

Jake finally asked what had been on his mind since meeting Kate in the yard the first day.

"I'm curious as to why, if you think so highly of your daughter, did you destine her for a life of hardship? Surely you must know it's far from settled or civilized out west and won't be for years to come?"

Elijah gave a wry smile. "Oregon is the perfect place for a woman of Kate's caliber."

"That remains to be seen," Jake muttered.

At this last statement Elijah's eyes narrowed. "My advice to you, young man, is to stay out of her way. I will ask her to stay out of yours. Now, do we still have a deal?"

Jake knew this family would be lost, or worse, within a week if he deserted them. The burden of their safety lay upon his shoulders. For better or worse he was stuck with Kate. He didn't have to like it, but he did have to accept it.

"Yes," Jake said, extending a hand to Elijah, who grasped it in a firm handshake. "I won't mention this again and would appreciate if you would do the same."

With things settled between them, they led the oxen and his horses back to camp.

****

Hours later, as Elijah and Kate talked in the wagon, Jake watched Ben wander through the camp, muttering to himself.

"Hi there," Jake greeted the boy. "You up for helping me check over the oxen's hooves?"

"Sir, you s-s-shouldn't talk bad to my s-sister anymore. Just b-b-because she does stuff wrong doesn't mean you get to be s-so awful to her." The boy took a trembling breath. "And if you k-k-keep it up you'll deal with m-me."

Jake hid a smile at the fierce protectiveness the boy displayed. He would grow into a fine man someday.

"Ben, it's my job to make sure nothing goes wrong, and your sister keeps doing things that could get her, or someone else, hurt. What do you suggest I do?"

Ben stirred his foot in the dirt. A family trait, Jake decided, since he'd seen Kate do the same thing. Silence filled the air, broken moments later by Ben's hesitant voice.

"I d-don't know." Ben raised his eyes with a hopeful look. "Maybe I could d-do more work so she wouldn't have to do so much?"

The boy was young, but eager to learn. Moreover, he'd stated his opinion and stuck up for himself in the stubborn way only a nine-year-old could in a battle with an adult. In doing so he'd earned Jake's respect.

"How about helping hitch and unhitch the oxen?"

Ben's face lit up. "Yes!"

With a chuckle, Jake led him to the wagon and began explaining how to smooth the oxen's yokes. He was well into his discussion, all the while patiently answering all of Ben's questions, when he caught Kate watching from across the camp. Curious, he stared at the boy.

"Did your sister send you to talk to me?"

"It was my idea." Ben's assurance was quick and honest. "I heard her c-crying again in the wagon after fighting with you. I felt bad for her."

Jake's heart sank. Kate was hiding to cry, and it was his fault.

Ben glanced up from the yokes almost as an afterthought. "You'll be nicer?"

Jake placed a reassuring hand on the boy's shoulder. "Without a doubt."

Chapter Eleven

Discarding the Past

Wednesday, May 31, 1843

Kate sat in the wagon, picking at another unraveling seam and eyeing the pile of her bedraggled clothing. Jake was right — everything she'd brought was completely impractical.

When condensing her trunks before they'd left, she'd taken only the finest dresses, thinking them the most appropriate to make a good impression in a new land. Now she was stuck with a wardrobe designed for sipping tea in sitting rooms.

The sewing bag hung from a nail, taunting her with its possibilities. Her mother had fallen ill before teaching her to sew, and her aunt had viewed it as menial work best left to servants. Now, despite her mending and washing attempts — and somewhat because of them — she wore rags that wouldn't last another month.

Kate sighed, thinking of the months to come.

Each morning their pace seemed maddeningly slow, yet within an hour she found herself racing to keep up. After trudging for hours, her legs grew wobbly and every step radiated through her heels and legs and ended in the base of her spine with a bone-jarring rattle. Thankfully, she and Ben had come to an agreement; he rode in the mornings and she rode afternoons and into the evening.

Trail life tested her resolve and stamina like nothing else. Before, she'd viewed herself as a capable woman, able to accomplish anything she set her mind to. Now, each day brought about new suffering.

Scorching sun ruined her fair skin, and tireless, vicious wind left her tender lips chapped and sore. As an added curse, her hair was a mess — the top slick with sweat and dust, the ends dried and frayed. No matter how tight her braids, tendrils always escaped and curled around her neck. Every night she battled matted curls.

With a sigh, Kate wiped sweat from her forehead with blackened, chipped fingernails. Conserving water meant sponge baths were now her only means of keeping clean, and at times even those were scarce.

Glancing through the canvas, she watched Jake instruct Ben how to crease the brim of his hat. Kate grabbed her hated bonnet, hopped from the wagon, and set off on the perpetual hunt for wood.

A month ago she'd lived a life of comfort and indulgence, yet hadn't given it more than a moment's thought. Now, she spent hours thinking of everything she'd had back home.

She missed lush, thick grass. She'd spent many a lazy afternoon as a child lying in the shade, running the strands of coolness through her fingers.

She missed trees. Their grounds back home boasted dozens; out here they traveled for days across dull, flat land with only an occasional shrub breaking the monotony. Aside from offering shade, she now appreciated their fuel for fire. Buffalo chips burned quickly and added a foul tang to meals.

She missed tall glasses of lemonade. She would give up ten of her favorite books, still secreted away in the wagon, for a single glass now. She could almost see it — ice dancing with cold water and freshly squeezed lemons, flavored with a touch of sugar, in a glass dripping with condensation. She'd spent many an afternoon savoring each sip as the coolness slid down her throat and enveloped her like a fresh breeze.

Kate licked her cracked lips, wanting for a taste of frosty sweetness. Trail life had certainly taught her to appreciate what she couldn't have. Like clean underclothes.

Back home, petticoats had been a pleasure. Servants kept them washed, pressed, and scented with perfumes. Out here they were nothing but a hindrance — flapping in the wind and collecting insects and needle-sharp stickers within the folds. Even worse, a torn seam left her kicking away the drooping fabric while she walked.

As if to confirm her thoughts, her foot caught in the hem and she stumbled. Again. Lifting her skirt, Kate looked down with a sigh of dismay to see the bottom edge caked with dirt.

"Why should I have to wear such a mess?" Lately she'd found herself staring wistfully at the men's clothing. Theirs certainly wasn't a burden — no corsets to restrict movement, and they seemed unbelievably comfortable.

Right then and there she decided propriety was overrated and shook her hips until the petticoats slithered down her legs to the hard, dusty ground. If it hadn't been so hot, she would have danced with sheer glee at the freedom. Why, she felt ten degrees cooler!

It was her secret, and no one would ever be the wiser.

Chapter Twelve

Tough Times

Tuesday, June 6, 1843

"Sweetheart, it's time to get up."

Kate groaned and rolled away from her father's voice. She'd drifted off to the pleasant hum of raindrops against the wagon canvas. The random splatters combined with the burst of fresh, cool air had provided the perfect backdrop for dreamless sleep.

An hour ago everything changed with the arrival of a torrential downpour.

Now, water seeped through a weakened seam in the canvas and fell to a cast-iron kettle on the floorboard beside her bed. Another pan protected the dresser. Kate lay curled around a third as it collected the steady drip from a tear above the bed.

The starless sky promised no end to her misery.

****

Hours later, Kate sighed as the wagon slid to a stop. The oxen were willing, but unable to continue through the slippery mud.

"Again?" she called to her father.

"Maybe this time it won't be so bad," he replied, looking at her through red-rimmed eyes. He was tired, just like the rest of them.

The weather had been brutal the past few days, alternating between blistering heat and roaring downpours. As a result, small ponds and crevices overflowed onto the dusty flatland, creating a widespread, muddy disaster.

Kate felt like crying but instead took a deep breath, familiar with what lay ahead. Forty minutes earlier they'd all been on their hands and knees working frantically to win the battle against the thick, sucking ooze trapping the front right wheel.

She pulled on her smelly oilskin rain slicker and joined Ben and her father at the back of the wagon. Leaning in, she grimaced at what she didn't see — the bottom of the left wheel.

"Seems we got done in by another rut," Jake said as he walked around the corner of the wagon, a shovel in each hand.

Immediately, she stepped away. Though she no longer avoided him outright, and he'd been nothing but courteous toward her, she still spoke with him as little as possible. Ben, on the other hand, clamored forward to take the extra shovel from Jake's outstretched hand.

One thing she couldn't fault Jake for was how he treated her brother. He endured Ben's incessant questions with a patience she'd thought impossible, and freely shared his knowledge during their nightly discussions at the fire. Ben happily referred to the time as "cowboy talk".

"Those clouds are getting darker by the minute," her father said from his crouched position beside the wheel. "What do you think, Jake?"

"I'll get a few digs in and we'll see how it goes. No need for us all to be filthy if we're stuck here waiting out another storm."

Filthy indeed.

When the rain had first begun, Kate had been overjoyed with thoughts of a bath. Unfortunately, her thoughts were short lived since most of the rain had ended up as mud. Conserving water was mandatory, and priority went to the animals, canteens, and water barrel. Over the past week they'd come across enough to keep them going, and not a drop more.

Their clothing suffered the most. Dirt caked everything they wore and made mending impossible. Not that her slipped knots, tangled thread, and gaps larger than her stitches could be considered mending. And washing clothes now consisted of wearing an item during a downpour, then hanging it — either before the fire or across a line in the wagon — to dry. Her arms and neck suffered many an angry scrape from the resulting stiff fabric.

A sucking noise filled the air as Jake thrust his shovel into the muck.

"Let's hope this hole doesn't fill up as fast as I empty it," he said, his biceps straining against his wet shirt. With a grunt, he brought up a dripping mound of earth and heaved it aside. Frowning, he leaned on his shovel to study the hole. When it didn't fill in he looked up with a triumphant grin.

"If we work fast, we can free this wheel and keep going."

Without hesitation, Kate rushed forward and dropped to her knees. In the time it took for Jake and her father to ready their shovels she'd managed to scoop and toss seven handfuls of mud. It wasn't much, but every bit helped.

She got to her feet again. "I'll wait up front for Ben's signal."

Shaking the sludge from her hands, she climbed into the wagon seat and gathered the reins. Though the oxen still intimidated her, the matter of who handled them during these moments had been decided by brute strength. Ben wasn't strong enough, and Jake and her father needed to push on the back of the wagon. So she drove.

Half an hour later, the drizzle changed to a downpour just as the wagon rolled forward. Their celebration was short lived, however, as despite her best efforts the oxen only managed a few steps before the front left wheel sank into another hidden rut.

****

With a mug of treasured coffee in his hand, Jake limped across camp to join Elijah and Kate at the fire. His left leg always bothered him in cold, damp weather and tonight was no exception.

"Long day, huh?" he asked, leaning back against a rock and positioning his leg closer to the warmth of the flames. The morning had been a waste, but they'd walked out the storm and made decent miles that afternoon. For once. "At least the ground isn't wet."

His cheerful effort at a conversation was met with only half-hearted smiles. The brutal realities of trail life had set in for the family. Long days, the rush to keep moving, and limited water ruled their lives and dictated his every decision. Jake saw worry in Elijah's eyes and knew the man doubted himself for leaving the comforts of home, and dragging his children along. He saw tiredness and boredom settling in for Ben. In Kate's eyes he still saw defiance — when he saw them at all.

For days after his talks with Elijah and Ben he'd been prepared to apologize, but she'd avoided his every attempt. In camp, she'd walk away as he approached, and she'd developed an uncanny ability to water her horses either downstream or at differing times from him. The only time they spent together was during meals and at the evening fire, and for what he wanted to say he didn't need an audience.

The woman was stubborn beyond belief. For some reason, it only intrigued him.

He stole a glance at her across the fire. She leaned against a wheel, biting her lip while she matched up the edges of a tear in Elijah's shirtsleeve. Her newfound determination impressed him. She'd dug out muddy wheels without complaint and kept up with her duties each day. It made him strangely proud of her and excited to share his good news.

"You two like swimming?" he asked.

Kate and Elijah exchanged a sideways look, and then both glanced across camp where Ben was brushing Old Dan.

"Why do you ask?" Elijah asked.

"There's a lake not thirty miles from here, but each day we fight this weather is another day it slips out of reach. We'll be able to swim, bathe—" he nodded to the shirt Kate had thrown aside in exasperation "—and do all the washing. So," he asked Elijah, "can you swim?"

"Yes."

"What about you?" He turned to Kate, hoping she was comfortable around water.

"Kate's a born swimmer," Elijah answered proudly, then his brow furrowed. "Ben's another story. He almost drowned two years ago."

Eager to change the subject, Jake decided some encouraging words were in order.

"It's been quite a month, but we're finally working well together and things are getting done right." He took a final swallow of his coffee and set the cup aside. "I figure we've come close to four hundred and fifty miles."

"It feels like forever," mumbled Kate.

Jake ignored the comment, but looked again at the six-inch tear in her skirt with rising curiosity. Why wasn't she sewing it? And why did she string together a series of sloppy stitches in her father's sleeve night after night? If she'd take the time to do the job correctly she'd be back to her usual activities at their evening fires — writing letters or reading one of the books she had hidden in the wagon — in no time.

She caught him staring and abruptly stood up, stepped over Elijah's outstretched legs, and headed toward the wagon.

Another day gone.

Chapter Thirteen

Interruptions

Jake watched, hidden and helpless, from the shadows of the woodshed as the gutless cowards who'd shot his family roamed his yard.

They'd killed his family. And though he was ten years old, he'd done nothing.

He'd stayed silent as one of the men kicked his dead father in the face, sending a spray of blood and teeth into the air.

He'd stood motionless as the man then snatched his baby brother's blanket from the dirt, wiped his face and neck, and dropped it to the ground again.

He hadn't stopped them when they'd rummaged through his home, emerging with blankets, food, and a rifle. Or when they'd led two saddled horses from his stable.

Only when they'd disappeared over the rise beyond the house did he gather enough courage to stumble from the doorway.

He reached his mother first. Her eyes, wide and unseeing, told of his failure to save her. He scrambled to his brother Michael, took him by the shoulder and rolled his lifeless body. The bullet had entered through his cheekbone and taken half his forehead on the way out.

Swiping away tears, Jake moved to where a corner of Teddy's blanket — now stained with his killer's filth — covered his head. Hoping against hope, Jake knelt and carefully pulled away the material, only to reveal blond curls resting within a widening pool of blood.

Pressing a fist against his mouth to dampen his sobs, Jake collapsed at his father's side.

When his family had needed him the most, he'd done nothing.

****

Thursday, June 8, 1843

A light rain had settled in by the time Jake woke the others. They departed, and when the oxen floundered into yet another rut, the group was so efficient they freed the wheel in fifteen minutes instead of the usual hour. The rest of the morning they made good time, and by late afternoon they reached the Wabash River.

When Jake halted Plug and dismounted on the edge of the steep riverbank, everything changed for the worse.

The swift current churned and fought its way over glistening rocks, leaving foamy whitecaps in its wake. A gnarled branch skipped over boulders and then disappeared beneath the roiling surface. With all the recent rain, the river would be impossible to cross; they were stuck waiting until it crested and lowered. Though Jake wanted nothing more than to keep going, a strong current was dangerous, and he had no intention of underestimating its power.

It was a horrible sight, watching someone drown.

Years ago, he'd come upon a man foolishly trying to cross a swollen river. The man had ignored Jake's shouted warnings, and after only a few struggling steps the current had pulled his feet out from under him. Jake had never forgotten how helpless he'd felt watching the man get sucked downriver. Listening as panicked screams faded to silence was even worse.

Jake led Plug back to where the others waited, eager and expectant, and grimly broke the news. "Get comfortable, because we're camping here until the river goes down."

Elijah and Ben handled their disappointment with sighs and shrugs. Then, amidst murmurings of a hunting expedition, they moved to unhitch the oxen. Kate, on the other hand, sprang from her saddle and headed toward the edge of the riverbank.

Why must this woman fight him on everything? He caught her arm, desperate to protect her from the temptation of the water. "Where are you going?"

She shook off his hand. "The river."

"Absolutely not," he said, shaking his head. "You can't go near it. For any reason."

Her eyes went wide with feigned surprise. "I need water to do a washing."

"Without a bucket?" His tone came out harsher than he'd intended and he took a calming breath before continuing. "The current is strong and could sweep you half a mile downriver within seconds."

"Fine, I'll just soak my feet."

"Funny." He cocked his head, angry at her deceit. "First you said 'do a washing', yet now you speak of going in. Which is it?"

"How dare you keep me from going down there! I'm a strong swimmer, so go find something else to do and leave me alone."

Jake swallowed hard as the image of her pale, lifeless body disappearing down a whirlpool flashed through his mind. She obviously had no idea of the danger this river posed, and he had to keep her from it at any cost.

"You can't be trusted. I'll bring up all the water you need."

"Fine. I want three bucketfuls." She started toward the wagon, then called over her shoulder. "Right away."

****

Kate prepared a hearty dinner of salt pork, baking powder biscuits, and beans. Her cooking wouldn't win any awards, but she was improving. After putting away the dishes, she decided to take advantage of the early evening and wash clothes. She gathered two of her worst dresses and the sewing bag. She'd done a passable job of repairing the rip in her father's sleeve; she might as well try to do other mending.

At least she'd be away from Jake.

Relentless in his insistence she not go near the river, he'd filled the wash bucket and set it, the soap, and the washboard about twenty yards from camp. After laying out her clothes, she examined a ripped side seam on one of the dresses. Washing it now would make the tear worse — better to fix it first. She carefully threaded the needle, tied a knot in the thread, and then promptly pricked her finger.

"Perfect," she said as a drop of blood fell to the fabric.

She sucked on the wound and then wiped her finger on the grass. After pinching the seam closed, she pushed the needle through the cloth and then pulled the entire length of thread, including the end knot, through the weakened material. Several attempts later, she closed the gap. Three loops of excess thread hung between the wide stitches, but it would do. She bit through the thread and tossed the freed needle back into the metal box with the others.

"At least I can make it clean," she grumbled.

With that in mind, she submerged her dress in the bucket, patted a stain with soap, and slid it down the length of the washboard with her fingertips. As she lifted the dress from the water to check her work, she saw Jake approaching.

Just what she needed — another confrontation.

****

Jake leaned against a tree trunk and watched Kate attempt to wash clothes. Obviously she had no idea what she was doing, but he admired her efforts.

The time had come for his well-rehearsed apology. Ben and Elijah were off hunting, and since both had declared they wouldn't return without tomorrow's dinner in hand he figured he had plenty of time.

As he stepped away from the tree and headed her way, she lost her grip on the dress, sending a cascade of water into her lap. Hiding a chuckle, he squatted at her side.

"You're doing fine," he paused, allowing a hint of a smile to cross his lips. "For a beginner."

"It's obvious?"

"No."

She shot him a sideways glance.

"Maybe," he replied while rising to wind twine between two sturdy trees. "Here's your clothesline. Now, let me show you how it's done."

He knelt again and took the soap and dress from her. As he plunged the material into the water, she sat back on her heels and wiped her forehead with the back of her hand.

"Sometimes I feel like I never do anything right," she said.

"Anything meant to be learned won't be learned in a day. With time and practice you'll do fine."

Jake scrubbed the material against the washboard, all the while trying to ignore the faint scent of roses in the air. Had she worn perfume to wash clothes? Leaving the dress to soak, he wiped his hands on his pants and reviewed his apology in his mind.

"I think I'll give it a try." With a tentative smile, she sank her hands in the soapy water. She began working the dress against the washboard, giving him the opportunity to enjoy the view of unruly curls swishing across her slim back. Moments later, she lifted the dress from the water, stared at it with a critical eye, then dropped it into the bucket.

Seeing her frown, he tried to reassure her. "It'll be much better after a thorough washing. And once you sew the rip it'll be as good as new."

"I already did." She brought up the dress and held it out to him. Jake saw an attempt had been made; long expanses of thread were stretched taut over the hole, and worn pinholes surrounded the seam's edge.

"Maybe try that one again," he said with a chuckle. To his surprise, her eyes filled with tears.

"Don't you dare make fun of me!" Her voice cracked and she choked back a sob. "I'm trying my best, but it's never good enough."

"Oh, Katie," he said in dismay as tears cascaded down her cheeks. "I didn't mean to make you upset. I just wondered why you weren't sewing it properly."

"I don't know how." Her cheeks flushed and she lowered her head. "We had servants to do such things."

"No time like the present to learn," he said with false cheerfulness. He reached for her sewing kit, retrieved and threaded a needle, and started stitching.

"You know how to sew?"

"My mother said a boy could learn to sew just as easy as he could learn to ride a horse or shoot a gun."

"My mother died before she could teach me," she said softly.

Jake clenched his jaw so he wouldn't blurt out anything else to make her upset. The next few minutes were filled with only the swish of the needle passing through wet fabric and the rustling of the grass blowing in the breeze. After he finished, he handed it to her.

"It's time I get around to what I came here for."

She looked at him warily. "What?"

"I've been—"

Small, rapid footfalls rushed up and seconds later Ben stood before them, sweating and gasping for air. Jake jumped to his feet and put a hand on the boy's shoulder.

"What is it?"

"I d-did it!" Ben crowed triumphantly. "I got my first pheasant!"

Forcing his pounding heart down from his throat, Jake listened to the enthusiastic, babbling tale of how Elijah had flushed the bird and Ben had downed it with only one shot.

The apology would have to wait.

Chapter Fourteen

Waiting

Friday, June 9, 1843

Jake stood on the edge of the river, arms crossed and jaw set, studying the jagged line he'd waded out to carve on a rock yesterday. He could see whether the river was rising or falling, and how fast, by checking the mark. This trip marked his third time down in the last hour.

At this point, he'd do anything to get away from camp.

They'd woken to blue skies and plenty to do. The morning had been spent organizing supplies, inspecting and repairing harnesses, and mending rips in the canvas. Washing clothes, bedding, and themselves had consumed their afternoon. By early evening he'd joined Ben in exploring the piles of furniture and treasures left at the riverside by previous travelers, had a lengthy conversation with Elijah regarding horse breeding, and spent plenty of time seeing what the insides of his eyelids looked like.

Boredom ruled the others now since there was nothing to left achieve, except to pepper him with incessant questions as to when would they cross. Judging by how water no longer swirled around the mark he'd made, the river had crested and would now slowly subside. They had one more day of waiting, two at the most.

However, Jake discovered a problem bigger than the swollen the river.

The barge.

The previous travelers had left it .on the other side once they'd crossed, so he hadn't been able to check it when they'd first arrived. But after he pulled on the ropes and brought it back over, he cringed as it came to a rest at his feet.

The structure consisted mainly of logs strapped together to make a platform, on which boards had been laid across and nailed. Thin wooden poles acted as railings on either side.

Once glance told him it wouldn't handle the crossing. The railings were twisted and brittle from exposure to the sun, and the platform where the wagon and animals would stand showed significant structural issues. The back right corner sat low in the water, two boards on the left side wouldn't hold his weight, and only a gaping hole remained where a third board should have been.

He and Elijah had some serious work ahead.

They spent the evening on the needed repairs. Elijah was a strong worker and surprisingly adept at carving wooden pegs, a task Jake abhorred. When darkness set in they'd replaced two railings with small, yet sturdy, tree trunks. Reinforcing the platform proved more difficult as they didn't have the time, tools, or trees to replace every board, but they checked over every inch of the barge and repaired what they could.

Jake hammered the last peg into the base, got to his feet, and joined Elijah in appraising their work.

"I'd say we've done a passable job here," Elijah said.

Jake nodded his agreement. "I had hoped to try tomorrow, but I'd like to wait another day for the river to go down."

"I agree," Elijah said. "Never hurts to play it safe."

The words were the perfect opening for Jake to bring up a subject he'd been dreading. "The oxen are tired due to excess weight in your wagon. We started out strong, but now we're making ten to fifteen miles a day when we should be doing twenty or more. At this rate, they'll die from exhaustion within the month. And given the condition of the barge, now is the perfect time to lighten the load."

Elijah took a cigar from his vest pocket, clipped an end, and lit it. After a slow puff he studied the smoke lingering in the air.

"You're sure there's no other option?"

Jake shook his head. "I know your property means a lot to you, but it can't be helped. We've got months to go, and we don't have time to rest the team simply because we're hauling too heavy of a load."

"I understand," Elijah said. "We can mention it to Kate when we get back."

Jake wasn't looking forward to that conversation or the fuss she would undoubtedly make. The woman's choice of words could be as biting as a whip when she was riled.

When they made their way back to camp, Jake was grateful to see Kate had already retired to the wagon for the evening. They hadn't disagreed over anything in over a day. But soon enough, their newfound truce would be tested.

****

Sunday, June 11, 1843

Early in the morning Jake came back from the river to find Kate waiting at the wagon tongue, shifting her weight from foot to foot with eager anticipation.

"Well?" she asked.

He nodded. "Today's the day."

From across the camp, Ben and Elijah cheered enthusiastically, but Jake only had eyes for the wagon. He'd hoped Elijah would have spoken to his family and they'd have emptied the extra weight by now, but the contents remained untouched.

So be it. His job was to make sure they arrived safely, and it was a job he would do, no matter how difficult. Tensing for the forthcoming argument, he broke the news.

"The wagon is too heavy to make this crossing."

Kate's joy faded. "What?"

Jake gritted his teeth and then said what Elijah should have said yesterday. "We can't cross unless you leave some things behind."

Her eyes and mouth went wide. "Certainly not! I abandoned nearly everything before we even began. I won't let you take away the last of what I care about."

"Going over with that load puts yourself, and everyone else, at risk."

The harsh warning brought a disbelieving shake to her head. However, those deep green eyes were like a window to what hid beneath her lightning temper. Though she would likely do her best to hide it, deep down she was scared he was right.

"I'll see what I can find." She started toward the wagon then called over her shoulder, "If anything." Moments later, three books sailed through the canvas and crashed onto the ground, followed by a footstool and a stack of ledgers.

Kate's head poked out from the canvas. "That's all I'm leaving, and nothing you say will change it."

"You've got a good start," he said, walking over. "What else can stay?"

"Nothing." She jumped from the wagon and landed beside him with a defiant glare. "We need it all."

Why couldn't she for once meet him halfway?

"No, you don't." Despite his best intentions, his voice rose to match hers. "Everything can be replaced once you arrive."

"Not everything." Without warning, her voice cracked, and he grimaced to see her bottom lip tremble. "Jake, my mother meant the world to me, and I can't bear to part with anything else. It's all I have left to remember her by."

Jake bit down on the inside of his cheek to stay strong and not retract his order. He knew what it was like to lose a mother at a young age, and he understood her desire to cling to anything and everything her mother had ever touched. But tough choices, not his sympathy, would get them safely to Oregon.

"Please." He lowered his voice to a whisper. "Don't fight me on this. It's too important."

Kate opened her mouth, then hesitated.

Yet just when Jake thought he'd gotten through to her, Elijah stepped between them.

"You two have had your say. It's my turn."

Chapter Fifteen

The Crossing

Jake fell silent upon hearing his employer's firm tone. They'd traveled together for over a month, long enough to get a measure of the man, and Jake's instinct told him Elijah was at the end of his rope. Not only with him, but with his own daughter.

"Father, I don't see how—"

"Enough," Elijah commanded, holding up his hand. "If Jake says you need to leave things behind, I'm sure you'll find pieces we can live without."

Elijah turned to Jake, his expression cold and unyielding.

"On the other hand, we've brought supplies to start our new business the moment we arrive. I don't plan on replacing them."

"You're not the only ones who've faced these tough decisions," Jake said, motioning to the piles of furniture and dishes previous travelers had abandoned riverside. "It's a common problem, and one you must fix."

"If we don't?" Kate countered.

Jake shook his head, amazed at how even with her brother shooting anxious glances between his family and the river, she still tried to undermine his authority.

"I won't go one step further until this load is lightened."

Elijah headed for the wagon, followed closely by Kate. After a furtive exchange, she climbed inside. Moments later a wooden chair with an upholstered seat appeared through the canvas. A matching one followed. Elijah set down one after the other, then reached inside and brought out a glass pitcher.

"Anything else?" Jake asked.

Kate's head popped out from the canvas. She glared at him before looking to her father in silent protest.

"Jake, I'm afraid I have to agree with my daughter. Everything else is either items we'll need once we arrive, or irreplaceable heirlooms."

Their stubbornness would be their demise in the west. Jake was sure of it.

"All right then," he answered with a forced shrug. "Since you insist on having your way, I'm willing to take the risk — as long as you can accept the consequences."

If they didn't agree with him now, they would within the month when the oxen were too weak to pull the wagon. Or dead.

He went to the toolbox and brought out a hammer and chisel. He then picked up one of the abandoned ledgers and ripped several pages from inside the leather cover.

"What are you d-doing?" Ben asked.

"Making this wagon box as water tight as possible," he said, dropping the ledger to the ground with a dark calm.

The sound of metal against metal echoed across the land as Jake lay between the wheels, pounding the hammer against the end of the chisel, forcing paper between the wagon's bottom boards. When Ben and Elijah offered their help he motioned them away, so infuriated he couldn't trust his own voice. When he finished, he tossed the tools back into the box and motioned the now solemn group closer.

"Your horses will be hitched to the wagon since mine have never pulled one. I'll drive. Ben and Katherine, you'll ride inside. Elijah, you'll go over on Nickel and lead Plug. If they panic, jump off and swim for it, but keep a good distance lest they give you a kick." Many a man had lost his life due to flailing hooves.

"The oxen won't be eager, but they'll follow your lead. Also, don't worry about how we're doing. Focus on getting across so you can have the horses secured and be ready to help when we hit shore."

"Why aren't the oxen pulling the wagon?" Kate asked.

With some satisfaction, he gave the answer. "Because if the barge gives way, the horses can swim and you might not lose everything."

For once, she had no response.

The group worked together, and within fifteen minutes Old Dan and Nina stood hitched and ready, and the oxen's three yokes were stored inside the wagon.

Elijah hugged his children and then led the horses and oxen down the riverbank. While he waited, Jake checked over the horses and made adjustments to their driving reins. When Elijah reached the river's edge, Jake swung into the wagon seat. As he reached to test the brake he felt the wagon sway, and turned to see Kate climbing into the back.

"Better go down on foot. This wagon's so heavy we're already risking toppling down the riverbank. I don't need the weight of you and your brother too."

With kind words combined with a few slaps of the reins, Jake urged the team over the edge. As the wagon tilted forward, he tried to ignore the noisy thumps from the shifting load. Hopefully a dresser wouldn't knock him from the seat.

Once the back wheels hit the top of the bank, Jake reached for the brake. The protesting squeal of the wheel's metal rims filled the air as he repeatedly set and released the brake, allowing the wagon to move forward inches at a time. Avalanches of dirt and rock traveled alongside the horses.

After the tedious descent, Jake maneuvered the team to the river's edge. Ben and Kate slid their way down as the choking dust cloud began to settle. Jake noticed her smug expression had disappeared, replaced by one of fear.

Good.

Jake eased the horses onto the barge. It would be brought across the river by a crude yet effective system — a rope strung across the span of the river and through two loops of rope connected to the left corners of the barge. All that was required of the rider was to keep hold of the span rope and guide the barge across, letting the current do most of the work.

After checking to see the wagon brake was set and the horses were calm, he motioned to Kate and Ben. "Climb up, slowly, into the back."

Once they were settled he tied the canvas securely, taking care to close the back so Ben couldn't see out. Satisfied, he turned to where Elijah waited.

"Give Nickel his head and he'll do fine," Jake said with a confidence he didn't feel.

"See you on the other side," Elijah called.

Never fearful around water, Nickel walked in and didn't hesitate when the water swirled against his belly. Plug tossed his head, resisting Elijah's repeated tugs on his lead rope, and then followed in after Nickel. The oxen obediently plunged in after them.

Once they were well on their way, Jake gave the barge a final push from land. The base logs grated against the riverbed and then went silent as they floated off. Propulsion now came from the current, while the looped ropes at the front and back left corners held the barge in place.

Jake paced around the platform, wiping his forehead on his shirtsleeve and his hands against his pant legs, cursing himself for sending his saddlebags over with Elijah without getting his gloves out first.

One minute ticked by, then another. Maybe he'd been wrong about the extra weight. They were doing fine so far with no problems in sight. Elijah and the animals were closing the gap to the other side, although the river had carried him farther away than Jake anticipated.

However, a quarter of the way across, the current grew stronger. A glance downriver saw Elijah in the water, one hand clinging to Nickel's saddle horn, the other leading Plug by the end of his reins. Not only had he completely ignored Jake's earlier warning to not get too close to the swimming horses, he was now in danger of being hooked and pulled under by their thrashing hooves.

Before Jake could shout a warning, the barge rocked wildly as a hidden undertow sent six inches of water over his boots. The river settled quickly, but when Jake headed to investigate an odd noise coming from the barge's back corner he saw the loop of rope attached to the barge unraveling, strand by strand.

Lunging forward, he grabbed and held fast to the rope spanning the river. But he was no match for the power of the current. The rope burned across his bare hands, slowing briefly as his fingertips curled against it, and then with a sickening *twang*, it arched free.

Kept in place only by the loop at the front left corner, the barge swung sideways. Jake scrambled toward the coil of rope attached to the wagon seat, but the barge lurched and he fell hard against Nina.

"Jake?" Kate's timid voice drifting out from the wagon was nearly lost in the water's roar.

A sharp *crack* halted his answer.

Hurrying around Nina to the right side of the barge, Jake cursed to find Old Dan's fidgeting hooves had snapped the edge board in half, allowing an unwanted glimpse of the logs underneath.

Without warning, the barge tilted. With a sharp jolt, the wagon slammed against the flimsy railing, the back right wheel stopping only inches from the water.

Everything happened within seconds, but Jake reacted immediately. Urging the horses forward by their bridles, he brought the wagon away from the edge and then hopped into the seat and set the brake with a grunt.

Hearing a gasp, he spun to see Kate peering through the front canvas, her wide eyes taking in the sight of the barge, now sideways.

"Jake, what's happening?"

Fear filled her voice, but Jake was relieved to see she wasn't panicking. Yet.

"A rope came loose and I need to retie it." He spoke quietly, trying not to worry Ben. "Stay in the wagon with your brother. It'll be fine."

She smiled weakly at his lie and pulled her head back through the canvas.

He shouldered the coil of rope and hurried to the front of the barge. Once he'd brought the end of his rope up and over the spanning rope and held it securely in his hands, he slowly worked his way to the back corner, fighting against the current as he walked. Within minutes, he'd brought the barge parallel to the rope spanning the river.

"No need to worry," he shouted as he quickly tied his rope around the railing, securing the barge once again. "I've got it all under control."

Then he saw Elijah.

Chapter Sixteen

A Reluctant Hero

From the moment the barge left the shore, Kate was excited by the damp air, the roar of the water, and the feeling of weightlessness as they dipped and swayed across the rushing river. It was a welcome change from the motionless prairie. There, the only noises were the groaning of the wagon, the creak of the leather saddles, or the whisper of tall grass parting to let the wagon wheels pass.

One look at Ben changed her elation. He sat on the bed, his small, white knuckles clenching the wagon box in a futile attempt to keep violent shudders at bay.

"Doing fine back there?" she asked.

A teary nod was his only answer.

As the view out the front canvas slowly changed from shoreline to river, Kate fought the urge to panic. But when the wagon shifted and then lurched to the right, it took everything she had to hold back a scream.

"I'm sure it's nothing," she assured him, all the while disbelieving her own words.

Ben shrieked as the wagon jolted forward and stopped hard. Kate rose to comfort him, and then froze when Jake scrambled into the wagon seat and set the brake lever. She thrust her head through the canvas and gasped to see Jake covered in sweat, his chest heaving.

"Jake, what's happening?"

"A rope came loose and I need to retie it." As he wiped the sweat from his forehead, her stomach churned at the sight of the angry welt across his palm. "Stay in the wagon with your brother. It'll be fine."

Grabbing a coil of rope, Jake hopped from the seat and hurried toward the horses. She ducked back inside and tried to ignore the strained muttering and heavy footsteps thumping along the barge.

She sank on the bed beside Ben and put her arm around him.

"It'll be fine." She echoed Jake's words. "Jake and father know what to do," she added and then hugged him close.

She spent the next few minutes clutching her brother to her chest while humming the same tune she'd sung to him as an infant. When the barge swung back into position she grasped him by the shoulders and pulled him away.

"See?" she cried triumphantly. "Everything's going to be fine. I bet we're almost to shore."

Ben rewarded the reassuring words with a weak smile.

"No need to worry," Jake's voice carried easily through the canvas. "I've got it all under control."

The tension slid from her body at his confident tone. Refined he was not, but when it came to leading them Jake had definitely proved his worth.

Seconds later, the silence was broken by Jake's urgent shout.

"Katherine, get out here! Your father's in trouble!"

Without hesitation, she charged through the front canvas and leapt into Jake's waiting arms.

"Hold tight to this and don't let go." He pushed her forward and curled her hands around a taut rope along the left side of the barge. "I'll be back for you!"

Without another word, he jumped over the railing.

Fear stole any chance at tears as Kate held the rope and frantically scanned the river for her father. With a gasp, she saw him. Rather, she saw the top of his head and one arm lying over Nickel's saddle horn.

She could do nothing but watch as, with Jake still at least ten feet away, her father disappeared under the water.

He didn't resurface.

Jake quickly closed the distance with long, powerful strokes. When he reached where she'd last seen her father his head tipped back, he sucked in a lungful of air and then dove into the river. Horrifying seconds and many prayers passed before her father's head came up, followed shortly by Jake's.

Jake rolled her father onto his back, grasped him by the shoulders, and pulled him toward the shore. Her father, coughing violently, attempted to sit up in the water several times, yet Jake continued.

"They made it!" Kate shouted to Ben as side by side, the two men joined several of the animals on the shore.

Jake had saved her father's life.

Kate's joy quickly changed to confusion as she heard a sharp noise.

"W-w-what's that?" Ben yelled.

"Don't worry," she called, fervently hoping he wouldn't dare peek out the canvas. How could she tell him the sound was from a board snapping in half? And gaps between the boards grew wider with each second? And the front corner sat under two inches of water?

The powerful current sent waves of water swirling around her legs. The barge swayed violently, yet still she held fast to the rope, hoping somehow it would keep them steady. When would Jake return?

"Kate!" Ben shrieked as the front of the barge rose from the water. His panicked screams continued as the wagon slid backward, and grew louder when the right back wheel crashed through the railing and landed in the river. The bottom of the wagon hit the barge — hard.

"Stay put!" she ordered while rushing to the horses, now struggling to keep their feet against the weight of the sliding wagon. After a hard fight, she managed to grab Old Dan by the bridle and urged the team forward. Inch by tenuous inch, they pulled until the wheel touched the barge. The hard drop had broken the board beneath, and despite her efforts, the bottom of the wheel remained submerged. Chest heaving, Kate climbed into the seat and reset the brake.

Jake said not to let go of the rope!

Frantic, she tumbled from the seat, splashed through splintered pieces of wood, and fell onto the rope while clasping it in her hands.

But she was too late.

With a recoiling snap the rope spanning the river, the same rope Jake had told her not to let go of, broke.

****

Elijah lay where he fell on the shoreline while Jake coaxed the final ox ashore. It was a miracle they hadn't lost any of the animals, much less Elijah. The man, who'd answered the question "Can you swim?" with a resounding "yes," now lay on the sand, retching up water.

Shrill screams brought Jake's focus back to the river and a horrific sight. The barge had broken from its tethers. Slowly at first, and then with chilling speed, it began floating freely downriver.

As it passed, Kate's eyes locked with his, her bone-white face flooded with sheer panic. Despite her efforts, the barge leaned hard to the right, Nina strained to get away from the sinking wagon, and one of the front logs was missing.

Grabbing his other rope from Plug's saddle, Jake ran down the riverbank, intent on getting parallel with the wagon and throwing Kate an end. It was the only way they could reestablish contact. Once he caught up, he found instead of being immobilized by fear, Kate was leaning over the railing waiting for his instruction.

"Grab hold!" Jake yelled while throwing her the end of the rope. She caught it on the second try. After she tied it to the railing, Jake looped his end around a tree. However, their success was short lived; the weight of the barge ripped the tied section of the weakened railing free.

Abandoning the plan, Jake dropped the rope and sprinted down the bank and into the water. He soon found his arm strokes were no match for the current and could only follow behind and watch helplessly while the barge spiraled down the river.

****

Kate balanced on the front of the tilted barge, desperately trying to calm the frenzied horses. Both pulled frantically against their harnesses as they struggled to keep their footing on the shifting planks. Their panicked movements slid the wheel further away from the platform.

"It's n-not w-w-w-working!" Ben sobbed as he bailed water from the wagon. "Our s-stuff is floating away!"

"Don't give up! Keep trying!"

Perhaps their best chance at survival would be unhitching the horses and letting everyone attempt a swim for shore. Surely if they stayed in place all would die.

****

Jake clung to the back of the barge, his chest burning from exertion. After summoning the strength, he pulled himself up and over what remained of the railing. Kate's scream of surprise greeted him as he collapsed against the wagon.

"You came back! Is my father all right?"

"He's fine," he sputtered, still gasping for breath.

"Please help us! The horses won't stay still and the whole thing is coming apart and Ben is so scared and we're spinning out of control." Her words were fast and garbled from fear. "Should we unhitch the horses and swim for it?"

"Listen to me!" He took her roughly by the shoulders. "Leaving everything is our last resort. If we work together, we can save the horses and the wagon." He lowered his voice so Ben wouldn't hear his next words. "There's a group of rocks in less than two miles. It's now or never."

Jake hefted Kate into the wagon seat as the final section of the barge sank beneath his feet. As the horses began swimming, he let go of the wagon and grabbed for Old Dan's tail. Then, using the harness straps as handholds, he pulled himself toward the horse's back. When he sat astride, he fumbled for the reins until he held them firm and then urged the horse toward the shore. Several tense seconds passed as both horses fought against his direction, but he persisted.

After what seemed like an eternity, he felt the unmistakable jolts of hooves hitting solid ground. Seconds later, Elijah's strong hand grasped his arm as he fell from Old Dan. Jake staggered forward and collapsed while Elijah guided the team to shore. The clatter of wheels against rocky ground was quickly followed by Kate's and Ben's excited shrieks as they tumbled from the wagon and ran to their father. The family clung together in a sodden embrace, weeping with joy.

When Jake finally recovered enough to rise to his feet, Elijah strode over, hand extended. "Words can't express my thanks to you for saving my family."

When the rope had slipped through Jake's hands it left a nasty burn across his palm, but he returned the handshake. "I'm grateful it ended well."

His words were calm, but Jake was furious at the role they had played in this disaster. Though weak, he was confident the barge and ropes would have held together long enough to get them to the other side if the wagon wasn't so heavy.

Squinting against the sun and fatigue, Jake's eyes swept the shoreline. Their supplies littered the bank for the next quarter mile, if not more. It would take the rest of the day to get everything cleaned up, dried out, and repacked. As he glanced around again his irritation swiftly gave way to cold fury. Sure enough, something was missing.

"Where's Plug?"

Wide eyes and open mouths stared back at him, but held no answer. Overcome, Jake threw his soggy hat to the ground. Money or not, he was done with their foolishness.

"Your disregard for my guidance stops now! From this point on I'm totally, and without question, in charge. Otherwise, I quit. No amount of money is worth what I've been through. We have more creeks and rivers to cross, and I won't have a repeat of the events of today. You *will* lighten this load!"

He shook his head in disgust.

"Plug likes to run and is probably long gone. With him went over half of what I own."

"What did you lose?" Kate asked weakly.

"Nothing as important as your precious mahogany dresser stuffed with linens, or the trunk of books you think I don't know about. Don't worry; it was just things I need to *stay alive*, like canteens and clothes. So if I can't find him, I'll have to buy another horse and more supplies at the next fort."

Another waste of valuable time.

"Since the other horses need a rest, I'll start searching for him on foot. While I'm gone you have some thinking to do." Ignoring the searing pain coursing through his left leg, Jake stalked away.

It would take the better part of the afternoon to find Plug. All the better — they could clean up the mess they'd caused.

Without his help.

Chapter Seventeen

Truce

Kate stood between her father and brother and watched Jake storm off. He had saved her family, the animals, their wagon, and their possessions. They'd repaid him by losing his horse and saddlebags.

"This is my fault," she blurted out once he disappeared over the rise. "I insisted on having my way and look what happened."

"No, sweetheart," her father said quietly, putting an arm around her shoulder. "He tried warning me, but I thought he exaggerated the danger and didn't take him seriously."

Kate held back tears as he pulled both her and Ben into a crushing hug.

"I'm so sorry," he whispered, and then paused for a long moment before clearing his throat. "To have put you both through something so terrible for mere possessions is inexcusable."

Kate shook her head against his chest. Though her father berated himself, she knew she was as much to blame. Some things were replaceable and some weren't. She'd almost lost her family for a few pieces of furniture.

"What's done is done." Her father stepped back and clapped his hands together with a definitive nod. "We're alive and unhurt, so let's move forward, starting with going through the wagon and keeping only what we need."

"What about Jake?" Ben asked.

"We'll give him time to calm down. In the meantime, let's get started."

No one said a word as they walked the shoreline, picking through rocks and mud to find their property. It was slow, tedious work but no one complained. Streaked with grime and carrying what they could, they made their way to the impromptu camp. Ben and her father started a fire while she headed for the wagon.

Once inside, she carefully weighed the value of each item in her mind, amazed at how her views had changed. Two months ago a bookshelf had taken precedence over everything; today she set it aside without a second thought. Now more than ever, she knew material things weren't worth the danger they caused.

Without discussion, she carried outside all the possessions she'd fought so hard to keep — two additional upholstered chairs, the wooden headboard with floral bouquets carved throughout, one of two side tables, the green velvet curtains from her mother's bedroom, a mirror — now broken, and her two-drawer mahogany dresser.

A glance over at Ben, dragging the other dilapidated side table into camp, confirmed her decisions. Although he tried to put up a brave front, she could tell he was still frightened.

"Where does this go?" Ben asked.

She pointed to the pile next to the wagon.

"Anything I can get for you, sweetheart?" her father asked as he stirred a pot of beans he'd started simmering over the fire.

"I need my green trunk from the wagon." Kate wanted to see how the contents had fared. It held her full wardrobe for when she arrived — dresses, petticoats, bloomers, nightgowns, and plenty of lace-trimmed underclothes.

"Consider it done," he said with his first smile of the day.

He dropped the trunk in front of her with a heavy thud. With trepidation, she clicked open the golden clasps and lifted the lid. On first glance, everything appeared fine. The top dress remained in immaculate condition and the tissue paper crinkled as she moved it aside. Flattening her hand, she slid it down the inside wall of the trunk, grimacing when she felt dampness halfway. Apparently the best money could buy didn't include waterproofing.

After careful inspection, Kate found each item just wet, not dirty. She spread the clothing out on the warm grass, thrilled all they needed was a good drying.

While her father and Ben went to recover the toolbox still lodged in the riverbank, Kate bent over the trunk of books. With deep regret, she brought her selection down from over forty to ten. As she placed the last one on the stack to be left behind, her father's shadow fell across her face.

"Jake is over the hill. I'm going to talk to him."

She shook her head. "Please, let me go instead."

After a brief walk, Kate saw Jake standing on top of a nearby hollow, staring out over the open land. Her battered slippers kept her footsteps soft, yet he glanced over his shoulder the moment her head topped the rise.

"Katherine, why are you out here?"

Unsure, she stopped several feet behind him. Mud covered his trousers to his mid-thigh and his shirt bore a jagged rip across the right shoulder. He'd paid quite a price for her stupidity.

"I owe you an apology," she said quietly.

He faced her, revealing a man all out of anger. "When I tell you something, there's always a reason. I hope you see that now."

Tears stung her eyes at the thought of a life without her father and brother. She was nothing without them.

"I'm truly sorry, Jake. I never meant to put my family—" she paused "—or you, in harm's way. I'm committed to this journey, and I promise I'll do what it takes to get to Oregon. From this point on I won't question your judgment, having seen firsthand the danger of doing so." She bent her head in shame. "This whole thing never would have happened if I had listened to you in the first place."

It was the perfect opportunity for him to berate her and she braced herself for the onslaught.

"I can't let you accept all the responsibility for what happened," he replied. "I knew better than to cross with an overloaded wagon. I should have insisted."

"I believe you did," she protested, astonished he shouldered the blame for what had happened. "And as usual, I wouldn't listen."

His lips twitched, but to his credit he merely shrugged.

"What I'm trying to say is…" She faltered and gave him a tentative smile. "I know I can be strong-willed and a bit headstrong, and I'm sorry."

Avoiding her gaze, he pulled off his hat and ran the brim between his fingers. When his eyes rose again to meet hers, his expression was one of chagrin.

"I owe you an apology as well. These past few weeks, and a few conversations, made me do some serious thinking. I now realize I tried so hard to convince your father you didn't belong on the trail I neglected to treat you fairly or with respect. I've been out of line."

She grew uncomfortable under his stare and he chuckled. "I hope now that I've apologized you'll stop fighting me like a cornered wildcat."

She blushed, but held his gaze.

"Katherine, I was wrong and I'm sorry. Will you accept my apology?"

"Yes," she said with a shy smile. "And you can call me Kate."

Chapter Eighteen

Moving On

As he escorted Kate back to camp, Jake dared another glance at the woman by his side. Her bravery when he'd left the barge earlier still amazed him. Most women would have fainted dead away at the mere prospect of such danger. Instead, she'd done what was needed and without hesitation.

"You handled the situation well when I went after your father."

"I didn't know I could until I did." She swung her arm across the wide expanse of bare land. "I guess it's like being out here. I didn't know such demanding work — work we'd designated to our servants back home — would be expected of me. I needed time to get used to the idea."

"You're doing a good job," he reassured her. "Taking care of your horses has lessened the burden on me, especially since you seem to know what you're doing."

"I *do* know what I'm doing," she corrected.

It was uncommon for a society woman to give her opinion so freely and without a concern as to what the men around her would think. The ones he had known only giggled, while hiding within dresses majestic in size and impracticality. How had it taken him so long to see the difference?

Kate was a rare woman indeed.

Elijah and Ben stopped wiping mud from the tools and openly stared as his and Kate's banter, now interspersed with easy laughter, continued after they'd walked into camp.

"Well," Elijah said, "this is a sight."

"What?" Kate asked.

"The two of you talking civilly," he replied.

"We thought we'd give it a try," Jake said, ashamed at how he and Kate having a civil conversation was such a noteworthy event.

"I knew you two would eventually come to an understanding of each other," Elijah said. "Besides," he added, "I was tired of being the middleman during your arguments."

"Yeah," Ben said, staring at them both in mock sternness. "Me too."

Jake nodded, realizing how their fighting had probably been a strain for Ben and Elijah. A glance at Kate's contrite expression revealed she held the same thought.

"How's it going here?" he asked, changing the subject. "Appears you've been busy."

"We're doing well," Elijah said, "but it will be an undertaking to clean and reload everything."

"Not everything," Kate added, pointing to a collection of furniture, a shockingly large stack of books, and a broken mirror. "This pile stays."

Jake let out a sigh of relief. She'd unpacked everything he'd asked for and much more. Her sacrifice meant they'd gain at least three miles more each day — five, if weather and landscape cooperated.

"I know you all counted on getting to the lake today," he said, "but I still need to find Plug. What does everyone think of staying here tonight?"

Three heads nodded their agreement and they eagerly delved into their various tasks while he saddled Nickel. He hadn't made it twenty yards out of camp when rapid footfalls came up behind him.

"Wait!"

Spinning in the saddle, he saw Kate hurrying toward him, his canteen beating a steady rhythm against her leg. In his hurry to start searching he'd left it behind.

"Glad you noticed my carelessness," he said as he leaned to take it from her. "It's bound to be hot out there."

With a tip of his hat, he set off again.

Several years ago he'd tracked Plug across open land without success. But if he was fortunate and searched far and wide, he would find the horse this time. He would start by making a wide circle, covering a few miles out from the river. Hopefully his eyes would cooperate.

****

Two hours later, Jake returned to a roaring fire with dresses, blankets, and a lace coverlet drying around it, Kate and Ben sorting sacks of beans and flour, and Elijah chiseling book pages into the cracks of the wagon.

"You found him!" Ben crowed with delight as Jake rode into camp with Plug, tethered to Nickel's saddle horn, following closely behind. Jake handed Elijah the reins as he dismounted.

"I've had Plug coming up on five years now. The day I bought him someone told me he wouldn't be worth a plug, so I named him that. On the other hand, Nickel sure earned his worth today. I might have to change his name to Dollar." Jake's grin widened. "He's the one who found Plug."

"How?" Elijah asked while helping remove the saddles.

"Leaving here, I headed south thinking he'd either followed the river or searched for the greenest grass he could find. Sure enough, about three miles out I saw Plug trotting along the slope above the river. Nickel let out a whinny and I whistled, but he was too far to hear. We followed him for a half-mile, then I tried whistling again, but the wind blew the noise away. Another mile passed before the wind changed. I was reaching my fingers up for another try when Nickel whinnied. Plug heard and came galloping back. Now we're here."

That night at the fire, the group talked well into the night. All of them.

****

Monday, June 12, 1843

Kate sat on the bed, her stable shoes in one hand and the flimsy slippers she'd worn on departure day in the other. Neither pair would save her feet until she could buy shoes at Independence — still weeks away — yet she couldn't fathom going barefoot.

While grimly inspecting her prospects, inspiration struck. She found two linen napkins, wadded them, and stuck one in each toe of her stable shoes. Perhaps she could stretch the damp leather enough so her toes wouldn't be bruised and swollen after wearing them.

With the promise of a deep, cool lake beckoning, she pulled on the slippers, finished braiding her hair, and jumped from the wagon.

She wasn't the only one eager to get started. Jake and her family were a whirlwind of activity. Within minutes their camp was stripped clean, her father sat with the oxen's driving reins in hand, and Ben and Jake waited mounted and ready in front of the wagon. She untied Old Dan's lead rope from the side of the wagon and swung into the saddle.

When nothing remained but to leave, Jake called back. "Ready?"

Biting her lip, she shook her head. She wanted one final look at her past.

She rode across their camp, halting Old Dan beside the jumbled pile of her treasured memories. Never again would she sip lemonade from the set of glasses with the gold rim, or run her fingers over the familiar books that for so long had eased the pain of her loneliness. The green velvet curtains weren't just material — for years, parting them had revealed her mother's wan, yet smiling face. She didn't see just a rocking chair; she saw the countless nights she'd spent soothing Ben to sleep after her mother died.

Jake rode over. "I realize this is hard, but it's for the best."

"I know."

After a long moment he spoke again. "It's time to go, Kate."

"I know."

Blinking fast, she rode away without a backward glance, unable to watch all she'd held so dear, and had fought so hard to keep, disappear into the vast land.

Chapter Nineteen

The Lake

Kate stopped Old Dan beside Jake and stared at the oasis spread out below. A stand of trees surrounded and shadowed the deep blue lake. A breeze sent ripples dancing across the water's surface and brought cool gusts of air to caress her warmed skin.

"How lovely," she murmured from her daze of contentment. However, the blissful silence was short lived once Ben rode up next to her.

Whooping and hollering, he tore off his shirt, kicked his boots free, and leaped from his saddle. Kate propped her elbow on the saddle horn, rested her chin in her hand, and watched in amusement as he sped toward the water, splashed in to his knees, and then sat with a shout of joy.

Jake dismounted and handed her Nickel's reins. "Got him?"

At her nod, he headed back to help unhitch the oxen. Working quickly, Kate removed the saddles from Old Dan,

Nina, and Nickel. Jake brought down Plug shortly after. Once she'd removed his saddle she led the horses to the shoreline.

"Watch them and make sure they don't drink too much," she warned Ben before gathering her skirt and trudging back up the rise. After the chances Jake had taken because of her yesterday, she wanted to do everything she could to make it up to him, which included putting off the long-awaited swim.

Once she'd helped to free the oxen and arrange the yokes and harnesses, she headed for the shore. After a quick check on Ben and the horses, Kate sat and whisked off her slippers. Her stockings followed and then she splashed in to her waist and dove beneath the surface.

Coolness slid along her body, soothing flushed skin and stripping away weeks of blistering heat and oozing mud. Once she came up for air she slowly arched her back and stretched her arms above her head, content for the moment to float and watch cotton clouds change shape against the crisp blue sky.

If she hadn't been so relaxed she'd have cried from sheer happiness.

Hearing Ben's shrieks of laughter, she shifted in the water and saw Jake and her brother splashing about near the shoreline. Her father waded nearby.

Fully refreshed and ready to play, she swam to her father, stopping just out of his reach. Giggling, she leaned back and kicked until waves of water cascaded down his chest. He cupped his hand and sent a spray over her head. Thus began a splashing match, which ended with her father soaked and both collapsing into a pile of laughter. During their play Jake retired to the shore, so they coaxed Ben further out and the three of them began to frolic about. Within minutes, she pleaded exhaustion and joined Jake in the sand.

"Having fun?" he asked.

"Oh, yes," she said, arranging her skirt neatly over her feet. "I just need to rest for a bit."

They sat in companionable silence, watching her father instruct Ben on the finer points of sending spurts of water out of clasped hands. Before long, Ben mastered the trick and began shooting streams into the air.

"It appears the student has surpassed the teacher," she said with a laugh. When Jake didn't respond, she glanced over. Instantly, her smile faded.

With his hands clenched against his mouth and his eyes filled with painful longing, he watched Ben and her father. His sadness overwhelmed her, and she laid her hand on his arm.

"Are you all right?"

Startled, he cleared his throat and ran his hands through his hair. "I'm fine."

"You're so serious. What were you thinking about?"

"My brother, Michael." He hesitated. "We used to play together in the water."

"Where is he now?" she asked, suddenly curious about his family.

"Gone."

Ben ran up to them, panting with excitement. "Come play!"

Jake jumped to his feet and chased her brother into the lake. She joined them, lounging in the luxury of the cool water until Ben began coaxing her to take part in the favorite game of their youth.

"Awww, come on, Kate."

"I'm too old," she laughed. "It would be improper."

"Who cares?"

She nodded her head in quick defeat. "Fine, but the loser has to make dinner."

"You're on!"

Her father sank into the water, hoisted her onto his shoulders, and rose. Jake did the same with Ben, then charged at them with a yell while Ben waved his arms. She and her father fought valiantly to keep standing and in the last moment Jake lost his footing, taking Ben with him.

They continued playing while the horses and oxen ate, then washed the animals together, as they were in need of a bath too. All were happy and content when they came ashore to lie in the grass and talk until their clothes dried. As the sun began its descent, everyone made their way back to the wagon, tired yet completely refreshed.

"What's for dinner?" Ben asked.

"I should be the one asking you." Kate said. "Remember our agreement?"

His eyes widened and he clutched his hands to his chest. "You'd make me cook dinner?"

"Certainly. And you have to do it by yourself," she added. "No fair having Jake's help." No need to forbid her father; he was nearly as hapless as her brother.

"What are you going to do?" Ben asked.

"I've got plenty of clothes to scrub clean." The task would be tremendous since she hadn't been able to wash anything dumped on the muddy riverbank yesterday. "Unless you want to help with those too?"

"No way!" Ben scampered off to the wagon, hollering about how having Jake start the fire wouldn't be helping. With a smile, Jake followed.

While they began preparing dinner, her father helped her bring an armload of clothes, the washboard, soap, and bucket down to the lake. After filling and bringing the bucket to her, he lingered close by.

"Are you sure you don't want help?" he asked, his eyes taking a slow perusal around the circumference of the lake.

"No," she said, kneeling to thrust a shirt into the bucket. "I want to be alone for a change. Traveling in a group gives me such little time to myself."

He stared at her with a hint of concern. "Any regrets?"

She sat back on her bare heels, brushed a lock of hair from her eyes, and considered her answer.

"A few days ago I would have said yes without hesitation. But today's the best day I've had in a long time. If the west is anything like here—" she paused and looked at the sunlight reflecting on the water "—I know I'm going to love it."

His relieved smile spoke volumes. "I'm glad, sweetheart."

****

While dusk set in, Jake crouched at the fire beside Ben and Elijah. All had taken a peek into the pot of lukewarm beans and poked at the slab of bacon Ben had dropped unceremoniously into the spider pan.

"She always says we'd starve without her," Jake said, grimacing as Ben knocked a spoon into the fire. "I think she might be right."

"Son, something's burning," Elijah said.

Ben whisked the pan from the fire, sending bacon flying by Jake's ear.

"Pretend you didn't see that," Ben instructed.

As the boy scooped up the meat and tossed it in the pan, Jake realized he'd be better off not knowing the details of how his dinner was being prepared.

"Someone should check on Kate," Jake said. "She'll need help bringing all the heavy clothes back and hanging them up."

"Since you're banned from cooking," Elijah said with a hearty laugh, "I vote you do it."

Relinquishing his duties to a nine-year-old made Jake laugh all the way to the lake — until the sight of Kate stopped him in his tracks.

The fiery sunset and exertion of scrubbing out the clothes created an explosion of color across her normally pale face.

Her hair had broken free from the braids she always confined it with, and now tumbled down her back. She'd been transformed into a soft woman with an inner glow.

She saw him coming and smiled, rendering Jake speechless by her beauty.

"Only a few more to go and I'll be done here," she said, then chattered on about the wonderful time she'd had earlier in the lake. When he didn't answer a question she glanced up at him and stopped in mid-sentence.

"Jake, what's wrong? Did something happen at camp?"

"Nothing's wrong." He looked away, certain his expression betrayed his thoughts. "I'm just checking on you. Dinner will be ready in half an hour."

"How's it coming along?"

"Badly, but we should be able to eat." He dared to look at her again, and was rewarded by yet another dazzling smile. How would his fingers feel buried in the soft curls of her hair? Suddenly desperate to dissuade the thoughts running rampant in his mind, he focused on the wet clothing strewn around.

"There's too much here for you to carry back alone. Want help?"

She beamed at his chivalry and pointed to the largest pile. "Those can go. I'll bring up the rest."

With a curt nod he grabbed the clothes and walked back toward the camp, berating his foolishness. Noticing Kate would only lead to trouble and jeopardize the money he needed from Elijah. Those earnings were his fresh start, his entire future.

He certainly couldn't take any chances on a woman.

Chapter Twenty

Trail Life

Tuesday, June 13, 1843 to Thursday, June 29, 1843

Wake up, pack up, move on, rest, move again, unpack, eat, sleep. Do it all over again the next day, the next week, and the next three months to come — the lull of everyday travel had set in.

Boredom began, the difficulties upon the body were realized, and the monotony of it all was mind-numbing. Blue, white, brown... blue, white, brown... all the eye could see for miles was blue sky, white clouds, and the continuous, undulating ocean of solid brown land. They were surrounded, with no end in sight.

After passing through St. Louis, they followed the Missouri River for over two hundred miles. Access to water and their lightened load made a dramatic difference, making a twenty-mile day a usual event.

Regrettably, it didn't last.

After they left Independence, where they'd resupplied and bought shoes for Kate, things got tough. Lack of water, rougher terrain, and blistering temperatures lessened their progress — mileage declined to fifteen, or sometimes even ten. The prairie seemed flat until urging their dehydrated stock up yet another rolling hill.

By now they were accustomed to the ever-present search for water. However, over the past few days the situation had become dire. Everything they'd passed had been cooked in the sun until brackish and stale. They were down to two full canteens, which meant only a few mouthfuls each day for man and beast. Coffee at each meal and washing the dishes were long gone — not a drop could be spared for anything besides drinking and cooking.

Unfortunately, as the one constant of trail life dictated, it would get worse before it got better.

****

Friday, June 30, 1843

Kate adjusted the material tied across her nose and mouth in a futile attempt to find a clean section to breathe through. All wore handkerchiefs as a shield against dust, and every few miles they stopped to wipe out the animal's nostrils.

Thud, creak. Thud, creak. Thud, creak.

The rhythmic steps of the oxen, followed by the slow spinning of the wagon wheels, brought puffs of dust into the air. One was tolerable, but the combination of six oxen, four horses, and a loaded wagon produced a relentless, suffocating cloud. It hung in the air, surrounding them, until finally settling upon everything in an invisible layer of filth. Dust forced its way into every crevice of the wagon, clothing, and body.

Above the noises of the animals, the creak of the wheels — turning, always turning — the quiet screamed in Kate's ears. It was a solid pressure, pushing and fighting for control. She found herself making noise for the sake of doing so — a scuffle of a boot here, humming a few notes of a song there. Sometimes, she had to fight the urge to scream, knowing the noise would only drift off with the wind.

The quiet always returned. The quiet always won.

That evening, as Kate was in the wagon putting dishes away by lamplight, she gingerly patted her rough, cracked lips. Pulling her fingertips back, Kate found them dotted with blood.

She brought out her mother's silver hand mirror for a further inspection, then immediately wished she hadn't. The reflection revealed eyes red-rimmed from exhaustion, sunken cheekbones, and hair coated in grime born of dirt and sweat. To her dismay, when she scratched the base of her neck her fingernails filled with a gray mixture of dirt and unwashed skin.

At this point, she'd abandoned thoughts of a bath. Such a luxury was out of the question. She wanted only enough water to give her feet a good, long soak. The sun had cooked every last drop of moisture from the grass until it felt like spikes through the soft soles of her slippers, and crunched like broken rock with each torturous step.

Perhaps if it rained, the grass would soften and she'd quit longing for the shoes they'd bought in Independence. A hopeful glance through the wagon canvas showed only clear black sky filled with millions of bright stars. Not a cloud in sight, no chance of rain.

Kate would have cried if she hadn't been so tired.

****

Sunday, July 2, 1843

Mornings were Jake's favorite time of the day. That morning, as usual, found him already dressed and Plug and Nickel saddled and waiting. With nothing left to do, he stood at the fire, watching the others get ready for the day. Today marked his fifth day with no coffee, and though he felt the effects, his main concern was how the others were faring.

Ben was young and could adapt easily; he was doing the best of all of them. Elijah suffered dizzy spells from lack of water, and his face showed the strain he carried from worrying about his children. Kate put up a brave front, but he couldn't miss her newfound limp. It mystified him since she'd gotten new shoes at Independence, but trouble walking meant foot problems, which always meant delays.

Grimly, he studied her as she emerged from the wagon and shuffled toward the fire. Fear of sparks setting off a wildfire forced them to keep the wagon twenty or so yards from the fire. The distance would give them a fighting chance at saving the wagon.

Only when Kate grew closer did he see she carried two pans, a bowl of flour, and a hunk of bacon. Cursing himself for not noticing her burden sooner, he rushed to take everything from her arms.

Watching her struggle past him, he had to fight back the urge to drop it all and carry her to the fire. Instead, he returned the items to the wagon and jogged back to where she now stood, staring into the flames.

"Try these instead." He handed her a small paper bag of dried apples. "Biscuits and bacon are tough on a body when water is scarce."

He turned to include Elijah and Ben in the conversation. "Speaking of water, our worries might be over soon." Three sets of desperate eyes stared at him with full attention. "We're about to enter a small valley, which usually means water somewhere near the base."

"How long till we get there?" Elijah asked quietly.

"If we have a good morning, we might be able to find a creek this afternoon. It should be enough to fill our canteens, both barrels, and satisfy the animals."

"Great," Elijah said, clapping his hands together in obvious relief. With a shout, Ben began dancing around his father. The two of them were so absorbed in their impromptu celebration neither noticed Kate's whimper as she took a step forward to join them.

Jake frowned. He had to figure out what was wrong, yet he didn't trust her to come clean in front of her father.

"Can the two of you check the back wheel while Kate and I finish up here?" he asked the joyful duo.

"I was thinking about doing that myself," Elijah replied. "I can't put my finger on it yet, but we'll figure out what's wrong soon enough."

Elijah put his arm around his son, and they headed for the wagon. Kate watched them leave and then sank to the ground, her face contorted in pain.

Jake studied her. "Doing all right?"

When she bit her lip and averted her gaze, it only confirmed his thoughts. She was hurting. Worse yet, she was hiding it.

He crossed his arms, figuring he'd begin with general conversation. "I'd give about anything for a cup of coffee right now."

"I know what you mean," she prattled out in a breathless spurt. "Sometimes I dream of a glass of cold, clear water. Everything is musty and stale."

Her voice went unnaturally high the last few words, and he lowered his tone to one he would use with a skittish colt.

"Tell me what's wrong with your feet."

She chattered on, ignoring his request. "Well, I better get going. Those horses aren't going to water themselves, are they?"

She leapt to her feet. Her hand broke her fall as she sank back down.

"Kate," he said softly.

She rose again, this time managing one lurching step before stumbling. Immediately, he was at her side. She leaned against him for a brief, wonderful moment before he felt her tense and try to pull away.

"Wait." He held her securely against his chest. "Isn't there something you need to tell me?"

"No."

"Prove it." He dropped his arms and took three strides backwards. "Walk to me."

"Fine." She squared her shoulders and lifted her chin. At her first step he heard a sharp intake of breath. Again, he rushed to her side. Before she could protest, he scooped her easily into his arms, walked across camp, and then lowered her onto Ben's bedroll.

"Tell me what's wrong."

She said nothing, but her eyes were heavy with tears as he put his finger under her chin and tilted her head to meet his gaze. "Let me take a look."

He crouched and put out his hand expectantly.

She blushed and needlessly pulled down the hem of her skirt. "I'm fine. They're just dirty and a little sore because I haven't been able to soak them."

"You're not fine, and I've seen feet before."

"Well, you haven't seen mine." Her eyes narrowed. "And I told you they're just dirty."

"And I told you I want to see them. Should I go under there and pull them out myself?"

Her eyes widened in surprise. "You wouldn't."

"Try me." He raised an eyebrow, half wishing she'd take the dare.

"Fine." The tips of her shoes peeped out from the fabric. "See? No problems."

"Kate, you're as headstrong as I am stubborn, but on this one I'll get my way. You've got my word."

She swallowed hard, then set her foot into his outstretched palm. Instantly the teasing stopped. Instead of the leather shoes he'd expected, she wore little more than slippers. Her foot had bled into the shredded fabric, which then hardened and molded to her delicate skin. As Jake inspected her injuries, he recognized the flimsy, soft-soled shoes as the ones she'd worn the first day of travel.

"What happened to the shoes we bought you at Independence?"

She bit her lip and shook her head. He started to push for an answer, then thought better of it.

"What are you doing?" she asked as he withdrew his knife from the sheath on his belt.

"Cutting these off."

Using the edge of the blade, he carefully peeled away the bloody fabric. The top of her foot felt soft as silk, but the underside was a swollen, abraded mess.

"I knew you were having trouble walking, but I had no idea it had gotten this bad. Let me see the other one."

A second bloody shoe appeared from under her skirt. After removing the useless material, he discovered a massive blister on the back of her heel. Across the ball of her foot was a deep, weeping crack. Gently squeezing the wound, Jake frowned as it oozed watery blood. He cursed to himself for having been so caught up with his own worries he'd failed to see one of the usual ones to befall newcomers. There was a reason they were called "tenderfoot".

"You should have told me," he murmured as he cradled her foot in his palm. "Kate, please know you can always tell me anything."

"I can handle it." Tears filled her eyes and she brushed at them impatiently. "Since it's my own fault."

"Why?"

"My new shoes gave me blisters, so one night I took them off and set them under the wagon. I forgot to put them back inside the next morning. I'd worn out my other shoes and those were all I had left."

"You've been wearing these—" he held up a strip of material in astonishment "—for two weeks?"

She shrugged. "I deserve it for being so careless."

"No," he said firmly. "Out here you are my responsibility, and I should have checked camp before we left."

"I thought I could make it until we got to the next fort." She bowed her head. "But when we grew so low on water, I tried to walk more to save the horses."

"At what cost? It could take weeks to recover from this."

"I know, but I didn't want the horses to suffer because of me. I've never seen Nina so sluggish, and I'm worried about the oxen too."

He carefully set her foot down, went to his saddlebag, and returned with a small jar and strips of cloth.

"You're a lot tougher than I gave you credit for, but the fact remains you won't be able to walk at all for at least a week. It will be another week until you can handle the pace necessary to keep up."

He wet a cloth from the mug at her side and pulled her feet into his lap. Once he'd cleaned them, he opened the jar and dabbed salve over her wounds. He wound a cloth over her foot, then tied the ends.

"Doesn't Ben have extra boots hanging from the side of the wagon?

She sighed. "They don't fit."

"Your father has a spare pair. They won't be comfortable, but you'll be riding all day and off your feet at night now."

"What about meals?"

His lips tightened. "Won't be a problem until we come to water."

"I don't want Ben to walk all day. Are you sure I can't ride in the wagon?"

"The oxen are thirsty. When they smell water they're liable to make a run for it. Your father might not be able to hold them back. Things inside the wagon could shift. Speaking of your father..." He focused on Elijah and Ben, who were returning to the fire. "How'd it go?"

"Well, the wheel won't give us any more trouble. I greased it up good. I'd be surprised if it makes any noise at all now." Elijah smiled until he noticed Kate's bandaged feet. "What's this?"

"Just some foot trouble, but she'll be fine in a week or two. In the meantime, she'll have to ride." He leaned forward and tousled Ben's hair. "You'll walk more, but you're pretty tough so you'll be fine."

"You bet!" Ben said.

"Let's move out now, so we can make the creek by tonight," Jake said.

Ignoring her protests, he lifted Kate and set her on Nina. Elijah resumed his position in the wagon seat, Ben took his place alongside the wagon, and Jake swung up onto Plug.

Wheels and hooves slowly plodded on.

Chapter Twenty-One

Doubt

Someone was following them.

Jake had seen no evidence, but long ago he learned to trust his gut. After leaving camp that morning, his gut told him there was trouble.

Within hours they would descend into the upcoming valley and become a prime target to anyone watching from a vantage point in the hills. Their dire need for water provided the perfect opportunity for a horse thief, or worse, to try for an ambush. Sound traveled far, and six oxen pulling a wagon with four horses nearby were bound to attract a lot of attention.

Kate, even more so.

Mid-morning Jake stopped Plug at the top of the hillside, dismounted, and looked upon his newest worry spread out below. The others arrived and gathered at the edge beside him.

Compared to the flat and barren prairie, the rugged landscape held plenty to explore. As the family's eager eyes darted over every crevice, treetop, and jutting rock formation, all Jake could think of was what was missing. The last time he'd been through there'd been a carpet of tender grass, perfect for satisfying the animals, and long stretches of wildflowers shifting in the wind — perfect for a woman like Kate. Now the valley was already losing color, and probably water.

He wished yet again he'd kept his mouth shut about finding a creek today. The weather they'd had the last few weeks only increased the chance of finding nothing but a dried-up bed of rocks. But they had to get there first. Though he could hold his own with a gun or in a battle of strength, a man could lose a fight simply by being outnumbered.

If trouble loomed, he needed a feel on how Elijah would hold up.

"What do you all say to a break?" Jake asked the group.

While they all murmured their agreement, he again scanned the nearby hills, searching for anything unusual. Time spent with his scope might ease his worries. Or not.

"Ben, can you check the oxen's yokes again?" he asked.

As the boy ran to the wagon, Jake focused his attention on Kate. She stood, flushed and delighted at the sights before her.

"You need to stay off your feet."

"I'm fine," she insisted.

"Rest," he told her firmly while pointing at a nearby rock for her to sit on. "You won't get any better if you don't."

Nodding her acquiescence, Kate shuffled toward the rock.

With the two of them out of the way, Jake faced Elijah. "Can I talk to you about Plug's leg? He's been favoring it most of the day."

Before he could answer, Jake gathered up Plug's reins and led the horse a good fifteen yards from the wagon. After they stopped, Elijah crouched to run knowing hands over the fetlocks.

"I hadn't noticed a limp," he said. "I hope it's nothing serious."

"He's fine," Jake replied quietly.

Elijah straightened with a look of confusion. "Then why are we here?"

"You have a gun in the wagon?" Jake asked.

"Rifle's under the wagon seat."

"Loaded and ready?"

"Always." Elijah frowned. "What's this about?"

"We'll likely reach water this afternoon, and horse thieves, or worse, have been known to lay in wait because they know you've got to have it. A loaded wagon and dehydrated animals don't make for a quick escape should trouble arise."

Elijah's eyes narrowed and his expression went grim. "What did you see?"

With one simple question, he'd unknowingly stumbled upon Jake's most pressing concern. Though he'd seen nothing, it didn't mean there was nothing to see. Throughout the past year, his confidence in his sight over long distances had diminished. The handicap was slight, but a man leading a naïve family needed every advantage.

Avoiding the answer, Jake nodded first to Ben, now dutifully inspecting the oxen, and then to where Kate stood, braiding Nina's tail. "Can either of them shoot?"

"Ben has some experience, but he's still mainly learning how to load and care for a gun. As for Kate—" Elijah managed a small grin "—unbeknownst to her mother, I used to take her practicing. She's an accurate shot."

Jake nodded at the confession. Perhaps Oregon would welcome this man after all.

Travel was uneventful for the next two hours, but just as Jake considered calling for the afternoon rest, the hair rose on the back of his neck.

Had a rock tumbled from the ridge above?

His unease grew as his eyes, and then his scope, followed the skyline. Still, even after the intense inspection, he found nothing out of the ordinary. Silently, they continued for another fifteen minutes, long enough to conclude his overstressed nerves were getting the better of him.

"I think we're fine," he called back to Elijah. "The creek should be about a mile ahead."

Less than half an hour later Jake found out how wrong he was.

Chapter Twenty-Two

Company

Jake stood in silence as the dry creek bed lay at his feet, mocking him with what it could have provided. They didn't have enough water to get through the next few hours, much less the next few days until they would reach, and then follow, the Little Blue River.

This was precisely why wagon trains left earlier in the year. On past trips through he'd found it a small, yet plentiful water source. Now, it yielded only a few drops per minute. Filling a canteen would take over an hour. Making matters worse was the dead coyote lying in the shallow pool of collected water. To drink from it likely meant illness. The risk was too great.

Jake removed his hat and wiped dust and worry from his forehead. Checking on the others, he found Ben horrified, Kate trying not to cry, and Elijah holding a dead stare to the dusty rocks in the creek bed.

"I'm not going to lie," Jake began, selecting his words carefully in the hopes of avoiding an outright panic. "The next few days will be hard. But it's been done before and can be done again. Half a canteen can last three days if need be and there are plants we can suckle from." The last option wasn't tasty, but when the choices were live or die, a person tended not to care.

A change on the hillside above caught his eye. A quick scan of the jagged rocks revealed little. However, Jake's movement had attracted attention. Three sets of eyes now stared at him, apprehension clear on their faces.

"I'm sure it was nothing," he said, willing his voice to remain calm, "and standing here will do no good. Kate, stay on Nina and watch for approaching animals. Ben, you look on the other side of the wagon. Elijah, come help me get this creek flowing again."

Jake dropped to his knees. After flinging the coyote aside, together he and Elijah scraped away the top layer of mud where the carcass had lain. The act wouldn't benefit them, but Jake couldn't stand the thought of animals needlessly dying from disease because they dared a drink.

"Hurry," Jake said quietly as they moved to dig out the source of the trickle — beneath a pile of boulders and rocks, large and small. "We need this too much to pass it by, but we've got to hurry."

"What's up there?" Elijah asked as he pulled another rock from the side of the creek bed.

"It could be a buffalo strayed from its herd, a lone animal, or just about anything."

"But it's not, is it?"

Jake's reply was grim. "Probably not."

They kept pulling and digging. After a few minutes Jake leaned back to survey the small, but steady flow of water. It would have to do.

"Ben, get a canteen, a cup, and a bucket and bring them over here. Quickly."

Ben scurried to the wagon.

"Should I get the barrel?" Elijah asked.

"No, we don't want to unpack anything."

Ben returned with the items. Jake put the cup under the water. Five tense minutes passed before he was able to hand it over to Ben.

"Take two sips and give it to your sister. After she's done, bring it to us."

Jake held the bucket under the trickle. Fifteen long minutes ticked by.

"Since there's only enough in here for one drink per animal you better give it to them," he said as he handed Elijah the bucket. "We can't chance them trampling Ben."

Thirty minutes and two full canteens later, the urge to leave was too overwhelming for Jake to ignore.

"It isn't much," he said, "but we can survive until Little Blue. Let's move on."

Mounting Plug, Jake led the group off. Minutes later, he swore softly when a glance at the skyline revealed the stark outline of a man on horseback.

Cursing again, he slowed Plug until he rode even with the wagon seat. Elijah sat stiffly, his eyes sweeping the terrain ahead.

"We've got company," Jake said quietly so as not to alarm Kate, who rode alongside the wagon, or Ben, who walked beside her.

"How many?"

"At least one. Others could be nearby."

"What's the plan?" Elijah asked, curling his fingers around the rifle lying across his knees.

"Keep going until we have reason not to," Jake replied. "We're not asking for trouble, but we'll be ready if it comes."

Jake urged Plug forward and held him to the right of the lead oxen. Intent on keeping watch on the shadowed figure, he reached for his scope.

A trail of dust down the hillside thwarted his plan.

It was hopeless. They were caught out in the open with a wagon, a hurt woman, and a child. The fact that he had Elijah on his side didn't reassure Jake by any means. A man could shoot one man dead and severely injure another before a single bullet was fired in return. If he and Elijah were killed or injured, Kate and Ben would be left alone and unprotected.

Grimly, Jake pocketed his scope, then twisted in his saddle.

The lone rider now followed only about fifty yards behind them.

Ben noticed first.

"Jake!" he shouted. "S-s-s-someone's back there!"

After a nod to Elijah — now holding his rifle at the ready — Jake spoke loud enough for Ben and Kate to hear. "Stay calm. He may want to trade supplies or warn us of upcoming danger."

He didn't believe his own words, but panicking them wouldn't help. Slowly, he eased Plug away from the oxen and glanced back again. The lone rider was approaching from the right, and slowly gaining. The situation called for a balance between needlessly scaring everyone and preparing for the worst.

Time to get prepared.

Jake slowed Plug until he rode aside the wagon. Leaning over, he deftly untied Old Dan's lead rope and held it out to Ben. "Get on and move over to the left of the wagon."

Once Ben mounted and did as he was told, Jake looked to Kate. "Ride next to your brother, and stay with him no matter what."

She was pale with fright but followed his request without question. Now at least they were in a better position, and both could help Elijah with reloading if needed. He kept Plug to the right of the wagon, putting himself between the group and the approaching stranger.

This family depended upon him, and Jake had no intention of letting them down.

****

Kate took yet another trembling breath in an attempt to keep calm. Ben rode beside her, small and quiet in the saddle. She had to be brave. It wouldn't do to faint.

The minutes crawled by and still the man followed, taunting them with his brazenness. Daring to look, Kate saw he wasn't wearing a hat. Another glance back and she stiffened. The horse didn't have a saddle, and the man's long black hair fluttered in the wind. A realization swept over her like ice water.

This was no ordinary man. He was an Indian!

She turned again in her saddle, aghast to see him only about twenty yards back, yet unable to tear her eyes away as he raised one hand in the air, and then brought it to his face.

A series of sharp whistles pierced the air.

Heart pounding, she stood in the stirrups, her eyes frantically searching across the endless terrain ahead. Within seconds, Jake rode up alongside her.

"There's nowhere to hide!" she cried out as strong whistles again filled the air. "What do we do?"

"Nothing," Jake said. "He's my friend."

"Your *friend?*" Her legs buckled and she collapsed into the saddle with a gasp. Her panic quickly changed to astonishment as Jake brought his fingers to his lips and sent duplicate whistles into the wind.

"Trust me," he said, leaning over to give her arm a gentle squeeze. "Most of what you read in those books is wrong."

She didn't have a chance to respond before he told her father to stop the wagon, and for them all to wait.

Rifle in hand, her father stepped from the wagon to stand at her side. Jake rode back to the stranger and held up his hand in a greeting. The two men dismounted and walked a short distance before the Indian began pointing over the hills.

Kate turned her attention to the horse he'd left standing. No reins, no saddle, or even a single strap to guide it along. The horse was either well trained or content to be wherever his master went. He stood peacefully eating grass and occasionally glancing around at the surroundings.

"However would Jake have known such a man?" she wondered aloud.

"I hired Jake because of his experience on the trail," her father said in clipped, low tones. "Perhaps they met on one of his previous times through."

"Look at what he's w-wearing," Ben said in awe, his face a mixture of anxiety and curiosity.

The Indian wore fringed leggings made of hide, and no shirt. One side of his waistband held a large knife, and the other a crude hatchet.

"I wonder if he's ever k-killed anyone," Ben whispered.

"Probably," she whispered back. The only references she had were the dime novels she'd read at home. This man looked just as they'd described. Tall, with muscular, tapered legs that disappeared within a pair of well-worn moccasins. The top portion of his glossy black hair had been pulled into a tight, high ponytail and adorned with several bright feathers. The leathery texture of his skin made it impossible to guess his age.

"Be quiet, you two. They're coming back," her father warned.

Jake and the Indian walked toward them. She heard their voices, but they spoke an unintelligible language. Her father stepped forward, motioning for her and Ben to dismount and join him.

"I'd like you to meet Whitehorse," Jake said solemnly.

Returning to the strange language, he then pointed to each of them. Throughout the introductions Whitehorse remained motionless, except for his eyes. They were as black as the deepest night, and Kate couldn't believe how they glittered in the bright sun. When they rested on her she briefly met his gaze and then lowered her eyes.

"Whitehorse knows of a stream nearby," Jake said, his smile jubilant.

As Ben threw his hat in the air and whooped with joy, her father stepped forward and extended his hand.

"On behalf of my family, thank you."

Whitehorse stood still. After a moment's hesitation, her father dropped his hand.

"How come your name is Whitehorse, but your horse is b-b-brown?" Ben asked before her father clapped a quieting hand upon his shoulder.

Jake broke the awkward silence. "Let's mount up and move on."

Twenty minutes later, as the six oxen smelled water, the wagon picked up speed. Soon, despite her father's best efforts and urgings, it clattered down the narrow rocky path. Upon sighting the stream they charged forward, thirst ruling all.

Quickly, Jake and her father jumped to unhitch the front pair before the back four pushed them, and brought the wagon along into the stream. The first pair lunged forward and met the water with heads down, tongues ready. The remaining teams stamped their hooves and strained against their yokes until they were freed.

Once all the animals were drinking comfortably at the water's edge, Jake climbed into the back of the wagon. He emerged with three metal cups, dipped each in the stream, and handed them over.

At the first sip, the refreshing coolness spread slowly over Kate's dry, swollen tongue. Then, filled with the overwhelming need to destroy the thirst that for so long had controlled her every thought, she gulped the rest. She then joined Ben and her father in greedily filling and drinking cup after cup. When Ben plunged his cup into the stream a fourth time, Whitehorse uttered a sharp, guttural noise, startling them all.

"Don't drink too much," Jake warned. "You'll be sick. Take it slow. There's plenty to last the next few days until we're following a river again."

All was silent until he spoke again. "He will stay for dinner if there are no objections."

None were made.

Whitehorse sat nearby, watchful yet expressionless, as they made camp. Dinner supplies in hand, Kate emerged from the wagon. She started the fire and the meal, all without a single glance toward Whitehorse. Ben, on the other hand, peppered Jake with questions.

"How did he know it w-was you when he was behind us?" Ben asked.

"I asked him that myself," Jake replied. "He said he knew by the markings on Plug."

"Why doesn't he wear clothes like us?"

Jake chuckled. "Clothes get in his way."

"Why was he following us?"

"I don't rightly know, but it's good he came along when he did. We were close to losing two of the oxen."

While flipping the salt pork over in the pan, Kate snuck unobtrusive looks at the man who'd helped them for no apparent benefit of his own. He sat near the wagon, still again except for his eyes. From her father feeding the horses to Jake and Ben reclining against the wagon wheels, he missed nothing.

Ben's questions continued. "Why d-doesn't his horse have a saddle?"

Jake tousled her brother's disheveled hair. "So you can ask about it."

"Quit bothering Jake and come get your dinner," she said.

"I better get going, or she'll yell at me again," Ben whispered loudly, and then scampered toward her with an impish grin. Kate couldn't hold back a smile as she dished up his plate. Life on the trail and Jake's patient guidance had him coming out of his shell more each day.

Once Jake and her father had gotten their plates, she hesitated a moment, then brought a full plate to Whitehorse, set it before him, and hurried back to the fire. As they ate, Ben ignored her warning and kept pestering Jake with questions. To her surprise, Whitehorse answered some in broken English. Jake translated the rest.

Late that night, as she finished soaking and wrapping her feet, a new thought settled in her mind.

Through Whitehorse, Jake had saved her family again.

****

Monday, July 3, 1843

For the first time in weeks, getting dressed wasn't an abysmal chore. Usually, the task involved picking through the soiled clothes piled onto the floorboards of the wagon and pulling the least offensive over her head. Today was markedly different.

Before retiring for the evening, Kate had scrubbed her dress clean and hung it in the wagon to dry. The fabric rustled pleasantly as it settled next to her body. Due to a secret late night bath, her hair shone in the early morning light as she brushed it, then confined the length into a topknot.

A peek through a slit in the wagon canvas revealed Jake alone at the fire. She heard only the crackle of the fire and her father's soft snores. Where was Whitehorse? Had he left?

She cautiously emerged from the wagon, breakfast items in tow. When Jake turned and rose to greet her in one fluid movement, she stumbled.

He was a man transformed.

Overnight he'd cut his hair. Shaggy waves had been tamed into a style reminiscent of the first weeks of the trail. Gone too was his ever-present stubble, revealing once again his strong, square jaw line. His shirt, still damp from recent washing, clung to his broad chest and shoulders. Long sleeves were rolled up to his elbows, exposing taut forearms. Crandall could have labored for years and still not have been half the man who stood before her now, his welcoming smile showing a hint of hesitation.

Willing her cheeks not to flush, Kate made her way to the fire. As she accepted the steaming cup of coffee Jake offered, her fingers brushed against his firm, strong hand. She faltered, and then blurted out the first question she could think of.

"Where's Whitehorse?"

"He left."

Kate exhaled a large sigh of relief, both at Jake's answer and to the fact that she'd made it to a nearby rock without falling and embarrassing herself any further. After a long moment, she ventured forth with the question she'd been wondering since their exchange of whistles.

"How did you meet him?"

Cobalt blue eyes reflected his uncertainty as they settled upon hers. "Years ago, he saved my life."

Chapter Twenty-Three

Revelations

It was a part of his life Jake had shared only once, with Valerie — and only after he'd withstood days of her pestering about his past. When he'd finally succumbed and told of the tragedy of his childhood and how it had shaped the rest of his life, Valerie's expression had been one of distress. Yet when he'd continued, telling of his time spent with Whitehorse, he finally recognized sympathy wasn't causing Valerie's misery. It had been the realization that his background would never be accepted in her social circle.

And now, by his own volition, he'd brought up his past to Kate. She sat across the fire from him, her eyes wide with anticipation to his coming words.

"Circumstances led me to the trail as a young man," he began, intending on rushing through the story. Though, what did it matter? After they arrived in Oregon their paths would cross rarely, if at all.

"This is my fifth journey across. First, I went with a wagon train. Our guide was short-tempered and didn't share knowledge easily, but by the end of the return trip, I knew the land. With only Plug for company, I headed out again the following spring. On the way back, I was hunting on the plains when a group of buffalo surrounded us. One scared Plug so bad he reared, knocking me off into a beginning stampede."

A glance under the wagon confirmed Ben and Elijah were sound asleep. Good. Sharing his past with Kate was one thing, but with her inquisitive family another entirely.

Jake refilled his cup and held out the coffeepot. "More?"

"No, thank you." She waved away his hand. "What happened next?"

"When the dust cleared, I lay helpless with a broken left leg. I couldn't chase Plug, who, incidentally, had run off. I was injured and alone in the middle of nowhere. No rifle, no supplies, and worst of all, no canteen."

He paused for another sip of coffee, but the bitter brew had barely hit his throat before Kate leaned forward, sending a splash of her coffee unheeded in the dirt before her.

"What did you do next?"

"Bandaged my leg with my shirt, made a crutch from a branch, and headed for a settlement I'd gone through about thirty miles back. Days passed. I couldn't find water or food, so I set up camp the best I could in the hopes another traveler would come by and rescue me." In reality, he'd known the chances of someone happening upon him were slim to none; death would be the more likely outcome. "Finally, delirious from dehydration, hunger, and pain, I mercifully passed out."

He stirred the fire, uncertain at the worry in Kate's eyes. Or was it tenderness he saw?

"I can't imagine why you want to hear this."

"You're leading my family across thousands of miles, and I know nothing about you." She stretched her legs, crossed her father's boots at the ankle, and gave him an encouraging smile. "Please, go on."

"I woke to find my leg set, and an unfamiliar face hovering above me while another poured bitter powder into my mouth. I lost consciousness again soon after. The next time I woke, I was lucid and curious of my strange, new surroundings — I lay inside a teepee on a bed of furs. Whitehorse appeared and told of how he and several of his tribesmen had found me, brought me back to their camp, set my leg, and dosed me with medicine."

"How did you understand him?"

"It was difficult at first, just a lot of pointing and grunting. But, eventually I picked up the basics. Over time, I learned Whitehorse belonged to the Kaw tribe, and he and the others had found me while on a hunt for buffalo. It took almost two months to regain my strength and for my leg to heal. During that time they taught me survival skills and the ways of the land."

Kate sighed. "All my life I've been taught to believe Indians are horrible, savage people. When I first saw Whitehorse yesterday, I thought…"

She faltered and lowered her eyes.

"Kate, something you should always remember is what the government and all the settlers are choosing to ignore. Indians were here long before us. Now, we're forcing them from the only land and lifestyle they've ever known because we want it for ourselves."

Suddenly uncomfortable at how much he'd shared, Jake shifted the conversation.

"I forgot the best part of the story. The day after Whitehorse rescued me, he found Plug." He chuckled. "Saddled, all supplies intact."

Though some would rightly view Plug's behavior as a hindrance, he'd always felt a connection to his horse's tendency to explore. After all, Jake spent his own life wandering, so he had trouble faulting his horse for doing the same.

"So," he added with a shrug and an uneasy smile, "that's how I met Whitehorse."

Quietly she studied him, her intense gaze evaluating his very depths, so much so that he had to force himself not to look away. Instead he sat silent and still under her probing scrutiny, his jaw clenched and his muscles rigid, and waited for her reaction, hoping he hadn't made another mistake.

"Thank you."

He frowned in confusion. "For what?"

"For sharing your past, and by doing so, showing me a different world."

Their eyes met, and held.

For weeks he'd tried to suppress his growing awareness of this woman who now sat across from him, her expression one of kindness and compassion. It was a far cry from the revulsion he'd seen from Valerie, and predicted from Kate, upon hearing his story.

"Kate, I've seen firsthand how dangerous it can be out here. That being said—" his tone grew husky with regret "—I must apologize again for my harsh words at the beginning of this trip. I was convinced you'd only be a liability and fall to pieces in a crisis. I now know differently." He paused, wanting her to see the truth of his next words. "I'm glad you came along."

As his unexpected compliment brought an enticing glow to her cheeks, their conversation was interrupted by Ben's arrival at the campfire. Soon after, the camp sprang to life.

Ben, bursting with questions about Whitehorse, tagged along behind Jake as he helped Elijah feed the animals. Kate's spoon clattered around the bowl as she mixed biscuit dough, and the hearty aroma of salt pork filled the air. Jake filled the kettle with water and set it over the fire to heat.

"I thought you might want to soak your feet before we left today."

"Yes, thank you." She peeked beneath the lid covering the biscuits and then looked up at him. "But more importantly, is there time to do a washing?"

Jake nodded. "Your father and Ben are planning on repairing some harnesses, and I'm going to repack my saddle bags, so it should work out fine."

After they ate and cleaned up, Kate disappeared into the wagon. Minutes later, Jake walked to the back and tapped a finger against the wagon box. She poked her head through the canvas.

"I'm here to carry your clothes. I've already got everything set up at the stream."

"Thank you," she said gratefully.

"Don't thank me too much," he replied. "I'm washing my own things."

As she climbed through the canvas and over the back boards of the wagon, her skirt fluttered in the wind. And when he caught a glimpse of skin while her leg searched for the wooden step, his suspicions were confirmed.

They knelt side by side at the stream. When they were done scrubbing and rinsing, he helped spread her garments on the warm grass. Glancing around, Jake couldn't help but notice what was missing.

"What did you do, abandon them?"

"What are you talking about?"

"Your petticoats." He laughed as her cheeks flamed. "Well, that answers my question."

"Please don't tell my father," she said with a frantic look over her shoulder. "He'd be so disappointed to learn I wasn't acting proper. Even out here."

"Your secret is safe with me." He finished spreading out his clothes, then bent to whisper in her ear. "I never did like them myself, and it seems like they'd just be in your way too."

Chapter Twenty-Four

Untimely Disruption

Wednesday, July 5, 1843

Jake woke late but stayed in his bedroll, his muscles still aching from the exertion of the past few days. Even though yesterday was the Fourth of July, they'd all agreed to travel hard. By nightfall they'd done over twenty miles. In one more day they'd reach the Little Blue River, and in about a hundred miles the Platte River. Even better, they were only about four hundred miles away from Fort Laramie, where they would resupply, rest, and get Kate new shoes.

Though they had months to go before reaching Oregon, Elijah and Ben sat shoulder to shoulder beside the fire, discussing plans for the first days after their arrival in Oregon City.

Jake had underestimated the man yet again. Elijah had goals for each week and subsequent months after their arrival. First, a store and land. Within two years he was confident in his ability to sustain a full-scale horse ranch.

"I'm telling you, Ben, what we have in our wagon will be sold at double the cost." Elijah paused to pat his son on the back. "And with what I've got coming out the following spring we'll be able to build a house and staff it properly within the year."

The offhand comment served as a vivid reminder to Jake of their differences. He'd spent his life focused on surviving each day and rarely made plans for longer than the coming season, while Elijah was a businessman prepared for — and fully expecting — success. Oregon would welcome this man, his wealth, and his family with open arms.

Jake poured a mug of coffee and walked to the wagon. After he scratched lightly on the weathered canvas, Kate pulled it aside.

"Good morning," she said, happily stretching her arms out to accept the offering.

Last week, he'd brought her coffee after a particularly long night. The irresistible sight of tousled curls and a sleepy smile encouraged him to make it a daily habit.

She took a slow sip and closed her eyes. "Thank you."

"My pleasure," he replied, and then headed back to the fire where Elijah and Ben were now discussing their first horse roundup. It was a definite pleasure to know this family.

Later, as they packed up camp, Jake gave some welcome news. "Today marks two months we've been on the trail."

"Already?" Elijah asked in disbelief. "It seems like we just left."

Jake shook his head. "We've gone nearly a thousand miles, and if things keep up we'll make it to Oregon in about three more months." Turning to swing his saddle up onto Nickel, he saw Ben trip over the wagon tongue.

Elijah rushed to the boy's side. "You all right, son?"

"I think so." Ben brushed himself off and got to his feet. "Just c-clumsy I guess."

As Ben returned to the chore of blanketing the horses, Jake noticed a limp. Just what they needed — another one hurt.

Elijah noticed too and crossed the camp. "Son, how's your foot?"

"It s-stings," Ben said, gingerly taking a step. "I must have twisted it when I fell."

"Sit down and let me check."

Elijah took off his son's boot and inspected his ankle, rotating and stretching it carefully. Watching, Jake couldn't help but wonder how his own life would have been different had his father not been killed. A boy needed a father, and Ben was fortunate to have such a caring one.

"It's not broken," Elijah declared, "but I think you should stay off it today. What do you think, Jake?"

Seeing no problem with his proposition, Jake agreed. "You can ride today. Mount up and wait with your sister while we pack up the rest of camp."

He and Elijah extinguished the fire, repacked the kettle, and secured the supplies. While they worked, Elijah kept glancing toward Ben.

"How about I ride beside him for a bit?" Jake offered, hoping to alleviate the man's obvious worry. "I'll make sure his foot isn't bothering him."

Elijah gave a relieved nod. Minutes later, the wagon pulled away, leaving Jake between Ben and Kate. They set out, side by side, riding behind the wagon.

"Jake, are you s-sure this isn't too much for Old Dan?" Ben asked with a worried grimace.

"He'll be fine," Jake assured him. "We have water to spare and we're coming up on more soon. But your concern shows the mark of a good horseman. Besides, I could use a scout up front today."

"What about me?"

Slowly, he twisted in his saddle. What was Kate up to now?

She answered his unspoken question with a tentative smile. "I need to learn how to survive out west, and I want you to teach me. Will you?"

Startled both by the request and the determination settling in her eyes, he let out an uneasy chuckle. But as their gaze deepened, his smile faded. This woman riding at his side was no longer the pampered, self-indulgent girl he'd begun the journey with. Months on the trail had worn down her brittle edges and transformed her into a confident, secure woman.

An exquisite, alluring woman.

How would it feel to hold her in his arms? To place his lips upon the curve of her neck? The curve of her hip?

He swallowed hard and spoke soft. "I'll teach you anything you want to know."

Ahead of them the wagon sped up, then slowed. Jake forced himself to focus on the trail.

"What's going on up there?" he muttered as the wagon lurched to a halt.

"Don't worry," Ben said with a toothy grin. "Father has the mark of a g-good horseman too. Or should I say, oxen man."

While Ben chuckled at his own joke, Jake frowned as the wagon surged forward. This time, instead of slowing again, the oxen broke out into a full run. All three fell silent as the wagon careened across the uneven prairie. Jake watched with growing dread as supplies flew into the air with each bounce.

"I'm sure he can handle it," he said, trying to reassure them. But within seconds it became apparent Elijah could not bring the runaways to a stop. "Or maybe not. Stay back!"

Kicking his heels into Nickel's side, he started after Elijah with the intention of getting ahead of the team, grabbing hold of the lead ox, and forcing them all to slow down. Due to the considerable lead of the oxen and the need to dodge wayward supplies now littering the ground, it took nearly a minute to catch up.

Plug was tied to the rear of the wagon and keeping pace step for step. Jake rode beside him and unsheathed his knife. Leaning over, he cut through the rope, setting Plug free. As he slid his knife into its sheath, Jake saw something that made his blood run cold.

The back left wheel was coming loose.

He yelled at Elijah, yelled at Nickel, yelled at the oxen, but it was no use. One second the wheel wobbled furiously against the axle, and the next it was off and rolling free.

With a loud bang, the wagon corner hit the ground, dragging a furrow in the dirt when it wasn't bouncing up then slamming down again. The noise was tremendous, but instead of slowing, the panicked oxen ran faster.

Jake urged Nickel closer to the wagon.

Ten feet to Elijah. How could the oxen keep such a pace?

Five feet to Elijah. Could the man make the leap?

Nickel thundered on and Jake reached Elijah, now on his feet and pulling back with all his weight on the reins. It made no difference — the oxen were runaways.

Jake stood in his stirrups, making room in the saddle behind him.

"Jump on! It's going to tip!" he shouted as hooves and wheels roared across the prairie at breakneck speed.

Elijah stayed in place. He either hadn't heard him or ignored the warning.

As the crackle of splintering wood filled Jake's ears, he knew Elijah had only seconds left.

"Jump! The front axle's cracking!" Jake yelled, desperate for him to heed his warning.

"Stay back! I can handle it!" shouted Elijah, stubbornly determined to save the wagon.

"It's going to tip!"

As if on cue, the wagon tilted dangerously to one side, then righted itself again. Jake heard the sickening snap of the axle and reached out with every last bit of strength, straining to grab Elijah from the seat.

But Elijah was gone.

Amidst tumbling oxen, supplies flying through the air, and a spectacular cloud of dirt, the wagon came to a final rest — upside down, with the canvas cover crushed beneath.

Chapter Twenty-Five

Dire Discovery

"Elijah!"

Jake shouted the name repeatedly while riding a wide circle around the overturned wagon and thrashing oxen in the hopes Elijah had been flung free. Seeing no sign of the man, he jumped from his saddle and hurried through the choking dust to the wreckage. Peering through the broken boards, he tried once more.

"Elijah, can you hear me?"

Nothing — although if Elijah had responded, Jake wouldn't have heard him over the bellowing oxen. A quick investigation found all six hitched to the wagon tongue; the lead team was dead, and a center ox convulsed beneath the mess of tangled chains and his twisted yoke. The whites of his eyes matched the jagged bone protruding from his front leg.

Knowing there was no choice once an animal was injured so severely, Jake ran to his saddlebag, seized his pistol, and shot the ox to end its misery.

Of their six oxen, three now lay dead.

Hurrying back, he found Kate and Ben crawling through the jagged boards and debris surrounding the wagon.

"Get back!" he warned.

Eyes wide with panic, Ben froze. Kate scrambled to her feet and spun in place, executing a futile search across the barren prairie.

"Where is he?" she shrieked. "Are you sure he wasn't thrown?"

"No, he's under there," Jake insisted grimly. He lay on his stomach and peered beneath the remains of the wagon. "I see a hand!"

Only he saw more than a bloodied hand. Before him in the settling dust was a ghastly sight. Elijah's head and torso lay hidden under splintered boards and burlap sacks, his lower body pinned solid by the five-hundred-pound wagon box.

Kate fell to the ground beside him with a soft grunt. "He isn't moving!"

Scrambling to her feet, she grabbed the end of the nearest board and began wrenching it back and forth. "Help me! Help me get the wagon off him!"

"Touch nothing!" Jake shouted. "One wrong move and everything shifts."

Wide-eyed, she let the board free.

Jake stood and grabbed her by the shoulders.

"I'll get closer and see how he's doing." He spoke quietly, trying to calm his panic and Kate's rising tears. "I'll hand you and Ben what I pull clear."

Releasing her, he began carefully stepping through the wreckage while heaving broken wagon parts and destroyed supplies out of his way. Jake grew increasingly worried by the minute. They still hadn't heard a sound from the fallen man.

Throwing aside the last sack of flour revealed Elijah's upper body and the reasons for his silence. Blood flowed from a gash on his left temple and pooled on the ground below. A steel hinge had lodged itself deep into his left bicep and bone protruded from his shirt at the elbow.

Suddenly, Jake realized he didn't even know if Elijah was alive. Dread roiled through him as he bent over.

"Elijah."

Nothing.

Jake tried again, but got no response. A glance toward Kate and Ben saw them standing hand in hand, their eyes filled with silent hope. He turned back and focused on Elijah's temple. The flow of crimson encouraged him — a dead man wouldn't bleed. Exhaling a long, slow breath, he tried once more.

"Elijah." He kept his tone low. "Your children are watching. If you can hear me, open your eyes." Relief flowed over him when Elijah's eyelids fluttered open.

"He's alive!"

At his jubilant shout they rushed forward before he could warn them. Kate recovered first.

"We have to get the wagon off him," she insisted in an urgent whisper. Ben nodded his tearful agreement.

"We will," Jake assured her with a confidence he didn't feel. "But we don't want to cause any more injuries in the process. Three of the oxen are still alive, and we can't chance their struggles moving the wagon. I'll stay with your father while you both go unhitch them. Be careful, but try to hurry."

As they ran to the front of the wagon, Jake pulled his handkerchief from his vest pocket, knelt, and held it to Elijah's head. Within seconds, blood soaked the material. He unsheathed his knife, pulled off his shirt, and quickly shredded it into sections. As he pressed a fresh cloth hard against the wound, Elijah opened his eyes. With a low moan, he struggled to sit up.

"Lay still," Jake said, while keeping solid pressure to Elijah's head.

"What happened?" Elijah murmured.

"There's been an accident. You need to keep quiet."

Elijah dropped his head against the ground. "Are they hurt?"

"Kate and Ben are fine. They're with the animals, but when they get back we'll get you more comfortable. A blanket and a few bandages will do the trick."

The words were encouraging, but Jake knew the situation was grim. Plus, there was still the unknown of what they would discover once they removed the wagon.

Groaning, Elijah tried to get up again. Jake held him down firmly, cursing as a trickle of blood appeared at Elijah's nostril and slid down his cheek.

"Lie still and save your strength," Jake urged.

"Can't be hurt. Can't leave them…" Elijah trailed off into incoherent mumbling before passing out again.

"You about done?" Jake called, willing his tone not to betray his alarm.

"We can't unhitch them. Their yoke chains are wound around the wagon tongue." Kate's voice was filled with fear. "And one of them is badly hurt — a wheel spoke is stuck deep in his side. The yoke is twisted on the back two so hard I don't know what to do."

Jake pressed another shirt piece against Elijah's head. "I'll handle it. Switch spots with me, but first grab as much fabric as you can find."

They returned with a shirt and a wool blanket just as Elijah regained consciousness and began moaning. Avoiding their eyes, Jake folded the blanket and slipped it under Elijah's head, then sliced the shirt into strips.

"Fold these into squares," he said, pressing the material into Kate's hands, "then hold them against his head and arm. I'll be back."

Jake headed to the oxen. The lead two lay dead, the center yoke held the ox he'd put down earlier, and the other one was as Kate described. The rear team lay gasping for air, but after a tense battle of wills he removed their twisted yoke. Once the two were up and moving, he reached into his waistband and stood over the struggling center ox.

A single gunshot echoed across the empty prairie, and then all was silent. Jake secured the gun and then returned to the others. "How is he?"

"Not good," Kate said tearfully as she wiped her brow with the back of her hand, leaving behind a bloody smear.

Kneeling, he placed the remaining squares of fabric against Elijah's head and tied them in place with a thin length of rawhide he'd taken from his saddlebag. He rose again.

"Let's get this off him," he said. "Kate, you and I will lift the wagon. Ben, when we do, I want you to take what you can find out of there—" Jake pointed to a pile of boards "—and prop it underneath. That way if we lose our grip, it won't fall. We'll lift again, and again, until we stand it up."

Ben stood motionless, his eyes frozen to the horror in the dirt before him. Jake hated for him to be so near his battered father, but it couldn't be helped. The boy wasn't strong enough to lift the wagon. Jake wasn't entirely sure Kate was either, but there was no other way.

"Ben, this is important. Can you do this?"

"Yes," Ben replied in a small, heartbroken voice.

"Are you ready?" Jake asked as Kate moved to stand beside him.

"Will he recover?" she asked quietly.

Jake opened his mouth to reassure her, and then closed it against the lie formulating in his mind.

"Are you ready?" he repeated.

This time, she merely nodded.

Together, they lifted the wagon a few inches. The rough, weathered boards tore into Jake's palms with each straining push, but now that they'd started, there wasn't time to fetch his gloves from his saddle.

"Ben, look under there and tell us what you see," Jake said, grimacing at the effort of holding the wagon steady. Immediately, the boy dropped to all fours.

"The water b-b-barrel is k-k-k-keeping the w-w-wagon off him. Hurry b-before it breaks!"

Another ten minutes passed before the wagon rested safely on its side. A glance at the splintered front axle, crushed tongue, and destroyed canopy confirmed it broken beyond repair. It would have been nearly impossible for even a skilled professional with all the necessary tools to repair it, and they were in the middle of nowhere with nothing.

Even more disheartening was what they'd uncovered.

Elijah lay unconscious, his right leg bent backward at the knee, bone protruding through his bloodied pant leg. And there was still the issue of likely internal injuries. The man needed a doctor's care, and as Jake glanced around the vast expanse of land, he unfortunately confirmed there wasn't another soul in sight.

Chapter Twenty-Six

A Path Diverged

Kate rushed to her father's side and dropped to her knees.

"Father," she whispered, placing her hand gently upon his good arm. "It's just a few broken bones, and you taught me how to set those. Stay strong and we'll be on our way again soon."

If only she believed her own words. Yes, she'd been in the kitchen when he'd splinted the broken arm of a cook who'd fallen down the stairs, but she'd been in the background as an observer and the doctor had arrived the same day. She sat back on her heels and cast her eyes across his injuries, unsure where to begin.

"Let's talk."

Jake stood beside her, his hand outstretched and reaching for hers. She shook her head against his unspoken request she leave her father, even if only for a moment. His expression unyielding, he leaned over, took her by the hand, and pulled her up before him.

"Walk with me."

Placing one hand on the small of her back, he led her away from the wagon. As they walked, he laid out his plan in slow, measured tones.

"We'll save valuable time if you tend to your father while I build a stretcher and repack what supplies I can salvage onto the horses. Can you do that?"

"What about the wagon?"

"No longer an option." Jake's voice grew tight and tense. "While I'm working, you keep pressure on his wounds and try and splint his arm and leg. Once he's ready, we'll head back for Independence."

"They'll have a doctor?"

Jake nodded uneasily. "They might."

She gasped. "Might?"

Firm hands gripped her by the shoulders. "Let's take one thing at a time. Above all, stop his bleeding. Then, we've got to load him onto the stretcher. Independence is about a hundred miles back, but if we push hard, we'll arrive in under a week."

Kate stilled beneath his hands, searching to the depths of her very soul for a glimpse of anything but Jake's resignation to her father's dismal fate.

"Can he make it so far?"

Deep in his eyes, she saw a faint glimpse of possibility.

"Katie, I won't quit until he does."

His answer proved she could trust in him, and above all, depend on him to do everything he could to save her father. She tightened her fists as a spark of determination lit and spread within her. Her father lay dying, yet the man before her hadn't given up and neither would she.

Together, they would save his life.

With a curt nod, she stepped out of his grasp and headed back to the wagon, wiping her eyes along the way. After her father was safe, she could cry. Right now there was work to be done.

As Jake headed off toward the horses, she began searching through the wagon's wreckage for boards and bandages to splint her father's wounds. Within seconds, she caught sight of her green trunk. She forced open both latches, grabbed her petticoats, and shredded the yards of white cotton.

Hearing her father moan, she snatched up the fabric and dashed to his side.

"Father, you've got nothing more than a few scratches. We'll get you to a doctor, and before you know it we'll be in Oregon."

His eyes opened, settled on her, and then blinked in sluggish confusion.

Doing her best to hide her rising fear, she untied the rawhide strip securing the bloodied cloths to his temple. Cautiously, she lifted away all but the last one, and then allowed herself a small victory upon seeing no fresh blood seeping through.

She added several folded squares of new cloth before retying the rawhide. Her father winced at the pressure, which brought her to near tears again.

"Just think," she continued, hoping her chatter would distract him from the pain. "Soon we'll have our own horse ranch, like you've always dreamed about. We'll be out in fresh air all the time, planting seeds for our garden and building corrals for all the horses we'll raise."

The last of the wishful words caught in the back of her throat, allowing nothing but a false smile to cross her lips. Thankfully, he closed his eyes again. As she tied the final knot around the splint securing his arm, she caught sight of Ben.

She'd been so preoccupied with Jake and then tending her father's injuries, she hadn't given her brother a second thought. Now he stood, staring vacantly at their father.

"Ben, sit for a minute. You've done fine. Rest."

Without a word he spun around, walked several yards, and then slumped to the hard, dusty ground.

Jake returned, bearing a long, angry scrape across his chest.

"You're bleeding!"

"It's nothing," he said, waving away her offer of a cloth. He set a brown bottle next to the blood-soaked clothing at her side. "Here, this will help."

"What is it?"

"Laudanum. It will dull his pain. Give him one sip at a time, slowly, so he doesn't choke."

She nodded and did as asked.

"How's he doing?" Jake asked once she'd recapped the bottle.

"Better, I think." No blood showed through the cloths on his temple, which she took to be a good sign. She glanced over at Ben, who sat small and alone, staring out over the open land. He'd been only an infant when their mother had died, so their father was the only parent he'd ever known. Determined to shelter him from the worst, Kate motioned for Jake to lean in close.

"Take my brother away from here," she whispered.

****

Forcing back guilt and regret, Jake crouched down before Ben. "How about you come help me?"

As if in a trance, Ben got to his feet and walked beside him to the boards and wagon parts he'd rounded up.

"Have you built anything before?" Jake asked.

"With my f-f-father…" Ben's voice cracked and he began to sob. Without thinking, Jake knelt and pulled the boy into his arms. Only when Ben's small shoulders stopped heaving did Jake release him.

"He's d-d-dying," Ben said, self-consciously wiping his tears and nose.

Jake took a deep breath. "We can build something to help him. Will you do that with me?"

Ben nodded.

Together, they created a pushcart using two wheels, a section of canvas, and pieces from the wagon. Chains and a spare harness wrapped tight around the boards were a poor substitute for nails, and the platform where Elijah would lay shifted as Jake lifted the two long boards serving as handles.

Time for a test walk.

Though his forehead broke out in a profuse sweat after pushing the cart only a few yards, it would have to do. Jake set the handles upon the ground and tried not to think of Elijah's added weight. Instead, he and Ben spread blankets and their bedrolls neatly onto the platform to act as a cushion.

The cart completed, Jake turned his attention to salvaging what he could from the destruction. Knowing there'd be no time to hunt over the coming days, he started a fire and gave Ben the task of roasting two hefty chunks of oxen rump.

Jake stood amidst burlap sacks of flour, beans, and cornmeal, trying to decide what would be the most practical to bring along, when Kate approached. Though her eyes were red-rimmed from crying, she appeared calm.

"My father wants to speak to you."

Jake followed her to Elijah, now deathly pale against the rivers of dried blood encrusting his forehead, cheeks, and mustache. Jake took in the remarkable job Kate had done to dress his wounds and splint his arm and leg. However, it was far from proper and he'd suffer greatly as they lifted him onto the cart.

"Jake's here beside us," Kate said, and then knelt to lift her father's good hand onto her skirt and quietly checked his pulse.

"Has he had much laudanum?" Jake asked, noticing Elijah writhe against a tremor of pain rippling through his body.

"I gave him another sip about ten minutes ago."

"Give him more," Jake said grimly. Given the extent of Elijah's injuries, all that mattered at this point was keeping him comfortable.

Kate bent again to put the bottle to his lips.

Elijah took a swallow, and then struggled to speak.

"Must talk to Jake. Alone."

Reluctantly, Kate backed away. When she was out of earshot, Jake went down on one knee at Elijah's side.

"Can they hear me?" Elijah managed the words between small panting gasps.

Jake shook his head. "No."

"Inside pocket."

Elijah's whisper was difficult to understand through the bloody froth sputtering from his lips. Jake reached for a cloth, but Elijah turned his head away.

"Let me help you," Jake commanded while wiping Elijah's mouth clear. He then tipped the bottle to administer more of the precious liquid. Elijah swallowed without resistance.

"Inside pocket," Elijah repeated, stronger this time.

Jake hesitated. Going through Elijah's pockets was the first step to both of them admitting defeat.

"Get it!" Elijah's voice was louder, as if what he was about to say gave him strength.

Jake reached inside Elijah's vest, and removed a small, careworn leather pouch. Two strips of rawhide were strung through the top and pulled tight.

"This?"

"Yes." Elijah's eyes bore into his own. "More."

Jake reached inside the pocket and withdrew a long billfold, several inches thick, made of well-worn deerskin.

"Open them," Elijah whispered as blood trickled from his nostrils yet again.

Jake pulled the pouch top apart, tipped it, and poured a gold ring, a silver pocket watch, and a hefty mix of double eagles and other coins into his palm.

After wiping sudden sweat from his forehead, Jake moved on to the billfold. It contained a gold letter opener and a staggering amount of money. Jake had known Elijah would need to bring his entire worth in cash, as bank drafts weren't an option until Oregon was settled and civilized. Though he'd vastly underestimated the man's wealth.

"Envelope," Elijah said with a long, low moan.

Jake searched the pocket again. It was empty, but another one revealed a butter-yellow envelope made of thick parchment paper, complete with a red wax seal.

With his good arm, Elijah motioned for the brown bottle. After a swallow, he continued.

"You're a good man, Jake. I trust you with my children, my money, and the envelope. I need your word you'll get them safely to Oregon and watch out for them after you get there."

"Don't talk like that. Your family needs you—"

"Give me your word!"

Jake nodded solemnly. "You have my word."

"Don't let them see me like this. Leave my pistol and one bullet and get them out of here."

"I will not leave you," Jake said with an adamant shake of his head. "And you won't get a bullet from me. I've made a rolling stretcher and—"

Elijah cut him off. "There's no hope. I know it. I feel it."

Jake sat back on his heels with a sigh. There was no use arguing once a man was certain about his fate. They'd had only the slimmest of chances to begin with, and now that Elijah had made peace with his impending death, the only thing left to do was be with him as he went.

"Bring them back."

Jake motioned for Kate and Ben to return.

****

When Jake beckoned them back, Kate grabbed her brother's hand and forced herself to put one foot in front of the other. Too soon they were kneeling, their broken father between them.

"We're here, Father," Ben said, silently brushing tears from his eyes.

"Both of you listen carefully." Her father looked first to her and then to Ben. "Son, I want you to have my pocket watch. Your mother gave it to me. Keep it close to your heart, just as I always have."

He turned his head to face her, his ocean-blue eyes revealing their usual perception, wisdom, and understanding. "Sweetheart, try to stop crying."

Attempting the impossible, Kate wiped tears away with the back of her hand.

"I want you to have the family Bible, and your mother's ring." He paused, and to her great surprise, he smiled. "And my hat. Wear it as often as you like, and think of the happier times."

A lone tear slid down his battered cheek.

"I'm so sorry. I thought I could give you a better life, and now look what I've done." A faint gurgle sounded at the back of his throat, and he gasped through several breaths before continuing. "Please, forgive me for leaving you."

"No!" She snatched up his bloodied hand and held tight, hating that he didn't have the strength to return her squeeze. It took all her willpower not to collapse against him, weeping from fear and helplessness. "It'll take a little time, and you'll be well again. You have to be!"

Slowly, he shook his head.

"Jake will watch out for both of you now. Do as he says and you'll be fine. Lord knows if I'd done that we wouldn't be in this mess to begin with."

Ben began crying in earnest and buried his face into his father's chest to muffle his sobs. Frantic, she looked to Jake.

"Please," she begged in a trembling whisper. "Tell me you can help him. Tell me you won't let him die."

Jake pursed his lips and looked away.

For the next few seconds, her father struggled through ragged, shallow breaths. Then he closed his eyes and spoke in a soft, joyful tone she'd heard as a child after he'd stepped over the threshold to meet her mother.

"My dearest Rebecca, I've missed you so."

Chapter Twenty-Seven

Moving On

Jake pulled the blanket from under Elijah's head and draped it over his lifeless body. Yesterday, he'd been leading a family in pursuit of their hopes and dreams to Oregon. Now Kate and Ben were orphans and dependent upon him for their survival.

He was their leader and he'd failed — to stop the oxen in time, to save Elijah, and perhaps most of all, he'd failed in allowing his wandering thoughts of Kate to interfere with his sole purpose on this journey. And then when she'd pleaded with him to save her father's life, all he'd done was look away. As with his own family so long ago, he'd failed. And now, two sets of grieving eyes looked to him for guidance.

Guidance he had no idea how to give.

Should he say a few words of reassurance or simply list out all that remained to be done before they could leave this place? Should he ask for their help or send them away while he worked? Perhaps a short ride would provide them a distraction, however brief, from the anguish of their new reality.

"We'll need to head back and retrieve the rest of the supplies lost this morning."

Kate placed a protective hand on the blanket. "I'd rather stay."

"Ben?"

With an expression of despair no nine-year-old should ever possess, the boy looked hesitantly to his sister and then slowly shook his head.

Jake rose to his feet, mired in uncertainty about leaving them alone, yet unwilling to force anything upon them. Finally, he made his choice.

"I won't be gone long."

Jake headed out with Plug. He retraced their trail for the better part of half a mile, picking up a kettle and pan first, and then a blanket, two shirts, and bag of cornmeal. As he stood beside Plug, securing his findings to the saddle, he saw something in the distance.

Elijah's hat.

It sat on the hard ground — the ultimate reminder of the responsibility now resting upon Jake's shoulders. Though he'd already planned on staying out west, he wasn't sure how he felt about the idea that because of a man's dying wish he *had* to stay. He'd roamed across the country for so long he didn't know how to live in one place long enough to settle in, meet the neighbors, and put down roots.

While he mounted up again, Elijah's hat in his hand, a thought crept into his mind. His pocket now held a considerable amount of money. He could keep riding, never look back, and no one would ever be the wiser as to how he became rich.

The thought left as fast as it had arrived. He'd given his word, so for better or worse, this was now his life.

His time as a wandering man was over.

Jake rode back to find Kate in an uproar — throwing things aside, dropping to her knees to peer through the remains of the wagon, then springing up to toss something else out of her way.

Jake dismounted and ran to her side. "What's going on? What happened?"

"I can't find his hat!" she cried. "It was my father's dying wish, and now I don't even have that!"

As she stood before him, covered in her father's blood, her eyes awash with panic and tears, Jake's heart ached with regret.

"I have it," he said quietly.

He walked to Plug, pulled the hat from the saddle horn, and returned to where she'd remained, motionless. When he held it out she collapsed to her knees, her head in her hands. Slowly, he knelt and placed the hat on the ground before her.

****

As dusk settled in, they all were dirty and sweat-stained from the exhausting labor of digging into the hard ground and lowering the coffin into the shallow grave. After they shaped the disturbed earth into a smooth mound, Kate and Ben helped him place three large stones atop the dirt. The coffin he'd built from splintered boards and bent nails could hardly be considered sturdy, and Jake wanted no chance of wolves digging up the body once they left. He completed the job by gently tapping a small wooden cross bearing Elijah's name into the head of the grave.

When he finished, they gathered around the mound.

"I figure this is as good a place as any to do this," Jake said while fumbling in his shirt pocket. "Your father wanted me to give you these."

He removed the gold ring and held it out to Kate. She closed her fist around the small circle. He reached into his back pocket, pulled out the silver pocket watch, and lowered it by the chain into Ben's outstretched hand. Then, knowing something needed to be said, he pulled his hat into his hands.

"Here lies a good man. Elijah Davis was courageous, brave, and I'm proud to say I rode the trail with him."

The silence was deafening as Kate stepped forward and bowed her head.

"Although I will miss him terribly every day for the rest of my life..." Her voice broke and she finished in a whisper, "I'm glad he's with my mother now."

She carefully placed a handful of wildflowers onto the grave.

"I miss him s-s-so much," Ben managed to utter before sobs racked his body. Kate put her arms around him, and together they cried for their father until well after dark. Finally, Jake took their hands and led them back to camp where they all sat silently around the fire.

No one offered to start dinner. No one was hungry.

****

Thursday, July 6, 1843

Jake watched over the camp and his charges throughout the night. Kate lay in his bedroll by the fire, and Ben lay wrapped in a heavy blanket at her side. The next couple of months would be difficult for them without the shelter and security of the wagon and all it had carried. The forts they would pass through now were small settlements at best, and no one would likely have a wagon for sale.

If that wasn't enough to contend with, there were three riders and four horses, leaving only one to act as packhorse. Even worse, they only had eight saddlebags. As a result, Kate and Ben would again have to sort through what they already considered their most valuable possessions in the world, and abandon the majority with the destroyed wagon.

At least they could trade the two remaining oxen — now useless without the wagon — at Fort Laramie for mules or horses to carry the supplies they'd purchase. Oxen would fetch a good price because tenderfeet would be eager to deal by then.

At dawn, he quietly built up the fire and brewed a pot of fresh coffee. By the time Kate and Ben woke, he'd prepared a small breakfast of reheated ox rump, beans, and cornbread. After they finished eating, Jake stood and slowly surveyed the camp.

"Kate, we'll need to start packing soon."

"I know," she said, absently wiping a cup and adding it to the stack in the kitchen box.

He grimaced, and then spoke the words that would crush her fragile world. "We're on horseback now, which means we carry only the bare essentials."

"You and Ben built a cart yesterday," she said, clutching a plate to her chest almost as if trying to shield herself from the coming words. "Why can't you build another?"

He shook his head. "Carts are for a flat prairie, not the rugged mountain passes ahead."

As the realization hit her, the plate slipped unnoticed from her fingers and fell to the ground with a soft thud.

"Leave everything?" she asked weakly.

"We'll take as much food and tools as possible. When we reach Fort Laramie we'll purchase more, but it won't be for another three weeks. Maybe longer. We need to pack light now because when we do buy food, we need to have room for it. Anything else will only be a burden."

As the harsh realization of his words set in, Kate stood, cheeks aflame, and began angrily pointing to her belongings.

"Of course it would be a *burden* to take the linens my mother made when she was a child," she said, flinging open the lid of an ornate wooden box and peering inside. "And the silver tea set that's been in our family for three generations, and the painting of my mother that hung over the fireplace in my father's study."

Jake swallowed hard. A full set of silverware and a tea set were only the beginning. This time, she'd have to leave the green trunk he'd picked out the first day long ago as the only one she could bring.

"When we started we had enough to furnish a home." She threw her hands up in despair as her voice lowered to a tortured whisper, "It's like the river all over again, except so much worse."

Jake put an arm around her slim shoulders, but when she stiffened he quickly dropped it.

****

Kate rummaged through the piles again and again, desperate to find everything she wanted. Jake had relented and given her free reign over two saddlebags. She intended to fill every inch.

After finding the painting of her mother, she cracked open the gold frame, removed the canvas, rolled it, and placed it into her saddlebag. She selected two dresses from her green trunk and wrapped them around her mother's china teapot — the matching cups and saucers would have to stay. She tied the bundle securely with a green velvet ribbon and then eased it in alongside the painting. Her mother's sewing kit followed.

First bag full.

Next, she took two embroidered pillowcases and folded them around her mother's silver brush, comb, and mirror. She secured the fabric with a camisole she'd twisted until it formed a silken rope. Her mother's lace coverlet would hold one cherished book, her family's Bible, and the silver jewelry box with red velvet lining. She then placed everything into her second saddlebag and cinched down the strap.

There was no more room.

Kate sat in her saddle, struggling against a horrible realization — once they left, she would never again see her father's gravesite. Fighting another rush of tears, she grabbed his hat from the saddle horn and slid to the ground.

"I can't leave yet."

"Take as long as you need," Jake replied.

She dug through her saddlebag for the small metal box usually reserved for her sewing needles, and then headed off. When she reached the mound, she gathered earth into her fingertips and carefully sifted it into the box. The lid closed with a soft click, and she slid the box into her skirt pocket.

With a deep sigh, she pulled her father's hat from under her arm and held it in both hands. As far back as she could remember, every thought of her father included a hat perched rakishly on his head. Growing up, the only time she'd ever seen him bareheaded was at the dinner table. That was, when he remembered to take it off. More than a few times her mother had to give a reminding look when he sat down without removing it first.

Her mother had kept a strict home in the way of propriety and manners, and insisted Kate dress in clothing suitable for a young lady. Even when the heat was enough to make her faint, Kate still had to wear the ever-constricting dress, petticoats, and bonnet. Of everything, Kate hated the bonnet most. It choked her neck, trapped heat against the skin it was meant to protect, and her hair always seemed to catch in the string's knot.

But her father had been sympathetic to her plight. When she'd been a child and her mother had been away visiting friends, he'd often let her use his hat for dress up. Once she grew older, he'd let her wear it while they rode throughout the grounds, checking on their land.

And now the hat was hers.

Kate looked back to where Ben sat in his saddle, faithfully waiting. Over the past day she'd tried so hard to be brave, but in reality she was frightened for their future. Though back home she'd helped in the store, she wasn't confident of her ability to manage one on her own.

Perhaps she should ask Jake to take them back to Charlottesville. People returned from the trail each year saying they couldn't make it or had changed their minds altogether. Aunt Victoria would likely let them live with her while Kate figured out how to earn a living on her own. But how could she even think of betraying her father so? He'd sacrificed his *life* for a dream.

A dream now up to her to fulfill.

As the burden of her new responsibilities settled heavily upon her shoulders, tears blurred her vision yet again. But this time she straightened and wiped her eyes. There was too much to do now, none of which included tears.

Slowly she untied her bonnet, laid it upon the grave, and then closed her eyes as her hair unfurled down her back and fluttered free in the wind.

"God help us, and don't let me fail," she whispered, settling her father's hat firmly on her head.

Chapter Twenty-Eight

Fort Laramie

Thursday, July 27, 1843

"We're here," Jake said, reining up his horse.

Confused, Kate pulled Nina to a stop beside him. She then twisted around in her saddle, searching for anything new, but saw only the usual endless miles of grass undulating in the wind. Not a tree or shrub in sight. What did he mean?

"Perhaps I should say we're almost here," Jake clarified as Ben joined her in looking around uncertainly. "Fort Laramie is a few miles away. We'll camp here, and go in tomorrow at first light."

They dismounted and removed their saddles in preparation for another night on the trail. Since her father's death they had traveled over four hundred miles, often doing twenty-five miles or more each day. Water access wasn't a concern since they now followed the banks of the Platte River. Making camp was markedly easier too. Ben got water, she cooked, Jake started the fire, and they all shared responsibility for the animals.

Lately the sights had been amazing. Kate's favorite had been the day they'd seen not one, but two rock formations. After they arrived at the first — Jake said travelers called it Courthouse Rock — she'd spent half an hour wandering around the gigantic base, much to Jake's amusement. Later that evening, they'd come upon what he called Chimney Rock, a massive stone column bursting from the earth to head straight into the sky.

Such a shame her father had only seen the rough times along the trail. At times, it was hard to believe he'd been dead for over three weeks. Kate still caught herself waiting for him to return from checking on the horses. Remembering why he wouldn't was the worst part of her days and nights.

With a sigh, she set the spider pan over the fire. As she reached for the salt pork, Jake squatted beside her.

The last three weeks had changed him. Physically, he was the same tough and capable man he'd always been, but it was plain to see his worry and concern. During the day he was rarely at ease, his eyes darting from crevice to hillside in a constant search for hidden peril. At night, she rarely saw him sleep. He stayed awake for hours, watching over their camp with a stunning intensity.

"I need to ask you something before Ben comes back with the water," he said.

"What?"

"Your father mentioned he was teaching Ben how to use a gun. If you have no objections, I'd like to continue the lessons."

His offer touched Kate. While she herself was a proficient shot, she knew her brother needed the additional knowledge only Jake could give — learning how to become a man.

"I wish Father was here to teach him," she said quietly, "but I'd like you to carry on in his place."

Jake nodded. "I've kept hold of your father's guns until now, but it's time for Ben to take them on. I'll start with the rifle and some target practice. Then in a few weeks we'll move on to your father's pistol."

Ben came up the rise with the water bucket, ending their conversation. Kate finished cooking dinner and passed out the plates.

"I've got some good news for you, Kate," Jake said as they all settled down on the grass to eat. "You'll want to get your letters ready tonight because you can mail them at the fort."

"Oh, how wonderful! I was thinking the other day about Marie Ann and Aunt Victoria and how—" Her hand flew to her mouth and her eyes widened in horror. "They don't know about Father. I have to tell them in a letter."

Jake's smile faded, and what had started out as a lovely dinner turned into a solemn affair. Her joy at reaching Fort Laramie was quickly dampened as visions of everyone they knew in Charlottesville reading such terrible news drifted through her mind.

But it couldn't be helped. There was no other way.

After dinner, she finished her letters by telling about her father's death, but omitting how they'd lost the wagon and were now on horseback — no use burdening anyone with more worries. Before sealing the envelopes, she added one final line about how they'd had made it to Fort Laramie and she would notify them of her final location as soon as they were settled.

Ben returned with more water. As he carefully filled the kettle and placed it over the fire to heat, Kate had to resist the powerful urge to hug him. Again.

Her brother was her entire life. She kept close watch over him, wanting him to know she would take care of him, even if she herself didn't know how it would be possible. Though the past few weeks had found her floundering in uncertainty, one goal remained crystal clear — she had to make a solid, secure future for them both.

****

Friday, July 28, 1843

Just after sunrise, Kate thrust her foot inside her father's boot for what she hoped would be the last time. The ill-fitting leather left furrows behind her trudging steps, but she didn't dare wear more than three pairs of socks. Sweating feet meant blisters, something she had no intention of suffering through again. The combination of daily cleansing and Jake's salve had long since healed her wounds, and the stubborn cut on the ball of her foot shrank each day. Soon only a thin scar would remain.

Kate pulled on the remaining boot and then bent to retrieve her father's hat from the edge of her bedroll. Lightweight and practical, it shaded her from the sun's beating rays during the day and kept her warm during the brisk evenings. Best of all, unlike a bonnet, no ties were needed to keep it in place.

With her eyes closed and face tipped toward the sky, she threaded her fingers through the length of her hair several times before settling the hat firmly upon her head. She stood from her bedroll, smiling at the thought of buying new shoes and so much more during today's visit to the fort.

After a quick breakfast, the group packed up and rode out of camp. Less than an hour later, Jake pointed to a river undulating in the distance.

"Though the upcoming fort is actually named John," he told them, "everyone calls it Laramie because it was built so close to the Laramie River."

As they rode up the bluff, the fort came into view.

"Where's the fence?" Kate asked, surprised to see the building out in the open, unprotected by the typical tall, sturdy wall of either logs or stone.

"Last time I came through I was told one is planned." Jake shrugged. "Guess they haven't gotten to it yet."

They arrived at the hitching posts, and after seeing to the horses and securing the oxen, they stood together in front of the large adobe brick building. Ben bounced on his heels in excitement and Kate had to stop herself from doing the same.

"Before I forget," Jake said, reaching into his pocket, "here's some money to shop today."

He dropped several heavy coins into her hand.

"Ten dollars? I won't need so much," she insisted.

"Trust me, Kate. Things are expensive out here."

Saying nothing, Kate secreted the money within the hidden pocket of her skirt.

"You can mail your letters and buy new shoes and heavier clothes right through there." Jake pointed to a nearby doorway. "The store owner is an honest man and he'll treat you right. Make sure to buy things that will last. The mountains ahead are unforgiving."

"Where can I find you two when I'm done?"

"First, we'll head to the livery and discuss getting all the horses re-shoed, then we're off to the blacksmith to see about a trade for the oxen," Jake said before clapping a hand on Ben's shoulder. "Then we'll see about getting this young man a bullet mold and lead of his own."

"You mean it?" Ben exclaimed in surprise.

"Yes." Jake smiled at her over Ben's head. "Your sister and I think it's time for you to learn how to use your father's rifle."

Ben whooped with joy. "Let's go then!"

Jake took a quick step, then turned back to her, his forehead etched with doubt.

"I'm having second thoughts about leaving you alone. Why don't Ben and I come in and wait while you shop?"

"Absolutely not," she said with a shake of her head. "I can take care of myself. Besides—" she gestured to the men standing at alert on the upper corners of the building "—there's not another traveler in sight. Only a few soldiers."

In truth, she was eager for a little time to herself. Plus, she had another reason for wanting to shop unescorted.

"I know, but I think—"

"I'll be fine," she interrupted, eager to begin her search for what she was after.

Jake reluctantly nodded his assent and walked away with Ben.

After they separated, Kate made her way down the walkway toward the supply store. When she walked through the door, a small bell pealed at her entrance. The noise was familiar, as were the rows of neatly stacked items. She dropped her letters in the wooden box marked Mail on the counter and then wandered her way between tables and shelves, noting prices and manner of display.

I can do this, she thought in wonder. *I can go out west, open my own store, and provide a life for Ben. It will take some doing, but with father's money to see me through while I'm getting settled, I'll do fine.*

Then another thought crossed her mind. Jake had given the ring and pocket watch back after her father's death, but what had become of her father's money?

The curtain on the back wall fluttered and a small, stooped man dressed entirely in black full-cloth shuffled out. His thinning salt and pepper hair, though neatly combed across his head, failed at concealing a glossy scalp.

"Hello," he called out jovially as a gnarled finger came up to prod his wire-rim glasses into place. "Everyone's long past through. You must have gotten a late start, or ran into trouble."

Kate hesitated. "Both."

"Sorry to hear. What can I help you with?"

It was the moment she'd been waiting for.

The dress she wore was highly impractical. It tore easily, was impossible to keep clean, and the mountains of fabric were forever getting in her way. The two in her saddlebags would be no different. She needed better clothes and shoes to finish the trip.

Her eyes feasted hungrily over the stack of men's trousers. The heavy fabric would hold up on the trail and keep her legs warm during the coming months. A glance over at the meager selection of flimsy shoes appropriate for women sealed her decision.

It was time for a change.

"I've been sent to buy some boots and clothes for my brother." Untrue of course, but Kate wasn't sure of his reaction to a woman purchasing men's clothes for her own use.

"Let's start with the boots," he said cheerfully. "What size?"

"A smaller pair should do nicely."

"I'll see what I have in the back." The man disappeared through the curtain and returned with two pairs in hand. Both were made of soft brown leather with white stitching. The wooden heels were sanded to a soft sheen.

Kate wanted them more than anything in the world.

"I have two choices here, but how you gonna know which'll fit? Boots can vary, and an improper fit will cause a lot of trouble." He checked out the front window then back to her. "Why don't you fetch him? Tryin' these on won't take but a moment."

"We're in a rush. I think I'll pick for him."

"I'd feel better if I saw for myself they were a good fit," he insisted. "I got a reputation to uphold, and it can't be said my shoes don't fit a person. Wouldn't be good for business."

The storekeeper's unexpected insistence made Kate even more determined to have her way.

"He's busy with our horses, but since we wear close to the same size I'll try them on for him."

He stared at her, saying nothing.

"We're in a real big hurry," she added, while holding out an expectant hand toward the boots.

He lowered his glasses with one finger and narrowed his eyes while looking her slowly up and down. After taking in her father's hat, her loose hair, and the tips of her father's boots peeking from under her skirt, he crossed his arms over his chest.

"Missy, you don't fool me none. I'm too old to care why a woman would want to wear men's boots. So have a seat on the stool and try this pair on for size. But first you'll need these." He tossed a pair of thick cotton socks over the counter.

"Thank you, sir," she murmured.

After trying them on and walking up and down the length of the store, she decided she couldn't do any better.

"I'll take them. How much?"

"Will you be needing anything else?"

"As a matter of fact, yes." Kate couldn't contain her joy at the thought of traveling in comfort. "I need riding clothes. Sturdy ones."

Ignoring his soft chuckle and watchful eye, she selected two pairs of men's trousers in the smallest size. After a quick inspection of long-sleeve shirts, she picked two. While walking back to the counter, she noticed a green vest made of wool and added it to the growing pile. Leather gloves completed her list of wants.

"These clothes were made for a full day's work," she said, placing the stack on the counter, "and that's what I'll be doing from now on. I'll take everything here, and another pair of those socks."

"Let's see," he said as he counted her selections. "Five dollars for the boots and another four for all the clothes, so nine dollars should cover it." He leaned in close to whisper, "I threw in the socks for free. It was worth it to watch you try to pass off such a lie."

She laughed with him as she handed him the money.

"Wrap them all up?" he asked.

"Everything but the boots. I'll wear those out."

Quickly and efficiently, he folded it all and secured it with string. As he handed the bundle across the counter, his eyes twinkled.

"Missy, you're lucky I'm not thirty years younger or I'd be packing you up and taking you home with me."

With a shy smile, Kate took the package from him. "You've been kind, thank you."

Carrying her father's boots, she stepped out of the store. Buying everything had taken longer than she expected. She needed to find Jake and Ben before they came searching for her.

As she walked, the heels of her new boots thumped against the wooden planks running the length of the fort. She was almost to the end of the walkway when she heard a low, quick whistle. Turning, she found Jake and Ben standing at the other end of the fort.

"Find what you needed?" Jake asked.

"Yes, thank you. How about you two?"

"We bought all the supplies we'll need for some time. Best of all, I worked out a trade of three horses, plus packsaddles, for the oxen. Oxen are like gold out here. By this point, horses pulling wagons are so worn out they can barely walk. Most travelers are eager to trade them."

Kate frowned at the thought of taking on downtrodden animals. "What condition are these new horses in?"

"It took some searching, but Ben and I found ones with spirit. We'll pick them, and all our new supplies, up after our own horses are finished getting re-shoed."

"What great news," she said, happy at the thought of giving Old Dan, Nina, and Jake's horses a much deserved rest.

"I saw some sunbonnets too, in case you were interested," Jake said with a smirk.

"This hat will serve me just fine, thank you."

Jake chuckled and led the group down the walkway. Kate followed, clutching the package against her chest in a futile attempt to calm her pounding heart. Replacing a bonnet with her father's hat was one thing, but what would Jake think when he saw her new purchases?

That she even considered Jake's opinion unsettled Kate more than the daring clothes.

"Where we headed now?" Ben asked.

"I figured we could go out a ways and fix lunch," answered Jake, "then come back and see what the locals are saying about trail conditions. Sound all right to you both?"

Kate nodded gratefully. It was already late in the afternoon and her stomach ached from lack of food. As they continued walking, Jake fell into step beside her.

"Those new shoes working out for you?" he asked while taking her father's boots from her hands and swinging them easily over his shoulder.

"Yes, they're comfortable."

Soon they reached the end of the wooden planks, and she stepped down into the soft dirt. After a few moments, Kate noticed she walked alone. Turning, she saw Jake and Ben standing side-by-side, both laughing at the well-defined imprints her new boots had made in the dust.

"What?" she asked with the same wide-eyed innocence Jake had shown moments earlier. "These were the only ones that fit."

"Sure they were!" chortled Ben before running off to join the horses.

After a slow perusal of the package in her hands, Jake's eyes rose to meet her own. Amusement lingered within their deep blue depths. "Did you find what you needed today?"

"Yes," she replied, before moving to follow her brother.

****

After a generous meal, they spent the next hours lounging under the shade of an oak tree. Jake spoke with a few passersby about the travel conditions ahead and seemed pleased at his findings. Warm and content, Kate dozed throughout the afternoon and woke to Jake packing up camp.

"Aren't we staying here tonight?" she asked.

"No. We'll want to fetch the horses and be on our way long before dusk settles in. The fort's not a place to mess with at night. The soldiers can get rowdy. It's best to avoid it altogether."

"Awww, I wanted to see," Ben said.

"Trouble will find you often enough," Jake replied. "No reason to go searching it out."

They headed back to the fort. While Jake and Ben went to pick up the horses, Kate went back into the store, package intact in her hands.

The familiar clerk shuffled out to greet her. "Everything fit?"

"I'm wondering if..." She stopped to glance around the store.

"Spit it out, missy. I don't have all day."

"I'm wondering if I could change here."

"Backroom has a curtain," he said. "Go ahead."

Kate stepped into the backroom, untied the bundle, and quickly changed into the dark brown pair of trousers, gray shirt, and green vest. Everything fit perfectly, and the material would last for months to come. She pulled the curtain aside and the storekeeper looked up from his paperwork.

"You'd probably look a sight better in some frilly clothes, but you'll do."

Kate gathered her clothes up in her arms. "I'd better get going."

"Best of luck to you," he said with a wistful smile. "If I was thirty years younger I'd be heading there myself."

****

"A gun is always loaded," Jake said as Ben stared up at him with a mixture of rapt attention and boyish enthusiasm. "Even when you're sure it's unloaded — it's loaded. A lot of men out there didn't respect that rule, and paid for it with their life."

Jake's heart sank seeing the boy's expression turn from joy to sadness. Ben should be learning this lesson from his father — not from the man who'd played a part in his death.

Guilt over the circumstances of Elijah's death tormented Jake. He'd spent hours mulling over that fateful morning, always ending with the fact that if he'd gotten to Elijah sooner, if he'd stretched farther and pulled him from the wagon seat and into his saddle, Ben would be learning guns from his father, Kate wouldn't bear such an enormous burden, and they wouldn't be orphans.

But in the end, berating himself wouldn't bring their father back. Jake had given his word at a dying man's side to watch over them and he was determined to see the job to completion and beyond. Which, for now, meant teaching Ben the ways of a gun.

"Bullets cost money and shouldn't be wasted. Make each shot count," he said to the boy now taking great care in loading his rifle. Soon he'd be ready to take on the size and weight of Elijah's pistol.

"When can we practice sh-shooting?" Ben asked eagerly, his earlier gloom now forgotten.

"We'll leave as soon as your sister gets back," he said with another hopeful glance around the fort, "and we'll have our first lesson after we put some miles behind us."

Where was Kate? As the minutes ticked by, Jake grew increasingly nervous. He'd been hesitant about letting her wander around unescorted, but she was so stubborn and insistent it was sometimes easier to let her do what she wanted.

After securing the last sack of flour, he looked for her again. Aside from a young man on the walkway, the fort was empty. As he turned back to Plug to tighten a strap, Jake heard the man approaching him from behind.

"You're getting mighty close, mister," Jake muttered before spinning around.

To his complete shock, he came face to face with Kate. She was dressed as a cowhand head to toe; the only thing missing was the gun.

This woman would never fail to surprise him.

Chapter Twenty-Nine

Ben

Wednesday, August 2, 1843

Jake stayed silent the first two times Ben swung his saddle into Old Dan's side, but stepped in before he could struggle through a third attempt. After all, there was a limit to a horse's patience.

"How you feeling?" Jake asked as he took the saddle from Ben's hands and lifted it onto the horse's back. Though the boy was short, he'd developed an efficient heave-and-swing motion over the past few months. Aside from today, he typically landed saddles into place on the first try.

"I'm a little t-tired."

"Could it be you've been staying up too late working on your aim?"

Since departing from Laramie a week ago, Ben had practiced his marksmanship each evening until long past dusk. Twice they'd enjoyed a tasty benefit of his dedication —

stewed rabbit.

"Probably," Ben answered with a half-hearted shrug of his shoulder.

"We've got an easy ride today. Sleep in the saddle if you can."

Jake tousled the boy's hair and then headed off to secure his saddlebags onto Plug. In the month since Elijah's death, life on the trail had changed considerably. After leaving Laramie six days ago, the rougher terrain became a welcome relief from the endless rolling hills. Water access was constant since they still followed along the Platte River, and now that the oxen had been replaced by three fresh horses, they traveled over twenty-five miles a day. And much to Jake's amusement, Kate continued to wear the clothes she'd bought at Laramie, along with her father's hat.

Jake led the group off and kept a close eye on Ben all morning. When they stopped for the noon rest he saw the boy's eyes were no longer clear and bright, his forehead bore a sheen of sweat, and he swayed in his saddle. The likely culprit of Ben's troubles worried Jake — forts could be rampant with disease, and less than a week ago they'd spent an entire day wandering around Laramie.

Jake dismounted and strode over to Ben, now slumped against Old Dan's mane. "How you feeling?"

"Fine," Ben replied with a weak smile.

Out of the corner of his eye, Jake saw Kate watching intently from across the camp. Not wanting to alarm her, he gave the boy a casual pat on the shoulder.

"How about you rest while your sister and I make lunch?"

"I'll get w-water first."

Kate stood with the packhorses, her eyes filled with concern as Ben retrieved the bucket and stumbled off toward the river. Jake joined her.

"Have you noticed anything different about Ben?" he asked, keeping his tone light.

"You've seen it too?" The question burst out, as if she'd been eager to unburden her own worries. "He says he's cold, but he's sweating. He's not eating much either."

"How long have you seen this?"

"It started yesterday, and it's gradually gotten worse. I thought maybe he was a little worn down, but now I'm not sure."

"We can take longer afternoon breaks until he gets better," Jake conceded, "but we'll need to keep a good pace or risk running low on food and supplies before we get to Fort Hall."

Ben returned. He drank little, ate nothing, and dozed during the majority of the rest. When they were ready for departure, he tried several times to mount his horse, all without success.

"Need a hand up?" Jake asked.

Ben gratefully accepted. While lifting the boy, Jake noticed beads of sweat dotted Ben's brow and his cheeks had turned ruddy. Jake held to an easier pace for the rest of the day and waited until after he'd dismounted to again ask the long-awaited question.

"How you feeling?" he asked as Ben slid limply from his saddle.

"I'm cold," Ben muttered through chattering teeth, "and I hurt all over."

He made it two steps before he went down on one knee. Without a word, Jake scooped him up and carried him to the blanket Kate hastily spread out.

****

Thursday, August 3, 1843

213

At breakfast Jake watched from across camp as Ben lay still in his bedroll. Despite Kate's repeated urging, he refused any food or drink.

"I'm not thirsty," he protested, pushing her hand away. "Leave me alone."

"Ben, you haven't eaten in over a day. You at least need water," Kate pleaded while trying yet again to put a cup to his lips. "Please, take a sip."

"No!"

Jake was relieved to see Kate ignore his objection and continue trying. She was rewarded for her efforts moments later when Ben took a drink — though more from spite than desire.

Jake went to Ben's side. "How you feeling?"

"Hot, and my head hurts." Ben complained. Jake placed a hand against his forehead. The boy was indeed burning up, and his flushed face was proof he'd been for some time.

"Let me rest." Ben closed his eyes.

"No problem," Jake replied, then stood and motioned for Kate to follow him across camp to where the horses stood saddled and waiting.

"We'll stay here for the day."

"You think he's sick enough to stop." It wasn't a question, rather a statement of acceptance. She inhaled a deep, trembling breath before continuing. "Even though yesterday you said we had to keep up the pace or risk running out of food, you think we should stop."

"I'm hoping if we rest today he'll be better tomorrow. No sense pushing it." If only Jake believed himself and wasn't trying to quell the fear in her eyes.

"You should tell him we're stopping. If he thinks it's my idea he'll say I'm babying him and will insist on continuing. Make an excuse so he won't know the truth."

"Will do," he said. "I'll be gone for a while getting meat for dinner."

After speaking briefly to Ben, Jake picked up his rifle, mounted Plug, and rode out of camp.

****

Over the next hour Kate kept the fire going and tended to Ben, who grew worse. Though the morning was cool, his skin grew slick with sweat.

"Tell me where it hurts and I'll help you," she said as she bent to wipe his brow, wanting so badly for her words to be true.

True that she could take away his pain and heal his body.

True that they weren't surrounded by hundreds of miles of unpopulated land.

True that his sister, the only family he had left, wasn't failing him.

"I'm tired, but my stomach hurts so bad I c-c-can't sleep," he said as he struggled against the damp blanket. "Take this off. I'm hot."

She did as he asked, knowing in a few minutes he would complain of being cold.

As the day passed, Kate did everything she could think of: wiped his forehead and chest with cool water, fed him a weak broth, and all but forced sips of water through his lips. Nothing worked. After the first few hours, he quit pushing the cup or spoon away. There was little fight left.

To make matters worse, thick grey clouds swarmed the sky and they had no shelter.

Kate scrambled to her feet in search of something, anything, to protect them from the coming storm. Working quickly, she went to a packhorse and untied the oiled canvas Jake had bought at Laramie. As she stood, pondering how to get the canvas off the ground, her eyes lighted on a collection of low shrubs about a quarter mile away.

It would have to do.

She headed out, a coil of rope on one shoulder and the roll of canvas on the other. Over the next half-hour she tied the canvas edges to the thickest of the shrub branches, and then spread out their blankets and bedrolls beneath. As she secured all the horses nearby, the clouds darkened and thunder rumbled in the distance.

Kate gathered an armful of branches and put them under the canvas for a later fire. Then, once the makeshift shelter was complete, she hurried back to Ben. As she knelt beside him, she saw he'd finally fallen asleep. He'd tossed and turned all morning, but now that it was time to move, he slept.

"Ben," she whispered.

His eyes fluttered open, then closed again.

"Ben." She bit her lip against tears and fear. "I need you to sit up."

"No," he protested feebly. "Leave me alone."

"I've made you a nicer place to lie down," she assured him while lifting him into a sitting position. As he leaned heavily against her, Kate pulled his bedroll out from under his legs.

"I'll be back," she whispered while easing him down onto the grass.

He didn't respond.

With his blankets clutched to her chest, she ran to the shelter. Inside, she dropped to her knees and quickly refolded two of the blankets so the dampness would be away from his skin. She didn't bother with the third — his sweat had soaked it through.

She ran back to Ben.

One last look over the rolling hills for Jake was to no avail. He could have easily carried Ben, but now her brother would have to waste precious energy by walking. Large drops had splashed down for the past few minutes, and at any time the sky could open up and catch them in a downpour.

With or without Jake, it was time to move Ben.

"Hey there," she said, kneeling at Ben's side to wipe his brow with a handkerchief. "Everything's ready. It's just a little walk and then you can lie down again."

"Carry me," he whimpered, seeming so small and frail in comparison to the sturdy, agile boy he'd always been. "I can't walk."

"Yes, you can," she insisted as she urged him to his feet. "It's not far and you can lean on me."

Lightning flashed in the distance as she put her arm around his shoulders and murmured into his ear, "Now, take a step."

His foot moved only a few inches before his knees gave way and he collapsed in a quiet heap. Feeling dizzy with helplessness, Kate slid her arms beneath his armpits and clasped her hands behind his back. To her dismay, she lifted him easily. How much weight had he lost from dehydration?

As they reached the covering, the rain began. By the time she got him settled it had turned into a torrential downpour. She rushed outside to check again if the horses were secure, especially since Old Dan didn't do well in storms. Once she was satisfied the knots were tight, she grabbed the last two saddlebags and headed to the canvas, pulled aside the front flap that acted as a door, then crawled in and lay next to her brother.

"I'm here," she whispered into his ear.

He raised his head. "Where's Jake?"

"Hunting. I'm sure he found shelter and is waiting out the storm."

Small, chubby fingers held tightly to her own. "Where's Father?"

Thankfully, he drifted to sleep before he could ask again.

The next hours were cold and miserable. The canvas offered little protection against the rain. Ben grew delirious and kept asking for their father. It tore at her heart to see him in so much pain, and to know nothing she was doing helped him.

She could only watch and pray.

****

Jake had given Kate an excuse; in truth, he'd left in search for a medicine man. When he'd broken his leg years ago it had been in the same area, and even though Whitehorse had moved on, his tribe was still known for helping ill or hurt travelers.

It had taken hours to find Shadow Dancer, and another one to convince him to help in the face of the coming storm. Two more hours had passed as Jake led the way back. By the time they rode up upon camp, the rain had slowed to a drizzle. He dismounted and pulled aside the canvas to find Kate huddled over Ben in a feeble attempt to protect him from the rain. Both were soaked.

"Where were you?" she demanded. "He's delirious with pain, and nothing I do is helping. He's even started asking—" She stopped when she noticed Jake wasn't alone.

"I brought someone who may be able to help," he said, stepping aside to reveal his companion. "His name is Shadow Dancer."

With the desperation of a cornered animal, her panicked eyes searched his own.

"Trust me, Kate."

****

Kate moved aside, but refused to leave. Shadow Dancer ignored her as he studied Ben with a frightening intensity, then spoke to Jake in a language she didn't understand. When he'd finished talking, Jake retreated and built a fire. Once he'd put water on to heat he crouched beside her.

"First, he'll prepare yarrow tea to help with the fever," Jake said while Shadow Dancer pulled pinches of an herb from a leather pouch strapped to his side and laid them on a small cloth. "Later, he will give rosehip tea for strength. If there is no change, he will give a larger dose of yarrow to reduce his pain."

Kate nodded, shrank against the sodden canvas wall, and watched as the man combined steaming water and herbs in Ben's cup. He then raised Ben's head and put the rim to his mouth. The mixture dribbled down his chin.

Shadow Dancer gave a sharp grunt before pulling a hollow reed from the leather pouch and inserting it far into Ben's slack mouth. Kate reached to snatch it away, but Jake caught her hand.

"This is the only way to get medicine into him."

Shadow Dancer inserted a crude funnel into the tip of the reed.

"Won't he choke?"

"Not if a few drops at a time are given. This will take all night, but hopefully in the morning Ben will be rested and alert."

"And then?" Ben had to get better. He was her entire life, her everything.

"We'll see," Jake said grimly.

Over the next few hours Shadow Dancer administered the series of medicines, some of which caused Ben to waken and babble incoherently, some made him fall into a fitful sleep, but as darkness surrounded them, he quieted.

Friday, August 4, 1843

Early in the morning, Kate slipped away for a much-needed walk. Ben had made it through the night, and now that he had the care he needed she was confident after a few days of rest they'd be on their way again.

She walked a wide circle around the camp, enjoying the simple pleasures of stretching her legs, breathing in the fresh air, and watching the sunrise.

With only the smallest rustle, Jake appeared at her side. "Mind if I walk with you?"

"Not at all. See what I found?" She held out the collection of wildflowers she'd gathered. "Purple is Ben's favorite color. I hope he likes them."

One look at Jake's forlorn expression and Kate knew something was wrong. "What is it?"

"I spoke with Shadow Dancer after you left. He believes his medicine is only holding off the inevitable."

"No. You're wrong," she said, shaking her head against the brutal truth she saw deep in his eyes. "You don't know Ben like I do. He's getting better!"

"No, he's not."

Kate gasped in horror. "How can you say such a thing?"

"Ben is sick," Jake continued, his tone void of any hope, "and there's nothing more Shadow Dancer can do except keep him comfortable until—"

"I don't believe you!" she cried, furious he'd given up so easily. "You fought so hard to save my father. Why aren't you trying to save Ben?"

Throwing down the wildflowers, Kate rushed back to camp and yanked aside the shelter's door. When she'd left Ben had been sleeping, but now his thin chest heaved and struggled with each gasping breath.

Pushing past Shadow Dancer, she curled next to Ben and began singing softly into his ear, just as she'd done when he was a child. It took three songs, but finally his breathing calmed. Lying next to her brother, watching his chest softly rise and fall, Kate knew Jake was wrong.

Jake crouched in the doorway and shook his head slowly when Shadow Dancer grunted at him. They went outside and began gesturing angrily to each other, but she ignored them and continued to sing, even as Shadow Dancer walked to his horse and rode away.

Soon, she joined Ben in sleep.

Kate woke to see Jake covering Ben's face with a blanket.

"What are you doing?" she demanded. "Leave him alone!"

She snatched the blanket away to reveal her brother — pale and lifeless.

"Oh, please God, no!" Her panicked screams echoed over the land as she shook his shoulders. "No! Ben, wake up! Ben, Ben, wake up!"

But her pleas went unanswered.

Chapter Thirty

Again

Jake spread out a sodden blanket on the ground and dropped a coil of rope beside it.

Ben's coffin.

And now, he needed Ben.

Jake walked to the shelter, crouched in the doorway, and peered inside. Kate remained as he'd left her — head down, cradling the boy's limp body against her chest.

"It's time," he said softly.

She pressed her cheek against Ben's forehead. "Please, don't take him from me," she begged, her voice a watery tremble. "He's all I have left."

Jake eased through the doorway. As he crept toward her, Kate's eyes locked on his and then slowly narrowed.

"No."

He hesitated, startled both by her refusal and the sight of her shrinking away from him as her eyes darted around the shelter like a cornered animal plotting escape. Murmuring apologies and reassurances, he tried again. As he inched closer she shook her head — slowly at first, and then with such fury her hair whipped across her face.

"No!" she shrieked. "I won't let you take him!"

He froze. "Kate, I have to."

She curled around the body and stared at the shelter wall, silent tears slipping unheeded down her cheeks. With a swipe across his own damp eyes, he reached for Ben's shoulder.

She slapped his hand away.

Jake sat back on his heels. As it was, she held Ben with a strength so fierce he had two choices — pry her fingers open and wrench her brother from her arms or wait for her to relinquish.

If time was what it took for her to see reason, he'd give her all she needed.

Cautiously, he lowered himself down beside her and slid his arm around her waist. Instead of pulling away at his touch, she collapsed against him with a disturbingly familiar cry of anguish.

He held her until there were no tears left.

****

This time, Jake dug the grave alone.

His chest heaved with exertion as he flung shovelful after shovelful of damp earth up from the deep hole. But though he tried to lose himself in the rhythm, he couldn't forget the devastation in Kate's eyes as he'd lifted Ben from her arms, severing her last connection to her family. Or his overwhelming regret as he'd walked out of camp, carrying a dead child against his chest and the taunting chants of all he could have done differently in his mind.

Jake tossed the final scoop of dirt onto the growing pile. The shovel quickly followed. He hoisted himself up until his waist teetered on the edge of the grave, then reached for the roped blanket lying nearby. After pulling the bundle into his arms, he gently lowered it into the earth.

Half an hour later, covered in mud and sweat, he stood at the head of the grave and methodically pounded in the wooden cross — a grim reminder of the one he'd made one month ago.

The trail had claimed, and now held, yet another victim.

Upon his return to camp, he found Kate in exactly the same position as when he'd left — slumped on Ben's bedroll, her Bible limp in hand. So fragile. So near broken.

"It's done," he said quietly.

She nodded through her tears.

How could Kate bear this? He'd seen strong men crumble at the loss of their mothers — something she'd already withstood — but to lose her father and brother in less than a month? Could she rise above such tragedy?

"We didn't have much for a marker," he continued, "so I put him atop a hill overlooking the river."

"Thank you," she murmured while reaching up to take his outstretched hand. He slowly pulled her to her feet and led her out of camp. Once the small mound came into sight, Kate let out a choking cry and stumbled into him. He caught her by the arm to steady her and then uncertainly withdrew when she shook off his hand.

Silent minutes passed as they stood, shoulder to shoulder, at yet another freshly-dug grave. The quiet crushed in around him, pulsing with whispered words of yet another failure. Only when the whispers grew to screams did he ease her Bible out from under his arm.

"I thought this would help you say a few words."

He held the book toward her, but Kate only glanced at it before settling her gaze on the ground once again.

Knowing she'd never forgive herself if words weren't spoken over her brother's gravesite, he began flipping through the pages. His mother had taught him well about the word of God, and he found and read several passages.

"Proverbs 3:5 Trust in the Lord with all thine heart; and lean not unto thine own understanding."

"Isaiah 40:31 But they that wait upon the Lord shall renew their strength; they shall mount up with wings as eagles; they shall run, and not be weary; and they shall walk, and not faint."

Kate sank to her knees, pinched a clump of dirt between her fingers, and placed it in a metal box she'd withdrawn from her skirt pocket. After snapping the lid shut, she looked to him.

"My family shouldn't be buried out here," she said, sweeping her hand across the endless brown grasses blowing in the wind. "They're so far apart, with only sticks marking their existence. I'll never see their graves again—" her voice cracked, and she continued on in a heartbroken whisper "—and now I'm all alone."

Blinking fast against the sting of threatening tears, Jake knelt down on one knee. Slowly, he slid her father's hat from her head, wrapped her in his arms, and cradled her against his chest. He wanted to offer words of healing, of wisdom, of reassurance. Most of all, he wanted to tell her no, she wasn't alone — that he would be there to comfort her and protect her.

Jake took a deep breath, and then, after a long moment, slowly exhaled. Nothing he did or said would take away this kind of hurt. Instead, he settled for holding her as she cried, wishing desperately he could shelter her from the pain of an uncertain future.

When her keening sobs subsided into soft whimpers, Kate pulled away from him. Taking the handkerchief he offered, she wiped her eyes.

"I don't want to go to Oregon anymore. I want to go back home."

Jake swallowed hard. Her plaintive words were the ones he'd longed to hear the first days on the trail, but now she asked the impossible. How could he explain to this distraught woman who'd lost nearly every possession in their pursuit toward an unknown land — the land that had taken her entire family — it was too late to go back?

Kate apparently mistook his silence for indecision and began pleading her case.

"I want to be with people I know, people who know me. I'll buy a wagon somewhere, and as we backtrack I can pick up everything I left behind. At least then I'll have more than memories."

"It's not possible," he said softly. "We're already three-quarters of the way there."

Her eyes went wide. "You're telling me you won't take me home?"

"No, I'm telling you I *can't*," he corrected. "At least not this year. We could get supplies, but it's still impossible. The weather won't allow it. It's warm now, but by the time we got back to the Missouri River it would be too cold to travel safely. Winter is coming. We'll see frost in a few weeks. As for the forts we passed along the way, they don't tend to put up civilians for the winter. They keep them for military personnel only."

"I can't go home?"

Hating the devastation he saw in her eyes, Jake regretfully shook his head. "Kate, we have to move on."

She stared at him a long moment, and then turned toward the grave.

"I'm going to pack," he said. He was reluctant to leave her, but wanted her to have a final moment alone with her brother. "I'll be right back."

She ignored him.

Desperate for her to know she could count on him and wanting to reassure himself she'd heard him, he held her by the shoulders until she faced him again.

"I'll be right back," he repeated.

He sprinted back to camp. After tucking Elijah's hat into Kate's saddlebag, he tied blankets, bedrolls, and the kettle to the nearest packhorse, shoved cups and plates in random saddlebags, and stomped out the dwindling fire. Within minutes of leaving Kate he was riding back again with all the horses trailing behind.

As he approached, he saw a chilling sight.

Kate lay beside Ben's grave, grasping fistfuls of dirt and letting it sift through her fingers.

"Kate?"

She didn't acknowledge him, not even when he dismounted and knelt beside her.

"Kate, it's time to go."

"I'm staying." Her voice was calm, childlike.

"I know this is hard," he said, cupping his hand over her arm, "but we need to be on our way."

"You go ahead. I can't leave my brother alone."

Yet another handful of earth rained down softly over the grave.

Never in his life had Jake been at such a loss for words. But after a few minutes of watching this same action over and over again, he knew he had to get her away however possible. In one fluid motion he scooped up her slight frame. Only when he held her securely in his arms did she meet his gaze.

The blankness in her eyes terrified him.

Though he'd been walking toward Nina with the intention of helping Kate into her saddle, he immediately pivoted and headed toward Plug. He held her tight against his chest as he mounted up, and didn't release his hold even after he'd settled her across his lap.

Through all this she didn't protest, didn't move. But, as they rode away she looked to the sky and whispered, "Goodbye, my brother."

They traveled the rest of the day in silence.

****

The rhythmic clopping of the horses' hooves against the hard ground created a song that echoed in Kate's head throughout the day.

My brother is gone, my father is gone.
My brother is gone, my father is gone.
My brother is gone, my father is gone.

She couldn't make the taunting words stop. She didn't cry anymore; there were no tears left. Instead, she lay limp and unresisting against Jake's chest, her only movement occurring because of the horse's steady gait beneath her.

With each step, the distance from everything that had ever mattered increased, but she felt nothing. She was beaten. The trail had taken all she had cared about, and all she had ever known.

She found comfort in numbness.

Chapter Thirty-One

Wandering

Tuesday, August 8, 1843

Jake set a plate loaded with beans, cornbread, and two slices of bacon in front of Kate.

"Nothing beats a good breakfast to start the day," he said hopefully, crouching beside her and easing the handle of a spoon between her curled fingers. Seconds later the utensil fell to the ground, unnoticed, while she stared blankly at the meal as if unable to comprehend its purpose.

She hadn't eaten but a few bites since Ben's death four days ago. Yesterday she'd stopped eating entirely. If she continued, he'd soon be at his last resort — forcing her. The thought sickened him.

With an anguished sigh, Jake rose and started loading the horses. While he worked he kept close watch on Kate, alert for any change, no matter how slight. As usual, she sat motionless in her bedroll, focused on the dwindling fire, oblivious to his every move. Even her eyes, which had always betrayed her hidden feelings, remained perpetually vacant.

Two days ago he'd checked the laudanum bottle, concerned it might be the reason behind the trance she'd fallen into after leaving Ben's grave.

Untouched.

Jake finished clearing the camp and then lifted Kate from the ground and placed her in Nina's saddle. He mounted Nickel, and with Nina's reins firmly in hand he began another day with a shell of a woman riding at his side.

Before Ben's death, Kate had taken an interest in the landmarks they'd be passing, how many miles they'd traveled, and what to watch out for. Now she merely nodded when she acknowledged him at all. Nonetheless, he still tried to engage her in conversation.

"We're coming up on some fascinating sights, Kate. We should see Independence Rock within the week."

She stared ahead, expressionless.

"We're making good time. We might even catch up to a wagon train."

As near as he could figure they were a few weeks behind a group of at least twenty wagons. Such high numbers usually meant women. Maybe another woman could provide the help Kate so desperately needed. Help he was unable to provide. Fort Hall was at least another month away, and he wasn't sure how, or if, she could continue on in her current state.

Jake tried again. "Wouldn't it be nice to meet new people?"

Nothing.

He rubbed his eyes, took a pull from his canteen, and settled in for another long day of silence.

****

Thursday, August 10, 1843

Jake sat on his bedroll, darkness at his back and a third cup of coffee warming his hands, willing himself not to fall asleep. He'd counted everything he could think of to stay alert through the night: stars, crunches from the horses' teeth as they grazed nearby, the snapping pops from a fresh log after he threw it on the fire. At least tonight he wasn't counting Kate's whimpering sobs as she suffered through her nightmares.

She lay curled in her bedroll, her back to him. But though her breaths were deep and even, he still couldn't relax his mind from the possibility she was awake and waiting.

His eyes burned with fatigue. He hadn't slept more than a few minutes at a time over the past three days, and now even counting wasn't stopping his head from lolling against his chest.

Underneath the clear, moonlit sky, he lost the battle.

****

Jake's eyes snapped open. Immediately, he looked to Kate's bedroll.

Empty.

Horrified, he scrambled across the dirt and tunneled his hand into her blankets.

Cold.

"Kate!" he shouted, clamoring to his feet. "Kate, where are you?"

Hearing no reply, he pulled his rifle from its scabbard and ran into the darkness. At the top of the nearest hill, he stopped and scanned the moonlit terrain. His vision blurred from the strain. Cursing, he rubbed his eyes and tried again. Nothing.

"Kate!" he yelled, frantic at the thought of her out there somewhere, alone and unprotected. He ran down the hill and up another. Squinting, he focused on a large expanse of rock in the distance.

He'd found her.

Jake sprinted toward her slim figure outlined in the moonlight. When he reached the rock she sat upon he stood before her, his chest heaving while he silently willed away the terror that had gripped him during his search.

"Can I join you?" he asked quietly once he trusted himself to speak.

To his surprise, she slowly nodded.

Encouraged by any response, no matter how small, he laid his rifle on the ground and eased himself down on the rock beside her. The wind whispered through the grasses around them, and the only other sound was the clicking of metal against metal as she opened and closed a small box in her hand.

"Kate, why are you out here alone? Again?"

Three nights ago, she'd left camp after he'd fallen asleep. He'd woken to stoke the fire and found an uneasy sight — her empty bedroll. Initially, he'd figured she was off attending personal needs. Several minutes had ticked by while he'd fought between respecting her privacy and needing to know she was safe. Finally, he'd surrendered and called for her. No response. After a frantic search for what had seemed like an eternity, he'd found her half a mile away, barefoot, staring at the stars.

How long had she been gone? What was she doing? He had no idea, and when he'd demanded answers, her sorrowful eyes had stared right through him. In the end he'd carried her back to camp, laid her in her bedroll, and covered her with her blankets. Then he'd brewed a pot of coffee and watched over her the rest of the night.

And now she'd wandered again.

"Kate, you know the risk of straying from camp." He'd warned her repeatedly how animals were known to attack those who left the protection the campfire and his gun provided.

Click open. Click closed.

"I panicked when I woke and couldn't find you. Why didn't you answer when I called your name?"

Click open. Click closed.

Jake gritted his teeth. He was exhausted. Frustrated. And enough was enough.

"You know how dangerous this is! It's as if you're pushing God to take you too. Don't let their deaths be in vain. You're alive. Make it count!"

Click open. Click closed. Silence.

"I can't..." She trailed off and closed her eyes against the tears slipping down her cheeks.

He froze, stunned at hearing her voice again after a week of silence. He had to act before she drifted away from him again!

"Tell me, Kate," he pleaded, falling to his knees on the ground before her. "Tell me how to help you."

When she didn't answer, he pulled her trembling hands into his own and held tight, wishing fervently he could snatch her up from the horrible void she'd tumbled into.

Slowly she raised her head. The moonlight revealed her delicate features, rife with uncertainty. He heard her sharp intake of breath and tensed with anticipation.

"I can't stop thinking of all I should have done differently to save them. If it weren't for my mistakes, they'd be alive today."

Her whispered words were like a fist to his gut. All this time she'd thought herself responsible? He shook his head, adamant that she understand she bore no fault in their deaths.

"No, Kate. You're not to blame — you did all you could, and more." Remorse at his own failures sat heavy on his chest, yet he forced himself to go on. "Trust me. You'll get through this. It will take a long time, but it will happen."

"What would you know about it?" Disbelief and anger clouded her features as she spat out the bitter words.

"I know plenty," he answered quietly. He'd tried to help her in every way possible — except one. Perhaps hearing his story would provide reassurance that survival and triumph were possible after even the worst of misfortunes. "I, too, lost my entire family through tragedy."

With a deep breath, he began the story of that horrible day so long ago.

"My father was a U.S. Marshal. When I was a boy, there were long stretches of time where I acted as the man of the house while he was chasing outlaws. The last time, he tracked two brothers over several territories until he caught and brought them back to face sentencing."

Kate sat before him, her eyes apprehensive, yet unwavering. Bolstered by her acceptance, he continued.

"They escaped while being taken to the courtroom. As they rode out of town, witnesses heard them swear revenge on the man who'd captured them. Word got to us too late. I was ten the day they murdered my father, mother, and two younger brothers."

She recoiled in horror. "Where were you?"

Jake swallowed back the bile roiling in his throat. What would she think of him once she knew?

"I watched it all from the woodshed." *Actually, I hid like a coward and they died — victims of my inaction.* "Afterwards, I was shipped off to New York City to live with my Aunt Caroline. At age fifteen I left to learn the land. And now," he added with a shrug, "I'm here with you."

Kate's wide eyes filled with empathy and she shook her head in wonder as the realization of their similarities took hold. "You know what this is like for me — what I'm feeling."

He nodded. "Eventually, you'll rise above what happened. You'll live with it forever—" he softened his tone "—but don't let it define the rest of your life."

"But what do I do now...?" She trailed off as he put a hand to her cheek and brushed aside a lone tear with his thumb. With a tender smile, he answered her unfinished question.

"You can start with promising you won't wander away from camp anymore. As for the rest, I can't answer that question. Only you can."

He tucked a wayward lock of hair behind her ear and then regretfully dropped his hands. In a perfect world, he would have arrived in Oregon and begun properly courting this beautiful, extraordinary woman. He'd have willingly spent a lifetime ensuring her happiness. But it couldn't happen now. Jake knew she'd always look at him and be reminded of what she'd lost — on his watch.

He rose and sat beside her again. Together they watched as the wind's light caress sent shadows of trees dancing across the moonlit land.

"Kate, I need to be perfectly clear about something. I'll take you back to Charlottesville if you want. We'll get to Oregon, stay for the winter, and come springtime we'll be the first party out."

"You'll take me back?"

Jake certainly didn't want to return. It would mean the loss of an entire year and a lot of money. But he had given his word to Elijah that he would watch over her, and if going back was what Kate wanted, he'd do it.

"Next spring, yes."

****

Hours later, Kate lay on her side watching idly as bright flames licked away burning wood. All was silent out on the desolate land and the horses had long ago settled in for the night. Across the fire from her, Jake slept. She didn't join him in slumber. Instead, for the first time in days, she wanted to stay awake. To feel, to think. His talk had lit a flicker of light within her, guiding her from the darkness of the past month.

She'd taken no time to grieve the loss of her father. When he'd died, she'd shoved aside her heartache in favor of taking care of Ben and plotting out their new lives. Then, when Ben died and Jake said no on going home, everything had crashed in on her. She hadn't been able to face the reality of life without her family and had willingly slipped into nothingness.

Now that Jake had pulled her from the hazy abyss she'd sunk into, she needed to face her future head-on and start making choices.

She'd asked him to take her back to Virginia, but deep down she wasn't certain of reverting to all she'd so willingly left behind. She had no family to take her in except Aunt Victoria. And aside from the unpleasantness of living under the same roof as the bitter, spiteful woman, there was also the size of the roof to consider — small. She'd be fortunate to get a bed shoved in the back corner of the parlor.

She couldn't be sure Marie Ann's husband would be willing to take her either. A houseguest would be an intrusion to a new marriage and new baby. Plus, the store had been sold and the owners would be under no obligation to offer her employment.

With her father's money, she could stay in Oregon. After all, the West was the land of opportunity. A place to reinvent yourself and create the life you wanted. A store, a ranch — the possibilities were endless now that she was free from all the expectations of her strict upbringing.

Being alone in Oregon wasn't something she would have ever chosen for herself, but Jake was right — she had to move forward.

Chapter Thirty-Two

Independence Rock

Wednesday, August 16, 1843

Jake stifled a chuckle as Kate yawned and shifted restlessly in her saddle. She'd been fidgeting beside him all morning.

"Problem?" he asked.

"I can't get comfortable." She sighed and then swept her hand across the desolate land ahead. "Plus, everything is the same. It's boring."

Admittedly, she was right. The days now passed slowly by, each identical to the one before. Sparse landmarks, sultry weather, and endless hours on the trail all combined to discourage travelers. But any guide worth his salt knew how to make the land interesting.

"There's a lot to see if you know where to look." Jake twisted in his saddle, shielded his eyes, and pointed behind them. "See the grass back there?"

Kate glanced over her shoulder. "Same as always."

He chuckled at her naivety. "A horse's hooves push the grass back down, pointing to where the horse has been, whereas a man's foot pushes the grass down to where he is going."

"I never noticed," she replied. She straightened in the saddle, her eyes bright with curiosity.

As Jake looked to the woman at his side, he was amazed at her tenacity. Not only had she accepted her situation, she was proving to be a strong-willed spitfire yet again.

"Tell me something else," she urged.

"Have you ever noticed how when you look from a fire into the darkness you're briefly blind? That's why an alert man—" he paused "—or woman, will never gaze into a fire at night." He shot her a sidelong glance. "Now, let's see how much you know about horses. What's the first thing you do if one breaks its leg?"

"Easy," she scoffed. "Shoot it."

"What?" His eyebrows raised in false astonishment.

"Shoot it." She repeated her words calmly, yet her fiery green eyes left no doubt of her rising determination to correct him. "There's nothing else you can do."

"You're matter-of-fact—" he smirked "—for someone who's wrong."

"I'm not wrong and you know it. A broken leg equals a dead horse."

"No, it doesn't," he retorted, enjoying the sight of her fighting for something she believed in so strongly.

"Yes, it does! There's no way you can honestly believe once a leg is broken the horse can be of use again! It's a terrible thing, but the fact remains a leg never heals correctly." She threw up her hands in exasperation. "You know I'm right, so why do you keep talking about this?"

His grin widened. "Because even as a kid I liked poking at a rattler to see if it'd strike."

She conceded to his teasing with a roll of her eyes and a loud, exaggerated sigh. But as she shifted her focus on the land ahead, he saw a faint smile cross her lips.

A lovely sight indeed.

Moments later, Jake spotted the ridge of low, rocky hills marking the impending Independence Rock. He said nothing, wanting Kate to discover it herself. Sure enough, a few minutes later she abruptly stood in her stirrups.

"Look at that huge rock!" She turned to him, her face flushed with excitement. "It must be fifty feet tall!"

"Probably closer to a hundred and fifty," he corrected.

She spun toward the rock again, sending her windswept hair whirling around her waist. She'd abandoned her braids along with her dresses, and he adored the sight of her hair flowing out from under Elijah's hat and trailing down her slender back. He'd spent many a recent evening watching her smooth her long curls and trying to decide which caught the firelight more — her heavy silver brush or the glints of red throughout her hair.

"Why didn't you tell me?" she demanded, startling him from his drifting thoughts.

"I wanted to surprise you. Did it work?"

She nodded enthusiastically. "It's a nice change to see something so strong and secure in the midst of all the low hills and grass."

He understood. The smooth dome rested upon the land, its sheer size both impressive and imposing. Walking around the base took over four thousand steps — children of the train on his first time through had proudly declared the number.

Since his last visit, someone had painted a large cross upon the rock; no small feat considering the sharp angle it took as it jutted up from the earth. Jake tensed as he realized the other difference — no one milled about the rock as they had in his previous times through. Reaching this point along the trail by Independence Day — hence the rock's name — was the goal of most travelers and wagon trains, and he and Kate were five weeks past.

They stopped several yards from the rock and dismounted. After helping him hobble the horses to keep them from wandering off, Kate walked to the base of the rock and ran her fingers across the surface. He rummaged through a saddlebag, and once he'd found what he wanted, he joined her.

"Someone carved their name," she said.

"Check over there," he said, pointing to a flat spot about fifteen yards further to the right. "You'll find a lot more."

She followed him, and then stood in awe before the etchings that spoke of those who had traveled before them.

"Why, there's at least a hundred names," she said.

"I left mine each time I've come past," he said, bending to trace his fingers along four sets of small indentations. "Over time wind, sun, and rain change the carvings. My first one is already different."

With a tentative smile, she placed her palm over an expanse of unmarred rock. "I want to do this."

"Here." He handed her the knife he'd removed from his saddlebag moments ago. "It's tradition. I've used this one every time I've been through."

While Kate slowly carved her name into the rock, Jake couldn't help but think what this moment should have been like for her, surrounded by her father and brother, the three of them filled with excitement while they left a lasting reminder of their time upon the trail. Instead, she was traveling with only her trail guide, and heading for an unforgiving land dominated by rough men.

Jake was at a loss as to what would happen once they arrived in Oregon and longed to clarify his role in her life. When she finished carving, he slipped the knife back into his pocket and gathered his courage.

"I have one more surprise," he said softly before reaching to take her hand.

****

As Jake's warm, strong hand enveloped hers, Kate felt her breath quicken, much to her astonishment. She looked away, trying to ignore the pleasant sensation of his thumb slowly caressing her knuckles.

"I want you to show you the view from the top." He gave her hand a final squeeze before releasing it and starting up the pathway. "Stay close to me and watch your step. Rattlesnakes tend to sun themselves in the crevasses near the base."

Kate followed him along the winding, narrow route, realizing yet again how her choice of clothing equaled an intoxicating level of freedom. Wearing trousers, she could explore the rugged landmark as she pleased instead of worrying about lifting, and ripping, petticoats and skirts. When they reached the peak she stood beside him in companionable silence, content to gaze upon the land spread out below and a far-off herd of buffalo.

"If we can keep up the pace, we'll make Oregon City by the middle of October."

His casual comment filled her with dread. In the beginning of the trip she'd only looked forward to the end, but now their daily habits were a comforting routine.

Each morning she started breakfast while he prepared the coffee. After they ate and cleaned their dishes, Jake packed up the campsite while she watered the horses at the river. By the time she returned, he had their saddlebags and canteens readied for the day, and while they loaded the horses he talked about whether they'd be seeking specific landmarks like a lake or a bend in the river, or if they would only be guided by the position of the sun.

When she didn't respond, Jake faced her with a frown. "What's wrong? I thought you'd be excited at the news."

"I'm thinking how trail life is so simple, and the days have a predictable routine," she said, all the while declining to mention how worried she was about the upcoming months. Making difficult decisions would soon be part of her daily life, as would living with the consequences if she chose poorly. And though Jake had promised her father he would see to it she was taken care of, she couldn't expect him to do anything besides help her get settled. Once he returned east next spring she would be on her own.

Pushing her uncertainties aside, Kate looked skyward and closed her eyes, happy to simply enjoy the warmth of the sun on her face. Being on this rock amongst countless names of kindred souls who had dared make the same journey brought on a feeling of contentment she hadn't felt in months.

"Kate?"

She opened her eyes and found Jake standing before her. With a shy smile, he slowly removed her hat, freeing her hair to blow in the wind. Her heart raced as his eyes, tender and uncertain, locked with hers.

"What happens when we reach Oregon?" he asked.

A breath she didn't know she'd been holding escaped in a rush. She'd known he'd pose the question sooner or later. He was a man of action, of planning. Undoubtedly he'd want to know if he'd be responsible for bringing her along when he headed east.

She took a deep breath and voiced the words that would solidify her future. "You won't need to take me back next spring, Jake. I'm staying in Oregon to take over my father's store."

His quick grin both confused and disheartened her. Was she so horrible to travel with? Obviously so. He seemed thrilled at the news he'd be making his return trip alone.

Willing her voice not to tremble, she continued. "I've given it a lot of thought and feel it's the right thing to do. For Father, and for me."

"Are you sure you're up to such a task?"

"What does that mean?" she replied, startled both at his question and the dubious scowl settling upon his face. "All those arriving in Oregon in the coming years will need what I can provide."

"You should know it's bound to be difficult. Out west, many people view store-bought things as a waste of money. They live off the earth." He waved his arm over the ground below for emphasis.

"But they'll need some items. Plows, seeds, and ultimately horses."

"I think you need to prepare yourself if you're not as—" he hesitated, as if trying to find the correct word "—prosperous as you hope right away."

She clenched her fists in an effort to fight back her growing irritation. First he'd been utterly bold with his elation at the news she'd be staying, yet now he wanted to question the wisdom of her decision?

"I knew before I left home it would be tough. But as I well know, anything is possible out here."

"Just don't expect too much."

"Why not?" she snapped, now livid from his repeated warnings. Did he take her for a fool with no business sense?

"My father expected a rush of business as soon as we opened. Why shouldn't I?"

"Let's just say the type of business men like a woman in charge of is not what you'll be running." His eyes, once gentle, now turned fierce. "It's a man's world out there, Kate. Rough and dirty. You'll do well not to forget it."

Wondering how they'd gone from holding hands to nearly shouting at each other in less than a minute, Kate glared at him while plucking her hat from his fingers. After setting it down hard on her head and pulling the brim over her eyes, she focused on the open prairie.

She spoke not one word as they wound their way down. When they were only a few steps from the ground she pushed past him and headed for the horses.

"I didn't mean to upset you up there. I only wanted you to understand—"

"Understand what, Jake?" She whirled to face him. "I'm a woman and therefore can't run a business?"

"That's not what I meant."

"Sure sounded like it."

Jake threw his hands up with a sigh of exasperation, gathered his horses, mounted up, and rode off. She followed, but took care to keep several yards between them. She had no intention of continuing their talk. His lack of confidence in her abilities had hurt her to the core.

****

An hour later they reached Devil's Gate — a V-shaped passageway through a massive rock. Trouble was, the river ran straight through the narrow space. Kate followed Jake's lead as he dismounted and led his horses into the river that was now the trail. Once they passed through the cleft, Jake urged his horses ashore and then waded in again to brace her arm as she stepped up from the river. She grudgingly accepted his help, still smarting from his earlier words.

While the horses milled about, grazing at will, he faced her.

"About earlier—"

"There's nothing to discuss," she snapped.

Jake let out an exasperated sigh. "There's a long way between here and Oregon. Hear me out and then we can drop it."

"Fine."

"What I was trying to say up there on the rock, though admittedly I did a bad job of it, was that though it will be difficult, I'm sure you'll do well." His voice grew soft as his eyes searched hers for forgiveness. "I'm sorry, Kate. I didn't mean to hurt you."

She studied him for a long time, wondering not at the sincerity of his words, but at her own apparent need for his approval. Since when did she care so much about what he thought? She smiled at the absurdity of such a notion, a gesture, which Jake evidently took to mean she forgave him for he smiled in return. Whistling merrily, he headed toward his horses.

"Now that we've gotten everything cleared up and out of the way," he called, "look back. It's one of the last times you'll see water heading for the Atlantic Ocean. Soon we'll leave the Sweetwater River behind, and with it the last of Eastern water. Oregon, here we come!"

Chapter Thirty-Three

The Cave

Thursday, August 17, 1843

"By the end of today, or early tomorrow at the latest, we should come upon an unusual sight," Jake said while carefully pouring the remains of their wash water on the morning fire.

"What?"

"You'll see," he replied, nudging dirt over the last of the smoldering embers with the tip of his boot. He had no intention of spoiling what would break the monotony of their hard travel over the past weeks. They were heading for the South Pass and he hoped once they completed the seventy-five-hundred-foot climb, they would spot the wagon train he estimated now to be only a day ahead.

With winter and mountain passes looming, he desperately wanted the security a wagon train could provide. Only two travelers meant little protection from, and fewer eyes to watch for, danger.

"Ready?" he asked once she'd gathered Old Dan's reins and the lead ropes to Nina and one of the packhorses in her hands. She nodded. They mounted up, him on Plug and leading Nickel and the two other packhorses. As the morning stretched on, a lively discussion ensued.

"I don't agree, Jake. Everyone knows packing ice in sawdust is the proper way to keep it from melting during the summer. Who taught you to use dirt?"

"My uncle. He always said good, well-packed dirt will let ice last just as long."

She laughed at his absurd notion. "Dirt will leave you with a pile of mud halfway into springtime."

"It seems you know a little more than I gave you credit for."

A flash in the distance caught his attention. Without a word, he reached into his nearest saddlebag and then brought his scope to his eye. Only when he was confident in what he saw did he raise his arm.

"Over there," he pointed. "Beyond the ridge."

"I don't see anything except what seems like a row of tufts of cotton." She paused, her stare intense. "Wait, they're moving! Do you think it could be...?"

"It's a wagon train! There's about twenty wagons and a few outriders. I'd say they're less than half a day ahead of us."

As the afternoon progressed, the air grew hot and thick. Dark clouds gathered in the distance and the mutterings of faraway thunder increased. While they stopped to water the horses, the wind picked up. By the time they departed, mighty gusts of air fluttered their pant legs and threatened to send unsecured hats rolling. Ominous black clouds formed across the sky.

Jake clenched his teeth when the first crack of lightning struck the ground less than three miles ahead. A storm meant they'd have to abandon tracking.

"Did you see that?" she asked in a hushed tone.

"Yes." Normally he liked nothing better than to settle in and watch a good storm, but they were in the open with no protection — something he doubted Kate had ever experienced. Being from town, she'd probably only seen storms from behind a windowpane. "We'll have to take shelter and wait this out."

Rain. Light at first, then it quickly turned into a downpour. Frigid drops changed to blinding hail. When the beads of ice began bouncing skyward after striking the ground, Jake knew the storm would wipe away all traces of the wagon train.

****

A rope of light writhed down less than two miles in front of them. Kate tensed in her saddle, waiting for the inevitable thunder. Old Dan reared at the first low rumble, nearly throwing Kate to the ground. He came down hard.

"You all right?" called Jake.

She nodded grimly as another burst of white raced across the sky. Seconds later a clap of thunder sounded, sending Old Dan straight up on his hind legs. As he pawed the air, she clutched the horn with one hand and held fast to the reins with the other. When he came down, she felt his muscles tense against her thighs.

"Steady, boy," she urged as she fought to hold him to a trot. Thankfully, Nina and the packhorse she led followed without a fight.

Jake rode up alongside her. "Storm's bound to get worse. I think it's time to dismount and walk them."

She shook her head. "I'll lose control over him the second my feet hit ground."

He frowned. "Kate, I've got the horses rigged harness to harness. What if he spins?"

"Good point," she agreed. While she did have better leverage in the saddle, a rearing horse tended to spin and bolt the moment they landed. She'd be crushed in the tangle of harnesses and hooves. Without a word, she slid from the saddle and grabbed hold of Old Dan's lead rope, taking care to leave plenty of slack for when he reared again.

"First chance we get we'll take shelter and wait this out," he said as he dismounted.

Together they spaced out their horses and started walking. They hadn't gone half a mile when a streak of lightning ripped through the air. Old Dan reared wildly and she scrambled to get out of his way. When he came down he fought the lead rope, but she planted her boot heels deep into the slick mud and held on. Several yards away Jake struggled to restrain a packhorse from jerking against the rope that connected it to Nickel's harness.

They got their horses under control and trudged on.

Rain roared down and then ricocheted, creating a haze a foot above the ground. Rivulets gathered into wide pools of water, some at least six inches deep. Kate slogged through each, thankful for every minute that passed without a strike of lightning.

Wind gusts whipped her hair against her face in long, stinging lashes and needled the rain through her thin coat so hard that tears came to her eyes. But nothing would be accomplished by complaining, so she pushed her father's hat firmly to her head and continued on without protest.

Ahead, Jake let out a series of unintelligible shouts. She shrugged and shook her head, unable to hear him over the wind. Undaunted, he cupped his hands to his mouth.

"Keep going! Shelter's about a mile ahead!"

She didn't attempt an answer aside from a quick nod. They moved on until he waved her to a stop and pointed toward a dark, craggy hill in the distance.

"Cave's in there."

She nodded through the stream of water cascading off the brim of her hat.

The cliff loomed closer, yet she saw nothing resembling a shelter as she followed Jake and his four horses up a small, rocky incline. Once they'd rounded a gentle curve she saw Jake whisk his rifle from the scabbard. After a look around, he tied Plug's lead rope to a low tree branch and walked to where she stood, waiting. He lowered his head until his mouth was inches from her ear.

"We might not be alone. Stay put while I check it out."

Kate nodded and then watched him disappear. Moments later he reappeared.

"All clear," he shouted, waving her forward.

She waited as he untied Plug, and then followed him to the mouth of a large, dark cave. Pulling off her hat, she urged her horses inside.

The walls were over ten feet tall. The shape reminded her of a triangle with a point at the back wall. There was a large opening to the storm, but an overhang ensured the cave was dry and protected. A stack of wood sat against a side wall, evidence of previous inhabitants.

As she checked over their surroundings, Jake started a small fire and then secured Plug, Nickel, and his two packhorses to a rope he'd strung across the cave. When he finished, he untied Old Dan from Nina's harness, and then freed Nina from the remaining packhorse.

"Tie your horses to the rope, and I'll build up the fire," Jake said as he took off his coat and headed for more wood. "While we wait for coffee, we can unpack and spread out our clothes and supplies to dry."

Kate stood shivering against the wall, unable to coax her icy fingers open enough to pull off her leather gloves, much less tie knots in wet rope.

Jake rushed to her side.

"I wasn't thinking," he said, steering her to stand before the crackling flames. "You get warm. I'll take care of everything."

She nodded, comforted by the fire's heat against her face. Meanwhile, Jake moved to Plug and unbuckled his saddlebags. They dropped to the ground with a heavy, sodden thud.

"I'm sorry I'm not helping," she said through chattering teeth. "I'll tie up the rest of the horses in a minute. I just need to—"

A bolt of lightning struck outside the cave entrance. With a loud crack and a wet sucking noise, a tree crashed onto the rock overhang, littering the entry with rain-soaked branches. Deafening thunder rolled overhead.

Old Dan reared.

"Grab him!" Jake shouted, trapped between the shifting horses straining against the rope tethering them to the cave wall.

Old Dan landed.

Kate lunged for his reins, missed, and then struggled to stay afoot as Nina and the last packhorse crowded around her, searching for comfort and guidance. She could do nothing except watch as, with her saddlebags fastened securely to his back, Old Dan bolted from the cave.

With a leaning heave of forearm against flank, she slipped past Nina and stumbled to the entrance. Three sharp whistles were to no avail. Aghast, she spun to see Jake heading toward her, his coat in one hand and hat in the other.

"Everything I have left is in those saddlebags!"

With his mouth pulled into a tight, grim line, Jake stared over her shoulder into the raging storm. His eyes glittered with an intensity she hadn't seen since his argument with Shadow Dancer just before Ben's death.

She caught him by the arm. "Don't."

He shook off her hand. "Take care of the horses and keep the fire going. I'll be back."

He leaped over a snapped tree limb lying at the mouth of the cave and disappeared down the rocky path.

Ten minutes passed.

While she waited, Kate secured Nina and the packhorse. Then, she tried to focus on getting warm instead of how Jake was out in the storm.

Thirty minutes passed.

She watered the horses, then pulled supplies off the packhorses and out of saddlebags. While she hung their clothes on a line she'd strung across one side of the cave, she kept close watch on the entrance.

One hour passed.

The leather saddlebags had protected the contents from the worst of the rain, so their clothes were damp but not soaked. After hanging in front of the fire, everything had dried except for one of Jake's shirts and a pair of his trousers. She folded their clothes.

With each passing minute her worry increased. The storm still raged, and with each strike of lightning the crackle reverberated throughout the land, followed by long rumbles of thunder. Gusts of wind whipped into the cave, scattering sparks and dirt across the floor.

Kate barely noticed. She was too caught up in haunting thoughts of what might have happened to Jake. The man was her lifeline. She'd lost so much already, and the idea that maybe she'd lost him too sent her heart pounding so hard the panicked rhythm pulsed in her ears.

With shaking hands, she stirred the fire. When another thunderclap boomed overhead she threw on enough logs to keep the flames roaring. Then, with nothing left to do, she paced the cave opening, shouting his name every few minutes until a new thought stopped her cold.

What if his absence was deliberate?

"He wouldn't leave me," she said aloud. "I know it."

But as the minutes ticked by, doubt crept in. What if he thought she was holding him back and had only been biding his time, waiting for a chance to disappear?

Kate sank to her knees and stared glassy-eyed into the fire, certain in the knowledge that he'd deserted her too. Soon grief, anguish, and sheer weariness took over and she collapsed into a ball next to the fire, rocking back and forth, her arms wrapped around herself for comfort.

****

Jake walked into the cave wearing a misshapen hat, soaked clothes, and a jubilant grin. Quickly he sighted Kate lying on her bedroll, her back to him.

"I found him! It was a long chase and he put up a struggle at the end, but I knew I'd get him."

She stayed silent, so he decided to let her sleep as he first secured Old Dan beside the other horses and then surveyed all she'd done while he'd been gone. The fire crackled lively between their bedrolls, the horses stood blanketed and calm, and their supplies and clothes were dry and organized.

Jake would have followed Old Dan to the ends of the earth before he would let Kate lose anything else on his watch. As it was, he'd tracked the fool horse for a mile before finding him. He'd spent the next mile cursing because each time he got near enough to grab reins, thunder rolled overhead or something — and at times, nothing — would spook the skittish horse enough to spin and bolt.

He'd followed, unwilling to return without those saddlebags. After he held Old Dan securely by the reins, they'd shared a long, cold walk back — he'd fallen off a rearing horse before and had no intention of risking re-injury to his leg by repeating the act, especially with Kate waiting.

Jake spotted his shirt and pants drying on a line near the fire. Though anxious to share the good news of his return, he'd rather do so while dry. Quietly, so as not to wake her, he lifted the clothes off the line and stepped behind the horses to the back corner. After he changed, he hung his wet clothes on the line. When he finished, he looked again to her bedroll.

"Wake up, sleepy. Your things are safe."

She didn't respond even though his voice boomed throughout the cave.

"Kate?"

He stepped closer and heard faint whimpering. At once the smile left his face and he dropped to her side. His chest tightened with fear when she turned to him — she'd been crying. Had someone found her? Hurt her? He choked out his next words, dreading the answer.

"What happened?"

"I thought you weren't coming back." Her face crumpled and she burst into tears. "I thought you left me too."

In one fluid motion, Jake pulled her onto his lap and cradled her within his arms.

"I'll *never* leave you. I'm here, and I'll keep you safe as long as we're together." Her cries only intensified and he pulled her close to his chest, all the while murmuring into her hair, "It's all right Katie, I'm here. I'm here."

****

Kate buried her head into Jake's chest and cried harder and longer than she ever had in her life. She cried for the loss of her mother, her home, and all she'd been forced to leave behind. She cried for her father, his brutal death, and the situation it had forced upon her. She cried for Ben. Poor, dear Ben and the painful, agonizing last moments before he'd slipped away, taking with him the final link to her family.

She cried the hardest because Jake was the only one left to hear her cry.

****

As Kate's violent sobs subsided into soft, feeble cries much like those of a kitten, Jake kept rocking her in his arms and whispering in her ear. Part of him wasn't sure what else to do — the other part didn't want to let go.

When her small, even breaths landed softly against his chest, he brushed away her remaining tears, taking care not to disturb her slumber. Firelight shone upon her face as he studied her soft, delicate features. Long, dark eyelashes fanned across her milky white skin, and her full lips held a hint of pink rose. Slender fingers rested against his shirt and her hair spilled over his arm in a glimmering tumble of curls.

She was exquisite, caring, and wrong for him in every way.

Jake closed his eyes and leaned against the cave wall. He'd been hurt before and didn't want it to happen again, but now the possibility lay within his arms. This headstrong, stubborn woman was indeed a splendid distraction from the dullness of the trail. But she'd been born with money and privilege, and neither had ever had a place in his life.

While the storm raged outside, Jake fell asleep with Kate nestled against his chest, enjoying, if only for one night, how wonderful it felt to hold her close.

Chapter Thirty-Four

Wagon Train

Friday, August 18, 1843

Kate woke slowly, her mind drifting through a hazy fog of confusion. The air felt cool against her cheek, yet warmth radiated throughout her body. Her other cheek pressed against something solid — definitely not her pillow. And why couldn't she move?

Slowly, her eyes fluttered open, focusing first on the coals smoldering nearby and then Jake's bedroll. His empty bedroll.

A tangle of blankets wasn't trapping her in place — it was Jake!

Her eyes widened in stunned disbelief. He lay behind her, one arm curled around her waist, his other arm supporting her head. Apparently she'd fallen asleep as he'd comforted her last night. But how did he think that gave him the right to share her bedroll?

And above all, what would he expect tonight?

"Good morning."

Her cheeks flamed as she realized his whispered greeting held no trace of sleepiness. In one quick motion, she grabbed his wrist and pushed his hand aside. Then she kicked her legs free from the blankets, jumped up and hurried to the other side of the cave searching for something, anything, to occupy her trembling hands.

Jake rolled onto his back, stretched his arms over his head with a groan, and then got to his feet. "Did you sleep well?"

She managed a nod.

"Care for coffee?"

She nodded again dumbly, unable to make even one word come out of her mouth. Jake ambled toward the fire ring as if nothing were amiss. Waking up entwined with a woman must not be an unusual experience for him. She, on the other hand, was twenty-two years old, but had rarely spent time alone with a man before this trip.

"Some storm last night, wasn't it?" he asked, crouching before the embers.

Yet another flustered nod.

Thankfully, he quit talking.

They ate a hurried breakfast of bacon and coffee, packed, and then led the horses from the cave.

"We'll have to take it slow," Jake said as they gazed across the land now covered with either glistening mud or shimmering ponds. "The storm wiped away any traces of the wagon train, but I figure they'll want to dry out and probably won't get far."

****

Late in the afternoon Kate slid from her saddle, grateful for a chance to stretch her legs. They'd skipped lunch and

afternoon rest in order to keep moving. Not that she'd minded
— little downtime meant little talking so aside from thanking
him for finding Old Dan, she'd kept quiet.

"Look!" Jake called from the top of a hill he'd walked to
after dismounting. "I found where they held out during the
storm."

She joined him in staring down upon a muddy mixture of
wagon and animal tracks, and the remains of several
campfires.

"Are you sure it isn't an Indian camp?"

Jake shook his head. "Indians don't use wagons, and they
typically return the earth to its natural state before they move
on. It's definitely the wagon train." He glanced from the open
sky to the small canopy of trees over the campsite. "A wagon
isn't dry during a hard rain. They must have had a cold night."

Kate blushed, thinking yet again of how she'd woken in
his arms. How he'd held her firmly against his chest, cradling
her, protecting her. The tickling, thrilling warmth of his breath
on the curve of her neck.

They were on their way again in minutes. Dusk
surrounded them when Jake stopped at the edge of a valley.
She halted Nina alongside him and followed his gaze to a
stretch of land dotted with white tufts less than a mile below.

Wagons!

Overcome with excitement and relief, she turned to Jake.
Instead of sharing in her joy, he stared at the distant canvas
tops with an expression of uncertainty.

"Don't tell me you've changed your mind about traveling
with a train?" she asked, incredulous at the thought.

His hesitation faded into a tense smile. "So, you see the
wagons? Good." He went to his saddlebag, pulled out his
scope, and put it to his eye. "I'll take a closer look and make
sure it's safe."

She waited, her heart pounding. She almost didn't care what these fellow travelers were like. She was so grateful to have caught up in only one day — thus eliminating spending another night alone with Jake.

Kate studied the far-off group. "Why are the wagons in a circle?"

"Protection." He lowered the scope. "Trains are vulnerable to attacks because they're easy to spot. Thieves track them with the intention of stealing animals during the night, so typically cattle, horses, and oxen are held inside the circle."

He stared at the wagons thoughtfully and then brought the scope to his eye again. "With a group that size men will be standing guard, and there'll be plenty more in bedrolls spread out inside the circle. We'll ride in, but be careful. They could be unfriendly — or worse — to strangers."

They mounted up and made their way down the valley. While they rode, Jake pulled his pistol from a saddlebag and slid it into the holster at his left side. A hundred yards from the wagons he pulled his rifle from the scabbard and laid it across his thighs.

Deep within the shadows on their right, a rifle hammer clicked into place.

"Hold it right there!" yelled a gruff voice.

Jake pulled Nickel to a stop and motioned for her to do the same.

"Follow my lead, and be ready to take off if I signal," he whispered, then shouted toward the hidden man. "Can we ride in?"

"Who are you and what do you want?" demanded a second deep voice from a stand of trees on their left.

"We're heading to Oregon," Jake replied. "We've followed you for a couple days trying to catch up, but last night's storm set us back some."

"You've got seven horses," the second voice barked. "Why you two got all those mounts?"

Kate's stomach twisted in fear. Could these men believe them to be thieves?

"We had more riders." Jake grimaced, then continued. "But it's just us two now."

"Stay right there," commanded one of the unknown men. "And keep your hands where I can see 'em."

Chapter Thirty-Five

Men

Kate sat motionless as a man stepped from the shadows on Jake's right, stopping directly in their path. Though his trousers ended in tatters at the knee and his shirt bore enough patches to rival a quilt, the pistol in his hand and hard glint in his eye showed he wasn't a man to tangle with.

Another crept out from the trees on her left, joining the first in blocking their passage. Faded red suspenders held up baggy trousers smeared with grime, yet the rifle he pointed at Jake's chest was polished clean. With a twitch of his lips, he spat a brown stream to the ground before him. Kate shuddered in disgust, then froze as his cruel glare settled upon her.

"I'm askin' again," he said, his tone as cold as his eyes. "Why you got all those horses?"

Beside her, Kate heard the familiar creak of Jake's saddle. A sidelong glance revealed his left hand curling around the handle of his pistol. Heart pounding, she looked back to the men as indecision roiled within — should she speak or keep silent?

"You're getting the same answer," Jake replied, his words clipped and tense. "We lost riders. Now, are we riding in or moving on?"

The suspendered one frowned. Instead of answering he took a few steps closer, craning his neck to peer at the string of horses tethered behind them. With a grunt of satisfaction he lowered his rifle and shifted his attention to her. After a long moment, his fierce scowl changed to one of astonishment.

"Hey Dreason," he called toward the first lookout. "This one's a woman!"

Kate shifted nervously as his thin lips stretched into a lecherous grin. He stared her down again, this time lingering far too long on her hips and chest.

"Nice," he muttered, moving closer. "Real nice."

Her cheeks flamed yet she kept still, mortified at the ruffian's brazenness yet unsure of what to say or do to stop his leering. Jake, however, had no such hesitation.

"That'll do," he commanded in a voice that left no room for uncertainty. The man dared a glance at Jake, then dropped his gaze as his partner approached.

The newest arrival wore his hat low, which obscured his eyes but not the mottled scar down his left cheekbone. A shiver of fear ran up Kate's spine and she forced herself to breathe. Yet, to her surprise, when he pushed up the brim of his hat, he revealed a friendly smile and kind, sympathetic eyes.

"Ma'am, I'm truly sorry about when you first rode up, but you can't be too careful nowadays. Last night we had a fellow lose a team of horses in the confusion from the storm. My name's Matthew Dreason. As for Lee over there—" he nodded toward the second watchman "—I'd like to apologize if he scared you. Thing as pretty as you are sure doesn't deserve to be frightened out of her wits by some stranger. And a stupid one at that."

Kate stifled nervous laughter at the insult. Meanwhile, Lee didn't heed Jake's warning or Matthew's last words — yet again his eyes roved her body from hat to heel.

"I'll be heading out now," Lee said with an impudent smile, oblivious to her lack of interest and Jake's muttered curse of irritation. "Sure was nice to meet you, ma'am."

With a curt nod toward Jake, he disappeared into the stand of trees.

Matthew shook his head with a sigh. "Pay him no mind. He's harmless."

"Thank you," she murmured. Jake said nothing, but apparently felt more at ease — his hand no longer rested on his pistol.

Matthew reached into his pocket and brought out a gold watch. "It's a bit past nine o'clock which means I got a break comin'. I'll take you in and get you settled."

With Jake close behind, Kate followed Matthew from the isolation of a rugged, desolate land and into a whole new world. A noisy world of children milling about the wagons, teasing one another as they tossed a cloth ball among them. A soft world of mothers lovingly cradling young ones in their arms, singing and rocking them to sleep. A dimly-lit world of dwindling fires scattered across the wide enclosure, holding the remains of dinner and heated wash water. A world of clattering dishes, jovial shouts at uncooperative animals, and above all, the togetherness of a group in pursuit of a common goal.

Kate sat in the saddle, so awash in the cacophony of sounds and sights she barely noticed when Jake stopped alongside her. His eyes darted across the circle, silently gauging each wagon and man before settling on her with a look of concern.

"Rough welcome aside, what do you think?" he asked.

"It's... different," she replied, unable to put her feelings into words. It was all so new. So loud. So incredibly lovely.

Jake's smile said he knew exactly what she meant.

Matthew directed them where to put their horses for the night. Soon after, Kate was sitting next to Jake in front of a roaring fire with a mug of fresh coffee in one hand and a plate of beef stew in the other.

She ate quietly, content to watch and listen while Jake and Matthew traded stories about the recent storm. As she looked around at all the wagons, supplies, and bedrolls filled with slumbering travelers, she felt a rising sense of security. Especially with Jake at her side.

Later, after a woman with a welcoming smile had taken their plates away and brushed off Kate's offer to help, Matthew launched into a lengthy, colorful description about a recent celebration the train had held. As he moved on to talk of all the food they'd eaten, Kate hid a jaw-splitting yawn behind the back of her hand. She didn't want to appear rude, but the sleepless night, the excitement of catching the train, and the warm food in her stomach had caught up to her. She concealed yawn after yawn until Matthew noticed her weariness and began glancing around the camp.

"Ma'am, I suppose you could bunk down next to Duncan's wagon for the night. I would wake my wife to set you up with a more proper situation, but she gave birth to our first child three nights ago, and I'd like to let her sleep."

Kate shook her head. "Please, don't wake her. I'm sure it will be fine. Thank you for your hospitality." She stood, picked up her bedroll, and then bent to retrieve her saddlebags.

Matthew sprang to his feet. "Let me carry those. They seem heavy."

She hesitated. While his chivalry reminded her of how men back home had jumped at the chance to do her bidding, she was in the west now. Once Jake returned to Virginia the following spring she'd be on her own — reliant only upon herself, not the goodwill of others. She'd refused Jake's offers of assistance for months, she wasn't about to backslide into helplessness again, especially over something she could easily manage by herself. With a surge of confidence, she waved away Matthew's hand.

"I prefer to carry my own packs, thank you."

His eyes widened, but he obligingly stepped back and pointed toward a blanket strung up between two nearby trees.

"You'll find the privacy and room to change over there."

****

Jake held back a chuckle as Matthew tried assisting Kate with her saddlebags and was subsequently told he wasn't needed. It was a lesson he'd learned long ago. And it appeared he had another lesson coming — judging by the reaction and attention she'd received from Lee earlier, he'd have to get used to men admiring Kate.

Matthew watched her walk toward the blanket, and when she was no longer within earshot he turned to Jake. "Independent little filly, isn't she?"

He nodded in agreement. "She's a tough one, and stubborn to boot."

"Didn't mean to jump in there," Matthew said. "But those bags looked so heavy, and she's so small."

"Don't let her pretty face fool you," Jake said. "She'll cut you in half with her sharp tongue."

"Aren't all women that way?"

"Most I've ever known."

Matthew added a log to the fire. "So you two heading for Oregon Territory?"

Jake nodded.

"We can take you as far as Fort Hall. We're all on our way to California."

"We'd sure appreciate it."

"How long you two been married?"

Jake knew this question was bound to come sooner or later. He'd been dreading it, along with all the subsequent inquiries and lectures that would arise from the answer — it wasn't considered proper for a young, unmarried woman to be alone in the company of a man.

"We're not."

Matthew raised a curious eyebrow, but said nothing. Jake was thankful for the silence. He didn't feel like explaining their situation tonight.

Across the circle, Kate emerged from behind the blanket and laid out her bedroll alongside the wagon Matthew pointed her toward. Once she'd settled in, Jake fetched his own saddlebags.

"Well, I guess she's got the right idea." He paused, glancing at Matthew. "Unless of course you need company on your watch?"

Matthew waved away the offer. "Don't worry about it. I only have another hour to go, and then it's Duncan's time." He tipped his head toward Kate's bedroll. "You'll be wanting to bunk down next to her?"

Jake hesitated. They'd be raising enough eyebrows tomorrow and during the next few weeks. He might as well have one last night by her side.

"That will be fine."

Chapter Thirty-Six

Friendly Strangers

Saturday, August 19, 1843

Kate woke early but stayed tucked inside her bedroll, eyes closed, enjoying the swirl of chaos as the camp came to life. Though the sun had barely shown first light she heard dogs barking, horses stirring, bacon frying, and children wandering about despite their mothers' admonishments to get dressed.

Hearing nearby giggles, Kate peeked out from a corner of her blanket. Three children stood beside Jake's bedroll, studying him as they whispered among themselves.

"Who are they?" asked a bare-chested, bare-footed boy with sun-bleached hair and grubby trousers held up by a frayed rope tied around his waist. He appeared to be about seven years of age.

"Don't know," answered a girl in a faded pink dress. Brown curls spilled from her bonnet and bounced along her shoulders as she rocked from tiptoe to heel. "Wonder where they came from?"

"Pa told me they got here last night," claimed the eldest of the group. The boy was no more than eleven, but spoke with the authority of a child beyond his years — a child well schooled as to the ways of the trail. "They had to sleep outside our wagon so's he could keep an eye on them."

Eager to meet such adorable interlopers, Kate sat up with a smile. "Hello there."

They shrieked in surprise at her greeting and scampered off between the wagons. She heard a chuckle from Jake's bedroll.

"The last boy talking must be Duncan's son," he said then groaned and stretched his arms over his head. "From the way the youngster tells it, we're dangerous scoundrels."

Jake sat up, glanced around the circle, and then looked to her again. "Wagon trains don't have the solitude you're used to. They're louder too," he added with a sleepy smile.

Twenty wagons made up the circumference of the circle. There appeared to be nearly one hundred men, women, and children in the group, with an average of four travelers for each wagon, and around fifteen outriders — those who had a bedroll instead of a wagon, and traveled by horseback. Together they created quite a ruckus preparing for the day. Travelers milled about, poking their heads into wagons and rooting through supply boxes. Pans were laid across freshly stoked fires and the smells of coffee, biscuits, and bacon mixed with the dust hanging in the air.

"It's noisy and full of life." She curled up her legs until her chin rested on her knees and watched the others begin their day. "And I love it."

Father and Ben would have loved it too. Her brother would have enjoyed frolicking with the other children, and from what she could see, her father would have fit right in with the men of the group. Several of them were crowded around a horse, debating the merits of a gelding versus a stallion. Seeing how her father preferred a mare to either, he would have participated in the discussion with gusto.

Kate sighed, wondering if she would ever quit comparing everything she saw and all she experienced to how it could have been if her family had lived.

"We'd better get ready," Jake said. "Each wagon train has a different routine. I'm not sure if this group lingers in the morning or departs after first light, but I know we don't want to hold them up on our first day."

In less than ten minutes their bedrolls and saddlebags were packed and their horses were watered and saddled. When they finished, Jake glanced uneasily around the circle.

"Matthew's expecting my help this morning, but I don't want to leave you unattended."

"I can take care of myself," she insisted with far more confidence than she felt. The thought of wandering amongst a hundred strangers made her stomach quake, but she certainly didn't want Jake to view her as a burden. "I'll find Matthew's wife. Certainly she could use some help."

She glanced over at their saddlebags. While they were strapped on the horses, they were still available to anyone determined enough to pry.

Jake was quick to reassure. "Don't worry. I'll keep a close eye on them, and you."

They parted.

On her way to find Matthew's wife, Kate passed by a harried woman trying to start a fire while minding two children. The younger child, little more than an infant, sat crying in the center of a quilt while a nearby toddler gleefully scooped up handfuls of dirt and threw them into the air. Abandoning her search for the moment, Kate approached.

"Anything I can do to help?"

"Yes, please." The woman swiped a wilted lock of hair from her cheek. "If you could get this fire going while I dress these two, I'd appreciate it."

Kate nodded, bent over the fire, and with a few expertly placed branches had it crackling lively by the time the woman returned with two freshly scrubbed children in tow.

"Thank you," she said with a curt nod.

"It's no trouble at all," Kate replied. "Glad to help."

"Name's Alice." She stared at Kate as if trying to place her face. "I haven't seen you before. When did you come on with us?"

"I'm Kate. I arrived last night. I'm searching for Mrs. Dreason — Matthew's wife. Do you know where I can find her?"

Alice shaded her eyes against the rising sun and pointed toward a willowy blond woman walking nearby.

"There's Ruth. She'll help you." She cupped her hands around her mouth. "Ruth!" Alice shouted before jerking a thumb toward Kate. "She needs to find Bonnie. Can you help her?"

"Sure!" Ruth called cheerfully. She strolled over, bent to tickle Alice's baby — now happily chewing on a blade of grass — and then straightened with a broad grin. "Hello, Alice. How's the day treating you?"

Alice, preoccupied with keeping her toddler from pulling sticks out of the fire, paid her no more attention. Ruth ignored the slight and turned to Kate.

"I'll be happy to show you the way."

And then, before Kate could even introduce herself, Ruth linked her arm through hers and they were off. As they walked amongst the wagons, Ruth called greetings to everyone they passed, all while keeping up a one-sided conversation with Kate.

"I see you're new to this group, but I'm certain we'll become fast friends. Don't worry about Alice. She's a bit snappy in the mornings because she's got too much to do and her lazy husband doesn't help with anything. You'll see for yourself he drinks too much. Did you know Bonnie is married to my brother, Matthew? We're all sharing a wagon. They had to bring me on this trip. I couldn't bear another winter back East. Where you heading to? California?"

Overwhelmed at the speed of Ruth's chattering, Kate's responses ranged from a nod to a smile, with an occasional "oh" thrown in for good measure. She stumbled when Ruth pulled her to an abrupt stop.

"Here we are," Ruth said merrily, banging on the side of a wagon. "Bonnie, we've got a visitor."

A petite woman with flaming red hair emerged from the canvas, balancing a swaddled infant in one arm and a wicker basket filled with linens, plates, and serving spoons in the other. Ruth reached up and carefully relieved Bonnie of the precious bundle. Kate followed suit with the basket. Once her hands were free, Bonnie eased down the short wooden ladder with slow, deliberate steps. When her feet hit ground, she collected her baby and looked to Kate with a tired smile.

"Can I help you?"

Contrite, Ruth turned to Kate. "There I go again. I've talked your ear off without even asking your name, or why you needed Bonnie."

"I'm Kate," she said, shifting the basket from one hand to the other. "We got in last night. Matthew was kind enough to let us join your group, so I figured I'd offer you my help this morning."

"I'm Bonnie, and this is our baby, Grace." Bonnie pressed a soft kiss to the newborn's forehead while humming a soothing tune.

"Can I do anything? My..." Kate paused, deciding what to call Jake. Trail guide sounded too impersonal; he'd become so much more to her. "My friend and I are packed and ready so I have plenty of time."

"Friend, huh?" chided Ruth. "Your friend wouldn't be the handsome man with the charming smile I've seen Matthew with all morning?"

Handsome? Charming?

"I'm not sure," Kate stammered, not wanting to inadvertently insult — or compliment — another man. "We've just arrived, and I don't know what any of the others look like."

"Leave the poor girl alone," Bonnie scolded good-naturedly.

Ruth smiled at her sister-in-law before skipping over to the wagon and up the ladder. After she disappeared through the canvas, Bonnie reached into the basket and pulled out a red-and-white-checkered tablecloth.

"You can set the table if you'd like."

It had been so long since Kate had seen a table, and even though this one was only two wide boards suspended between an upended travel trunk and a water barrel, it was a lovely sight. She unfolded the cloth and snapped it into the air. The crisp material unfurled and then drifted down, concealing the rough wood. When Kate reached into the basket and pulled out a stack of plates, Bonnie broke the silence.

"Ruth's brash, but she's got a heart of gold. She's still young — probably about your age — and with me pushing thirty and Matthew well on his way to forty, we enjoy her impulsiveness."

Kate nodded, yet again unsure of what to say. Bonnie solved the problem by calling for Ruth, who quickly popped her head through the canvas.

"Yes?"

"Bring out two extra plates," Bonnie said, facing Kate with an expectant look. "You two will join us for breakfast, won't you?"

"I'd hate to impose."

Bonnie smiled gently. "I insist."

Ruth emerged from the wagon, her arms loaded with a frying pan, a thick cut of salt pork, and two plates. She hopped to the ground and strode over to the fire.

"Good thing I made extra biscuits this morning," she said with a satisfied nod. "And this pork won't take long to cook. We'll be eating in no time."

Kate felt awkward and intrusive at joining this family, especially since she didn't have much to offer them.

"I could get some coffee if you'd like," she suggested to Ruth, now hustling serving bowls and platters between the wagon and fire ring. "Or perhaps you'd prefer bacon?"

"Oh, Heavens no! We've got more than enough food," Bonnie said from where she now sat cross-legged on the ground, rocking the baby in her arms. "We started with too much, and pick up more at each fort. It's a wonder we've made it this far. Though I would give almost anything for a fresh, juicy peach or pear. I'm so sick of dried."

"I'd settle for anything except beans." Ruth wrinkled her nose. "I can't stand beans."

"I could go the rest of my life without another bite of beans," Kate agreed, then focused on adding forks and tin cups beside the plates. Minutes later, Ruth set a bowl overflowing with high-rise biscuits in the center of the table between the platter of sizzling salt pork and jar of strawberry preserves. As a final touch, Kate added a bouquet of wildflowers she'd picked from beneath the wagon. They both stepped back to check over their work.

"Almost seems civilized, doesn't it?" Ruth asked. Kate nodded her agreement. It was a far cry from balancing a plate on her knees and scooping in hurried forkfuls while Jake mapped out their day. *Civilized indeed.*

"Here come the men," Bonnie called, taking a seat at the table with Grace cradled in her arms. "They're right on time."

Kate turned to see Matthew and Jake crossing the circle. Jake spotted her and his arm shot up in an enthusiastic wave. With Ruth watching, she shyly returned the gesture.

Introductions were made, and then the group sat on the two benches flanking the table. After a moment of prayer, they began eating. Chatter was polite, yet minimal.

"Well, Jake, we'd better get moving," Matthew declared after he'd emptied his plate and taken a final swig of coffee. "The captain of this train doesn't tolerate starting late." He stood and leaned to kiss his wife on the forehead. "Breakfast was great, as always."

"All thanks to your sister and Kate." Bonnie sighed as Grace's fussiness erupted into outright wails. "It sounds like someone else is hungry — again."

Matthew turned to his sister with a worried expression. Ruth patted him on the arm, then sprang up and began gathering the plates.

"Brother, those oxen aren't going to yoke themselves. And Bonnie, you go and take care of my niece," Ruth insisted. "I'll clean up everything after I fetch more water."

Humming a cheerful tune, Ruth deposited the stack of plates into the wash bucket sitting near the fire. She then picked up the kettle and sauntered off toward the river. Bonnie rose and with Matthew's help, climbed into the back of the wagon. Matthew then headed off toward his oxen, leaving Kate alone with Jake at the table.

"I'll be right there," Jake called to Matthew's departing figure before facing her again. "I've spoken with the leaders of the train. They've agreed to take us on — with the expectation

I'll help out during the day where I'm needed. And spend a few hours each night on guard duty."

Kate stared at him as a myriad of feelings washed over her. Spending one day at a fort swarming with other travelers was one thing, but living with them was another. And while she was delighted at their acceptance into the train, she quickly realized what Jake's obligations meant for the remainder of their trip. In essence, she'd be on her own and surrounded by strangers. Friendly strangers, yes, but strangers all the same.

Unwilling to share her rising anxiety, she gave him a weak smile. As usual, he saw right through her bravado.

"I'll still be around for anything you might need," he said, giving her arm a reassuring squeeze. "And I'll always watch over you." His hand — warm, powerful, yet still so gentle — lingered before slowly pulling away. "Are you planning on riding today?"

"I don't know," she replied. "Ruth made mention about getting to know each other. Perhaps I'll be with her."

"Very well. I'll tie the horses to the Dreasons' wagon." He stood, put his hat on, and walked a few steps before turning back. "See you tonight."

Once Jake disappeared into the chaos, she rose and made short work of cleaning the breakfast dishes, dumping the last drops of wash water over the fire, folding the tablecloth, and repacking the wicker basket. She brought the basket to Bonnie, along with the remaining pans and supplies. Jake returned, horses in tow, and she helped tether them, minus Nickel, to the wagon.

After he strode off again Kate considered dismantling the table, but since she hadn't a clue where, or how, the boards, trunk, and water barrel should be stored, she dismissed the idea. She crouched before the fire ring and began poking at the watery ashes, unsure of what to do next. Ruth was nowhere to be seen and she didn't want to bother Bonnie again.

Matthew arrived, and in a matter of minutes he'd hoisted and secured the pieces of their makeshift table onto the wagon. With a tip of his hat, he climbed into the driver's seat and took up the reins.

Then, with a guttural shout from the captain, the train came alive.

Wagons, livestock, riders, and walkers began a lumbering gait toward the horizon, eventually thinning into a winding line. The sounds of wheels creaking, animals grunting, and canvas flapping in the wind all blended together, creating the symphony of a wagon train.

Kate walked alone, overwhelmed and wishing for a familiar face. She found one in Nina — perhaps she would ride today after all.

As she untied her horse, Ruth rushed around the corner of the wagon.

"I'm so sorry I didn't get back in time! I had to use the privacy and then learned Alice's oldest child had wandered off, so I helped with the search. We found her though, sitting right in the middle of a patch of berries, stuffing her face. Thank goodness they weren't poisonous! By the time I got back we were moving." She glanced at Nina's reins in Kate's hand. "Walk with me instead?"

"Don't you want to ride in the wagon?" Kate asked, unsure of their routine.

"No! Too slow, and besides I'd much rather get in all the sunshine and fresh air. Bonnie had to ride back there for the past two months and now she's with the baby, so I'm glad to have someone to walk with. It gets boring after a time."

Kate retied Nina.

Ruth pulled her bonnet from her head and swung it nimbly from her fingertips, chattering on about various members of the train. Kate stayed silent, content to listen. They walked for over an hour before Ruth caved to curiosity.

"I promised Bonnie I wouldn't," she said with a roll of her eyes, "but I have to ask. Why are you wearing men's clothes?"

Kate couldn't help but laugh. "Everything I brought was impractical, so I bought these at Laramie. Of course, I'll go back to skirts when I get to Oregon Territory."

"It doesn't sound half bad." Ruth felt the leg of Kate's trousers, thoughtfully rolling the material between her fingertips. She then motioned to her own faded calico dress. "I can't believe how much time I've wasted mending this ragged thing."

Kate shrugged. "Sewing isn't my strong suit, which is another reason for the clothes I have now."

With Ruth at her side and other women joining them throughout the day, Kate continued walking alongside the wagons. Their conversations flowed easily, especially with all they had in common. Each had faced and survived the hardships of the trail.

****

Jake spent his morning keeping a watchful eye out for Kate while undertaking a variety of duties. With Matthew Dreason usually not far from his side, he checked on a rattling wagon wheel, brought back a runaway horse, and helped secure a loose wagon cover. While not strenuous, the work — coupled with constant dismounting and mounting — demanded much more than his past months of watching for danger from the comfort of a saddle. By the time the captain called a stop for lunch early in the afternoon, a dull ache plagued his left leg and his temple.

He saw Kate eating with the Dreason girls, but only had time to wave at her as he and Matthew headed to assess an ox they'd seen limping into camp. It wasn't until later in the night while they cared for their horses that he was able to speak with her.

"So, how was your first day?" he asked while they brushed Nickel.

"Wonderful," she replied, her face shining with such blissful joy it almost made him forget the pain throbbing throughout his leg. Almost.

"The women are nice, and Matthew's sister, Ruth, is quite lively. In fact, I was invited to sleep in the Dreasons' wagon tonight with her and Bonnie. Do you mind?" When he didn't answer, she stopped brushing and studied him, her happiness fading into concern. "Is something wrong?"

Oh, how he'd missed her today! He'd missed her companionship, her enthusiasm, and most of all her smile. But seeing her delight at being around others, he realized the soreness in his leg would eventually fade — he'd willingly work until he collapsed from exhaustion if it meant keeping them members of this train.

"No, not at all. I've got night watch with Matthew, so it's good you'll have their company. Besides," he added with a forced laugh, "it's not as though you'd want to be sleeping in the dirt beside me again."

****

Hidden behind the blankets of the latest privacy, Kate held her threadbare dress in one hand and the trousers she'd bought at Laramie in the other.

Clawing her way out of the gilded cage she, and all women, were thrust into from birth had been a hard-won fight, so why was she retreating now? The wide-eyed stares as she walked by? The whispered comments behind cupped hands?

No. Yes. Maybe.

Back home she'd eschewed society women and all they stood for. She'd hated her aunt's teachings, shunned frivolous parties, and detested the vicious gossip-fests others had thrived upon. However, deep down, she'd always loved dressing the part.

As her eyes flitted between the vastly different clothes clutched in her hands, she ultimately decided to accept with grace that even on the desolate trail, propriety still won over comfort.

Resolute, Kate folded her trousers and placed them into her saddlebag. She removed her shirt and vest and tucked them away too before slipping into her wrinkled dress. Her father's hat, however, stayed firmly in place.

After gathering up her saddlebag, she crossed the circle and knocked lightly on the Dreasons' wagon. Ruth popped her head out from the canvas.

"Hello there. Come in!" Ruth said, pulling the material aside and holding out her hand. Silently cursing the skirt tangling around her ankles, Kate climbed the short stepladder and slipped inside.

A bed littered with blankets, pillows, and a wicker basket of linens spanned the width across the back. Just past the end of the bed, on the left side, was an oak dresser with the top drawer missing. The space was filled with a frying pan and a sack of coffee. A wooden rocking chair nestled in the front right corner. Tools, bags of flour and other foodstuffs, and an assortment of kitchen supplies were piled beneath the access to the wagon seat. An oil lamp sat atop the dresser and clothing hung from nearly every bow.

Ruth lounged on the end of the bed while Bonnie sat in the rocker with the baby in her arms. As Kate settled herself cross-legged upon the opposite corner of the bed, Ruth began fussing over her.

"This will be so much fun! We've finished arranging things. You'll sleep on the bed with Bonnie and I'll be on the floor — don't step on me if you get up."

"Oh no," Kate said, dismayed at the thought. "I wouldn't dream of taking your place. The floor will be fine."

"Don't worry," Ruth paused with a playful glint in her eye. "The bed is lumpy. Besides, Bonnie snores."

"I do not!" Bonnie protested.

"Yes, you do," Ruth said, bringing up a hand to hide a giggle.

"I most certainly do not." Bonnie's tone was haughty, but a twitch of her lips showed her displeasure as feigned.

"How's it going in there, ladies?" Matthew's voice rumbling through the canvas sent Ruth into a fit of giggles. Bonnie shook her head in amusement, first at her sister-in-law, and then to Kate.

"Remember," continued Matthew, "I want you to let me know if you need anything. Anything at all."

"We're fine," Bonnie replied, now fighting back a snicker of her own.

"Oh, and one last thing?"

"Yes?"

"Honey, you *do* snore."

Ruth and Bonnie erupted in peals of laughter. Kate joined in, unable to keep a straight face amidst such high spirits. Matthew departed, and the gaiety continued as they readied for bed. By the time Grace was snuggled into the blanket-lined missing drawer and the lamp was blown out for the evening, Kate felt a kinship with the two women. Their easy banter reminded her of lazy afternoons with Marie Ann, where no matter the topic their conversations had inevitably included giggles.

When the wagon quieted, Kate learned Bonnie did in fact, snore. Though only softly, it was enough to keep her awake.

That, and thoughts of how the feather bed complete with sheets, quilt, and a pillow was a poor comparison to sleeping in Jake's arms.

****

Jake walked along the train's outer perimeter with Matthew until long past dusk, feeling a strange mixture of relief and loneliness each time they passed the Dreasons' wagon. Once they were certain all horses, oxen, and livestock were secure for the night, they headed for the Dreasons' campfire. Their responsibility for the next several hours was to handle any situations arising within the circle — four teams of watchmen stood guard beyond the camp.

In the wagon behind him, Kate and the two women talked and laughed for a time, but as the night progressed their sounds tapered off.

"So what brings you out here?" he asked Matthew after the camp had long since gone quiet.

"My sister has trouble breathing in damp weather. A year ago her doctor said she would eventually succumb unless we got her to a dry climate. California is warm and Bonnie was willing, so here we are."

Jake nodded, not wanting to pry into specifics. Instead, he laid out his pistol and rifle and began giving each a thorough cleaning.

"We've had a fairly easy go of it so far," Matthew said. "I'm partial to oxen myself, seein's how well they shoulder the burden of a wagon. Not a bad herd of horseflesh you've got for yourselves — though I'm thinking it's a bit much for two riders?"

Matthew spoke casually, but Jake understood the implied questions. He and Kate weren't married, so why were they traveling alone? And where was their wagon?

It was only a matter of time before such inquiries were raised. Wagon trains were notoriously full of tall tales and innuendo, and their situation was a prime target for finger pointing. No matter the cause, others would consider an unmarried woman alone with a man highly indecent.

"I hired on as trail guide for Kate's family. Six weeks ago we suffered a horrible accident — the wagon overturned, killing her father and four oxen. We abandoned the destroyed wagon and nearly everything else and traded in the remaining team of oxen for packhorses at Fort Laramie." Jake paused, unable to speak through the sudden tightness in his throat.

"You said 'Kate's family'." Matthew frowned. "What about the others?"

"Her mother died years ago. Her younger brother took sick soon after we left the fort." Jake swallowed hard. "We lost him two weeks ago. It's just us now."

Matthew shook his head sympathetically. "Rough."

Jake crouched before the dwindling fire, using the cover of tossing on a log to dissuade further questions. As the flames darkened, then consumed the once unsullied wood, a grim realization hit him hard.

If he wasn't careful, Kate's reputation would end up just as charred and broken.

Chapter Thirty-Seven

Preparations

Thursday, August 31, 1843

After a late dinner, Kate stood beside Ruth in the wagon circle. They and the hundred other travelers were waiting for Jeffery, their captain, to speak. All day the train had buzzed with anticipation over the promise of a special announcement rumored to be made that evening. Excitement rippled through the crowd as a lanky, rugged man with a green felt hat hopped up onto the trunk of a fallen tree.

"I know I've pushed you hard these past few weeks, but as a result we've got time for a reward." Captain Jeffery waited for the camp to quiet again. "Tomorrow we'll stop at Soda Springs. Saturday we'll rest during the day, and then we'll have us a celebration late into the night." Cheers erupted and men's hats filled the air, yet Kate didn't join in their enthusiasm. Arrival at the springs meant their separation point, Fort Hall, was soon to come. Leaving the security of the group and the deepening friendships would be difficult.

Over the past two weeks Kate had become acquainted with many of the families, but she'd spent nearly every moment with Ruth and Bonnie. Jake continued his duties with the men, and the only time she spoke with him was over meals.

Kate had, however, seen more than enough of Lee, the lewd watchman she'd encountered the night she and Jake had joined the train. He'd since paired his forwardness with a fondness for riding in close proximity to where Kate walked during the day.

Yet, though the mere sight of him was enough to make her cringe, she never felt truly threatened. Not because Matthew had deemed him harmless, but because Jake still watched over her. He'd shown an uncanny ability at appearing the instant Lee did and held no reservations on rousting him away with a stern glare or harsh words.

As the captain stepped down, members of the train dispersed, still lively with talk of the celebration. Children were dispatched to hunt for berries while the women gathered, busily making plans for the food they would prepare over the next two days. Even though supplies were dwindling, there was enough sugar, flour, soda, and baking powder for pies and bread. Meanwhile, the men discussed strategies for a group hunt.

As everyone readied for bed, the air still crackled with energy and anticipation. The Dreasons' wagon was no exception.

"Oh, Kate, it will be grand!" Ruth said, her eyes shining with delight as she bounced in the seat of the rocking chair. "Our last celebration we had a bonfire, the men roasted a side of beef all day, and we all danced until the wee hours of the night. I can hardly wait to hear the sounds of the fiddle and banjo again."

"I'll just be grateful for the added rest," Bonnie said. "Being on the move day after day is tiring." She lay upon the bed, the baby cozy against her chest. Both had done well over the past weeks — Bonnie's strength was returning, and Grace nursed mightily and slept for hours at a time.

Kate found herself caught up in their excitement until a glance down at her ragged excuse for a dress sobered her smile. As Ruth and Bonnie chattered on, she tried smoothing out the numerous wrinkles in the skirt, but quickly realized the futility. The folds were long since permanent. The same fate awaited the two dresses she'd saved. They'd been stuffed into the bottom of her saddlebag for so long it would take hours to iron one properly, if she had an iron.

It couldn't be helped.

****

Saturday, September 2, 1843

That afternoon Kate volunteered with Ruth and Bonnie to set up the long table they'd use to hold the food. As she and Bonnie discussed where to place the silverware and plates, Ruth stalked over from the wagon and dropped a stack of tablecloths onto the table with a thump.

"Bonnie, I've held my tongue for two weeks, but I won't go along with this absurdity any longer. I'm asking her!"

"What?" Kate asked, curious as to what could be bothering her so.

Ignoring Bonnie's warning glare, Ruth turned to Kate. "How is it you're out here alone, with only an unmarried man accompanying you?" She leaned closer and whispered, "Did you two run away together?"

Kate's fingers tightened around the cluster of spoons and forks in her hand. Though she wasn't surprised in the least by

Ruth's bluntness, her relationship with Jake was a subject she had thus far managed to avoid and wasn't eager to discuss.

"Ruth, I told you not to bring it up!" scolded Bonnie. "When will you learn to keep your mouth shut?"

"I just wondered," Ruth replied weakly, her eyes wide with shock at her sister-in-law's vehement tone.

"I tell you things for a good reason," Bonnie snapped, her cheeks flushed in anger. "Next time, listen to me."

With a sigh, Bonnie swung around to face Kate. "Matthew told me." She paused, her eyes filling with sympathy and tears. "Sweetie, you don't have to explain anything to us."

No, she didn't.

But Ruth's questions were valid, and for the first time Kate realized the assumptions others would make about her and Jake. Assumptions she would need to correct. And if she couldn't explain what had happened to these two understanding women, how would she explain it to strangers once they reached Oregon?

Kate focused on Ruth's uneasy gaze. "Jake and I didn't run away together. My father hired him to guide our way to Oregon."

"Where is your father?" Ruth frowned in confusion. "How come he didn't come out with you?"

Kate took a deep breath and the words flew from her mouth in short bursts. "My father died on the trail. So did my younger brother. It's just Jake and me now."

Ruth gasped and a hand flew to her mouth. "Oh! How horrible!"

Kate nodded, striving for calm even as her eyes roamed the area, searching for an escape from further questions. "I see we're low on water. I'll go."

Grabbing the empty bucket, she bounded out of camp. As she stumbled along the path to the river, Kate wept for the first time since joining the wagon train. She'd been so busy and had so much fun there hadn't been time to dwell on the loss of her family. But with one question, all her pain surfaced again.

By the time she reached the riverbed she'd regained her composure and wiped away the remaining tears. Dwelling on the past accomplished nothing, especially when there was work to be done.

Kate crouched and dipped her bucket into the river. As the water cascaded inside she closed her eyes, enjoying the warm sun against her face and the water swirling against her palm.

"Hello there."

Her eyes flew open at the familiar deep voice. Jake!

She saw him lounging upon a nearby boulder; hat off, muscular legs stretched out and crossed at the ankle, unbuttoned shirt revealing his broad, tanned chest.

"What are you doing?" she asked, focusing again on the river as she willed her voice not to betray her racing heart. What was wrong with her?

"Catching up on my sleep," he replied. "I had watch duty last night."

"I'm getting water."

"So I see," he said smartly, but when she faced him again he sat up so fast his hat fell to the ground. Instantly his expression changed from teasing to one of concern. "You've been crying. Is that fool Lee bothering you again?"

"No," she murmured, shaking her head.

"Remember what I told you when your feet were hurt? If you've got a problem, you can always tell me."

With a sigh, she sat on a rock and absently stirred pebbles with the toe of her boot. "I was thinking of Father and Ben. Ruth asked about you, and their deaths came up. I didn't want to go into details," she finished with a shrug. "So here I am."

"I'm glad," he said softly. "You're great company."

The next few minutes passed in inane chatter while Kate summoned the courage to ask the question that had been on her mind since Captain Jeffery's announcement of the celebration.

"Will you be there tonight?"

Jake cocked his head as a playful smirk danced across his lips. "Depends."

"On?" She fidgeted with the handle of the bucket, finding herself strangely nervous for his answer. Could he have volunteered for night watch?

"If you'll save me a dance."

Jake's confident reply sent Kate's breath into her throat, and she could only nod before hoisting up the bucket and scurrying off to camp. Upon her return, she didn't see Bonnie or Ruth so she grabbed a tablecloth from the stack and spread it over the long table. When she reached for another cloth, she saw Ruth marching toward her, undeterred by several of the travelers who called her by name. Eyes bright with unshed tears, she stopped before Kate and pulled her into a fierce hug.

"I'm so sorry," Ruth whispered in her ear. "I didn't mean to pry, and I certainly didn't mean to make you upset. Please, forgive me."

Kate returned the embrace, happy to have such an understanding friend. "Of course."

Ruth stepped back, clapping her hands. "Time to get ready!" She plucked a limp curl from Kate's shoulder and twirled it around her finger thoughtfully. "You know, if you take off your hat we can fix your hair up real pretty. And Bonnie has a dress that will fit you perfectly."

Kate thought about protesting, about insisting Bonnie shouldn't be bothered with such trivial matters when she had the chance to rest, about declaring such effort wouldn't be worth the hassle. Then, she thought of the man she'd promised a dance.

"It sounds lovely."

They strode off arm in arm, whispers abundant between them. As they neared the Dreasons' wagon, Ruth abruptly spun and headed for the nearby woods.

"I have a surprise. Follow me."

"What's with you?" Kate laughed as she stumbled along beside the determined woman. "You're bouncing along so fast I can barely keep up."

"You'll see." Ruth giggled as she stopped before a sheet strung between two trees.

"What is this?" Kate asked.

Ruth ignored her. "Bonnie, she's here!"

Bonnie's fingertips came into view. Seconds later the sheet was pulled aside to reveal the blanketed enclosure held a metal bathtub filled to the rim. Purple and gold flower petals drifted through the steam rolling off the water. A brush and comb rested upon a stool beside the bath, and a towel hung alongside a white satin robe over a nearby tree branch.

Kate gasped in delight. "Is this for me?"

"Yes," they chimed together.

"We took ours early this morning while you were tending to your horses," added Ruth.

Bonnie handed Kate a small rectangular box. "I save this for special occasions, and if this isn't one, I don't know what is."

Kate eagerly fumbled the flaps of the box open. To her astonishment, a bar of store-bought soap slipped out. Such a luxury was unheard of on the trail; homemade was the norm. She put the soap to her nose, inhaled deeply, and nearly swooned as the clean scent of lemon verbena washed over her.

"I declare, this may be the best thing I've smelled in all my life."

"Enjoy this, and come back to the wagon when you're done," Bonnie said before slipping through the sheet.

Ruth whispered loudly, "Yes, do hurry so we can get you all prettied up for him."

Kate's chin went up a notch, as did an amused eyebrow.

"Ruth!" Bonnie's scolding shout resonated through the curtain. Giggling, Ruth skipped from the enclosure, pulling the sheet closed as she left.

Kate couldn't get her dress off quick enough. She stepped into the tub and sank down through the sultry waves and into utter and complete luxury. Her daily baths back home were no comparison. There she hadn't gone weeks without a decent washing, hadn't spent months covered in grime. She soaked until her fingertips were wrinkled, scrubbed her skin until it was creamy white, and then leaned her head back against the side of the tub.

Time to relax and enjoy this moment.

"How's it going in there?" Ruth called out from the other side of the curtain.

"Perfection," Kate replied, delighted beyond all reason.

Ruth poked her head in and held up a steaming kettle. "I came to take your clothes, add water, and bring a rosemary rinse for your hair."

After Ruth left, Kate began washing her hair. What had been a nightmarish chore for the past four months was now a luxury with soap, warmth, and privacy. When her hair was clean, she soaked a while more and then emerged from the tub. She patted herself dry with the towel, donned the robe, and headed for the Dreasons' wagon.

Once inside, she settled herself on the bed. Ruth sat in the rocker, mirror in hand, inspecting her hair, now pulled into a sleek up-do. Bonnie laid the sleeping baby into her drawer-bed and then began a noisy, disruptive search through two large trunks. As usual, Grace slept through their latest ruckus.

"The dress is here somewhere," Bonnie said, now headfirst into the first trunk. Dresses and linens flew onto the floor as she pawed through the contents. "I just can't remember where I packed it."

"You're making a mess," chided Ruth as she pulled two hairpins from her hair, allowing it to fall free. So much for the up-do. "She can wear one of mine."

"You're too tall," Bonnie scoffed, diving into the second trunk. With a crow of triumph she sat up, blew a lock of hair from her forehead, and held a dress aloft for inspection. "This will fit, won't it?"

"Oh, yes. It's beautiful!" Kate gushed. The dress was a brilliant emerald green with exquisite black beading around the ends of the capped sleeves and across the hemline. She reached out to touch the silk — so different from the grungy calico she'd worn the past weeks.

Cautiously, she stepped into the fine dress. Once Ruth finished securing the hooks down the back, Kate looked down with a sigh. She'd lost so much weight on the trail. Her normally trim waist was now even smaller. At least she needn't worry about corsets. The neckline however, was a concern. The material fit snugly across the curves of Kate's chest and dipped far lower than anything she'd ever worn. Bonnie noticed her blush and secured a black velvet ribbon around Kate's neck.

"This will draw attention upward," she said quietly. Then, with a knowing smile, she bent to the closest trunk and plucked out a shawl. "Or, this will prevent it entirely."

Once they were dressed, they took turns doing each other's hair. Ruth and Bonnie brushed Kate's until it shone and wove ribbons within the mass of curls they'd produced from heating a small steel rod over the flame of a candle, and then wrapping sections of hair around it until it cooled.

Bonnie had sent one of the children out earlier to find them a collection of wildflowers, which they each now wore in their hair. None had shoes appropriate for a fancy affair, but it couldn't be helped. They would have to conceal their sturdy traveling ones beneath their skirts.

"I can't believe the baby slept through the commotion of us getting ready," Bonnie said. She carefully tucked Grace into a Moses basket and picked up the handles. "Are we ready?"

"Wait, I forgot one last thing." Ruth rummaged through her own trunk and emerged holding a perfume bottle. After carefully dabbing each of their wrists with the scented treasure, Ruth beamed with joy.

"Now we're ready," she declared.

Weaving through the travelers, they made their way from the circle of wagons to the clearing the men had created by chopping down trees earlier in the day. The freshly cut trunks formed a seating ring around the celebration area. The bonfire was over five feet tall and promised to last the evening. Food had been set out while Kate and the women were getting ready. Men and children alike hovered near the table, waiting for the signal from Captain Jeffery to eat. In the meantime, music and dancing were already well underway.

Kate stood quietly, only partially listening to Ruth's chatter as her eyes searched for the one thing missing from the beginning celebration.

Where was Jake?

Chapter Thirty-Eight

Lingering Thoughts

Jake walked through the quiet wagon circle, his saddlebag clutched in his hand and a fresh shirt slung over his shoulder. He was heading to the river for a dip and a scrub before he joined the growing celebration in the nearby logged-off clearing. As he strolled by, festive music and the smell of roasting meat lured him closer. He stood in a group of outlying trees, content to watch the other travelers.

Then he saw Kate.

As she stepped into the clearing, the sun was taking leave of the sky and the fading light only accentuated her beautiful features. Her hair, normally hidden beneath her father's hat, now tumbled down her back, adorned with flowers and ribbons. Her dress revealed silken shoulders and accentuated every curve.

Jake's saddlebag slipped from his fingers and fell to the ground with a thud as he stared, mesmerized by the woman who had been his sole companion for nearly a month, and who he'd fought so hard against bringing at all.

Kate rose up on tiptoe and scanned the crowd swarming around her. Who was she searching for? His eyes swept across the throng of people, but he saw no one heading her way.

Before long, Matthew's sister grabbed Kate's hand. Together they headed to the edge of the clearing and claimed their place on a tree trunk to watch the festivities. Jake heard rustling and spun to see Matthew heading toward him, frowning and scratching his jaw.

"Problem?" Jake asked.

"Our milk cow's limping. I checked her fetlock for a sprain or a bowed tendon and found neither, so I'm figuring it's an abscess. I'd like to put a poultice on, but she's fighting me pretty hard. You up for helping?"

Jake glanced at Kate, now clapping her hands and tapping her foot along to the rhythm of the music. With a sigh of regret, he tore his gaze away and focused on Matthew.

"Of course."

"Don't worry," Matthew said with a grin. "We'll get you back to that pretty lady."

A full hour passed before Jake was able to wash, don a clean shirt, and return to the celebration, now in full swing. Children ran underfoot with squeals of laughter, the food table had been picked over, and the music and bonfire roared.

The clearing thumped with rhythmic footsteps as circles of travelers stepped in unison to the caller's shouted directions. Jake hopped onto the stump of a fallen tree and quickly spotted Kate whirling around the circle. Her eyes snapped and sparkled against the last rich colors of sunset.

After a word with the caller and musicians, he wove his way through the swirling crush of women's skirts. He waited, timed his steps, and within seconds Kate spun into his waiting arms with a gasp of pleasure.

He lowered his lips to her ear. "I've come for my dance."

As per his instructions, the beginning notes of a waltz floated across the circle — he had no intention of sharing her for their first dance together. While holding her closer than required, he led her through the intricate series of gliding spins across the trodden grass. After only a few steps, his eyebrows raised in astonishment — instead of the stiff corset he'd expected, he felt the warmth of her skin as her torso twisted against his palm.

"Where have you been?" Kate asked once he'd regained his rhythm.

"Helping Matthew. You look pretty tonight." In the waning light he saw her blush, adding a rosy glow to her beauty.

"Thank you," she murmured, shyly dipping her head. "I'm glad you made it back."

"I wouldn't miss it for the world," he said, all the while reveling in her scent as he guided her around the clearing, in how she trembled beneath his touch as he slid his hand around the curve of her waist, and above all, in how fulfilled he felt as he held her again.

At Kate's gasp, Jake turned to see Lee heading toward them, a lascivious smirk plastered across his face. Lee's behavior toward Kate had infuriated him from their first night with the train, but he vowed not to make a scene. Not much of one anyway.

Lee halted before them, but only had eyes for Kate. "Let's dance."

"I'm already with my partner," she replied, her tone pleasant but firm.

"Him?" Lee scoffed, jerking his head in Jake's direction. His lips pulled into a cruel sneer. "Seems you didn't hear me. I wanna dance with you."

In a gesture well familiar to Jake, Kate raised her chin a notch. "No."

Lee's eyes narrowed and he reached for Kate's arm.

Jake was faster. Three quick punches — one to his nose, one to his gut, and a final one to his jaw — convinced Lee of his error in judgment. He slithered to the ground with a whimper, but Jake helped him to his feet. By his hair. Then, with one hand gripping the back of Lee's collar and the other clutching a fistful of shirt, Jake escorted the blubbering cur across the clearing and deposited him in a heap before the captain and two lieutenants.

After washing his hands and adjusting his shirt, he searched for Kate. He found her leaning against a tree, watching the dancers.

"Lee won't bother you again."

To his surprise, she chuckled. "After that little incident, you're bound to be more the talk of the camp than you already are."

He frowned. "What do you mean?"

"Oh, come now." She shot him a chiding look. "From bringing in fresh meat for three days in a row to finding a lost child, you've certainly earned your reputation as an excellent guide."

"I suppose you think you're clever?" He raised an eyebrow. "How about this?"

Before she could protest, he caught her by the waist and spun her around at a maddening pace. To his amusement, Kate could barely keep up. She collapsed against him, breathless from exertion and laughter.

"You win!" she conceded, her eyes sparkling with delight.

Without warning, the music slowed. He shifted his feet nervously at the change, unsure if she'd be willing or if she'd prefer to sit it out.

She was willing.

His breath caught as she ran her hand up the contours of his arm and then cupped his shoulder. He closed one palm around hers, and splayed the other across the small of her back, imperceptibly pulling her closer. Their eyes locked, and as they began their first steps he couldn't help but to wonder things he had no business even considering.

If he tunneled his hands deep into her hair, would it feel like silk against his fingers? How would she react if he pressed his cheek to hers, and whispered his deepest thoughts into the scented curve of her neck? What would it feel like to succumb to his rampant desire to kiss her full lips now parted so seductively?

Far too soon, a closing note of music floated over the clearing and the musicians called for a break. Dancers split off and milled around them as he and Kate stood still, hands connected.

Their fingertips lingered, then parted.

As night settled in the musicians quit playing, the dancing subsided, and the crowd thinned as the little ones were put to bed, all the while protesting weakly against the tentacles of sleep. Soon it was just the adults and the hum of many conversations.

Jake took a seat directly across the fire from Kate, which made it easy to sneak glances her way. She and Ruth sat on one of the many benches surrounding the dwindling fire and listened as Captain Jeffery kept everyone amused with his tales of past travels, including one about a new night watchman who'd gotten spooked by the shadow of a tree. Kate laughed hysterically when the stories got taller and more unbelievable.

After a few hours, the night air took its toll. Kate yawned then laughed to see Ruth doing the same. They stifled more for the better part of an hour before giving in to their sleepiness.

"Good night everyone," Ruth called as she and Kate stood up, a shawl now wrapped around them. Kate glanced his way with a shy smile and then shuffled off toward the wagons with Ruth glued to her side.

Without a word, Jake stood and wound his way through the crowd. He followed the duo to the Dreasons' wagon and watched until they disappeared beneath the canvas. Then he returned to the bonfire and joined Matthew, who sat with his tobacco box and pipe in his lap.

"Seems like Bonnie had the right idea to retire hours ago," Matthew said, taking a pinch of tobacco and pressing it firmly into the bowl of his pipe. "Getting up and going tomorrow will be rough after such a late night."

Matthew set the box on the ground and rose. "I like to walk when I smoke. Care to join me?"

Jake nodded in agreement. From force of habit due to night watch duty, they began walking the circumference of the wagon circle while Matthew lit his pipe. After several draws and a contented sigh, he spoke.

"Kate's mighty pretty and sure to be snatched up quick, what with the shortage of women out here."

"I can't say you're wrong."

"Got any designs on marrying her?"

"She wouldn't have me," muttered Jake. "I was horrible to her when we were first starting out."

He grimaced, recalling the speech he'd given Kate their first week of the journey. If only he hadn't tried to scare her with his talk of all the things that could go wrong! At the time he'd been trying to get her to go home, but now, to his shame and regret, the worst of what he'd said had come true. The terror in her eyes as she'd held her dead brother would haunt him forever.

"I could buy Kate a mansion, and it wouldn't come close to making up for how I treated her and what I said to her the first month of the trip."

"Never underestimate a woman's power to surprise a man," Matthew said with a wry smile. "Though, you better act fast. Once you two hit Oregon there'll be plenty of men waiting, and willing, to snatch her away from you."

"I know," Jake said. As he'd held Kate tonight, he couldn't help but think what he'd desired in a woman, a partner, and a lover, was right in his arms.

Matthew tapped the ashes from his pipe. "You're probably worrying over nothing. I saw the passion between you two tonight plain as the nose on my face."

Matthew's glib words brought Jake crashing down to reality.

What was he doing? He was supposed to be watching over Kate, not taking advantage of a naive woman who was all alone in the world — thanks to him.

****

"Kate, are you asleep?" Ruth whispered loudly from the floor of the wagon.

"No," Kate whispered back. She'd been dozing for the past hour. "It's hard to sleep after all the excitement."

"Did he kiss you tonight?" asked Ruth.

"Did who kiss me?"

"Jake, silly!" Bonnie's sleepy voice drifted out from under her pillow. "Did he?"

"Did he what?"

"Kiss you!" Ruth and Bonnie chimed together.

"No, and I don't want him to either. It would confuse everything."

Ruth sat up and lit a candle. "I saw the way he was eyeing you tonight, especially by the bonfire. And if I'm not mistaken, you were looking back as well."

"I was not!" Kate exclaimed, shaking her head for emphasis.

"You were too." Ruth got to her knees, leaned on the bed, and stared at Kate. "You're blushing."

"Am not."

"Yes, you are," Ruth said. "Bonnie, you better check. Kate's face is so red she might be ill."

Bonnie raised her tousled head and peered at her sister-in-law. "You're one to talk. What about Frank? He doesn't take his eyes off you."

"Frank?" Ruth laughed. "He doesn't know what marriage means. He just wants a wife to keep his house and bear his children. I want those things too, but if I can't have a marriage with love and respect like you have with Matthew, I'd rather stay alone."

"Me too," Kate agreed. Her Aunt Victoria had taught the art of putting on simpering ways to catch a husband, but Kate knew to do so would earn her a man who wanted only a pretty toy, not an equal. Crandall had been safe and predictable, but there had always been one nagging problem — the promise.

Long ago she'd promised her mother to never sink to acting coy and unintelligent to attract a man. Any man that would fall for such foolishness, or desire a woman of such nature, had no place in her life.

"What about you, Kate?" Ruth asked. "What do you want in a husband?"

Kate picked at the lace trim on the sleeve of her nightgown. She'd always been a bad liar and two realizations had come to her tonight — she hadn't wanted to leave Jake's arms after their last dance, and she didn't want him to leave her next spring.

"Okay, we'll stop talking about this." Bonnie silenced Ruth with a look. "In all seriousness, Kate, what are you going to do once you get to Oregon?"

"Run the store my father bought. After a few years, I hope to sell it and put the profits into a starting a horse ranch. It was my father's dream for our family and his whole reason for coming out here. Now, I'm going to see to it his dream becomes a reality."

Both abandoned all teasing.

"Is Jake going to help you?" asked Ruth.

"No. After we get to Oregon he's going back East."

"What for?"

"He makes his living guiding people on the trail. So he'll head out again next spring."

Chapter Thirty-Nine

Separation

Tuesday, September 5, 1843

The days following the celebration were the toughest since Kate had joined the train. Their captain settled for nothing less than twenty miles per day. While the majority of the group was agreeable and willing, a few began grumbling about the trail and the hours of endless travel.

Kate noticed most of the complaints came from Ralph. He was married to Alice, the woman Kate had started a fire for the first morning on the wagon train. When the wagons circled for the night, Ralph's wagon was often positioned next to the Dreasons'. The closeness allowed them to easily overhear his bellowing rants during meals.

This morning was no different.

"There he goes again," Bonnie said, cringing. "Loud enough so everyone has to hear. I don't know what he thinks he'll accomplish, but I know I'm tired of listening to him."

"Maybe you won't have to for much longer," Matthew said, nodding toward where the captain and two lieutenants were completing their daily rounds of the circle. After a cursory glance over Ralph's wagon, Captain Jeffery checked his pocket watch with a frown. He then walked to the center of the circle and cupped his hands around his mouth.

"We're burning daylight, people," he called to the entire train. "We've got to get moving and get those miles behind us. And Ralph?" He gestured to where Ralph sat in a bleary-eyed slump beside his fire. "I'm getting real tired of waiting on you. Pack up!"

From her position at the Dreasons' table, Kate saw Ralph's face stretch into an ugly sneer. "Lay off and let me have my coffee first."

"See those?" Jeffery thrust a finger toward the mountains jutting across the horizon. "They won't wait, the weather won't wait, and I *definitely* won't wait for you to have your coffee. Let's move out!"

He spun to address the men who had congregated behind him as he'd torn into Ralph. "As for any of you who think differently, you're welcome to head out on your own."

Ralph stumbled to his feet and the crowd dispersed as quickly as it had gathered.

"Typical tenderfoot," Matthew said.

"I feel so bad for Alice," added Kate. "She was so nice when she helped me find you all on my first day. With those two young children, she's got her hands full as it is. It's too bad Ralph won't do more to help."

"A man and a woman have to be a team out here," Bonnie said, smiling at Matthew. "Both have to pull their own weight or their marriage, and their lives, won't work."

Kate snuck a glance at where Jake leaned against the side of the wagon, his fingertip tracing the rim of his coffee mug.

When he caught her watching, he bowed his head and disappeared around the corner of the wagon.

With a lump in her throat, she rose and began gathering plates, wondering yet again at Jake's distance toward her. Over the past two days she'd told herself repeatedly nothing was wrong. That his aloof silence only stemmed from exhaustion due to the long hours and extra miles, and not because of something she'd done.

But deep down, she knew something between them had changed.

****

Thursday, September 7, 1843

Kate stepped from the Dreasons' wagon for the last time and joined everyone in the usual hustle and bustle to get fed, packed, and ready for departure. As she placed dishes into the basket, women from neighboring wagons came to say their goodbyes. After all the well-wishers drifted away, the wagons were ready to go and Jake waited nearby with their saddled horses, Kate dared a glance to Ruth and Bonnie.

"Well, I guess it's time," Kate said, blinking back tears. Bonnie answered by stumbling forward and pulling Kate into a crushing hug. They both began sobbing in earnest.

"Are you sure you won't come with us?" Ruth cried as she joined in their embrace. "I know it isn't Oregon, but at least you'll have us to help you until you get settled."

Kate pulled back, wiped her eyes, and laughed when she saw them doing the same thing.

"I can't say I didn't think about it, but no, I'm going to Oregon. My father paid good money for a store, a house, and land. I can't let it all sit empty."

Except it was so much more. Fulfilling the dream her father had set in motion would be her one chance at independence. She wouldn't have to depend on anyone else to take care of her and she'd be free to do as she pleased, to explore new possibilities. Maybe somewhere down the line she'd regret her decision. But she'd regret it more if she didn't even try.

"Take care of yourself," Ruth said through her tears. She gave Kate one last hug before rushing to board the wagon. She and Bonnie had agreed the previous night to start their first day without Kate in the wagon together. Once Ruth climbed through the canvas, Bonnie turned to Kate.

"Matthew speaks highly of Jake, and I've seen things too these past three weeks. You stick with him, Kate. He's a good, solid man, and out here that's everything."

"Let's move out!"

At Captain Jeffery's shout, Bonnie ran to her wagon. As the wagons formed into a winding line, she and Ruth popped their heads through the canvas.

"Goodbye, Kate!"

"Goodbye!" she yelled in reply. "Write when you get settled!"

It was like leaving Marie Ann all over again. She'd shared a common bond with these women. They knew what it was like to survive on the trail. They knew reaching their destination would take every ounce of strength and tenacity they could muster. They knew the odds were against them. What they had in common had made their friendship fast and pure, and that much harder to lose.

Kate blinked back tears at the thought of watching Jake leave for Virginia next spring.

Chapter Forty

Alone Again

Kate stood beside Jake, watching silently as the wagons passed by. When the last one disappeared around the bend, she wiped her damp cheeks and took a calming breath.

"I'll be back in a moment," she said, heading for their horses. She lifted her saddlebag from Old Dan, flung it over her shoulder, and walked into a thick stand of trees.

The day she'd reverted back to her dress, she'd told herself propriety was more important than comfort. But deep down, she'd known the real reason she'd changed was to appease others. And she'd hated herself for succumbing to her need for approval, for acceptance, and most of all, for not fighting the flawed belief that appearance mattered more than ability.

When she reappeared dressed again in the familiar trousers, shirt, and vest she had purchased at Fort Laramie, Jake's lips twitched in amusement, but he made no mention of the different clothing. He merely watched from his saddle as she tied her bags in place and then pulled herself onto Nina. Once she was settled, he broke the silence.

"We've got less than six hundred miles to go until Oregon City. Today we'll do fifteen and then stop early so the horses can get plenty of rest. Tomorrow's a twenty-five mile stretch of rough, barren terrain. I'd like to do it in a day."

She nodded. "Sounds good."

Jake led them off. Over the next hour he made several attempts at conversation, but no matter the topic, each discussion eventually waned into silence. Finally, after yet another failed attempt, Jake stared at her for a long moment.

"You're quiet today," he said. "I know the Dreasons asked you to go with them to California. Are you regretting your decision?"

"No," she replied, adding a decisive shake of her head for emphasis. "I still want to go to Oregon."

"Something else on your mind?"

"No, I'm fine." She hesitated and then blurted out the first excuse that came to her mind. "I'm just getting used to the saddle again."

She was a liar.

Jake always said she could tell him anything. But she couldn't tell him she'd done nothing but giggle over him like a simple schoolgirl for the past three weeks. Or how she'd been consumed with thoughts of how such a rugged, bold man could touch her so gently — first on top of Independence Rock when he'd caressed her hand, and then when he'd held her as they'd danced the night away. But most of all, she couldn't tell him how memories of waking cradled in his arms in the cave so long ago had her heart pounding every time she thought of being alone with him tonight.

"I'm fine," she repeated, tilting her head so he couldn't see her blush.

****

Friday, September 8, 1843

Jake dozed throughout the night and was out of his bedroll before dawn. The full moon against the clear, dark sky provided enough light to check on the horses and begin packing up camp. They had a hard day ahead and he was anxious to get started. Wincing at the stiffness in his leg, he crouched and stirred up the remains of their fire. He added a handful of pinecones and small branches to the glowing coals and then shifted to study Kate's sleeping form.

She'd had a rough night. Though he'd given her both his blankets, she'd tossed for hours before succumbing to exhaustion. Over the past weeks she'd enjoyed the comforts of a wagon, and he had little doubt the brisk air and unyielding ground would leave her with tense, aching muscles when she woke.

Now she lay huddled in her bedroll, her hair fanned out across the dirt. Jake resisted the urge to gather the silky locks and tuck them beneath her blanket. She'd been skittish enough their first day alone together; what would she do if she woke to find him running his fingers through her hair?

As he watched her sleep, he couldn't help but think Matthew was right — once they reached Oregon, men were going to scramble at the chance to sweep her off her feet.

But what did she want?

All he'd ever heard her speak of concerning her future was about her father's dream for the store and a horse ranch. He didn't doubt she'd be a success; she had a head for business that equaled any man. But what about her dreams? What did she want aside from what her father had planned for her life? Was she interested in getting married? Did she want children?

Kate slept soundly as he watered the horses, built up the fire, and warmed and ate a portion of last night's dinner — coffee and rabbit stew. Then, when he could avoid it no longer, he knelt and gently shook her shoulder.

"What's wrong?" she whispered, glancing from the moonlit sky back to him in bleary-eyed confusion.

"We need to get an early start."

"Oh, of course." She sat up with a sleepy yawn and then shivered as she gazed upon the nearby shrubs glistening in the moonlight. "Did it freeze last night?" she asked, clutching one of his blankets around her shoulders.

"Barely," Jake said. "Unfortunately, it'll only get colder in the coming weeks."

"I suppose I may as well get used to it." She whipped off the stack of blankets, pulled on her boots, and sprang to her feet. Clasping her hands together, she stretched her arms over her head with another yawn. "I was getting soft sleeping on the Dreasons' feather bed."

His mouth dropped in amazement. "They had a feather bed in there? No wonder you couldn't sleep last night!"

Kate smiled. After she secured her saddlebags and bedroll to Old Dan, she joined him in front of the fire.

"Sorry breakfast couldn't be better," he said as she accepted the mug of coffee and plate of warmed stew.

"What about you?" she asked.

"I ate while you were asleep."

"Then I'd better hurry." She scooped a heaping spoonful, shoved it in her mouth, and chewed.

"Let me know if you get too tired today and we'll take a break."

"I'll be fine," she mumbled around a second spoonful. "Let's get it over with. What time is it?"

"Ten minutes to five."

She gulped her coffee, scraped the remains of the stew into one final bite, then rinsed her plate and packed it away. After clapping her father's hat firmly onto her tousled hair, she wiped her mouth, brushed her hands against each other, and headed for Old Dan.

He led them off. The day was long and included crossing the Snake River twice. But come nightfall they'd gone the entire twenty-five miles.

They set up camp and cared for the horses. As he built a fire he heard Kate fumbling with the coffeepot lid, then her whispered curse as it dropped to the ground. A sidelong glance at her shaking fingers confirmed his suspicions.

He rose, retrieved the lid, and took the pot from her hands. "We'll get you a heavier coat at Fort Boise, but in the meantime you'll wear mine."

She tried to protest, but her chattering teeth betrayed her need for warmth.

Wishing he could clothe her in the finest of furs, he shrugged off his coat. As he draped the tattered wool around her narrow shoulders, his fingertips brushed against her cheek. Startled at how icy it was, he led her to the rising flames and then hurried to fetch another blanket.

If someone had told him the woman he'd met in Elijah's yard so long ago would have made it through today without a single complaint he would have bet, and lost, a year's salary.

Chapter Forty-One

Fort Boise

Tuesday, September 26, 1843

Three weeks and three hundred miles later, Kate breathed a sigh of relief at the sight of Fort Boise looming in the distance. By the end of the day they'd have supplies, and hopefully warmer clothes. As with Fort Hall, Hudson's Bay Company ran this fort, so she had high hopes as to the goods available.

They rode through the entrance. Once their horses were secured to two hitching posts, she followed Jake into a cramped, but clean and organized, store. Kate scrutinized the merchandise, noting displays and quantities. A scruffy man appeared from a back room, studied them, and slapped the counter with a broad smile.

"Well if it isn't Jake Fitzpatrick!" He strode over and grasped Jake's hand with a hearty shake. "I sure didn't think I'd be seeing you this late in the year." After catching sight of

Kate, he stared at Jake in astonishment. "You got married?"

Jake's cheeks reddened. "No."

To her surprise, Kate felt Jake's hand on the small of her back, gently propelling her forward. "Captain Payette, meet Miss Davis. She plans to open a store much like this one."

"Not here I hope." Captain Payette chuckled. "I'm planning on running this place for at least another year."

"No, in Oregon," she replied.

His smile disappeared and he cocked his head, staring at her thoughtfully, as if trying to gauge if she were serious. When she didn't flinch under his inspection, his look of doubt faded into one of curiosity.

"I can't say as you'll have any easy time of it out there — not on account of you being a woman, but because it's rough and lawless."

"Do you have any advice?" she ventured.

Captain Payette crossed his arms and thought for moment. "The west is filled with good folks, right alongside liars and thieves. Watch out for yourself, and be careful who you trust."

As her lips parted to ask another question, he pointed to a new arrival entering the doorway. "I've got another customer. While I'm busy, you both make sure to check over the trade table."

"Will do," Jake said.

Captain Payette walked over to a wall stocked with dry goods and began to pull burlap bags off a shelf, all the while talking with the newcomer. Kate was astounded as she overheard him relaying the cost of various goods.

"He's charging an outrageous price for flour," she whispered to Jake.

"Don't forget, he pays an outrageous price to get it here." He pointed to a jumble of clothes sitting on a nearby table. "Payette is a soft-heart, and known to take items in trade if a traveler's low on money. Dig through and get yourself a heavier coat, or at least a sweater. Grab any socks you find."

"What about you?" she asked.

"I'm hoping he's got some blankets hidden away for his favorite customers." He tapped his chest with a grin, then headed for the counter where Payette was finishing up with the other customer.

As she searched through the mishmash of clothes — some threadbare and some pristine — she listened as Captain Payette assisted Jake with dry goods and other supplies. The man was exceedingly polite, knowledgeable, and full of suggestions. Aside from flour and sugar, everything seemed priced fairly considering the remote location.

"I'd have to ask Kate," she heard Jake say. Curious, she turned and saw both men motioning her over. Picking up the scarf and wool coat she'd selected, she headed to the counter.

"He's interested in a trade. All these supplies for a horse," Jake said, waving a hand across the pile of new foodstuffs, a log cabin quilt, and now her clothes.

"Which horse?" she asked.

Captain Payette tilted his head. "Oh, how about the scrawny filly out there twitching and fussing?"

He wanted Nina.

She snorted in disgust. "The 'scrawny filly' is the nicest-bred horse this side of the mountains. You know it and I know it, so you'll want to set your sights a mite lower."

Payette shot Jake a sideways glance. "Sounds reasonable enough."

She faced Jake. "What do you think?"

"I think you're doing fine on your own," he replied.

She focused her attention back to Captain Payette. "I'll trade you the brown packhorse. And to show I hold no hard feelings over your first offer I'll let the packsaddle go too, but only if you agree to throw in one more blanket and another bag of coffee."

"So you're easy on the eyes and a shrewd businesswoman to boot? Well, seeing how I've always been a sucker for a pretty face, you've got yourself a deal, little lady."

"Don't say yes to my offer because you think I'm pretty," she admonished. "Say yes because you think it's fair."

Payette slapped his knee and let out a mighty laugh. "You are a feisty one, aren't you?"

"So I've been told." This time she was the one to give Jake the sideways glance.

"Deal," said the captain as he stuck his hand out and firmly shook hers. He wrapped their purchases and sent them on their way with his best wishes for a good trip.

****

Thursday, September 28, 1843

After Fort Boise, Kate realized there were more aspects to operating a store than doing the books in a backroom. To succeed, she needed to know how business was done out west.

"Who brought up trading a packhorse the other day?" she asked as they slowed their horses through a stretch of rocky ground.

"Captain Payette. I'm glad he did, it saved a lot of money."

She broached another topic she'd been pondering lately. "My father bought land from someone who gave up and returned to Virginia, but what about those who aren't traveling with a deed in hand? How do they own land out there?"

"For now it's a free-for-all since there isn't a country that can officially claim the Oregon Territory as their own. But in

May of this year, people calling themselves the Provisional Government of Oregon passed something called the Organic Laws of Oregon. It's basically a constitution to govern out there until it becomes an official part of the United States."

She frowned. "So these laws were passed in an area that doesn't belong to any country?"

"You've described the problem perfectly. You won't arrive to an organized system of laws and order. It's going to be tough." He flashed a teasing grin. "But you're tougher."

The trail narrowed, forcing them to ride single file, which made further conversation awkward. A mile later when the trail widened, she urged Nina forward until she again rode beside Jake in comfortable silence.

"You're quiet," Jake said. "Is something on your mind?"

Kate considered bringing up the biggest concern plaguing her since her father's death — money. Specifically, how much she'd have left after paying Jake's guide fee. Her father hadn't discussed with her the details of his and Jake's arrangement, and she wasn't sure how to broach the topic. So once again she decided to wait on the discussion until they were closer to Oregon City. After all, she had plenty else to worry about.

"I'm thinking about how I hope the store my father purchased is profitable, the house livable, and the land able to support horses."

"I'm not sure how close my property will be to yours, but I'll be around if you have questions or need advice."

He was staying?

"You never mentioned plans for Oregon," she said, fiddling with the reins in a valiant effort to hide the flicker of hope he'd ignited. "I assumed you'd head east come spring."

"No. I decided before I left this would be my last trip out."

"But after Ben died you said you'd take me back to Virginia..." She trailed off.

Jake shrugged. "I would have, but you chose to stay."

Kate silently pondered the implication. His offer would have meant sacrificing his plans for Oregon and squandering an entire year by doing nothing but riding the trail. Yet instead of complaining or trying to influence her decision, he'd willingly put her needs before his own.

And now they'd be neighbors.

Chapter Forty-Two

Sudden Descent

Saturday, October 7, 1843

Jake woke at dawn and got the fire roaring. He wanted another early start to keep their momentum of the previous week. They'd averaged fifteen miles per day, which was good considering they'd left the Snake River and were heading into the Blue Mountains where the temperature dipped near freezing most nights.

Kate joined him at the fire for a breakfast of leftovers — beans, cornbread, and roasted pheasant. As she ate, she shot furtive glances at the mountains they'd cross in the next few days, but she waited until they sat in their saddles to ask the question he knew was coming.

"How are we going to make it over those?"

"Not over them," Jake said. "Through them. The trail switches back and forth which makes for a steady, manageable incline instead of a steep grade."

Her doubting eyes swept over the craggy peaks in the distance.

"Don't worry," he said, forcing a cheerful tone to his voice in an effort to mask his own apprehension. No use worrying her with everything that could happen. "We'll dismount when conditions warrant."

He led them off.

Two hours later found them in a light, yet bitterly cold rain. The ground grew slick, and before long Plug slipped, landing hard on his front knees.

"Whoa!" Jake jumped from his saddle. When Plug regained his footing Jake stroked his mane and then bent to examine his legs.

"How is he?" Kate asked.

"All right, but it's too dangerous to continue on horseback. We'll have to walk them."

Jake took his hat off and wiped the sweat from his brow. The situation wasn't good. They were stuck on a dangerously narrow path with a steep rock wall to their left and a massive drop off to their right. Another stumble and one of their horses could slide over the edge.

He had to find shelter. Fast.

"I've heard rumors of a cave in this section of the trail, but we'll take the first decent shelter we find. It's getting colder by the minute, and we don't want to get caught in the open if this sleet changes to snow." He helped Kate dismount and then squeezed her gloved hands. "How are you doing? Are your hands or feet tingling?"

"No, I'm fine."

"Follow me, and mind the horse's steps over the icy patches."

They walked for nearly half an hour before he found what he was searching for — a dark area within the steep outcroppings of rocky ledges above. Jake narrowed his eyes, trying to decide if what he saw was merely a shadow or the opening to a deep cavern.

"There's a promising spot ahead," he called. "You up for staying put while I investigate?"

Instead of a response, he heard a panicked cry.

He spun around to a horrific sight.

Kate was sprawled on the icy ground, her fingers scrambling madly for traction as her legs and then torso slid over the edge of the trail.

"Kate!"

Shoving past the horses, he ran to her, skidding to a stop on his stomach with one hand outstretched. He caught her by a fingertip.

But it was too late.

Before his other hand could take hold of her wrist, she slipped from his grasp. Powerless, he watched as she tumbled down the hillside — screaming his name until a tree trunk stopped her cold.

Then all went silent.

Chapter Forty-Three

Accusation

"Kate! Can you hear me?"

She'd fallen at least twenty feet. He could barely make out her silhouette through the dense forest, but thought he saw her arm shift.

"Don't move! I'm on my way."

He ran to the horses and grabbed a rope and a canteen. After tying one end of the rope to a tree and the other around his waist, he sidestepped off the trail and down the mountainside. Getting to her took agonizing minutes, but when only a few feet remained, he breathed a sigh of relief as her hand reached for him. He took the hand in his, knelt, and brushed her hair aside to reveal a scrape on her forehead and a face pale with fright.

"Hi," he said. "Are you alright?"

"My leg hurts," she replied in a teary whisper.

"Which one?"

She winced. "The right."

He unsheathed his knife. Cutting open the bloodied rip in her trousers revealed a gash along her calf nearly two inches in length.

Don't let it be broken, don't let it be broken, don't let it be broken.

With gentle, probing fingers he tested the depth of the wound. To his relief, he saw only dirt instead of the bone fragments he'd feared.

"Is it bad?" Kate asked, wiping her sleeve across red-rimmed eyes.

It wasn't life threatening, but stitches were in order. He grimaced at the debris he'd have to pick out before closing the jagged flaps of skin.

"Only a cut," he said, opting to skip the details of what was ahead. For now. "I'll throw a bandage on it here, and then fix it proper once we're back on the trail."

Kate bit her lip and nodded.

He reached into his coat pocket and brought out a handkerchief and two rawhide strips, each about an inch wide and a foot in length. Setting the items aside, he uncapped his canteen and dribbled water over the wound. Kate groaned, but held still as he pressed the folded cloth against her calf, and then tied it firmly in place with the strips. When he finished, he held the canteen while she took a sip of water. He then picked up her father's hat, brushed it off, and set it on her head.

"I don't know what happened," she said, staring up at the tracks she'd made as she'd fallen. "I must have lost my footing."

"No harm done," he replied with a cheerfulness he hoped hid his fright. "I'm going to rig this rope so it holds both of us. Can you stand?"

"Yes."

She grasped his arm and he eased her to her feet, steadying her as she swayed against the angle of the hillside. After enlarging the loop of rope around his chest, he positioned himself behind her. Once the rope encircled them both, he directed her every step as they inched up the hill. Her cheeks grew pale, then ruddy from the exertion.

Back on the trail, Jake spread out a blanket and helped her down onto it. The temperature had dropped, and the rain had changed to a light snow. Given he had no idea when they'd find shelter, and not wanting her leg to grow worse while they searched, he decided to tend to her wounds then and there.

He dug in his saddlebags for a spare shirt, ripped off the sleeve, and then gathered a needle and thread. Thankfully he wouldn't have to use hair from one of the horses' tails. He started with the scrape on her head — superficial, but coated with grit. It needed nothing more than a few splashes of water and time to heal.

Her leg wasn't as easy.

As he picked debris from deep within her leg, he heard her draw several shaking breaths and then let them out slowly. As he flooded the wound with cleansing water and then patted it dry with his shirtsleeve, he heard a faint gnashing of teeth. As he pierced her tender skin and tightened the first stitch, he heard only the creaking protests of her leather gloves as her hands clenched into fists.

Ten stitches later, he finished. He'd sutured more than a few cuts in his day, but only on hard men who'd gulped whiskey by the mouthful first, and then swore furiously with each poke of the needle.

Never had he seen someone bear the pain so stoically.

Cursing the thickening snow that demanded he find cover instead of cradling her against him and comforting her until her pain subsided, he got another blanket. After wrapping it around her shoulders, he crouched and peered into her wide, trusting eyes.

"Stay here while I search for shelter."

He rose and hurried up the trail, cursing his poor eyesight as he searched for the dark area he'd been focused on before Kate slipped. In less than half a mile he located the entrance to a cave hidden in the deep recesses of a rocky overhang. Upon inspecting it, he breathed yet another sigh of relief. It wasn't spacious, but it would do. There was enough room to make a fire, and the horses could crowd in and be out of the weather. He trampled the snow at the mouth of the cave and hurried back. As he rounded the final corner, he saw Kate's snow-covered figure sitting right where he'd left her.

"I found a cave," he said as he approached. "It's small, but it's close and it's dry. I'm going to take the horses there, get a fire started, and lay out your bedroll. I'll be back for you when I'm done." He knelt to check her knee and forehead. "How are you?"

"C-cold."

Jake clenched his jaw, disgusted with his own thoughtlessness. She'd waited for him to return, trusted him to care for her, and yet here he was considering leaving her again. He fought back the sudden desire to gather her in his arms and whisper apologies and promises of safekeeping into her hair. Instead, he settled for pulling off her gloves, capturing her hands, and bringing them to his mouth.

"Never mind that plan," he said, blowing warm air over her fingers and then rubbing her hands between his. "Let's get you to shelter. The horses can wait."

"What if they wander?"

"Then I'll find them. You're what matters most. Do you need me to carry you?"

"I can walk."

Replacing her gloves, he pulled her to her feet and tossed both her blankets over his shoulder. He led her to the cave, step by limping step. He spread out the first blanket, sat her down, and then tucked her securely in the second one.

"I'll be back with the horses as soon as I can."

He charged out the entrance and down the trail. Minutes later he returned, dropped the horses' lead ropes on the ground, and rushed to her side. "Do you have pain anywhere beside your leg and head?"

"No."

Jake crowded the horses along one wall and started a fire. By the time he had her bedroll laid out, the chill was leaving the cave. Soon she was sipping a cup of steaming coffee and nestled beneath several blankets.

"Are you warming up?" he asked, throwing another hunk of wood on the fire. "Let me know if you need anything, and I'll get it for you."

"I'm fine. Truly I am."

Perhaps. Perhaps not. Nasty injuries like a sprain or even a fracture might not appear for hours. He checked her stitches. Again. "Nothing else hurts?"

"Jake," she said softly. "I'm *fine.*"

He told himself to stop hovering. That she was fine. That he hadn't almost lost her. Resisting the urge to ask if she needed another blanket, he leaned against the wall and watched as curls of smoke rose from the flames and then drifted through the cave entrance.

"Why Jake," she teased. "I believe I caught a glimpse of worry back there when I fell — though how I saw it through all your hair is beyond me."

At least her sense of humor had returned.

"You don't like my beard?" he asked, playfully stroking his jaw. Normally he was clean-shaven, but he'd let it grow in preparation for the last leg of the journey. He liked the protection it gave against the bitter mountain winds.

"I'm not used to seeing you with a beard."

"I could say the same thing for you."

Eyeing him warily, she ran a hand along her own cheek. "What do you mean?"

"You have to admit, it's unusual to see a woman in a man's hat instead of a bonnet." He paused, suddenly curious. "Planning on wearing it in Oregon?"

"Of course."

He raised an eyebrow. "Petticoats too?"

Kate's mouth dropped open and he chuckled. "Catching a glimpse of bare leg when you mounted your horse was the highlight of my days early on."

"You're terrible." Rosy lips twitched with hidden laughter as she snuggled deeper into her bedroll. "How much further?"

He welcomed the change in topic. Anything to banish the image of her smooth, creamy skin, both back in the petticoat days and tonight, when he'd held her leg steady as he'd stitched. "About three hundred miles."

"Should take three weeks?"

"Four at the most. Getting nervous?"

She fidgeted with the corner of a blanket. "Is it obvious?"

"Only to me," he murmured.

Instead of responding she rolled over, ending the conversation.

The fire sputtered, then grew dim, but still Jake couldn't sleep. Maybe it was the danger she'd faced today, or something else entirely, but the thought of Kate starting a new life without him made his heart ache.

"Are you asleep?" he whispered.

"No." She rolled over and propped her chin on a slender hand. The glow of the firelight played across her hair. Their eyes locked and he felt it was time.

"Did you leave a beau behind in Charlottesville?" he asked.

"No."

"What about the man I saw you fighting with in the apothecary?"

"Why do you ask?"

"Curious." He went for a nonchalant shrug, but his heart pounded so hard it was an effort to speak.

"Crandall was a childhood friend who at one time wanted more," she ventured quietly, "but I was too busy taking care of the store, the house, my father, and Ben. In the end, he found another woman who could devote the time and attention he thought he needed, and as it turned out, become expectant with his child. What you saw was our last conversation before I left."

Jake cursed his stupidity. All he'd wanted to do was find out if she had anyone serious back home, and instead she was now recalling memories of a spineless rogue who couldn't see the treasure in a woman like herself.

"I'm sorry. I'd thought a woman like you would have had men lined up just to get a glimpse at you."

"Not hardly. You were there when he told me I'm not the marrying type." Her lips pursed together in a tight line. "It seems Oregon is the perfect place for a woman like me who's destined to be alone."

****

Kate's cheeks flamed as she recalled the conversation with Crandall. Jake had heard everything, so why was he bringing it up?

"Kate, do you understand what you're setting yourself up for in Oregon?"

"What do you mean, setting myself up for?" She paused, increasingly confused by both the conversation and the hard, condemning edge that had suddenly crept into Jake's voice.

"Remember what Payette said? He hopes to stay in business another year. One. Year. It's something to consider, since you're basing your entire future on a successful store. What happens if you fail like so many others?"

"Then I'll get a job," she snapped, feeling her temper rise.

"You've got a lot to learn about life out west, starting with the fact most business owners aren't going to hire a woman when a man wants the job."

"Then I'll live off my father's money until I get settled." Before she knew it, the words she'd held back for so many months burst forth. "What's become of my father's money?"

"What's that supposed to mean?" He sat up so fast the blankets fell from his body. "Did you think I wasn't going to give it back to you?"

"I knew there should be some left," she joined him in sitting up, "and wondered why you were so happy to trade the packhorse back at Fort Boise instead of paying cash..." She faltered, not wanting to go on.

"So you thought I was going to steal it! You thought I would get you to Oregon and abandon you without a cent to your name?" His eyes grew cold and narrow. "Quite an accusation, Kate."

"I never said you would steal it!" Panic crept into her voice and reverberated around the cave walls. What had she done?

"Kate, I may be a lot of things but I'm not a thief!" A thick vein in his neck beat a steady rhythm as he shoved aside his blanket and got to his feet.

After he stomped off, Kate sat in stunned disbelief. How had a simple conversation escalated into such a fight so quickly?

"Jake?" she called out after several anxious minutes passed and he hadn't come back.

No response.

The mouth of the cave revealed his boot prints in the snow and her eyes followed them until they disappeared in the night.

"Jake?"

She waited then tried again, louder this time. "Jake?"

"I'm here, Kate. Stop calling my name."

She drew back into the cave, silent.

An hour later she squeezed her eyes shut as Jake's footsteps approached her bedroll.

"I know you're not sleeping. Look at me."

She opened her eyes to see Jake standing over her.

"Kate, all a man has is his word and his honor. When your father died, he made me promise to get you and Ben to Oregon, and he gave me the money to hold onto until I did." He held up his saddlebag with a white-knuckled fist. "It's all right here. Every cent your father gave me the day he died, less supplies we've purchased since, and all of those are accounted for with receipts."

The bag dropped to the ground. "If you don't believe me you can check for yourself."

Chapter Forty-Four

Clarifications

Sunday, October 8, 1843

Kate dozed fitfully beside the untouched saddlebags. When the pain shooting down her calf ruined any hope of sleep, she stared at the cave ceiling and wondered how she could have implied, even for a minute, Jake would keep the money. He'd more than proved he was a man of honor; the fault lay with her.

Even though sunrise was over an hour away, she slunk out of her bedroll and built up their fire. Jake slept with one hand draped above his head, his tousled hair evidence of frustrated fingers. The early morning quiet was broken only by his soft snores, but not for long.

Jake stirred and glanced sleepily over to her empty bedroll. Immediately he sat up, his eyes wide and anxious. Once he spotted her sitting nearby, he lay down again, this time facing the cave wall.

"Jake," she spoke cautiously.

No response.

"Jake, please."

She settled for speaking to his back. "I'm sorry. I let my thoughts get carried away. I didn't mean to suggest you'd done something improper with the money."

He sat up with a look of disbelief. "You can't cross back over a bridge you've burned."

With a heavy sigh, Kate laid another branch on the fire. For the next few minutes the only sounds came from the soft drips of thawing snow, the crackling of the fire, and the occasional shift of the horses' hooves against the cave floor.

As he accepted her offering of coffee, she attempted to start a conversation again.

"Seems like it might be a nice day. At least the snow seems to be melting."

Jake glared at her over the rim of his cup.

"Do you think we should wait until it warms up?"

"Certainly not," he said, yanking his bedroll into his arms. "I'm not staying any longer than I have to."

They were on their way soon after. Uncomfortable silence dominated the next hour as Jake brooded and she replayed last night's events. Finally, she could stand the silence no longer.

"If you won't accept my apology, at least answer a question." Kate waited for him to respond, but when a minute passed without a word from him, she continued. "Jake, something you said about a promise to my father kept me up over half the night. The day he died, he spoke to you alone while Ben and I waited nearby. Do you remember?"

The saddle creaked as he shifted to stare at her, his piercing blue eyes revealing sorrow and pain. "Yes."

"What did he say?"

He turned away. "I don't want to talk about this."

"Why? I don't think knowing my father's last words to you is too much to ask."

Jake grabbed Nina's reins and pulled their horses to a halt. "Why are you doing this?"

She felt horrible about the fight and her role in it, and thinking of her father made her even more upset. But she'd started this conversation and didn't want to let it go.

"I want to know."

"Really?"

"Yes." She nodded, her resolve firm.

Jake dismounted, pulled her from her saddle, and took her by the shoulders. "Your father knew he wasn't going to make it, and he asked me to take you and Ben away before he died. He didn't want you to see him suffer."

Kate stifled a sob. "Is that it?"

"Then he said I was a good man, and he trusted me with his children and his money."

Her knees buckled. Jake caught her solidly against his chest.

"Jake, I'm so sorry," she whispered through instant tears. "It all came out so wrong."

"Don't cry, Katie," he murmured while stroking her hair. "I shouldn't have reacted the way I did. I know now you didn't mean any harm."

Craving his warmth and tenderness, she buried her face into the folds of his coat, loving the feeling of being held. Then, cold reality set in. A relationship with Jake could jeopardize her newfound freedom and could also halt the fulfillment of her father's dream.

With great regret, she pulled away.

Chapter Forty-Five

Henrick

Tuesday, October 17, 1843

Kate stood at the top of the embankment, studying the deep, wide river below. She then eyed the opposite embankment. It appeared steep and, like everything else since they'd parted ways with the wagon train, impossible to climb.

"We'll cross here," Jake said.

She watched the water churn and froth against a boulder near the center. "Are you sure?"

"Since someone cut the ropes to the barge, we don't have a choice." Jake ran his hands through his hair in frustration. "We've searched for a better option for half the day. This is as good as it's going to get." He faced her. "Scared?"

"Yes."

"It'll be all right," he said. "We'll take it slow." With a doubtful nod, she watched as Jake mounted Plug. With the lead ropes for Nickel and a packhorse firmly in hand, he urged

Plug down the bank. Once the horses were situated below, Jake climbed the embankment again. Breathing hard from the exertion, he bent at the waist and put his hands on his knees.

"It's a lot steeper than I expected." He straightened and ran a sleeve across his brow. "I'll take Nina and the packhorse. Old Dan listens to you, so I'd like you to lead him down."

She followed Jake down the bank, their every step dislodging a slew of stones. Rocks bounced through Old Dan's front legs and he pulled against the reins. Coaxing him forward with dried apples worked for the first half of the descent; brute force brought him the rest of the way.

When they reached the river's edge she closed her eyes and breathed deep, reveling in the small pleasure of the fresh, clean air and the soft mist caressing her skin. Though her clothes were grimy and she hadn't bathed in weeks, she felt refreshed.

She opened her eyes and found Jake staring into the water. He threw a branch and watched as the current swept it away.

"There!" he declared with an extended finger. "There's where we'll cross. See how the branch lingered? It means the current isn't as strong around that point."

She nodded, uncertain. It all seemed the same to her — too swift.

"I've secured the packs, so don't worry about them. Ride Old Dan, and take Nina by the reins. I'll ride Plug and hold the reins of a packhorse. Nickel and the other packhorse can follow on their own."

Jake rode Plug into the water. She waited for Nickel and the packhorse to go, and then urged Old Dan to the water's edge. As Old Dan waded in, she had to fight to keep him straight against the swift current. Downriver, Jake shouted back to her.

"It's deep! Hang on tight!"

His warning came just as Old Dan lost his footing and began to flounder, plunging Kate into water so cold it took her breath away. She held fast to the saddle horn and Nina's lead rope as they were swept along at the whim of the current.

Ahead, she saw Jake near the shore, his hand wrapped around Plug's halter as he led the flailing horse toward the riverbank to join Nickel and the two packhorses. She cried out in relief as Old Dan regained his footing.

Powerful arms locked around her waist, and then she felt Jake pulling her from her saddle.

"I've got you." Jake's voice rumbled in her ear. "You're safe."

He carried her to shore while Nina followed close behind. Once he set her down he pointed at Nina's lead rope still clutched in her fist.

"You can drop it."

She tried, but couldn't open her hand. Jake watched her struggle and then pried the rope from her fingers. Then, as Jake checked over the horses, Kate sank to her knees on the rocky shore. Minutes later, Jake joined her.

"I'm glad it's over," she said with a dubious glance at the river. "I certainly didn't expect the water would be so cold."

"It's worse in the spring with the snow runoff. At least none of the horses got hurt, and all the saddlebags stayed in place." He faced her. "What about you? How are you feeling?"

"Wet, but fine. How about you?"

"Good." He gazed at the clear blue sky. "Lucky for us it's such a warm day since all our spare clothes are probably soaked. We'll dry everything out tonight by a fire, but first we've got a hill to tackle."

Kate turned around to evaluate the climb and her breath caught in her throat. Mossy rocks nestled at the base of an embankment that was ten feet high and glistening with mud.

"That looks fun," she said grimly.

"That's what I thought," he said, his tone matching her own.

****

Jake leapt out of the way as yet again Nickel scrambled and clawed his way toward the top of the steep hill and then slid down again. Regardless of his efforts, the horses couldn't catch solid footing on the thick, oozing mud.

He'd rolled aside the rocks piled at base of the embankment — no use risking a thrown shoe or even worse, a broken leg. He'd stripped the horses of all gear but their bridles to decrease their weight and created a diagonal path to lessen the severity of the climb. He'd covered the mud with what little grass he could find to give traction to slick hooves.

But his ideas proved futile.

After this last grueling attempt he collapsed on the riverbank, exhausted from coaxing, pulling, and ultimately pushing them up the steep hill, only to have them balk at the last few feet and slip down again.

"I can't believe I got us into this situation." He looked to Kate in exasperation. "Night is coming, our clothes are wet, and we'll freeze if we don't get in front of a fire. And we certainly can't make one here. There's no dry wood and all the mist would put it out anyway."

Jake searched around for any other option, but saw nothing. The danger of the current was tame compared to what they were up against now. And traveling downriver to find an easier climb would be foolish, if not impossible — thousands of rocks covered the riverbank, guaranteeing at least one of their horses would fall, risking a snapped leg.

Their only choice now was for him to climb the bank, send down a rope, and physically pull the horses up. The problem was Kate. Though she was strong, he wasn't sure if she had the stamina to help him haul up six horses.

"You need a hand there, boy?"

Startled, Jake looked up and locked eyes with a grizzled man staring at them from the top of the embankment.

"Why'd you cross here?" The stranger grinned through tobacco-stained teeth. "There's a barge not two miles north."

"Couldn't use it," Jake replied. "The ropes were cut."

The man held up a coil of rope. "Need a hand?"

Jake swiped off his hat and tipped his head back, intent on getting a better look at the man, but he'd already disappeared.

A long length of rope flew into the air. The end landed at Jake's feet.

Kate looked at him in eager astonishment. "What a great coincidence!"

"Let's hope that's what it is," he said grimly.

"What do you mean?" she asked, her eyes filled with confusion and unease.

He spoke low. "Kate, for all intents and purposes we're trapped down here. And those cuts to the barge ropes are recent. You do the math."

Resigned to the fact that he had no choice but to accept the stranger's help, Jake gritted his teeth and tied the rope to Nickel's halter.

"Ready!" he shouted before turning to Kate. "Stand with the rest of the horses. I'll go up with each one and come back for the next."

"Talk em' up!" the stranger bellowed. "I'll have you out of there in no time."

As Jake urged Nickel forward he tried not to think how pale, small, and alone Kate looked. Or what would happen to her if something went wrong. Instead, he took a deep breath and grabbed Nickel's tail in preparation for the laborious task ahead.

When the rope went taut, Jake chased Nickel up the hill, shouting directives and their progress to the man above. With a final heaving scramble, the horse made it to the top of the embankment. Jake followed, hopping to his feet to check over Nickel's legs, hooves, and stomach.

As he worked, he studied the man now gathering his end of the rope he'd wrapped around a tree for leverage.

He was older, and if the condition of his clothes meant anything, he'd lived in the woods for some time. A thickened, yellow toenail protruded from a hole in his boot and a worm-like scar ran from his forehead over the bridge of his nose and then continued down one cheek. His long, gray beard had collected a fair amount of tobacco stains and dirt since his last washing, which by the looks of him would have been weeks, if not months, ago.

Jake tied Nickel to a nearby tree and then walked to the edge of the embankment, joining the man in staring down at the remaining horses bunched together below. Kate sat on a rock, her head down with a blanket pulled over her shoulders.

Jake crossed his arms. "You've got good timing. I was thinking of crossing back over the river until you came along."

"You need a rest, or you ready to go again?"

"I'm ready," Jake said.

"Lucky for you I was here."

"Appreciate it." Jake grabbed the rope and sidestepped down the hill. They were in it now for better or worse.

With some difficulty Old Dan went up, and then Nina went up without a problem. Plug scampered up the hill with little assistance, but one of the packhorses kept sliding down. Only after much panicked scrambling did it reach the top.

As Jake checked again to make sure the horses were safe and secure, he realized it wasn't the man's clothes or appearance that bothered him — it was the way he kept peering over the hill at Kate. He couldn't decide whether it was worry or something else in the man's eyes.

"One more to go," Jake said before sliding down the hill yet again. When he walked the rope over to secure it to the final packhorse, the man yelled down.

"Better send the girl up before she freezes!"

Regrettably, the stranger was right. If the last packhorse was a problem, she would be surrounded by damp, cool air for as long as it took to bring it up. And even five more minutes was too long for someone in her condition. Already her lips held a tinge of blue.

Though he hated the idea of sending Kate up before him, he trusted in her feisty spirit and steadfast courage to let him know if trouble brewed. And in his own ability to get to her no matter what.

"I'm c-cold, Jake. Let me go."

Jake nodded and bent to whisper in her ear. "Be careful. Keep this close—" he pressed his sheathed knife into her hands "—and I'll be right there if you need me."

Her eyes widened, but she said nothing as she slid the knife into her pocket. He showed her how to grab hold and use the rope and then watched as the man towed her up and over the bank.

****

The strange man reached out a gnarled hand and hauled her roughly over the edge. "You good now?"

"Yes, thank you."

He eyed her as she stood up, brushed mud and grass from her coat, and straightened her hat. Then he grunted and focused once again on the rope. It was her chance to study him unobserved.

As the man spit, then ran his sleeve along his mouth to soak up the tobacco spilling from his mouth, Kate decided he must be one of the men she had heard about who lived in the mountains and shied away from people. And apparently never washed.

Filthy or not, Kate didn't care; he had helped them.

Unaware of her scrutiny, the stranger braced his feet against the tree he'd wound the rope around. He grunted, and with a straining heave of his arms the final packhorse appeared. Jake followed close behind. Ignoring the man, Jake took Kate by the arm and all but dragged her to the where he'd tethered the rest of the horses.

"Are you all right? While I was down there did he talk to you? Bother you?" His eyes narrowed. "Try to touch you?"

She stiffened, unsettled both at where his questions were headed, and his insinuation the man who'd helped them out of a predicament that had been Jake's fault to begin with was anything less than honorable.

"He did nothing of the sort," she said, allowing her rising irritation to creep into her tone.

"Good. Now sit tight while I bring up the saddles and rest of our gear."

Jake headed back to the packhorse. After walking it in a circle and running his hands down each leg and over each foot, he tethered it with the others. He spoke briefly with the stranger and then disappeared over the embankment, rope in hand.

She wanted to defy him, to follow him down the hillside and ask what he meant with such risqué allegations when the man had done nothing but assist them. He hadn't so much as glanced her way since pulling her up from the ground, and yet Jake had immediately thought the worst.

Several minutes passed before Jake struggled up the hill, holding the rope in one hand and her saddle in the other. She rushed forward to relieve him of her saddlebags he'd thrown over his shoulders and then walked beside him to the horses.

"Saddle Nina while I fetch our gear. It shouldn't take more than a few trips before we're on our way."

"Why are you so eager to leave?"

"Gut feeling."

Without stopping for a rest or even a swig of water, he trooped up and down the hill, carrying packsaddles and all their supplies along with his saddle and bags. The man assisted without complaint. After the final trip up he followed Jake to where Kate was hoisting the last of their supplies onto a packhorse.

The stranger thrust his hand out toward Jake. "Name's Henrick."

Jake shook the outstretched hand. "Jake."

She waited politely, and when she realized Jake wasn't going to bother introducing her she stepped forward.

"I'm Miss Davis. I sincerely thank you for taking the time to help us today."

"No problem. I was getting water when I heard you down there." Henrick's missing front tooth, as well as a few others, caused a soft whistle as he spoke. "My camp is up a-ways. Fire's going and supper's ready. You're welcome to stay a while, or for the night."

Jake shook his head. "We'd rather be getting on our way again."

Henrick frowned. "Those clothes ain't gettin' no drier."

"We're plenty dry," Jake said. "We'll be moving on."

Kate was stunned at Jake's outright rebuff. Yes, Henrick was peculiar, but there was no reason not to accept his offer of hospitality.

She turned toward Henrick. "Would you excuse us for a moment?"

He tipped his hat toward her and then retreated to the tree where he'd dropped his rope.

"You've got no call to be so rude to him." She pointed to Henrick, now coiling the length of his rope around his forearm. "Why would you say no to his fire, especially when we haven't eaten since breakfast and we've been stuck in the same sodden, filthy clothes all afternoon?"

"I can't explain it, but there's something about him I don't trust."

She let out an exasperated sigh. "You're willing to risk injury to the horses by riding them only an hour after hauling them up the hillside based solely on your feeling that the man who's done nothing but help us isn't to be trusted? I won't hear of such nonsense."

"Listen to me." Jake's expression grew fierce as he stepped closer, towering over her. "We're riding on and that's final."

Yet again he wouldn't budge.

Well, this time neither would she.

She was done submitting to the will of others. Soon she'd be on her own, and in her new life her decisions would be based upon her need to survive and succeed. And now, with darkness looming, she had every intention of sitting before a fire so she could get warm, get dry, and eat.

"Jake, I'm cold. I'm tired. I'm hungry. And I want to stay!"

Her words of disagreement must have carried over to Henrick, for he craned his neck toward them with a crooked grin.

"Got a fire and supper going right now," he repeated.

Jake clenched his jaw for a long moment before turning to Henrick.

"Much obliged."

Chapter Forty-Six

Trust

As they followed Henrick through the dense forest, Jake slid Elijah's money and paperwork out of his saddlebags and into the front pocket of his shirt. He'd shoved his pistol inside his coat pocket before he'd brought up the first horse, but now he wore it at his hip in a tied-down holster. The change alone might be enough to cause Henrick to reconsider any trouble he may have planned.

For now, Kate's suffering took priority. However, he had no intention of staying after she got warm. Sunset was over three hours away — plenty of time to get a few miles between them and Henrick before they made camp.

Ahead, Henrick weaved through the trees and ducked under low branches with practiced ease all the way to his camp, which was at least a mile from the river and set at the edge of a clearing about a quarter-acre in size. Beans simmered in a kettle over a crackling fire, four horses were picketed nearby, and supplies were scattered around in haphazard piles. Far too many supplies for one person.

While Jake stayed on his feet and declined all Henrick's offerings, Kate only had eyes for the fire and the plate of beans and mug of coffee Henrick handed her. To Jake's dismay, she sat cross-legged before the flames and ate and drank freely, all the while answering each of Henrick's probing questions as to their travels.

Jake's misgivings grew.

"You stopped for the night?" he asked as Henrick scooted beside Kate to refill her coffee.

"No," Henrick replied. "I've had a run of bad luck, so I figured I'd camp here for a while and get things together again."

Jake reevaluated the camp, taking special note of the horses and their gear. Everything was of the highest quality, not something he'd predict for a man stating he was down on his luck. Plus, he would hazard a guess a nearby saddle was military issue, which would be nearly impossible for a civilian like Henrick to obtain.

Time for a smooth, fast retreat. No sense riling Henrick with observations and accusations. A fight would serve little purpose and endanger Kate.

"Our horses need water," Jake said, hoping the flawed logic of returning to the river wouldn't dawn on Henrick until after he and Kate were long gone.

"No problem." Henrick took a scoop of beans, filled his mouth, and then pointed over his shoulder with the spoon. "There's a creek over yonder. The walk won't take but a minute."

Jake tensed. If Henrick was camped so near water, then his earlier statement about coming to the river for water was an outright lie.

Time to go. Now.

He crossed the camp to their horses, untied each, and headed back to the fire. He locked eyes with Kate, hoping to convey all his concerns and the urgent need for her to stand and walk away. Without questioning him.

"Kate," he said, his tone and expression deathly calm. "Let's water these horses."

Startled, she rose.

Without a word, he pressed Old Dan's and Nina's reins into her hand and then gathered the reins of the remaining four. She walked beside him until they were out of Henrick's earshot and then halted.

"Why on earth did we leave? And even more importantly—" She gasped when he seized her by the arm.

"Not another word until we're at the creek," he muttered, glancing back toward the camp. To his dismay, he saw Henrick standing with his arms crossed over his chest, staring at them.

Kate jerked her arm from his grasp but stayed silent. Pressing his finger to his lips, he motioned for her to keep moving. He fell into line beside her. Less than a minute later, as the horses bent their heads over a small, but plentiful creek, Jake checked on Henrick. He'd returned to the fire and now sat with his back to them.

"Why did we leave in such a rush?" Kate's eyes flashed with irritation as she stood before him, her hands planted on her hips.

"Because Henrick is up to no good. I think he cut the barge ropes. I think he waits for travelers to get stuck on the bank, offers them his help and camp, and then robs them — or worse — during the night."

She brushed his concerns aside with a wave of her arm. "Jake, I swear you think the worst of everyone. He's a harmless man seeking company."

"No, he's not!" Jake grabbed her shoulders and spoke with a fierceness that surprised them both. "We need to leave. Trust me."

"We can't," she said, wriggling one shoulder from his grasp and then shoving his hand from the other. Narrowing her eyes, she began ticking off the reasons for staying on her fingers. "Our clothes aren't dry, the horses aren't rested, we aren't rested, and most importantly, your suspicions are absurd."

Realizing rationalizing with her would instead likely lead to a fight — something he didn't want Henrick overhearing — he gritted his teeth, bent his head, and spent the next moments checking over his pistol and his knife. Only when his breathing and anger had calmed did he dare raise his eyes to Kate.

But she'd already started toward camp. She was now a good ten feet away from him and wouldn't turn around despite his urgent whispered demands to do so. Unwilling to shout, he followed her back. Once he'd secured the horses, he stood by the fire, furious with Kate's willingness to trust a man like Henrick over him.

"Jake, would you mind getting more wood for the fire? It gets mighty cold at night and I'm running low." With a rueful shake of his head, Henrick hitched up his pant leg and pointed to a bloody scratch on his knee. "I'd go, but I hurt myself helping up your last horse."

Kate now had all of her sewing supplies out of her pack and was busy mending her coat.

"Kate, I need you to help me get the wood."

"I'd rather stay and patch this sleeve," she replied without looking up. "I ripped it coming up the hill."

Either she had missed the hidden meaning or was trying to spite him.

"It shouldn't take you long. I got some already cut over there," Henrick pointed across the clearing, "but with my leg being hurt I can't walk so good."

Arousing Henrick's suspicions would only cause trouble.

"Fine," Jake replied. "I'll go. But Kate, while I'm gone I want you to think about Captain Payette's advice to you back at Fort Boise." Jake repeated Payette's warning to himself and hoped she was doing the same.

The west is filled with good folks, right alongside liars and thieves. Watch out for yourself, and be careful who you trust.

She didn't move. Didn't even raise her eyes.

Furious, he stalked across the clearing. When he reached the area Henrick had pointed out, Jake saw only an axe sunk into a felled, but intact, sapling. Well, he wasn't about to chop a woodpile for a scoundrel like Henrick. Loose branches would suffice.

He retreated into the woods and circled around the camp as he gathered branches so he could keep Kate within his sight. Her head was bowed as she stitched up the coat on her lap, but he heard an occasional snippet of her conversation with Henrick. Why was she acting so stubborn and making such stupid choices?

The forest was dense with old growth, so while ferns, moss, and rabbit holes were plentiful, branches were not. It took a good ten minutes before he had an armful of burnable pieces. On his way back one fell from his grasp and he bent to retrieve it. As he rose he heard a frantic, garbled scream.

Branches tumbled from Jake's arm as he raced through the trees toward Kate, now pinioned against Henrick's side, immobilized yet still fighting valiantly to break free from Henrick's left arm encircling her shoulders, his left hand crushing her mouth quiet while his right hand restrained her wrists against his upper thigh.

Jake pulled his pistol seconds before he leapt over a fallen log and landed before the fire.

"Kate, keep still," Jake said, leveling the barrel at Henrick's chest. "Henrick, you vile, pathetic excuse for a man — let her go and keep your hands where I can see them."

"Boy, there's no need to get twitchy," Henrick said. "Me and the girl was gettin' better acquainted is all."

Jake's trigger finger tensed as he noticed Kate's shirt ripped down the front and the corner of her mouth bloody and swollen.

"Let her go!"

"Nowadays a man can't have any fun," Henrick grumbled, releasing his grip.

Kate sprang up and stumbled toward him, her eyes wide with fear. When she fell into his side, he curled his free arm around her waist and pulled her against his chest. His eyes and aim never wavered from Henrick's chest as he lowered his lips to whisper in her ear.

"Can you gather your things and mount up on your own?"

Deep within the folds of his coat, where she'd buried her head, he felt her nod. She pulled away from him, filled her saddlebag, and gathered reins. Only when he saw her in Nina's saddle, holding Old Dan's lead rope in hand, did he speak.

"Henrick, the one thing saving you from a bullet is I don't do a man's work when there's a lady present. You so much as sneeze I'll make an exception."

Jake wanted nothing more than to rid the world of a man like Henrick — a man who would prey on a defenseless, naïve woman like his Katie. The man cowering before him was little better than the Gilroy brothers who'd attacked his mother and then killed his family so long ago.

But though he yearned to shoot a furrow across the top of Henrick's skull and then stare into his eyes as he begged for his life, he had no intention of allowing Kate to watch the gruesome sight of a man dying by his hand. He motioned for her to ride from the camp and waited until she reached the center of the clearing before speaking again.

"You move now, you die quick. I catch you following us, you die slow."

Henrick nodded his understanding.

"And this is for stealing her innocence," Jake said.

As Henrick frowned in confusion, Jake swung his forearm to the left and slammed the side of his pistol against Henrick's temple. The man fell to the dirt with a satisfying thump.

Jake centered his barrel on the unconscious man's chest once again and kept his aim steady while he pulled himself into Nickel's saddle, gathered the reins and lead ropes of the remaining horses, and then rode off. He met Kate in the clearing and together they headed into the forest and the growing darkness. A good three miles passed before he called out to stop.

"We'll camp here for the night. Don't take your boots off. If we have to leave suddenly, there won't be time to get dressed. Also, we can't chance a fire." If Henrick woke and chose to follow them, flames would be a dead giveaway as to their location.

They picketed the saddled horses and changed into their spare clothes. While she laid out her bedroll, he finally asked the question he'd been dreading.

"What went on back there?"

Kate tearfully shook her head, and he didn't pursue it.

****

Jake paced around the edge of their makeshift camp, cautious and alert for signs of Henrick lurking nearby. The moonlight filtering through the treetops revealed Kate curled in her bedroll — frightened, skittish, and watching him as he prowled.

The change in her eyes tore at his soul. No longer shining with ambition and an unrealized sensuality, they were now fearful and filled with sorrow and the cruel realization that lecherous cretins like Henrick existed in this world.

Watching her cringe at every rustle in the forest, he longed to cradle her in his arms until her shivers of fear subsided, to smooth her hair as he reassured her not every man was a depraved abuser. But as much as he wanted to comfort her, he was terrified of saying the wrong thing, of doing the wrong thing, and ultimately making the situation worse. So he did what he knew for certain was honorable — he guarded the camp, protecting her from harm.

Just before dawn, when he'd returned from checking over the horses and their gear, he heard Kate whisper his name. Taking a deep breath and praying for the right words, he walked to her bedroll and knelt beside her.

Her eyes met his and then overflowed with tears. "Jake, I'm so sorry."

"You've got nothing to be sorry for."

"You warned me. Repeatedly. And still I didn't listen." She sat up in a rush, wiping her cheeks with her fingertips. "You said several times I should trust you, and I want you to know I do. Above all else, I trust you."

He breathed a sigh of relief hearing the words. "It means a lot to me, Kate, and I promise to never take such a precious gift for granted." He reached for her top blanket and pulled it around her shoulder. "Morning isn't far away. Try to get some sleep."

Once she'd lowered herself back into her bedroll, she slowly slid her hand over his. "Will you stay with me?"

"Of course."

As the sun rose he remained beside her, holding her hand long after she'd fallen asleep.

Chapter Forty-Seven

Surprises

Wednesday, October 18, 1843 to Monday, October 23, 1843

Blue sky dotted with cotton clouds stretched above them. Tree-covered hills numbered in the hundreds below. Snowy peaks jutted through the haze on a far-off ridgeline. Traveling the mountains allowed a person to discover nature in all its glory.

Fresh, crisp air brought about a newfound energy. When they led their horses through the thick canopy of trees, startled birds flew from their nests while squirrels first stared in wonder, then chattered angrily at the invasion. Rocks mingled with soft earth and lofty grasses to create a feeling of cozy seclusion.

But while the mountains were beautiful, they were grueling, too. Early each morning Jake and Kate were up with the sun, walking the horses across steep ravines, over treacherous rocks, and sliding down hills. Gnarled trees left brutal scrapes on skin and horseflesh alike. Each evening they cared for the horses, cooked a half-hearted meal, and collapsed into their bedrolls.

Tuesday, October 24, 1843

Kate watched Jake from the corner of her eye as they rode, wondering yet again the reason for the change in his usual calm, steadfast demeanor. All morning he'd fidgeted in his saddle, grinned for no apparent reason, and she'd even heard him humming. When he pulled his feet from the stirrups to swing his legs alongside Plug's flank she could stand it no longer.

"What's with you this morning?"

"I was aiming to keep it a secret," he said with a sheepish smile, "but it seems you can tell I've got something on my mind." He raised an eyebrow, daring her to ask more.

With an exaggerated sigh, she succumbed. "Well?"

"Right now we're about a day away from The Dalles — the point where we'll leave the trail for the Columbia River. A lot depends on the weather, but if all goes well we'll ride a raft for a week until we reach the mouth of the Willamette River. Then we'll have about a two-day ride until Oregon City."

Though his news was great, one word caught her attention. "You said raft. Can't we keep going on the horses?"

Pursing his lips, he shook his head. "The land's too rugged. Someday someone will discover an alternate route, but until that happens we have to go by river, which means a raft."

"Please tell me we don't have to build one?" She almost couldn't bear the pleading tone in her voice, but the thought of such an exhausting, laborious undertaking made her want to lie down and take a nap. For a week.

"Building our own is one way to go. However, the Hudson's Bay Company rents them."

Thrilled, she straightened in her saddle. "How perfect!"

"Not really. Their price is high."

Her smile faded into a grimace of frustration. "So we can't go around, we don't want to build a raft, and renting one is expensive. Is there another option?"

"Maybe. I'm hoping we can hire a local as our guide. Money isn't the true issue here — it's safety. I'm confident in our abilities, but the two of us negotiating a heavy raft down the Columbia isn't a risk I'd like to take. The majority will be a smooth ride, but at times there'll be wind gusts and submerged rocks. And there are rapids. I'm no fool, and if we don't have to go it alone we won't."

No, Jake was a lot of things, but a fool certainly wasn't one of them.

"Kate, don't let what I've said worry you. I'll be right there with you."

They settled into a comfortable silence. As always, Jake's eyes scanned their surroundings in a constant search for game, trail markers, and danger. Despite her nervousness at what he'd said about the upcoming river, she always felt safe with him by her side.

Soon she'd be on her own, in a land dominated by rough men. Men like Henrick. The chilling thought kept her awake most nights, shuddering from revulsion as she recalled how one second she'd been chatting with a friendly stranger, and the next she'd been stunned to feel his hands pawing at her, his fingers ripping open her shirt and grabbing her tender flesh so roughly. The smell of his tobacco-stained shirtsleeve as he'd slapped her cheek in an effort to quiet her, and then clamped his hand over her mouth once she'd fought him. Her terror as he'd declared his plan to kill Jake, and then proceeded to mutter a litany of detailed, lewd desires in her ear.

Most of all, what kept her awake at night was wondering how could she have missed Henrick's true intentions? How could her instincts have been so wrong? But ultimately, each bout of wondering always ended with the same realization — she'd been so intent on getting her way that her inexperience had nearly led to disaster. Her father had always said pride and diligence had a hand in a person's success, but ego and ignorance did not.

Yet for no other reason than wanting to exert her independence, she'd failed to do the one thing she'd need to do to succeed in her business, and in her new life — follow the advice of someone more knowledgeable than her. Someone who had proved time and time again to have only her best interest at heart.

She wouldn't make the same mistake again.

Chapter Forty-Eight

Waiting

Wednesday, October 25, 1843

Kate's breath caught in her throat as she stared down upon the vast river, stunned at the power of the current as it sped by in an undulating dance through land and rock.

The Columbia River — strong, silent, and a hundred times the size she'd imagined.

Jake waited ahead, halfway down the hillside, his elbow resting on his saddle horn as he gazed at her with an expression of pride and uncertainty. Drawing in a shaky breath, she forced away her rising trepidation and turned her head left — toward Oregon and her new life, now less than two weeks away.

Two weeks!

With a shriek of glee at the realization she stood in her stirrups, yanked off her hat, and pumped her arms to the sky.

Jake cupped his hands around his mouth. "Happy?"

Nodding, she slapped her hat to her head, tightened her fingers around the reins, and dug her heels into Nina's side.

"Race you!" she yelled as she thundered past Jake, with Old Dan and her packhorse in close pursuit. She reached the riverbank, pulled her horses to a stop, and spun in her saddle to watch Jake lose her impromptu contest. Seconds later he stopped Plug beside her and leapt to the ground. Grabbing her by the waist, he pulled her from her saddle.

"Kate, we've reached The Dalles!" He swung her around so fast her feet flew into the air. "We're almost there!"

She joined in his shouts of excitement as he whirled her around several more times, and then in his giddy laughter as he lost his balance and they tumbled to the ground. Once they got to their feet again, she pulled up her coat sleeve and held out her arm.

"I'm so excited I have goose bumps. The back of my neck is tingling too." Lowering her sleeve, she eyed the empty riverbank. "So it's just us?"

"For now. Others may show up in the next few days. And there's always a chance we'll pick up travelers along the way once they realize their mistake in trying to go over the mountains." Plug nickered and began pawing the ground, his usual signal for attention. Jake went to him and scratched his mane. "I think the horses are feeling left out. What do you say to brushing them and wiping down their gear?"

She agreed, happy to once again partake in such a simple, routine task. They worked in silence, removing saddlebags, saddles, and harnesses.

"Is it me or is this afternoon warmer than usual?" she asked, shrugging off her coat. It was a muggy day for late October and the extra exertion left her flushed.

"It is a warm one," agreed Jake as he too removed his coat. "It's hard to believe only a few weeks ago we were in the mountains and it was snowing."

Once the horses were clean, watered, and happily grazing, they set up camp. After she finished laying out her bedroll, Kate sat on top of the blankets and wrapped her arms around her knees. "What's the plan for the rest of today?"

"Wait for the raft."

She looked at the coffee brewing over the fire, the horses chewing grass nearby, and a bird gliding lazily on a breeze in the sky above. Turning, she took in the sight of Mount Hood etched against the sky. She felt content, something she hadn't been in a long time.

"I don't mind the wait."

Stretching her arms and legs like a cat in the sun, Kate curled on her side and drifted to sleep. She woke to see Jake removing a pan from the fire. Rubbing her eyes, she stared at him. "How long have I been asleep?"

"Long enough to get out of helping me catch and cook dinner." Chuckling, he handed her a plate loaded with cornbread and two fillets of fish.

After a leisurely meal complimented by relaxed, easy banter, Kate washed and put away the dishes. When she finished, she took happy note of the sun's position — high in the sky. The evening stretched out before her, ripe with possibility.

"My clothes are long past filthy — a condition I plan on remedying tonight," she declared in an effort to persuade herself to take on the daunting task. "What are you going to do?"

"Mend Plug's bridle and then watch the sunset with you." Whistling, Jake picked up the kettle and pointed toward the river. "I'm going for water."

Kate walked to where her saddlebags lay, hoisted the one holding her clothes and her mother's sewing kit over her shoulder, and then returned to her bedroll. Once she'd pulled out the jumbled collection — a pair of grimy trousers, two shirts crisp with dried sweat, and several pairs of socks, each stained with filth — she surveyed the items strewn about with a sigh. Everything she owned, including what she wore at the moment, either needed a thorough scrubbing or bore tears so large it would take hours to sew each properly. She'd start with the stubborn rip that kept reappearing in the sleeve of her coat.

Jake returned as she was threading a needle. She studied the tear on the side of his shirt.

"If you'd like, I'll mend the rip for you."

As Jake rummaged through his saddlebag on a search for another shirt, she bowed her head and focused on lining up the edges of the thick material. Seconds later she burst out laughing as Jake's torn shirt landed in a heap at her feet.

"Nope," she said, wadding it in a ball and flinging it onto his bedroll. "I only sew clean things."

"Is your coat what you mean by clean?"

Kate had to admit he was right. A streak of dirt caked the front, the bottom hem was stained, and since she'd worn it day and night during their weeks on the mountains, the wool held a definite unwashed odor.

"While I can't argue the logic of needing to make our clothes presentable again, I have a better idea of how we can pass the next hour or two."

Curious, she raised her eyes.

"I found the perfect spot to watch the sunset," he said with a shy smile.

"Given how cold the weather has gotten lately, I need to finish this." She nudged her coat sleeve. "Plus, I want to catch up with my letter writing."

Jake waved away her concerns. "You'll have plenty of time to write tomorrow. Besides, there aren't any forts to drop your letters at between here and Oregon City." When she hesitated, he resorted to teasing and cajoling her. "Come on, Kate. There's plenty of time to fix your clothes and write some letters, but the sun is setting right now."

"You're incorrigible," she said, signaling her defeat with a half-hearted sigh.

She allowed him to pull her to her feet and followed him up a nearby slope. After he spread out a blanket, she settled in beside him. Across the river, the ground rose and fell in soft, grass-covered humps, reminding her of ten fingers side by side, playing the water as if it were piano keys.

"Was there a fire over there?" she asked, pointing to a darkened area on the otherwise bare hill.

"Look up," he replied. "The clouds are big enough to block the sun."

Both were silent as the sun slowly descended, burning a brilliant red hue across the fluffy clouds hanging low in the sky. Rocks and leaves shimmered and appeared almost on fire as the sun clung to the top of the mountain range to the west, then slipped behind the peaks. She waited to speak until the sky faded to dusk.

"I had no idea how lovely it would be," she murmured. "Thank you."

Jake jumped to his feet with boyish enthusiasm. "It's still warm out. What do you say to a swim?"

She protested, but Jake had perfected the art of teasing and continued to do so until she finally gave in and followed him toward the riverbank. When they arrived at an inlet where the water calmed, he flung off his boots, socks, and hat. He then walked in, ducked his head, and paddled around the cove. She did the same. They swam for a few minutes, then got out and sat on the rocks nestled along the riverbank.

Moonlight filtered through several trees lining the bank, casting shadows onto the smooth water below.

"Watch yourself," Jake warned as she scooted across the rock to hang her feet in the water.

"I'm fine," she replied, swinging her legs against the cool stone.

"It might be slippery." He rose and stretched his leg as if preparing to jump to another rock. His foot shifted; he lost his balance and fell into the river with a tremendous splash.

Kate squealed in delight. "Look who's telling me to watch my step!"

"Oh, you think this is funny?" he demanded. With a mischievous grin, he pulled back his hand, cupped it, and snapped it forward, showering her with a cascade of water.

Kate responded by tossing her head back and laughing.

"Maybe you need to join me in here, little lady." He stepped closer and grabbed her ankle.

At once her laughter ceased. "You wouldn't."

"I would." He grinned and then pulled her in with a splash. She came to the surface sputtering, then quickly swam several yards away.

"I can't believe you did that," she protested. "I was almost dry!"

"Yes, but you're clean now, aren't you?"

"I was clean before. You're the one who smelled."

"Who, me?" Jake laid his hand across his chest in mock distress. "I've never smelled."

"I beg to differ." She giggled. "At times you can be downright pungent." Leaning back in the water, she kicked her feet and sent frothy waves over his head.

"Now you're going to get it."

She was no match for his powerful strokes. Within seconds he caught and held her forearms against his chest. "Give me one good reason not to dunk you."

She struggled briefly, then gave in to laughter.

"Where's the tough talk now?"

Kate couldn't speak through her giggles.

"One reason or under you go," he taunted.

Gasping for air, she managed to sputter, "You stink."

"Here you go!" With a gentle push, he sent her under the surface. When she came up, they tussled briefly before he lost his footing, sending them both under again.

****

Jake wanted to stay in the river forever.

The moonlit sky, the breeze whispering through the leaves, the air thick with a heady fragrance of pine and fading blooms — all of it paled in comparison to the beautiful woman standing before him, water swirling around her waist.

Kate stood flushed and breathless, tempting him with her nearness. As she brought a slender hand up to smooth her hair, her shirt clung to her soft, full curves. The taut fabric nearly drove him senseless.

Pushing his remaining reason aside, he moved closer and tilted her chin. Her green eyes widened with surprise, then drifted closed. After a long moment, he brushed a lock of hair from her cheek and then took her hand in his.

He felt her shiver. "Cold?"

"No," she murmured. "Just nervous."

"Me too."

Cupping the back of her head with his free hand, Jake swept his lips across her forehead in a light, lingering caress.

She pulled away. "I think we should get back."

"Me too."

They walked to camp, changed into dry clothes, and slipped into their respective bedrolls — all without a word spoken between them.

Chapter Forty-Nine

Columbia River

Saturday, October 28, 1843

"There it is!" Jake pointed to an immense wooden raft floating around a far-off bend in the river. Kate scrambled to her feet, forcing herself not to shriek from excitement.

The raft was here!

They'd waited for three days with their supplies packed and horses saddled. Now she had nothing to do but stand beside Jake and watch as a wiry man with dirty blond hair, torn overalls, and new boots expertly guided the raft toward them, hopped ashore, and looped a rope around a nearby tree. Once he'd stretched the knot firm, he turned to Jake.

"Name's Pete," he said with a curt nod. "Horses go in the middle three across, supplies and packs in the back. Price is thirty dollars a person — cash. I ain't arguing the cost, and I won't take your animals in trade for the amount. If you're coming, be loaded when I get back."

He walked up the hill without a backward glance. Kate's jaw dropped as she stared at the retreating man.

"People get to the point fast out here. They don't have time to waste on words."

Or manners, Kate thought as she bent and grabbed up her saddlebags. Before she could rise, Jake lifted them from her hands.

"I'll get all this. Handle the horses."

As she led Old Dan aboard, Kate thought it trusting for Pete to leave his raft with strangers, but then noticed a man reclining against the left side railing. Despite the large plug of tobacco in one cheek, his beard was tidy. His clothes were not. Holes at the elbows and knees showed he was used to hard work and little washing.

"Hello," she greeted him warmly as she tied Old Dan's lead rope to the rear hitching post. The man tipped his hat in her direction as she passed by him, but when she returned with Nina he ignored her. By the time she'd secured their remaining horses, Jake had all of their supplies in a tight pile against the back railing. Kneeling, she helped him tie a coil of rope over their things.

Pete came back from the woods. "Ready?"

Jake nodded. Kate said nothing.

As an afterthought, Pete pointed to the sitting man. "There's Angus. He don't talk much."

Pete moved to the front left corner of the raft, untied the rope holding them to shore, and threw it in a heap at his feet. Picking up a long pole, he used it to push the raft away from the bank. Angus grabbed a second pole. Leaning against the left rail, he helped Pete steer them out onto the river.

Jake crouched before where she sat, her hand resting protectively over her saddlebag. "Excited?"

"A little, but I'm also—"

"Hey!" Pete shouted. "Quit jawing with your woman and help get this thing downriver."

Jake gave her arm a reassuring squeeze and then moved to the right railing, pole in hand. Pete hadn't told her to do anything, so she stayed put and watched the scenery as the current propelled them downriver.

At first the men were kept busy steering the raft away from rocks that looked like tables standing atop the river, but soon the raft glided along the wide expanse of smooth water. Rolling hills gave the impression of pillows, but as the hours passed the mounds gave way to cliffs.

Vibrant green moss carpeted the rocks while the cloudless sky was a brilliant blue as far as the eye could see. A soft breeze brought birds to play overhead, and the raft glided by more birds bobbing along with the waves.

The ride was smooth for the better part of the day, but as the sun began its descent, the wind increased. Frothy water splashed across the raft deck.

Pete turned to her with a wolfish grin. "Scared?"

"A little," she replied, trying not to stare at his yellow teeth.

"You think this is bad? Soon you'll be clinging to this raft and fearing for your life." He let out a cruel laugh. "Though, you could always press those sweet curves of yours against me instead."

Furious, Kate scrambled to her feet. Apparently, men of the west needed a refresher on proper decorum around a lady. She'd start with this one. "You are a rude, disrespectful fool. I won't stand for such insolent talk."

Pete snorted.

"Leave her alone," Jake said, his tone quiet, but forceful.

Pete's eyes narrowed. "Or?"

Jake's glare went fierce. "Leave her alone!"

Pete hesitated and then returned to watching the river.

Kate let out a breath she hadn't realized she'd been holding as she sank to the deck. She had a lot to learn about life, and men, out west. Though this time she'd defended herself, it was Jake who'd ultimately kept her from a stranger's unwanted advances — again.

The night she and Jake had watched the sunset and then played in the water, Kate had been sure of one thing — he'd wanted to kiss her. She'd shied from his advances not because they were unwanted, but because she felt torn at the thought of deepening their relationship. While her immediate future would undoubtedly be easier with Jake by her side, for the first time in her life she was a free woman. Free to do as she pleased, speak as she pleased, and go where she pleased. Why would she want to limit all the possibilities before her when she had experienced none of them?

****

Tuesday, October 31, 1843

"Look!" Kate pointed to the right at a perfectly formed rock slope shaped like a backward S. The men glanced over, shrugged, and then returned to navigating the raft between two islands.

After the brief interaction yesterday, no further troubles had ensued between her and Pete. Meanwhile, he and Jake had settled into a wary understanding of each other. Angus said nothing to anyone.

Kate leaned against their pile of supplies tied to the back railing, happy to rest and enjoy nature's beauty. The rocky cliffs were gone, replaced by tree-covered mountains rising sharply from the shoreline on both sides of the river. They varied from brown and sparsely treed to areas so dense with trees the eye was deceived into thinking no ground lay beneath. The river was blue in spots and green in others.

As the morning progressed, Kate found herself succumbing to yawn after yawn. The previous night had been cold and damp, and now beneath the warm sun she struggled to stay awake.

Until the noise.

Kate couldn't place the odd sound. She listened for a moment, but didn't hear it again and dismissed it as a bird's chatter. But less than a minute later as they floated slowly by a large outcropping of rocks, she heard it again.

"Does anyone else hear something strange?"

"I don't hear nothing," Pete grumbled.

"There it is again." She cocked her head, listening intently. "It sounds like a bird screeching, but different."

"I said I don't hear nothing," Pete repeated as the mysterious noise sounded again.

She frowned. "It sounds like someone yelling."

"First it's a bird and then it's someone yelling." Pete smirked at her. "You best get your ears checked."

Kate heard only rushing water churning against the raft and conceded defeat. "Maybe you're right. I could have sworn, though..." She trailed off when movement flashed in the corner of her eye. Suddenly, a woman crashed through a line of bushes high on the hill above, stumbled, fell, and then rolled down the hill, coming to a stop at the bottom. She sprang up quickly and began running along the river, waving her arms.

"Wait! There's a woman over there!"

"I don't see nothing," Pete said, not even bothering to move his head.

Kate turned to Jake. "We have to stop!"

Jake shielded his eyes from the bright sun and focused on the shoreline. "Pete, there's someone over there. We better head ashore."

"I ain't stopping for nobody," Pete groused. "There's only one place I pick up travelers, and this ain't it."

"But you have to!" Kate grasped an unused pole. "We can't go on without seeing what she needs."

"Put it down!" roared Pete. "We're not stopping until tonight."

"We'll stop now," Jake said firmly.

"Of all the…" Pete turned to Jake with a snarl, but when he did, he saw for himself the young woman running alongside them. "Well, what do we have here?" His expression changed to a leer.

Pete and Angus began steering them ashore while Jake held fast to the rope. Once they hit the shoreline, Jake jumped off to secure the raft near where the woman stood drenched in sweat, hands to her heaving chest. Kate followed, canteen in hand.

"Thank you so much for stopping," she uttered between deep, gasping breaths. "I thought you didn't see me."

Kate offered the canteen and watched in surprise as the woman drank gulp after greedy gulp.

"Take your time, ma'am," Jake said. "We've got plenty."

The woman sheepishly handed over the empty canteen.

Jake waited patiently until her breathing had calmed to speak again. "What are you doing out here alone?"

"My husband cut his foot on a rock. Now his leg is infected and he has a fever. We couldn't make it any further, and I came down to the river for water." She placed a hand to her chest and looked to Jake. "Sir, you've saved us for sure."

"Now wait a minute," Pete hollered from the front of the raft. "We ain't taking on a sick man. Who knows what kind of disease he has? Best we can do is send someone after you once we get to Oregon City."

The woman's face paled as she shot frantic glances between Jake, Pete, and Kate. "My husband needs attention right away. You have to take us!"

She leapt onto the raft and reached for Pete's hand, but he jerked it away. "Woman, I ain't taking on no one with a fever. I'll send someone back and that's final." Pete's narrowed eyes bored into Kate. "You and your man better get back on. We're leaving."

"What if they paid you?" Kate ventured. Pete seemed like a greedy man, unlikely to turn down money no matter the perceived danger.

"Well now," Pete said, eyeing the woman. "There's an interesting proposition. I think double the usual charge would do." His lips stretched into a nasty sneer. "After all, there ain't another raft coming down this river anytime soon. Maybe not till next year. In fact, I think triple the charge would be even better."

"Nearly two hundred dollars?" Kate said. "Now you wait a minute—"

The woman held up her hand, interrupting Kate's tirade.

"It wouldn't matter if the price was only two dollars. We were robbed last week. They took every cent, our horses, and most of our supplies." She stepped from the raft and walked to Jake. "Perhaps you would be good enough to spare me your canteen and a bit of food before I go?"

"I'll do better." Jake said, crossing his arms and eyeing Pete. "If what she says is true, then his fever would be from an infection, not from disease. I'll pay their fare, but I won't have you taking advantage. It will be the same amount you charged us, or we'll be getting off with our money, too. So what's it going to be? Four paying customers, or none?"

"I said I ain't taking no one on this boat with a fever for less than double the fare."

Kate could no longer hold her tongue. "Shame on you for trying to take advantage!"

"Now hold on." Pete held up his hands. "I've almost changed my mind, but I need a little incentive is all."

"You degenerate! What you need is a good swift kick on your—"

"Kate, get the horses and take them ashore," Jake said, calmly hopping onto the raft. He untied a saddlebag and lifted it onto his shoulder. "We'll no longer ride with these men."

When Jake jumped off the raft and dropped his saddlebag to the ground, the woman shook her head.

"Sir, I can't let you do this. You should go ahead. Just please remember to send someone for us."

"Ma'am, he's not being truthful with you," Jake said. "Rafts come by every few days or so. We'll get your husband fixed up while we wait."

Kate took the woman's hand. "Don't worry. We have enough supplies to share with you and your husband, and we've got horses to spare."

"Now wait a minute." Pete had apparently realized she and Jake were serious and he was about to lose money. "There's no way I'm leaving without my fares from you people. I gotta make money too, you know." He glared at Jake. "If you agree to pay their way then we'll be done with this."

"Regular fare?"

"Regular fare," Pete muttered.

Jake faced the woman. "Ma'am, where can we find your husband?"

"He's over the hill under a large evergreen tree." She burst into tears. "Thank you so much! We'll repay you the minute we step foot in Oregon City. My husband's uncle runs a hotel there and is good for the money."

"Kate, stay here with her while Pete and I fetch him."

Pete grimaced but followed Jake up the hill. They returned, supporting a tall, ashen man between them. It was easy to see why — his foot was swollen to twice the normal size and covered with an angry rash.

They eased him onto the raft. Once he was settled against the back railing, the woman sank to his side, buried her head in his chest, and sobbed.

Pete rolled his eyes. "We've wasted enough time. Let's get moving!"

Jake thrust a small satchel in Kate's hands. "This is theirs. Give them water and whatever food they need." He returned to his side of the raft and grabbed his pole.

Unwilling to intrude on the newcomer's happiness, Kate quietly put a stack of leftover biscuits and a canteen of fresh water in front of them. She added bandages and Jake's salve then quickly retreated to her corner of the raft.

They floated on down the river.

****

Later that night as the group made camp, the woman approached Kate. "You helped save my husband's life, and I don't even know your name."

"I guess we didn't have time for formal introductions back there today. My name is Kate."

She stretched out her hand, but the woman grabbed her into a fierce hug.

"Thank you so much. I don't know if we could've lasted another day out there." She released Kate and stepped back again. "I'm Margaret, and my husband's name is William. But I must confess I've forgotten your husband's name already."

"He's not my husband," she said, looking to where Jake was hunkered over a circle of rocks, starting a fire. He saw her watching and winked.

Margaret stared at her, curious. "Your brother?"

"No, he's a good friend traveling to Oregon with me."

Chapter Fifty

All Set

Sunday, November 5, 1843

Dawn found Kate sitting beside the fire, pondering the last five days on the river — five long days. She'd spent her time at the back of the raft, her hand or head resting against the tied pile of her and Jake's supplies. With nothing to do, she filled her days by watching.

She watched the scenery along the river transform from gentle, grassy hills to vertical cliffs bursting from the water's edge, offering no shoreline or opportunity of rest.

She watched Pete and Angus keep to themselves, except at mealtimes.

She watched Margaret's devotion to her husband as she nursed him back to health. Each morning she washed his cut, applied Jake's salve, and then bandaged his foot. With her excellent care, combined with plenty of rest and nourishment, William steadily improved. Yesterday morning he'd walked a few steps with the aid of a crutch Jake had fashioned for him.

Most of all, she watched Jake. He'd spent his days at the front right corner of the raft, always quick with a well-timed push against a rock and a reassuring grin when he caught her staring. Though he never complained, Kate worried about how his leg was holding up under the strain. His position bore the brunt of the waves, and he spent hours standing in the frigid overspray. At the end of each day he'd limped from the raft, his face tight with weariness and pain. She eyed his bedroll now, relieved to see him still asleep. He needed the rest.

When Kate saw the others stirring, she quickly poured two cups of coffee she'd made fresh that morning. Yesterday Angus and Pete had drunk every last drop while she and Jake had been reloading their supplies. She wouldn't make the same mistake today.

Kneeling beside his bedroll, she skimmed her fingers along Jake's arm, hesitated, and then shook his shoulder. "Time to get up."

Eyes closed, he let out a low groan of protest. "Already?"

"Already," she replied wistfully. He'd been working so hard. She wished he could sleep the day away. "I have a surprise for you."

His eyes fluttered open, focusing first on her and then the steaming cups in her hands. He chuckled softly as she passed him one. "Nicely done."

She winked at him, then rose and headed across camp.

****

After breakfast, Pete set his plate aside and motioned for Kate and the others to gather in close. He sketched a crude map of the river in the dirt.

"Today's gonna be tough. The river narrows between two rock walls, and gusts of wind whip through there so hard they'll knock a man clean off his feet. Even worse—" he pointed to a sharp angle in his map "—we've got to make it past this."

Pete paused, his eyes flitting over each of them. "Usually, I've had five or more solid men with me by this point. Today we'll do with what we've got, and hopefully no one dies in the process."

Kate swallowed hard and tried to focus on Pete's directions. His words were a brutal reminder of the two graves she'd left behind on the trail.

Pete hastily drew a diagram of the raft and tapped the upper corner. "Since Jake is the strongest, he'll ride front. It's the roughest ride. Angus and I will each take a side. Women, you'll stay in the back with the gear."

"What about me?" William asked. "I'd like to help."

Pete hesitated, then shook his head. "Too risky. Stay with the women."

"I suppose I'd rather be out of the way than a hindrance," William said.

"You got that right." Pete grunted. "I'm not gonna lose my life for anyone else's carelessness. I've seen grown men sucked into a whirlpool, and there wasn't anything we could do. We had to let them go lest we lose the entire raft."

Margaret gasped. "I can't swim!"

To Kate's surprise, Pete's expression softened. "Don't go getting all hysterical. I built this raft with my own two hands, and it's as sturdy as they come."

"Don't worry," Kate whispered as she patted Margaret's trembling hand. "All we have to do is hang on tight and everything will be fine."

The day progressed without a problem, even as the river changed from blue to green to brown, punctuated by rising whitecaps. Late in the afternoon, Jake checked on the horses' lead ropes, securing them to the hitching posts. With his trousers soaked to his mid-thigh, he knelt beside Kate and pulled hard against his saddlebag, testing yet again the rope tethering everything to the raft floor.

After retying a loose knot, he pointed to where William dozed against the railing. "I see you ladies are keeping him calm."

Kate chuckled at the joke, but Margaret only grimaced and closed her eyes.

"Jake!" Pete called. "Get up here, quick!"

Jake stumbled as he got to his feet, but recovered his balance and hurried to the front. Seconds later, Kate felt the raft pick up speed as it rounded a sharp curve.

"Here we go!" Pete yelled.

Chapter Fifty-One

A Warning Ignored

Kate's heart pounded as the raft shot into a narrow passageway. Towering cliffs on both sides left no room for error. She heard Pete's shout above the deafening roar of water and Margaret's howling.

"William, take my spot!"

William scrambled to his feet, grabbed a pole, and hopped to the right side of the raft behind Jake. Pete rushed to the front left corner while Angus remained on the left side.

Waves crashed against the raft and then the men. They braced their legs wide and strained against their poles to stay upright.

"Jake, William!" Pete called. "Hurry!"

Kate's breath caught in her throat at what she saw ahead — the top half of a submerged boulder. Jake leaned against the railing and shoved his pole against the wall created by the cliff at the edge of the river. William followed suit. Their adroit push spun the raft back on course. Collision avoided.

"Angus," Pete yelled. "Up ahead!"

Angus joined Pete in maneuvering them away from a whirlpool. Jovial shouts rang out from the men as the raft returned to the river's center. The next several minutes they worked tirelessly together. Commands shouted by one and followed by the rest kept the raft steady.

All went well until a wind gust sent Pete crashing into the horses and his pole into the river. While he lay tangled and helpless beneath panicked hooves, his unprotected corner scraped against a hidden rock. Wood chunks flew.

Pete rolled to safety, scurried to his feet, and grabbed another pole. Seconds later, the raft dipped sharply as the men clustered at the left corner and battled a series of whirlpools.

Ahead, Kate saw what appeared at first to be another ordinary rock, but when she rose to her knees to get a better look she gasped in horror.

"Jake!" She pointed toward a massive boulder sitting directly in their path.

The men cursed and fought to reposition themselves and their poles. But there wasn't time. There was nowhere to push. They were traveling too fast.

Margaret's screams filled the air as the right corner slammed against stone with a sickening thud. The impact tumbled everyone to the raft floor. As they regained their footing an earsplitting crack rang out.

The splintered right railing twisted free, and then crashed into the river.

"It's coming apart!" Margaret shrieked, grabbing hold of Kate's arm. Hard.

Kate barely noticed. All her attention was on the far right floorboard. The front edge floated at least a foot from the raft, while the back end — hidden beneath their supplies — was held in place only by the rope tethering their supplies to the raft.

Kate glanced at Margaret, now babbling incoherently between chest-heaving sobs. She'd be of no use. Neither would the men — brutal waves demanded their full concentration.

Yanking her arm free from Margaret's clutches, Kate crawled past her and headed for the loose board. Lying on her stomach, she stretched her arms over her head, fighting against the current stretching the ropes and submerging their supplies. The raft jolted and her chin hit the floor so hard her teeth slammed together. Thankfully, no blood. Within seconds, only a few inches of rope and her desperate grip prevented the board from escaping. She couldn't do this alone.

"Jake, help me! I can't hold on!"

Seeing her plight, he dropped his pole and rushed past William. He fell beside her with a grunt and she felt his icy hands graze hers as he grabbed hold of the board.

"There's a coil of rope under our blankets," he said. "Get it."

She got to her knees. After shoving her hands beneath the blankets on the right side of their supply pile and finding nothing, Kate scurried around to the left side. Nothing. Another frantic search ensued, this time in the center. She cried out with glee when her fingers brushed against course rope.

The raft tipped to the left.

"Jake, tie it up," Pete yelled as the raft teetered further. "We've got rapids coming!"

"William!" Jake shouted. "Take over for me here."

William limped back. Once his hands replaced Jake's on the board, Jake raced to the front of the raft. Meanwhile, Kate struggled to loosen the knot securing the rope coil — no small task since it was soaking wet. Finally, she wrenched it loose.

Kate crawled unsteadily past Margaret, now sitting with her fists clenched against her forehead, and returned to where William had lost the fight. The front edge of the board now rode at almost a ninety-degree angle from the raft. Two blankets floated nearby, irretrievable, and the kitchen box seemed soon to follow.

William took the rope from her and quickly fashioned a lasso.

The first throw overshot the end of the board.

The second throw the loop tangled in the air.

"One more time and I'll go in after it myself!" William hollered in frustration as he pulled the dripping rope onto his lap. Setting his jaw, he threw a third time. The rope looped neatly around the end of the board.

Kate braced her feet against the hitching post, and together they pulled the board snug against the edge of the raft and tied it fast. When they finished, William collapsed on his back, panting heavily. She flopped down beside him.

As her breathing calmed, Kate realized the river had calmed as well. Opening her eyes, she saw that though the raft still careened along at a stunning pace, the waves had subsided.

It was over.

She relished in the thought — until she focused on their supplies. Actually, the empty space where a portion of their supplies had been. She investigated, and found in addition to the two blankets she'd seen swept away earlier, they'd lost Jake's bedroll and the lid to the kitchen box.

Kate broke the news. "Jake, we lost some things, including your bedroll."

Jake spun around, his face pale. "Where's my saddlebags?"

She froze, recalling their fight in the cave. How he'd dropped his saddlebags before her. How he'd stated she could count the receipts if she didn't believe him.

Father's money was in his saddlebags!

She scurried around the edge of the pile, yanking at knots, thrusting her hands over, under, and through it all, desperate to find the one thing she needed, the one thing that would provide for her future.

"Find them?" Jake yelled.

"No!" She'd already lost so much on this trip; could she survive losing the money too?

"Keep searching."

"Where did you pack them?" How could this happen so close to the end?

"Under a blanket!" he shouted, thrusting his pole against the cliff wall. The force put him off balance, and with no railing to catch him he fell, his left leg crumpling beneath him as he went down.

Kate hesitated, her search abandoned as she poised to leap to his aide. "Jake?"

Waving away her concern, he stiffly got to his feet. But as he bent to retrieve his pole the raft abruptly tilted. With a guttural shout, he crashed to the floor, facedown, his right leg fully submerged. His left leg fought for purchase, then skidded over the edge even as his fingertips scraped the boards in a frenzied search for something solid. Something to hold on to. Something to save him.

"Jake!"

Kate dove across his arms, pinioning them to the raft. But her weight was no match against the fierce current. Within seconds, his waist and then torso disappeared into the river until his armpits rested on the raft's edge.

To her horror, she felt his arms writhing beneath her. He was trying to pull free!

"What are you doing?" she shrieked.

"Kate, I won't let you lose your life for me. Get the money and let me go!"

She gasped. How could he think she cared more about the money in his saddlebags than she did him? That she'd abandon him for something so meaningless?

"The money doesn't matter!"

"But you do." He stared at her with resignation in his eyes. As if he'd already accepted his fate. As if he was already prepared to die. "Let me go, Kate."

Ignoring his repeated plea, she gripped his wrist, struggled to her knees, and wrapped her fingers around his shirt collar. Though she pulled with all her might, he didn't budge.

And there was no one to help her. Pete and Angus were on the other side, intent on keeping the raft afloat. Margaret clung to the supply pile, her eyes wide and unseeing to anyone's plight. William was trying to reach Jake, and had already crawled half the length of the raft, but his earlier exertions had sapped his strength. Now his progress came in inches — he'd never make it in time.

"Stop!" Jake bellowed as she leaned over his back, plunged her hand into the frigid water, and grabbed hold of his waistband. "You'll pull yourself in!"

Agonizing seconds passed with several failed attempts, but amidst his grunts and her screams, she finally pulled him to safety.

Chapter Fifty-Two

A Confession

Jake lay in a heap on the edge of the raft as searing spasms rippled down his leg. For once, he relished the pain. Pain meant he was alive. Alive because of the woman lying beside him, her hand still clutched around his wrist. Propping himself up on an elbow, he gazed down at her.

"You could have been hurt..." His voice broke and he finished in a whisper, "Or worse. Why didn't you listen?"

He searched her eyes, finding tenderness and uncertainty in their depths. After a long moment, she raised her hand to stroke his cheek with trembling fingers.

"Jake, I can't lose you. Not today. Not ever."

To his astonishment and joy, she wound her free arm around his neck and nestled her head against his chest. And there she stayed, her body pressed to his, as they swayed as one to the rhythm of the waves. Until Pete's taunting shout ruined everything.

"Finish up yer lovin', cuz we need help up here."

Kate stiffened against him then scurried away.

****

At dusk, they stepped off the raft for the last time. Jake, Pete, and Angus hauled saddlebags, packs, and supplies off the raft and dumped them in wet, disorganized piles. Meanwhile, William helped Kate and Margaret lead the horses from the barge. Once the animals were secured the women headed for the woods, arm-in-arm, whispering between themselves.

Jake unloaded the last of the supplies, which thankfully included both his saddlebags. Hours earlier, Kate had unearthed them and held them aloft with a triumphant shout. Though Elijah's money had always been safe inside his inside coat pocket, he too had been relieved to note both his bags were intact with their buckles fastened tight. Their kitchen box hadn't fared so well. After a quick search, Jake determined they'd lost three dinner plates, two mugs, the lid to the iron kettle, two canteens, and all but one of the serving spoons.

"Where's the women?" Pete asked.

"Off to gather blackberries," William said. "They said something about trying to make a pie."

Pete snorted. "Don't they know the growing season's long since past?"

"I tried to tell them, but they were determined." William threw his hands in the air. "Far be it for me to dissuade two ladies on a mission."

"Just as well. I don't like doing business in front of women," Pete said before facing Jake. "Well, this is it. You've traveled the Columbia and lived to tell about it. Now I'll take my money. Thirty dollars a person."

Jake reached into his pocket and removed his black leather wallet. Slowly, he peeled away bills totaling one hundred twenty dollars, and set them into Pete's outstretched hand. Pete counted the money again, then shoved the wad into his back pocket and walked onto the raft. Angus followed.

Once they were alone, William faced Jake. "I'll pay you back as soon as we get to Oregon City."

"I'm not worried. Glad to have you along, especially after all you did to bring the board in today."

"I may be weak as a kitten right now, but after all you've done for us I wasn't about to let anything go without a fight."

"Kate holds tremendous value on what's in her saddlebags — losing them would have devastated her. So I reckon we're even now, don't you?"

William grinned. "Reckon so."

****

Kate and Margaret returned to camp empty-handed but cheerful and began rooting through supplies while discussing what to make for dinner. William made himself comfortable against a tree trunk and promptly dozed off. Angus and Pete slung their guns over their shoulders. Grumbling about finding meat, they headed into the woods.

Jake tied a rope between two trees and began spreading out blankets, clothes and supplies. It was a mindless task, perfect for deep thinking and for sneaking glances at Kate, now studiously building up the fire.

He wanted her. For the rest of his life. And judging by what she'd said to him on the raft, and how she'd clung to him after, she wanted him too.

Jake, I can't lose you. Not today. Not ever.

As he hoisted another blanket over the rope, he considered whether a man like him, a man who couldn't give her the lifestyle she'd been raised in, could make Kate happy for the rest of her life. She'd said the money didn't matter, but what if weeks, months, or years from now she wanted more than he could provide? What if she regretted her life with him?

He sighed, knowing he was resorting to plucking excuses from thin air. Such nonsense about money would have been true of the woman he'd met in Elijah's yard at the beginning of the trip. But the woman Kate had become over the past months was so much more than a decorative chatterbox whose main concern was the size of a man's wallet.

But though he longed to sweep her into his arms and confess his love for her, hesitation and doubt kept him still. What if she'd gotten caught up in the moment and spoken out of fear and not love? What if she regretted saying those words?

Jake sighed again. While not being certain of her true feelings was a valid concern, in truth something else worried him even more — Elijah.

Would pursuing a relationship with Kate be taking advantage of the promise he'd made to watch over the man's daughter?

Chapter Fifty-Three

Clearing an Obligation

Monday, November 6, 1843

After breakfast, Jake readied the horses while Kate, William, and Margaret broke down their camp. Pete and Angus had said their final goodbyes late the previous night, and were now walking back to get ready for next year's travelers.

Once the group was mounted and ready, Jake led them off. He held Plug to an easy pace to save everyone's strength, especially William's. Oregon City was still two days away, and if William fell ill again it would be tough to ration food while they waited for him to regain his strength. Jake's heart leapt as his other reason for the slower pace turned in her saddle and smiled at him.

He had two days to figure out what to do about Kate.

****

After a chilly, yet uneventful day on the trail, Jake wanted little more than to warm his leg by the fire. However, a lingering issue remained. One he had no intention of letting slide.

He'd waited all day for the perfect moment to speak to Kate alone and decided he wouldn't get a better chance. Dinner was long since finished, the horses were cared for, and William and Margaret were engaged in a lively conversation about farming. Kate relaxed near the fire, tucked into a blanket so only her hands and face had to fight the cool night air. He hated to disturb her, but this was something he had to do in private.

"Kate, would you take a walk with me?"

She slipped from her blanket and followed him out of camp. When he stopped at the edge of a clearing, he sat on a log. Instead of joining him she stood nearby, biting her lip and clutching the ends of her sleeves in her fingertips. Seeing her nervousness, he patted the spot beside him with what he hoped was a confident smile. She sat.

Taking a deep breath, reached into his coat and pulled out Elijah's deerskin pocketbook.

"Your father gave this to me just before he died. I've already taken out my payment, and you'll find the rest of the money has all been accounted for. All of the financial records from the trip, including receipts for all the purchases I made, are in here, along with the original contract for my employment signed by myself and your father."

"I remember this," she said in a hushed, reverent tone. "When I was young he would give me money for candy from here. Then, when I got older, money for clothes."

"I also have this," Jake said, withdrawing the careworn leather pouch. Pulling open the two strips of rawhide strung through the top, he shook out the pocket watch he'd taken off Ben before burying him and a mix of double eagles and other coins into his palm. After a long moment, he eased everything back inside and gave it to her.

Her eyes glistened as she rubbed the soft brown leather between her fingertips.

"I have one last thing," he said, handing her the butter-yellow envelope made of parchment paper. Someone had already torn an edge open, presumably Elijah.

"I've never seen such an elaborate seal." She ran her fingertips over the red wax. "It isn't my father's, or anyone else we dealt with regularly at the store. Did he tell you what's inside?"

Jake shook his head. "No, and I didn't think it was my place to ask."

"I'm frightened."

"About what?"

"Oregon. The store. The ranch. Everything. I know it's what my father wanted for me, but now that I'm almost there, I'm scared." She dropped her gaze. "What if I'm not strong enough? What if after all this, I can't make it?"

"Kate, you've got the desire and fiery spirit it takes to make it out here. You can do anything you set your mind to, so don't let anybody tell you different."

She wiped her cheeks with the back of her hand. "Is there anything else?"

Jake paused. Time was rapidly running out until their arrival into Oregon City, but he couldn't make himself bring up the second subject. He wanted the moment to be perfect — for Kate to be happy, not teary-eyed and missing her family.

He finally spoke. "No."

Chapter Fifty-Four

Arrival

Wednesday, November 8, 1843

Kate lay awake in her bedroll, planning her future. They were due into Oregon City early that evening, and decisions had to be made. For each, she analyzed every detail as well as the potential consequences. Then, when she felt confident enough in her choice, she compared the outcome to what her father would have done.

Overwhelming.

Though she had nothing to sell, she had every intention of opening the store by the end of the week, if only to introduce herself to townsfolk and her potential customers. And thanks to her father's business sense, the shelves would soon be fully stocked. Contracts were already in place with trusted suppliers, and next spring two wagons loaded with provisions would be making their way to Oregon. An additional three wagons were expected to arrive later in the year.

However, the horse ranch was the ultimate goal. If the store wasn't successful, she could hire on as a nanny, a cook, or even work in a hotel in town to save up enough money buy additional land and hire experienced ranchers.

Kate sat up and slid a hand into her trouser pocket. Her future lay heavy and reassuring against her leg in the form of a pocketbook, leather pouch, and envelope with a strange seal. Once a peek at the others confirmed she was the only one awake, she withdrew the envelope and slid two documents onto her lap — the bill of sale to the new store, and the deed to the house and land. After several attempts at deciphering the numerical codes written along the top corner of each paper, she gave up and returned the papers to the envelope.

Her father's pocketbook was next.

She opened the flap and ran a thumb over the money. The amount was more than she'd expected. It would cover her needs for the coming years, and if she managed it properly, for the rest of her life.

She noticed a familiar piece of paper tucked away in the back. With a smile, she carefully removed the note written to her father so long ago.

My Dearest Elijah,

It is the night before we are to wed, and I am overcome with happiness at my good fortune to have found such a caring man to spend the rest of my days with. I promise to love and cherish you with all my heart, and stand strong by your side as we move forward in our new life together as husband and wife.

All my love,
Rebecca

Kate ran her fingertips over her mother's precise handwriting. Her parent's love had been deep, pure — the kind poets could only dream of capturing with mere words. A perfect love, one she'd always envisioned sharing with her own husband someday.

And now she knew she wanted that man to be Jake.

Here she sat, less than a day away from Oregon City, with all her plans in place and her new life about to begin, but the one question she cared about most remained unanswered.

How did Jake feel about her?

On the raft she'd said she couldn't bear to lose him, ever. She'd spoken from her heart and he'd said nothing in return. Done nothing in return.

Across the camp, William began to stir. Kate folded her mother's note, eased it into the pocketbook, and then stowed everything back in her trousers. As she rose to build up the fire, William bolted upright, rubbed his eyes, and nudged his sleeping wife.

"Time to get up, honey!" Hopping from the blankets, he danced a brief jig.

"Seems someone's feeling better," Margaret mumbled, her eyes firmly shut.

"How can I not?" William exclaimed. "The sun is shining and look how rich and dark the dirt is out here." Reaching down, he dug out a fistful of earth and held it aloft. "It's a farmer's dream!"

Margaret yawned.

William dropped to his wife's side and began nuzzling her neck and tickling her until she giggled. Soon, both were laughing uproariously.

Kate watched them. For days the couple's murmurs of adoration and tenderness had filled her ears, leading her mind to wander to thoughts of her own life. Would she ever share such blissful love?

****

The last day proved tedious, and due to the narrow trail that demanded single-file riding, it was populated with long stretches of silence. But as the sun was taking leave of the sky, Jake halted at the top of a hill.

"Why are we stopping here?" William called forward. "You said we'd be in Oregon City tonight."

"I thought you all might want to see something," Jake said, moving Plug aside. Kate dismounted and joined the others in their silent stares at the shops and houses spread out below.

They'd arrived.

At once Kate was overcome with emotions — elation at having completed such an incredible journey and a crushing sadness that her father and Ben weren't at her side, sharing in the moment. But it was when she looked to Jake with the realization that once they reached the bottom of the hill he'd go off to start his own life, without her, that her throat tightened and her heart began to pound. Finally, her feelings conspired against her and she burst into tears.

Margaret and William looked at her in dismay, then to Jake in confusion.

"You two go on ahead," Jake said calmly. "We'll be right there."

Without a word, they mounted up and made their way down the hill. As the sounds of the horses' hooves faded, Jake faced her.

"I'm sorry," she murmured. "I'm ruining this moment for you."

"No, you're not," he said with a tender smile. "Besides, I've seen the city before."

She took a deep breath and dried her tears. "Thank you, Jake."

"For what?"

"Getting me here. I feel like I'm a completely different person now," she ventured.

"I agree. You've grown from a pampered, unsure girl into a strong, competent woman."

Hearing this, Kate yearned to touch him. He was so near she could feel the warmth of his skin, but she wavered, still uncertain where their conversation was leading.

****

Jake gazed into those enormous green eyes he'd grown to love.

Yes, he loved her.

It wasn't even a question anymore. From the furthest reaches of his mind to the depths of his soul, he ached with hidden longing for this woman who was everything he'd ever desired.

Had Elijah been alive, Jake would have asked for permission to court her properly. But Elijah was dead. Nothing would ever change the fact, and it was time to move on. He wasn't about to let what had happened on the trail affect his future. Their future. If she would have him.

"Kate, you're the most incredible woman I've ever met, and I'd love nothing more than to be by your side and share a life together with you."

Her smile of pleasure was the invitation he'd been waiting for. After a long moment, he brought the back of her hand to his mouth and kissed it softly. When she didn't protest or pull away, he brushed his lips across the inside of her wrist, then lingered, breathing in her scent.

Her soft sigh was his reward.

Reveling in her sweetness, he locked eyes with her as he first kissed each of her fingertips, and then laid her palms against his chest. His breath quickened as she slid her hands around his waist and pulled him closer with a sensual, willing smile. Lowering his mouth, he swept his lips along her jaw. As he reached the creamy skin below her earlobe he paused, allowing his breath to warm her. When her body trembled, he lifted his head but kept one palm splayed across the small of her back, enjoying the feeling of her arching against him. Her eyes drifted closed and he ran a thumb over her bottom lip.

Her whimper of frustration sent him over the edge. Tunneling his hands deep into her hair, Jake bent his head and finally did what he'd waited so long to do to the woman standing before him.

He kissed her.

When their lips parted, he pressed his forehead against hers and whispered the first words of their new life together. "Katie, let's go down there and see what the future holds for us."

Kate and Jake thought conquering the Oregon Trail was tough — until they tried to build a life together in Oregon City.

Their journey continues in

Tainted Dreams

Saturday, November 11, 1843

Kate rode into the settlement of Champoeg with Jake at her side and the familiar butter-yellow envelope hidden deep within her pocket. At the end of the main street sat the land office; a weathered building that held the details of all claims made in Oregon City and the surrounding area.

Though the trail had taken nearly everything from her, two shining glimmers of hope had survived. Deeds that were the key to her new life—a life that would begin the moment she learned the locations signified by the string of numbers scrawled across the top of both papers.

They secured the horses at the hitching post and then headed for the door. Jake knocked twice to announce their arrival and then pushed it open, revealing a room with a sagging cot on one side and a freshly polished stove on the other. A wrinkled man with a trim white beard stood up from his desk, walked over, and clapped a hand on Jake's shoulder.

"Jake! What a surprise!"

"Kate, I'd like you to meet a friend of mine, Jim."

"It's a pleasure to meet you, ma'am." Jim nodded to her and then motioned to two scratched but sturdy oak chairs opposite his desk. "Please, make yourselves comfortable."

Jake pulled out her chair and waited until she was settled before sitting beside her. After they'd exchanged a few rounds of inane chatter about the weather, Jim rested his elbows on the desk and laced his fingers together.

"What can I do for you today?"

Kate dried her palms on her trousers and took a deep, calming breath before speaking the words she'd waited over four months to say.

"My father purchased a building in Oregon City and a house two miles outside of town. I'm here to learn their locations."

"I don't understand," Jim said. "Why didn't he get this information when the claims were first made?"

"He bought the deeds in Virginia, from a man who'd changed his mind about living in Oregon Territory." She slid a trembling hand into her pocket and withdrew the butter-yellow envelope with the red wax seal. Tucked inside were the two pieces of parchment paper that represented her father's dream for the rest of his life.

And now his unfulfilled dream was hers.

Her house. Her land. Her future.

"I see you've got something there," Jim said. "Let me take a look."

She set the first paper — the one she surmised was the deed to the store — into Jim's extended hand.

He pulled the oil lamp closer and leaned over the desk, peering at the paper with a deepening frown. After a long moment he pressed and slid his thumb over the numbers written at the top, grimacing at the smear of ink left behind.

"Jim, is there a problem?" Jake asked.

"The plot numbers don't match anything I've ever seen and the wording is all wrong. Give me a minute." With the paper in hand, Jim crossed the room to inspect three plot maps nailed to the wall.

While they waited, Jake placed a calming hand upon her bouncing knee and gave her a reassuring grin—a grin that slowly faded when Jim resumed his seat with a heavy sigh.

"I'm sorry, ma'am, but this deed is forged. It's worthless."

About the Author

Christi Corbett lives in a small town in Oregon with her husband and their twin children. The home's location holds a special place in her writing life; it stands just six hundred feet from the original Applegate Trail and the view from her back door is a hill travelers looked upon years ago as they explored the Oregon Territory and beyond.

Christi's Sincere Thanks To...

My family and friends for your encouragement and pep talks.

My critique partner, Artemis Grey for your keen insight into Jake and Kate's actions and reactions, for sharing your vast knowledge about horses, Virginia, and the details of death, and for rooting me on all the times the going got tough. And most of all, for just getting it!

My critique partner, Margo Kelly for pushing me to go over it again and again and then once more to make sure I got everything right, for your stellar technical advice on the mechanics of writing, and for your willingness to drop everything to review yet another draft.

The Ridge Writers for listening to the same story week after week, and for always offering insight and advice with a smile.

Authors Kaki Warner, Jillian Kent, Reid Lance Rosenthal, Eve Paludan, and Shelley Houston for your unwavering support, wisdom, and encouragement.

My Beta Readers: Tracy, Jenny, Angela, Heidi, Amy, Sarah, and P.D.P.
for giving up your free time to share your opinions and suggestions.

Martha Gaines for your wonderful advice on stuttering and speech patterns in children.

The staff at Mazama Sporting Goods for sharing your knowledge about guns of the 1840's.

Attic Media, for creating a book trailer that brought my words to life.

"TV" Jeff for keeping my computer going as deadlines loomed.

And finally, Stephanie Taylor for making my writing dreams come true.